"Irresistible . . . The heist is ingenious and spectacular, described in enough detail that Zagel confesses in an afterword that he 'misdescribed' some aspects of the Federal Reserve so he wouldn't provide a road map to robbing the place. . . . An intelligent thriller with the most likable bad guys since *The Sting*. What distinguishes *Money to Burn* is the fascinating glimpse into the mind of a dedicated judge. Any lawyer who feels guilty for reading Grisham can proudly be caught with *Money to Burn*." —*USA Today*

"Fabulous . . . As the crime unfolds, the book becomes a funhouse-mirror morality tale as well. . . . Like novelists John Grisham and Scott Turow, Mr. Zagel is himself a veteran player in the justice system, a Chicago circuit court judge. Thus he brings texture and grit to his beat cops and Midwestern heroes gone awry." —*The Wall Street Journal*

"*Money to Burn* is wonderful. At one level, it is an engrossing fast-paced tale of an amazing caper, envisioned by an entirely unlikely mastermind. At another, it is a discerning portrait of the moth-and-flame mentality that often grips those who enforce the criminal law. In all ways, it is thoroughly compelling."

—Scott Turow, author of
Presumed Innocent and *Reversible Errors*

"When James Zagel—who in his assortment of careers has been an investigator, a police chief, a lawyer, and a judge—turns his attention to writing a crime story, the results are explosive. He brings the excitement of a heist, the intelligence of a legal thriller, and the suspense of detective fiction to his compulsively readable debut novel."

—Nicholas Pileggi, author of
Wiseguy and *Casino*

continued . . .

"A sleep-depriving page-turner."　　　*—Chicago Sun-Times*

"This summer's sleeper could be James Zagel's *Money to Burn*, a darkly hilarious tale of a federal judge who sets out to rob the Federal Reserve Bank in Chicago of $100 million in cash. The story is all the more delicious because first-time-novelist Zagel is himself a U.S. district court judge in Chicago . . . brilliantly conceived and beautifully executed—a winner all the way."

　　　　　　　—The Washington Post Book World

"*Money to Burn* is so smart, sharp, and full of wonderful characters and action scenes that everybody is going to want to read it and then see the movie it's certain to become. As a bonus, the book is as deeply rooted in the rich soil of Chicago crime literature as the best of Sara Paretsky . . . fascinating . . . beautifully choreographed . . . In between working out the intricate but plausible details of his robbery plan and its unexpected aftermath, Zagel also lets us in on the many ways a federal judge can change (and even subvert) the course of justice from a sitting position. Some of it is reassuring; other parts are frankly a little scary."　　　　　　　*—Chicago Tribune*

"Think of *The Taking of Pelham 123* occurring inside the Chicago Federal Reserve Bank to grasp the underlying action of *Money to Burn*. However, what engages the reader with the story line is the thought processes of the judge, a model citizen who seems to have allowed his darker side to take charge. James Zagel provides an intriguing debut novel that will hopefully not be the last because this author has plenty of talent."　　　　*—Midwest Book Review*

Money to Burn

James Zagel

BERKLEY BOOKS, NEW YORK

MONEY TO BURN

A Berkley Book / published by arrangement with
the author

PRINTING HISTORY
G. P. Putnam's Sons hardcover edition / July 2002
Berkley mass-market edition / August 2003

ISBN: 0-425-19121-4

BERKLEY®
Berkley Books are published by The Berkley Publishing Group,
a division of Penguin Group (USA) Inc.,
375 Hudson Street, New York, New York 10014.
BERKLEY and the "B" design
are trademarks belonging to Penguin Group (USA) Inc.

PRINTED IN THE UNITED STATES OF AMERICA

10 9 8 7 6 5 4 3 2 1

"First-time novelist James Zagel, himself a former police chief, prosecutor, and trial court judge, tells a story with the sort of detail only an insider can bring with such facility. Equally engaging is Mr. Zagel's vivid description of the city of Chicago in both its physical structures and the feel of the town."   —*New York Law Journal*

"Judge Zagel gives readers an interesting perspective on the legal system . . . a complicated thriller with a difference."   —*Mystery News*

"When [a] first-time thriller writer explains in explicit detail how to rob the Federal Reserve Bank in Chicago of $100 million in used money about to be destroyed, you might . . . think of the latest Bruce Willis movie. But when the writer is a Chicago federal district court judge, you should probably sit up and take notice, especially if he writes as well as Zagel. . . . Zagel incorporates enough scenes of Devine at work in his courtroom to convince readers that there are more subtle ways to influence and even short-circuit the judicial system than are dreamt of in our darkest *Law and Order* fantasies."   —*Publishers Weekly*

"Both morally irredeemable and close to irresistible, [Zagel's thieves are] an engaging cast of scoundrels. . . . A deft, elegantly written tour de force."   —*Kirkus Reviews* (starred review)

"What a thrill."   —*The Newark Star-Ledger*

"Compelling."   —*Booklist*

Money to Burn

Part One

Voir Dire

IT WAS MY first time inside the Federal Reserve Bank of Chicago, and I entered with the hope that the next time I was inside I would be carrying a hundred million dollars out to my nice Jeep.

I wore a fine dark gray chalk-stripe custom made by Fallan & Harvey in London. Leaving the courthouse, I had walked two blocks west to LaSalle Street. The Corinthian columns on the imperturbable Federal Reserve Building were rock solid but badly in need of a cleaning. I softly recited the Corinthian order: modillion, dentil, volute, rosette, acanthus leaf, flute, fillet, torus, scotia. I think I missed one or two; it had been some thirty years since Brother Mueller disciplined us at Mater Dei Preparatory School by making us memorize each of the parts of the Ionic, Doric, and Corinthian.

"It's good to meet you, Judge," the bank's public-relations director said as she handed me a blue plastic nameplate. "You might be surprised to know you are the first judge who ever asked for a tour. Tell me why you're interested in the Federal Reserve, and then I'll know what to show you." I clipped the nameplate to my right lapel so that everyone who shook my hand would know I was "Hon. Paul Eamon Devine."

"I'm trying to figure out how to rob the place," I told her. "We haven't had a pay raise in a long time." I waited a beat for the bank officer to laugh and then joined her.

I was telling her nothing but the truth. That is a good operating principle in lawyers and in certain kinds of lives, in particular the life I had always led. It worked out well as long as you understood that the rule is "speak nothing but the truth," not "tell the whole truth."

"Well, if you're going to steal our stuff, Judge, I better show you our security systems. I bet that'll change your mind." With an amiable wink, flattered to be humoring a federal judge, she could conspire with me, secure in the knowledge that the federal government had spent all the money necessary to protect the five to seven billion dollars in cash that comes to rest every day in the bank; no one would dream of challenging its security. Did she choose her clothes to look as impenetrable as her employer's walls? She wore a dark nailhead fabric without a visible crease and, a slim woman, she looked as solid as an armored car. Her own nameplate was perfectly squared against her jacket. "Orla Scorzo" she was, Irish mother and Sicilian father, I would bet.

We stopped first in a small viewing room to observe the counting floor through a glass panel. Dozens of employees were examining bills, stacking them, wrapping them, setting aside old and torn bills to be destroyed. Each employee had plenty of work space, not because the Fed was a considerate employer, but so the guards could keep an eye on each of them. Nothing an employee did seemed to fall out of the range of surveillance cameras.

"Our employees are usually very long-term. It's a good job. They get used to surveillance."

"They never wave at the camera?" I asked

"No, it would be a breach of etiquette."

"The very word." I was in my attentive-judge mode, gravely acknowledging her information, which I already knew to be true.

"We inspect all the bills. A lot of them are in very bad shape. We destroy them, about twenty to thirty million dollars a day. The rest are repackaged and sent out to banks. I'll show you."

We wound our way to the vault. The guard gravely opened several heavy doors for us, glancing at my escort's figure, then my face, my visitor's badge, and, last, my suit.

"Judge, you'll notice there are a lot of locked doors around here. There is no one—I mean, no one person—who has a key to every door. No single person can go from the vault to the counting room by himself. Whoever goes that way will need help with the keys and the locks. Here's the vault."

It was a simple room. All the electrical and ventilation systems, she told me, as if it were a great secret, were self-contained under the raised floor. The walls were very thick, and where there were no walls there were bars and huge vault doors.

"The vault rests on solid earth. No way to tunnel in from underneath—I mean, no way to do it without being pretty noisy for a pretty long time. We have sound-detection systems." She spoke like a mother convinced her child will walk on water any day now. "Somebody could try to tunnel in quickly from the side, but take a look here."

The vault was not flush against the walls of the building. There was a six-foot gap between the sides of the vault and the outside walls. I had known about that, too. An idiot could see this was not the most propitious way to crack this place.

"You could take power drills or bazookas and hammer a way into what you think is the vault and, after all that hard work, Judge, you wind up in this little corridor looking at a camera, and knowing the security guards are looking at you and laughing. But the vault is tempting." She patted my arm.

And it was. I looked, discreetly, at the cash piled on steel-and-glass cases set on wheels resting in the vault. My guide was speaking to a guard. I took the opportunity to stare directly at the money. One of the carts might, by itself, contain twenty million dollars. This was the cash that the banks were going to get back. It would be quite an accomplishment to walk away with it.

Orla Scorzo showed no concern that a big theft would ever occur. She seemed to have faith in the Fed, honest confidence in the way it did things. I think she was happy at work. I was, once, that way myself.

"And the worn-out money?" I asked my guide, who had come back to my side.

"We shred it. It goes on those conveyor belts to a shredder. In the old days, we burned it, but the Environmental Protection Agency complained. Shredding makes less pollution, and we can weigh what we shred to make sure we get it all. We try to reduce the temptation to steal." She turned on her one-inch-square, solid-black heel. "Let's go to the security monitors."

Standing among dozens of monitors and two officers whose eyes darted from one screen to another was the Wheezer, Secu-

rity Chief Ernest Corman. I had already determined that Lieutenant Charity Scott was off work this particular day, and the
man who despised her, the Wheezer, showed me how the monitors covered every square inch of the rooms containing the
money.

I looked closely at the monitors. They were everything that
Charity Scott had said they were when she described her operations to me. Corman said the same things. I could hear the little
wheeze whenever he took a breath, the sound Charity had
acidly mimicked.

I was beginning to feel warm. There might be ways to defeat
this system. I wondered how far away I was from Redding
Prindiville's office. I wondered what my tour guide thought of
the bank's new president, but I was not going to ask about
Prindiville. Then I saw Trimble Young's image cross one monitor. I gauged more than a little disdain in the Wheezer's face as
he, too, watched the screen. Charity Scott was proving to be the
perceptive observer for which I had pegged her.

"Thank you, Chief."

Corman nodded his suspicious face, his brows tightening as
his eyes met mine.

As we strolled past the hallways and locked doors, we
moved at a moderate pace while Orla recited various obscure
and semi-interesting facts about the Federal Reserve system. I
paid just enough attention so that I would notice when she
paused, which she did often, so that I could say "I see" or "really" at appropriate intervals. My mind was blazing with the
possibilities—the opportunity to break Prindiville's bank, the
ache to do it, and the knowledge that I was an idiot even to pon-
der it. Finally we were in the lobby.

"Thank you very much. It was a fine tour," I said in my
courtroom voice.

The armored car of a woman gave me a public smile.
"That's great, Judge. We have a little souvenir you can take
with you, even if you never figure out how to knock over our
bank." She handed me a little sausage-shaped item of compressed gray and green flakes. It looked like a squared-off lobe
of brain, and it took me a moment to realize what it was. "It's a
little gift we make out of the shredded money. Could be as

much as a few thousand dollars there, but it's impossible to put back together."

"No, it's only good for public relations." This time she grinned, the security guardian of the PR realm acknowledging her own conspiracy to create goodwill.

I rolled the sausage between my palms, warming it.

"What do you do with the shredded money that you don't use for souvenirs?"

"We shred it and dump it in a landfill—good, clean waste."

I thanked her, left the Fed, and went back to the courthouse. Right on LaSalle and then left on Jackson; the front of the Board of Trade Building was gleaming in the sunlight. I stopped to look and then went in to pick up a sandwich at the cafeteria. I saw the thing, myself, running through the Fed, un-escorted, my arms somehow wrapped around a hundred million very hot dollars.

I like my courtroom, but sometimes I wish it were more ornate. It is a large, paneled cube. The great architect Mies van der Rohe designed the exterior of the building. Someone who was less great than Mies designed the interior. The ceiling is twenty feet high; the wooden panels are each ten feet high and six feet across, stacked one on top of the other. The wood is oiled every so often to preserve it. For one year after each oiling the light gleams faintly off the wood, usually at the bottom of the upper panel, a narrow shining band about eleven feet above the floor. The ceiling is a light metal grille, an expanse of two-inch squares hiding dozens of fluorescent light fixtures and ventilation openings and ducts. If it weren't for the concealing grille, the ceiling would look at home in a factory. When a case drones on before me and I allow my eyes to fall about the room, I find no warm place to rest my gaze. A few judges put lamps on the ends of their very long benches, and if someone remembers to turn them on they create two small pools of warm light. I have no lamps.

The old federal courthouse, now torn down, was gratifyingly ornate. I have seen the photographs. The surfaces were rarely plain; crenelation, curlicues, carvings, moldings, multicolor, marble, and painted walls provided a rich canvas along with the wood. While your eyes followed the complicated patterns all over the courtrooms and marble hallways you could have lost yourself for a few moments. You could wonder if anyone ever bothered to clean the grooves and the hidden spaces behind the decorations. You shared your space with the dust of decades—dust present when Al Capone stood trial.

This afternoon after I returned from my tour of the Fed, all I had to do was sentence a man. When I entered the courtroom, the defendant was holding hands with a striking woman in her late thirties, presumably the new wife I had read about in the presentence report. I peered at her on the sly. What kind of woman would marry Massachusetts Slim, the hustler I was about to sentence?

Three months ago Massachusetts Slim had quietly entered a plea of guilty to mail fraud. On that day I knew only that he was a very handsome man who now lived in Massachusetts, and who once did a convincing impersonation of an investment advisor and blew a lot of other people's money. It's an old story in this courthouse.

Now I knew more. Slim plead guilty to a single count of mail fraud, which limited his maximum sentence to five years. A good prosecutor would have settled for no less than a ten- or fifteen-year ceiling on a plea bargain. If Slim had said no to that deal, a good prosecutor would have taken him to trial and convicted him of dozens of frauds. Slim was lucky not to have a good prosecutor. Years ago, when I was in the United States Attorney's office, I approved hiring him. He made a good beginning and then got lazier every year. After I read the presentence report and some letters from his victims, I guessed what happened. There were over a hundred victims scattered over the country, and Slim's records were a mess. The prosecutor had an easy choice for him. One, spend a lot of nights at the office taking pains to reconstruct the record and then haul himself around the nation to find out which victims would be good witnesses. Two, forget about all that hard work and take the one count where he happened to have good records and two decent local witnesses and offer a quick deal for a plea to that count. The defense lawyer had Slim take the deal within an hour of the time it was offered. Under the law, I could not even order restitution paid to any victim but the two involved in the single count of fraud. If another victim wanted to get money back, that victim would have to pay a lawyer to do the work the prosecutor should have done.

At sentencing I had to put this prosecutor's incompetence out of my mind. I had accepted the guilty plea; it was too late to undo it. Besides, so much money had been taken and spent that no restitution could likely be paid. You can only sentence for what has been proved, and his other crimes were not proved. I had to act as if I thought justice were being done.

Under an older law that applied to this case, I could give a sentence as small as I wished or as much as five years. Walking into court, I had in mind a sentence of one year. Defense counsel and the prosecutor expected something like that sentence to result from the plea deal. In my presentencing notes I had written two years as my maximum. You never know what might set you off at a sentence hearing, particularly when you are irritated with the way the case was handled. If you commit in advance to an upper limit, then you can avoid sentencing in anger. A good judge taught me this moderating strategy.

Testifying for the prosecution were Tim and Kathy, a married couple in their mid-forties and once close friends with Massachusetts Slim. Slim's first wife and Kathy taught high school together in Evanston. Tim started a company that made and distributed findings, small parts for watches and jewelry. Everything they had went into the company. "It was hard, boring work," Tim said haltingly, "and you never get really rich, but we did wind up with four million dollars when we sold the company." They did a lot of worthwhile volunteer work and attended to their three children. They had no reason to worry about their financial future because they had given most of their money to Slim to manage under the terms of very conservative trust agreements. Tim and Kathy told all their friends about Slim. Some gave money to Slim; some referred their friends. Slim sent them an eight-percent return on their money. The reports he mailed to them reflected the conservative investments they had agreed upon, and those reports were fictitious.

Slim spent about half the money he received to live his own

fine life, and the rest of it he invested in high-risk stocks; "inartfully selected" was the phrase his lawyer had used when I heard the guilty plea. When the bubble burst, Slim had only a fraction of the capital his investors had put in his care.

Tim did low-paid temporary work before he finally got a job with decent health insurance and a pension. "I'm on the road four days a week," he whispered now, his eyes fixed down on the prosecutor's shoes. "I'm gonna have to work until I'm sixty-eight to get a modest pension." Kathy went back to teaching, without her previous seniority. The life that they had planned for themselves was gone. They had lost not only their money but also their friends; everyone who might have supported them during this time was blaming the two of them for bringing Slim into their lives. Their pain was audible, but they did not ask me to be harsh with Slim. They just wanted to tell their tale. They made the plea bargain seem better. If they, who knew Slim, were not outraged, then he might not be that bad a man.

"Your Honor," Slim's lawyer said, "my client will speak first, and then we will hear from his wife." Why? I wondered. The defendant usually speaks last.

I watched Slim as he walked slowly to the lectern, wearing a well-cut dark blue suit and looking downcast. When he reached the lectern, he put his hands on the side rails and took a deep breath. He looked up and showed me his sad blue eyes and spoke softly.

"Your Honor, I'd like to say I was mentally ill when I hurt all the people who were dear to me, or that I was drinking, or that I was a drug user or a compulsive gambler. I'd like to give you a good excuse and I'd like to believe in that excuse, but I can't do it. There's no excuse in the world, not for this. I stand before you, a man who accepts his guilt."

He paused to look at me—really, I think, to force a nod. He won. I nodded.

Then he breached protocol. He turned away from me, from the court. He looked at Tim and Kathy and let his shoulders slump. "Tim and Kathy, I want you to know that I am sorry beyond words. I deserve your condemnation. I can never respect myself again because you are always in my thoughts."

He turned back to me. "Your Honor, I will work hard to pay

everyone back, even if it takes the rest of my life to do it." His words were surpassingly earnest. "I will be straight for the rest of my life because I can't live with the pain I have caused. Thank you, Your Honor."

He lied. He didn't mean a word of his apology. I knew because of the little piece of theater, turning to Tim and Kathy. From that transparent gesture I would have known what he was, even if I had not had a cleverly written report from his own psychiatrist that said nice things about him but described, in fact, a manipulative man without a conscience or a scruple. As a prosecutor and a judge I had seen enough sociopaths to know one. The only good thing about this one—he was not murderous. He would ruin you but leave you alive.

Slim was a natural criminal. Intelligent enough to make a fine living without violating the law, a natural criminal would commit a crime if he could see a way to do it without getting caught. He would cheat you out of fifty thousand dollars rather than earn a legitimate hundred thousand from you, even if both methods required the same amount of work. Honesty is too plain for him and crime glitters.

He retreated from the lectern as his wife walked toward it. He touched her arm, a light touch, performed so that I would see it.

Massachusetts Slim's wife had long ash-blond hair, not carefully done but not neglected either, the set of hair you see on women who devote their lives to good works. Her face was patrician, long and narrow, everything very straight with intense brown eyes. One of her ancestors, I had read in the presentence report, had been among the first white people to see Plymouth Rock.

The woman stood away from the lectern while she talked to me; she stood up straight and smoothed her long skirt before she began. She faltered at first and when she did, her face reddened slightly. "When I met my husband, my loving husband, I was a widow raising two small sons," she began. "We met when he enlisted to work as a driver at the Boston Women's Center, an unpaid driver, a volunteer. One evening, I had coffee with him. The first thing he told me was that he was under investigation for fraud, that he had caused many of his friends to lose their money, and that I would be better off if I stayed with him—excuse me, if I stayed away from him." She reddened more. "He has never lied to me, never." She glanced toward me, but her eyes didn't rise the whole way. "When I disregarded his advice and we grew closer, I saw what a good man he was. He spent more time with my sons than he did with me and brought them all the things they had lost when their father died."

Was it a set piece much like the one I had heard from her husband? No. I knew she was speaking in honest defense of her man, just as my wife, Ellen, would have defended me. She occupied space the way Ellen had, firmly but not overbearingly, and she drew me in as Ellen had. As a woman, honest but not innocent.

"For months and months, the investigation went on, and I know he was tormented by it. He never raised the question of marriage, even though he knew I was financially secure and could have helped him. When we did marry, he insisted on signing an agreement surrendering any claim to my estate. Since our marriage, he has lived in my house and, of course, I have paid the household expenses. But he has never asked me for money." She paused in distress. "He is the love of my life. He has always told me that he had been a bad man. He is not a bad man now. He is a good man. I need that good man with me and my sons as soon as I can have him back." She cast her eyes my way. "Thank you for your patience in hearing me out."

This last part was so heartfelt, her need and her devotion so real, and I was moved by her so strongly that I knew I ought to keep the sociopathic and coldly calculating Slim away from her for as long as I could.

I gave him five years in prison. It was not justice, but it was the best I could do. The one thing I could not do was to tell her I was giving him that sentence as a blessing to her.

The image of Slim's wife stayed with me. When I went home I walked directly to the basement office sanctuary that I had shared with Ellen.

The two of us had bought an antique partners desk. I had kept her side of the desk as she had left it on the day she died, except for the rough draft of a line drawing she had begun. She had a fair hand at broad portraits. I was the subject of this one and I could not bear to see myself in her lines, so I placed the drawing in the wide center drawer.

Ellen was thin and beautiful with dark red hair and bright green eyes. Her cheekbones were high and her eyes set deeply in her head. She was a couple of inches shorter than I—nearly six feet, a very tall Irishwoman. She could make her face say anything she wanted it to say. Her range of expression could go from absolute zero to the intensity of the sun's corona.

Ellen had been twenty-seven when we met. The Illinois State Police had found a single car wrecked against the huge stone footing of a viaduct. The driver was unconscious and the car trunk had popped open, revealing several thousand dollars visible in the trunk. The state police, honorable men and women, carefully inventoried every bill and secured the property for the unidentified driver, then on his way to the hospital in Joliet, Illinois.

The police ran his fingerprints against their computer and found they matched a record of a battery arrest over a dozen years earlier. The arrestee was Peter Alexiev, who did not have an Illinois driver's license or a phone number. Detectives who checked state police intelligence found that Alexiev cropped up as a possible money launderer.

When Alexiev woke up, the detective told him the car was totaled. Alexiev asked about recovered property and was informed there was only an empty suitcase in the trunk. Alexiev exploded. "There was a quarter million bucks in there!" he cried out. The detective gave him a slight nod of the head. Alexiev exploded again. "You guys stole it."

The detective smiled coldly. "Who's going to believe that the state police stole it?"

Alexiev started begging. He would be killed for losing the money. Couldn't they blow up the car so he could say the money was blown up, too? Too late, he was told; the car was already in a police lot.

When Alexiev looked his most depressed, the detective suggested that Alexiev could save himself by becoming a police informant. "But you guys stole the evidence," Alexiev protested.

"We could give some of it back to use in court," the detective suggested.

The money launderer led the state police to four separate

criminal organizations employing him. Alexiev was an effective snitch, even though he was really put out when he learned the state police had never stolen any of his money.

An assistant state's attorney in Cook County, Ellen Doherty was on the brink of charging an important group of organized-crime figures. They were the same men I was pursuing as a federal prosecutor. I had a much larger case, but it was not ready for indictment. I wanted her to wait. But thanks to Alexiev, she had stronger evidence. Alexiev would be hell on wheels as a witness, and I wanted him.

When Ellen and I met in my office to iron out the jurisdictional issues, she wore a dress, not the typical suit of women lawyers. It was a summer kind of dress, mostly turquoise with a little pattern. She wore perfume. I was optimistic. I had the federal army of law enforcement to back me up, and she would have trouble even finding a police officer to give her witnesses a ride to the airport. My opponent was a pretty girl in a flimsy dress.

"Hi, I'm Paul Devine."

"Your voice. It's nicer in person than on the phone," she said, smiling. "I'm Ellen Doherty."

My charm was working. "This work your office did was really good, and it fits perfectly with our case. If it is all put together in one prosecution we can take down the entire south suburban outfit."

"Congratulations. Why are we having this conversation?" Her voice was clear and her diction sharp.

"We need the assistance of this Alexiev, your witness. We need his testimony and the conversations he recorded."

She got up and started toward the door. "I don't want to rush this, but if you want Alexiev, he's yours. Give me a half a day's notice and he'll be waiting for you in my office."

"I really appreciate this. May I call you Ellen?"

"Of course, Paul," she said as she grasped the doorknob.

"Wait," I said.

"Not for long."

"What exactly do you want, Ellen?"

"Nothing. Why would I want anything? I'm ready now. My grand jury is going to indict in four weeks. We'll convict, and eight big boys from the outfit go to state prison."

"But we'll prosecute the same guys in six months," I found myself having to say. "We can't leave them out of our case—it'll create a giant hole for the jury."

"I think you are bright enough to figure a way to fill it."

"Two cases do not serve law enforcement," I said.

"Can you stop me from indicting?"

"No. But why would you do it?"

"Because my prosecution was handmade by a bunch of state troopers way out in the sticks and then up here in the city, and the federal government had nothing to do with it. The troopers and my office should be recognized for that effort, and it won't happen if I let you fold my case into yours."

"But this will be an example of federal-state cooperation."

"What cooperation? We have our case without any help from you. Did you ask us to help you develop your case?" Her voice was sharper now, her diction even more acute. "Come on, Paul. You'll have a sweet little press conference, my boss will stand shoulder to shoulder with your boss, and there will be a nice photo op. But our office will be shut out of the case and the FBI will get all the investigative credit."

"This is all about credit?" I shot back.

"Oh, Lord, can I be hearing this?" Her hand came off the doorknob and she was facing me, very tall and beautiful. "When was the last time you returned an indictment like this without any recognition from the media? My boss runs for election, he deserves the credit, and he needs it. Your boss, is he actually going to run for senator?"

"He might," I allowed.

"Then why should your boss get credit for our work? I'm indicting in a month."

I stopped talking and breathing. I realized I was still sitting down, looking up. I took a breath and asked, "What do you want?"

She had the leverage. I agreed that the state would indict the defendants the day before we did. After we indicted, the two prosecutors would meet and agree there should be only one case, the federal case. It would be prosecuted by both offices, and the state prosecutor would become a special federal prosecutor.

She tried the case, and I found myself another trial. We both won. Despite my desire not to see her, I found myself seated next to her at a bar association dinner. She seemed a different woman, no longer handmaiden to the devil. We had lunch every few weeks.

She changed jobs, leaving the state prosecutor's office on the west side of Chicago and coming to the Loop. She was an associate general counsel in one of the city's largest banks, a short walk from my office. It was easier to meet for lunch. I fell long before she did. Finally she came around. She started calling me Paulie.

Sometimes when I sit at my side of our partners desk I believe I see her sitting there in her chair, wearing her slightly off-center smile. "Ellen, I'm not crazy," I said now. "I think I'd like to rob a bank."

Dave Brody called at eight. His paramedic shift at the Chicago Fire Department ended at seven. "Hey, Paulie, need to see you about a job. Be there in an hour."

"I'm here as usual. Jazz later?"

"Jazz."

Dave had been my close friend since Mater Dei. He went to college—everyone at Mater Dei goes to college—but he loved action and joined the fire department, becoming the only blue-collar worker in our class. Refusing all promotion, he had more medals for heroism than he could count on both hands.

Heroism was not, however, part of the job he wanted to talk over with me. He had a little sideline that I had not known about until I had quit as an assistant United States attorney and had been a partner in a law firm for a few years.

He started his off-duty work in his quest for Bridget Ryan, his unattainable princess. In his way, he was still doing it for her. Although he has not spoken to her in years, she is, in her way, as big a part of his life as Ellen has been of mine. Dave was twenty-six years old when Bridget engulfed him. Small and aggressive, she fit a carload of clichés—pretty as a picture, thin as a reed, sharp as a tack and, with Dave, as wild as the wind. Even now he would stop in his tracks at the sight of a woman with Bridget's pale hair. The prominent Dr. Ryan did not want his daughter, the Belle of Sauganash, to marry a fire-fighter without enough ambition to take the lieutenants' examination. Dave would not ask Bridget to defy her father until he had enough money to buy the life she was used to living. That is how Dave became a torch.

He started fires, one or two a year, so that poor unfortunate owners of burned-out buildings could collect insurance money. Insurers were up in arms about some very large claims for fire damage and they suspected arson, but the fire department had declared the blazes to be accidental. In the small world of fire insurers and arsonists, a few independent consultants were able to arrange for a difficult-to-detect torching of a building. The consultants also gave advice on how to make the claim plausible, how to manage the business to make it look profitable for a few months before the fire, how to let some truly valuable things, like family mementos, go up in flames. Dave became highly valued in his field and known to an extremely select clientele. He thought he could continue setting his fires for profit as long as he did it seldom and well, and never worked for anyone but the three insurance consultants he knew to be safe. No firefighter had ever been hurt in a fire that he had set. No insurance company had ever refused to pay the claim on one of Dave's fires.

Five years after he started torching buildings, he had enough money to buy a colonial in Sauganash and pay for the good life, as defined by Dr. Ryan. In those same five years, he held his breath every time Bridget or her father found some surgical resident or big-firm lawyer; but all those relationships died. Bridget never stopped seeing him, not entirely, and their evenings always ended with her ritual of tearing his shirt off. I laughed when he told me that, but it was no joke.

The night he told her he had invested wisely, and had enough money for her to be his wife in style, "She gave me a little kiss, Paulie, on the cheek and said that we weren't really well matched, lived in different worlds, were uncomfortable in the other's world, blah, blah, blah. Marriage wouldn't work. 'I love you, but if we married, we'd learn to hate each other.'" Dave knew she was serious because she, who never set foot on public transport, insisted on taking the bus home. She departed the bus when the driver would not take her American Express card, and Dave hailed a cab for her.

"You were just a good lay to her, really. That's it," I told him.

"Yeah."

"You're fortunate to know the truth, Dave."

"Yeah," he said.

His life after Bridget seemed to have three functions—he saved lives, destroyed buildings, and prowled the clubs at night. He had the money for an endless tour of the Gold Star Sardine Bar and its fine music and Andy's and the other jazz clubs. If he could stand the volume, he spent time at places with names like Glow, Drink, and Shelter, where he picked up fast young women. The sex was fine, and it usually got better when they found out he was a fireman. I always wondered whether they would find him more exciting if they knew he was a torch.

After Dave told me his story, I finally understood why he would never let me bring him into my or Ellen's circle of friends—police officers, federal agents, bankers, and prosecuting attorneys. He knew he might get caught someday, and he did not want me to be seen as the best friend of a criminal.

I never shared any of this with Ellen. I was afraid she would disapprove of Dave Brody. Maybe I was wrong.

When he arrived I took Dave to the basement, the safest place in the house. He sat in Ellen's chair, across the desk from me. He was the only person who could do that. "Paulie, there is a job for me," he said. "Let me give you a detail or two."

"Don't bother," I said. "My advice is don't do it."

Dave's dark brown right eyebrow raised; he was amused. "Let's say, hypothetically, I don't follow your advice, that I just want your opinion on some details."

"Dave, I'm a judge, not a lawyer. This conversation isn't privileged. I would have to tell the truth if I got served with a subpoena."

"I'm not going to tell you that much about it. And, besides, if they know enough to start interviewing you, then I'm already charged, tried, and sentenced."

I just sat there. I had my own thoughts about crimes.

"The problem, Paulie, is that the job can be done only during two hours of one day of the week. It's the only time there are no people around."

I kept silent, but he outwaited me. "Can you do all of your setting up and all the rest of it in two hours?" I asked him. "Are you going to be in the place only the one time?"

He turned back and forth in the chair while he ran the thing through his mind. "I don't know."

"If you have to set up on one day and then come back later to pull the trigger, you know someone could find out what you've done—say, on a routine inspection of the heating system. The police could be waiting for you when you come back a week later. So don't do it."

Dave gave me his good-old-Paulie smile. "That's good advice. If I have to be there twice, I won't do it. But if I could do it all in the two hours? It's a hell of a challenge, Paulie."

"But you do this over and over again, Dave. Nobody bats a thousand. Even one strikeout is the end of you."

"Okay. Thanks, Paulie." Dave grinned at me and swiveled the chair, ready to bound up, to do something, to move so he could move.

"Have you seen Bridget lately?" I asked. He laughed at me. "I see her now and again," I told him. "Her shoulders have rounded, her chin has fallen, and she fights with her kids." Dave's eyebrow came up again, but he said not a word. "Okay, this job, it's wrong, Dave, a bad act with no justification."

"Yes it is, Paulie, and that's always bothered me—even if it hasn't stopped me."

Dave and I went to see Henry Butler at the Green Mill. The pianist went from modal streams to gospel. The man has very strong hands; his drummer was loud as hell, and we could easily hear Henry through it even in the so-so listening room that is the Green Mill. The place, a nightclub since the early 1900s, had run full tilt during prohibition and remained an odd historic landmark sitting in a bad uptown neighborhood. The club was half full. Henry Butler deserved a bigger crowd but, since he is sightless, they might have told him he filled the house.

From there we went downtown to Andy's. A few in the

crowd were there for the music, but most were there for the
character. It was an old club that limped along for years offering
Dixieland to conventioneers until the neighborhood around it
became trendy: the small industries moved out, the lofts were
converted into tony brick residences, and new buildings rose
up. Now people began to realize that the wrong side of Michigan Avenue was just a short walk away from the very right side
of Chicago, the big office buildings of the Loop and the glitter
of the Magnificent Mile. Richer, older people moved in from
the suburbs. Younger lawyers, doctors, commodities traders and
MBAs made their first homes there. At Andy's, Dixieland re-
ceded and the music advanced all the way into the 1950s. It was
packed with young professionals unwinding after work. When
a particularly good musician played, the later crowd included a
few gray-haired men who showed up to nurse drinks and listen
closely to the solos. In twenty years, Dave and I would be two
of them.

The music tonight might not draw in the older crowd. They
had a jazz singer, a guy from Seattle, Woody Woodhouse, not
very young, not very handsome, not known to me, and not
recorded on any major label. He was fabulous, but few in the
crowd paid enough attention.

Dave and I talked about old times—high school, girls we'd
escorted to jazz clubs twenty-some years ago. A couple of
women came up to the table. One of them knew Dave and they
sat for a while. It was nice but then they went away.

"You know, Paulie, those were very nice women," Dave
murmured to me at a point when the music went low.

"I agree."

"Some day, in the very distant future, Paulie, you might
want to meet somebody like them."

"I know, Dave."

"Women today are better than they were. They're stronger,
they look good, they use their minds—you know, like Ellen."
Whatever slick rejoinder I might have summoned was cut off
by a thundering drum solo.

We left after a fine up-tempo version of "Come Back to Me."
When Woodhouse sang Alan Jay Lerner's verse the image of
Ellen, in those last gorgeous days, came to me.

Money to Burn   21

From the hills, from the shore,
Ride the wind to my door,
Turn the highway to dust,
Break the law if you must,
Move the world, only just
Come back to me.

At three in the morning, Dave and I ate cheeseburgers at Weiner Circle on Clark Street. We looked across the dimly lit commercial street at the small, trendy shops for kids with green hair and kids with recent law degrees and we talked baseball. Sitting there with Dave and facing an empty home for the rest of the night, I felt like robbing the Fed.

2.

CHARITY SCOTT WAS a sergeant of the guards of the Chicago Federal Reserve. Her husband, Trimble Young, a master electrician, often worked in the vaults. She was a supervisor, so he could not be in the vault when she was in charge of everyone who was guarding the money. The Fed had a rule against spouses working in any assignment that might compromise security. One of them had to resign, according to the edict of Redding Prindiville, newly appointed president of the Chicago Fed. The decision was either made by Prindiville or approved by him. In his newly august position, he never needed to appear in court, so it surprised me when he bothered to present himself at this pretrial conference in the Scott case. By the luck of the random assignment of cases, this was his third one in my court. There was history between us, and he must have believed I thought well of him.

Scott and Young's complaint maintained that the Fed could easily devise a system that would keep husband and wife apart at work. As it was, whenever Trimble had to go into the vaults, Charity would change places with a guard in the lobby to remove herself from the vaults. Trimble was never in the vault for more than an hour or two. All of this, said their lawyer, was a reasonable accommodation between the interests of the married couple and the interests of the Fed.

The little twist in the case was this: Charity was black and her husband was white. The couple charged that the Fed supervisors were refusing accommodation because both black and white bosses were hostile to their racial intermarriage.

I had seen them first a month earlier. Charity Scott and Trimble Young had appeared without their lawyer, and I talked to them while the Fed lawyer waited in another room. I was trying to settle the case, and everyone agreed I could confer alone with each side.

They looked like photographs from an ad in *Vogue*. Trimble was a beautiful sort of man—his hair was fair, almost white, and thick and straight, and he had bright blue eyes and a small, aquiline nose. A thirty-year-old, he was very thin. He said nearly nothing but he looked bothered, put out.

Charity Scott appeared to have the color and texture of a deep noir Godiva chocolate, the ones with the white fondants that Ellen liked. Her face and her frame were geometrically correct in all proportions. All the elements of Charity's face partook of the classic golden mean. When she spoke, there was audacity in her eyes and a resonance of truth in her tones and timbres. She might be the world's most effective liar.

"Why are you willing to go ahead here without your lawyer?" I had asked. "You don't have to. We can reschedule."

"She's a really good lawyer, Your Honor. I met her when I was in the Army. She's very honest," Charity said. Trimble said nothing.

"So why isn't she here?"

"Judge, she told me that we didn't have much chance of winning. She told me she would like to take my ten thousand dollars but I would be better off in the long run if I kept it my-self."

"Your lawyer is very honest," I said. "But why is the case so weak? All you ask for is a reasonable accommodation?" The judge should never look surprised; it is inconsistent with the image of omniscience that makes the job easier to do and gives comfort even to the losers.

"Not really, Judge. Tell you why." Charity leaned forward, her face intent. She shimmered a little in the light with her high albedo skin. "The workers at the Fed have a lot of pride, like good soldiers. Everybody there has some little role in keeping America strong. But there's all that cash and, Lord in Heaven, you see it every day. Our mission is to keep the employees from stealing. We take it seriously. Even the employees appreciate us. Like even the surveillance cameras are a protection for the honest ones." Charity smiled, pleased. "One girl told me that if they didn't have those cameras, her boyfriend would make her steal a pack of bills a month."

"Yes," I answered, "but . . . ?"

She cocked her head toward her husband. "About ten per-cent of Trimble's calls are emergencies. We're short of staff, if you count only the people who do the real work. If I were them, I could prove that there is no way—I mean, no way—that the Fed can work it so that Trimble will not be in the vault when I am in charge of security." She shrugged. "They can't accommo-date."

"So why did you sue?"

"Trimble is white, I'm black, and the old boys don't like it. You can see the disgust on their faces when we walk out of the building. There's one guy, Mr. Prindiville's personal pet, the head of security, name of Corman—behind his back, everyone calls him Wheezer—who's really pushing this."

"This intermarriage—it bothers them that much, in this day and age?"

"Hey, some blacks think marrying a white guy is an insult to black guys. This Corman hates me because I'm black and tough and better educated, too. I went to college. I was an officer in the Army. I think he hates Trimble, too. He calls him 'pretty boy.' " Trimble nodded slightly as if to say thank you. "This

Corman has pinned a target on my back," Charity went on. "I can't prove it. No one ever says this stuff out loud and no one ever writes it down."

Her eyes happened into mine and contained them. "So, Judge, I'm trying to bluff them into some kind of deal we can live with. I lose authority to supervise when Trimble's around, and the most senior guard takes over—something, anything."

Maybe she was calculating that I would eventually learn why reasonable accommodation would not work and that she might not be able to prove racial animosity. If she told me first, and thus demonstrated her intelligence, then I would trust her. Then there was the way she looked, and she knew how she looked. If I met her face-to-face, I would be taken with her and want to help her. The first two moves, demonstrating unforced candor to a complete stranger and a clear understanding of the situation, were military skills. These are the ways a junior officer learns to deal with a new commander.

She was precisely the kind of person who, if God were paying attention, would never end up at the mercy of a despicable fool like Redding Prindiville.

"I will try to help your bluff." I must have done a good job because the Fed lawyer brought Prindiville with him for this second meeting with Charity and Trimble.

Prindiville stood and shook my hand. He looked grave and wouldn't let go for a moment. "Let me say first of all, Judge, how bad we in the legal community felt about the loss of your wife. I spoke with her at some ABA conferences, and she was a fine lawyer and a fine person. You have my deepest condolences."

Was it possible that he had forgotten what he had done to her? I could barely thank him for his expression, although this escaped his notice. He went on, "She was at United Airlines, I think? Then I remember she went to Choctaw Chip and took them public. That company is worth a couple of billion dollars now. What an extraordinary opportunity for her and to have it taken from her so inexplicably . . . as well as everything else. Such a shame."

"Yes," I said, "a shame."

He evaded mention of her work at the bank, the job she had just before United. She was at the bank when Prindiville accused the bank and Ellen, in particular, of a breach of trust. Prindiville was a team leader then with the Comptroller of the Currency. His failure to mention the bank probably meant that he did remember that he had hurt her.

Prindiville did not state the Fed's own case as well as Charity Scott just had. This prince of darkness was not so hot at his job. Prindiville was worried about Trimble being in the money-loading areas. Neither he nor his lawyer understood how intense the institutional concern with employee theft was. They acted as if the Fed security was primarily there to stop armed men from robbing the place and escaping in a hail of gunfire.

I trundled out of the study and back into my main office to ask Charity about both her and Trimble being on loading docks at the same moment. "Not an issue, sir," she said promptly. "If an electrical problem occurred at the docks, security would just shut down the area and stop operations until the problem was solved. They wouldn't have to open up until Trimble went back to his workroom.

Back to Prindiville I went. "You know, " I said, "I forgot to congratulate you on your appointment to head the Fed here. I know it must present different challenges from the ones you had as the Fed's general counsel in Washington. It's not lawyer's work now. You are the chief executive officer running a big bank and getting to sit with the Federal Reserve Board. A big job and the public is finally beginning to understand how important the Fed is to us all." I felt the slightest touch of fire in my throat.

Prindiville turned his ear to me, so as not to miss a word. "Why, thank you, Judge. It is an honor and I welcome the responsibility. I agree that the public is beginning to appreciate us."

"If it doesn't break any confidences, I would like to have lunch with you after this case is over. You can tell me what it is like to work directly with Alan Greenspan." I was currying favor with this swine. He gave me a small tip of his head. I felt as dirty as if I hadn't bathed in a month. It was then that I first thought of robbing his damned bank. But I pushed the thought away.

"An honor, Your Honor," he said. Was this a sample of his wit?

Time to make my pitch. "Now, regarding this case—if you could agree to an order that allowed the two plaintiffs to continue working as long as they were never physically in each other's presence at the bank, then the case could be settled now without anyone having to pay out any money and without anyone having to admit to doing anything wrong."

Prindiville nodded sagely, but I could tell he did not actually know whether this was good for him. So his lawyer piped up. "Judge, what happens if they violate the agreement?"

"There will be an order that gives me continuing supervision over the case to make sure that the agreement is honored. They know it would be easy to catch them violating the agreement. It makes sense to me."

Like only a few government representatives in court, Prindiville, as head of the bank, actually had the power to do something, to decide. "What advantage is it for the Fed if I accept this agreement?" he asked.

I put my palms out in front of me. "If you catch the two of them together at work, you can fire them. There won't be any arguments about your motives. Look," I told Prindiville and his lawyer, "you really don't know what these people will say. They could make up a story about how a supervisor said something terrible, as in a racial insult or racially based threat, something about uppity black women or racial intermarriage. Of course the only witness will be one of them. Maybe what they say will be believable even if it never happened. That wouldn't be good for your work at the Fed."

"A valid point, Judge," Prindiville said. "We accept your proposal, if and only if the two of them agree to the terms."

I stated the terms of the agreement aloud for the record, and Prindiville said yes. Then I went to Charity and Trimble and stated the terms again. They both said yes. The case was over. If you tell the judge yes, you have no right to take it back. After the deal was made, Prindiville gave me a little direct look, eye to eye, a bonding between two men of high principle. Then we parted with a firm handshake.

My craven performance complete, I went back to the people for whom I had undertaken it. Charity thanked me for my efforts; but she could not see how the order would help her. "The

Wheezer is gonna know that the problem isn't the loading area, and he's going to tell Mr. Prindiville."

"Probably, but Mr. Prindiville is going to be too embarrassed to come in and tell me that they made a mistake, that he didn't know what he was talking about."

"But what happens the first time Trimble and I are together in the vault area?" Trimble's eyes were following the conversation back and forth, like the net judge at a tennis match.

"I think you're still all right if you are in separate rooms, not physically in each other's presence," I said.

"Eventually, Judge, they'll catch us in the same room together more than once. It's only a matter of time."

She was quite right. "Think of this, Sergeant: If it takes a year, you have had that extra year at the Fed. And what if it takes two years or five? You'll have had those years, and maybe the bigots will retire or get transferred. It can be good to buy time." I thought of robbery again, and I looked closely at her.

Charity and Trimble left my office, and a moment later Prindiville popped his head into my chambers.

"I'm sorry to interrupt, Judge, but I believe I have a picture of myself and your wife at the corporate counsel dinner last year. I'd like you to have it, if it would not create an ethical problem for me to give it to you."

It might, I thought—a lawyer should not give anything to a judge who is in the middle of hearing one of his cases. But I wanted to see Ellen's face in that photo, to look for a sign of what I knew she was thinking as she stood next to Prindiville. So I told him to send it.

Ellen would have said, "Paulie, dear, you have finally learned how to push the jerks around in the right way. Good for you, and if you get a little sick to your stomach, it's all for a worthy cause. Let me give you a kiss to make it better."

In a minute Monsignor Royce would start talking about me to the all-class convocation for students and parents, also called Alumni Honors Day. He would praise me as he was now praising Thomas J. Tully, the mathematical genius. I was sitting in the huge new auditorium/indoor athletic facility of what was in my youth, and may still be, the best high school in Chicago, Mater Dei. Then as now, St. John Royce ran the place—seeing to its excellence and advancing its prestige.

Tom Tully accepted his distinguished-alumnus award, making a bad joke about how the complete orderliness of Mater Dei actually hindered him when he set out to find out why snowflakes looked the way they did and, along the way, perfect the mathematics of chaos. All nine of his children had come out to see the ceremony. Three of them laughed at the chaos joke. Tully sat down next to me.

Behind the Tullys sat Dave Brody, my classmate and my oldest and only friend at Mater Dei. When you go through school with the nickname Perfect Paulie, it is hard to find many friends. Dave wore his Chicago firefighter's dress uniform and against the dark cloth, I could see all his decorations. He had quite a lot of them; he had a penchant for running into burning buildings and braving gunfire in order to give CPR to people caught in crossfires. I had never seen the medals before. He had told me more about arson than heroism.

Dave grinned at me when Monsignor Royce began to declaim the virtue of myself. Paul Eamon Devine. "Like Professor Tully, young Paul Devine was one of the boys to whom I taught the calculus. I thought I had another Tully in my class, but it was not to be. It took Tommy about a month to learn more math than I was capable of teaching him. Paul, on the other hand, took a whole six weeks before he figured out the entire calculus."

Tully whispered in my ear. "So slow, Paulie."

"Paul did one thing that Tommy did not, that no other student before or since has ever done; he maintained a perfect record at Mater Dei. He received the highest possible grade in every course he took, and he took the most difficult courses we offered. He read Greek and Latin as well as St. Jerome, and he was our best student in the sciences and in the literary arts."

I whispered in Tully's ear. "One-trick pony you are, Tommy."

"And his achievements were not solely academic. He and his friend, Dave Brody, who I see here today, led Mater Dei to the first state championship in any major sport won by a school from the Catholic League—when they defeated all comers, public and private schools alike, to win the state high-school baseball championship two years in a row. I am sure he will forgive me for telling you that he did not have athletic gifts to rival his academic talents"—he nodded my way, to keep me in my place in the world—"but he worked as hard as he could to improve himself, and he never backed down. The only high-school athletic record he holds, I think, is the record for most times being hit by a pitch. I am sure he could have dodged a few of those pitches, but he was willing to take the blow in order to get on base for our team."

I worked a bit at keeping my face attentive and neutral because now I was thinking how the best way to break into the Fed would be to keep it from looking like a break-in at all, the way a good torch makes the fire look like an act of God.

"From Mater Dei, Paul Devine went on to graduate summa cum laude from Harvard, from which school he received a full scholarship despite his absence of need for the funds, and then, before his further education, he spent two years in the intelligence corps of the Army. . . ."

I heard "Yale Law School" but lost my concentration at the moment I was discovering a way to convert my act-of-God theory into something doable, all the while managing, I think, to keep an interested yet modest expression on my face. The modesty came from a slight smile on my lips and slight bow of my head as if all this pleasant praise was too much to bear.

I stopped thinking about the Fed and its guarded treasure when Monsignor Royce looked down to read the words on the plaque he was to give me. I knew it was the last thing he would do before calling on me to speak. I knew what I would say when it was my turn. I don't deserve this, but if I did deserve it, most of the credit should go to my parents, my family, and my school whose crushing tuition fees are, in fact, a bargain. All you students should know that if I could do this, you could do it too if you would just try hard enough. And all you parents should know that your children's chances of doing so well would improve if you gave the school more money to build a new science center—all this said gracefully enough to avoid giving offense and plainly enough that the point is not lost.

There would be no hint that I had it in mind to become Mater Dei's most perfect criminal.

I had learned a new lesson and found a new truth. I knew how to get away with stealing millions and millions of dollars from the Federal Reserve Bank of Chicago. I would have help from the inside, but the key to success was known only to me. I wanted and needed Dave Brody to help. I thought about the rightness of asking Dave to help and about how I would ask him. I thought about why I wanted to become a criminal. I knew I wanted this, but Mater Dei teaches its scholars to ask why.

Prindiville must be a good part of the reason why I would rob the Fed. I had wanted retribution for Prindiville for a long time, more so since Ellen had died. I thought this as I walked to the podium after the good Monsignor beckoned me forth. I nodded to Dave Brody.

I knew I would do it. I was elated with the criminal secret I held. I glided through my short plea for money for the new science center.

Monsignor Royce practically danced up to me while I was speaking with Dave. "Hello, Brody! Still with Paul Devine. You two still close friends?"

"Yes we are, Father," Dave answered.

"Wonderful thing, your friendship. Such different boys you were. What was it now, Brody—you won twelve letters here, football, basketball, and baseball, every year you were here?"

"It was sixteen, Father. Shotput and broad jump in track-and-field."

"And you look to be in fine shape still," Monsignor Royce said as he lightly punched Dave's stomach and then pretended his hand was in pain. "So, Brody, what are you doing with our fine fire department?"

"I'm a paramedic." Dave kept on his solemn, just-doing-my-duty-ma'am face.

"Oh, I didn't know," the Monsignor replied. "That must be rewarding work," he added a little drily.

Both of Dave's eyebrows came up, and I hustled him off. We strolled by big lawns and little patches of wildflowers—it is the thing in Chicago to re-create little islands supposed to look like the prairie that was here in the nineteenth century before Jean Baptiste Point DuSable decided this was a good place to live. The football stadium was larger and fresher now; they had knocked down two of its walls and rebuilt them to accommodate a soccer field. At the baseball diamonds a new computer laboratory rose beyond the left-field fence.

"You knew then why we called you 'Perfect Paulie,' did you?" Dave asked in a voice as dry as the one Royce had used with him.

"Well, Dave, could it be because in a class of four hundred boys, in the best high school in the city, I was the best student and I was a big kid who picked up Tubby Houlihan and threw him through the gym door when he ran me into a wall in gym class? Because my father had money and my mother had mystery and glamour? Because I never misbehaved, I never challenged any of the teachers, and I was nice to adults?"

"Could be, Paulie." A smile flickered on his face.

We stopped and sat on the home-team bench. "You were beyond belief on this field, Dave. Not just that you were so fast you were grabbing ground balls on my side of second base, but it was all those hitches and lurches—it was hard to believe what I was seeing. You were absolutely ungraceful, and you fooled a lot of opposing players. You were so fast you didn't need to be smooth."

Dave laughed. He was as big and solid as he had been then; age showed only around his eyes. Then he looked away and grew quiet.

"It was easy for me. I was lucky," Dave said as he kept his gaze toward right field.

"I wasn't so good, but I loved baseball because it was running and jumping and smashing the ball and close games." I said this to myself more than I said it to Dave. "And then we won the championship, and I still think of it; you can never get that kind of thrill after you've grown up."

What I thought was that packing many millions of dollars away as fast as we could when the two of us were side by side in the vault required choreography and practice just like the double play.

3.

A WEEK OR so after Paul E. Devine Day, I saw Charity and Trimble. The settlement I had brokered was inscribed as a court order for me to sign.

We had some time in chambers. The Fed lawyer had brought the wrong version of the consent decree. He decided to walk the short distance back to his office and get it himself, so I asked about how Charity had decided to join the Army. Nearly all people I have ever met want to tell you about themselves.

Charity shrugged, wary. "The Army would pay for college, and train me with heavy equipment. That's why I went in."

"Why heavy equipment?"

"My Uncle Edgar, my Dad's brother, my favorite man, was the neighborhood mechanic. He liked to show me things, and it just stuck with me."

"The Army keep to its deal with you?" I asked her.

"We got along great, me and the Army. I had the right genes for it. I got in shape fast, I liked the weaponry, and I liked the stress. The Army tells you exactly what it expects and when. No extra Bible classes like I had to go through with family back home. And if it had wheels or tracks and an internal-combustion engine, I learned how it worked, how to use it, how to fix it, how to make sure it stayed up and running, and how to handle the paperwork for it. I had something the sergeants needed—I could repair everything from a motorcycle to an armored personnel carrier. Plus I was quick about it."

She was warming to her story, I could tell. Trimble watched her adoringly, which seemed to be his chosen role in life. "How did you become an officer?"

"I was good. I made sergeant. They sent me to the desert combat training base. I had a squad of soldiers. Then the base commander changed, and the new guy was a colonel who really hated blacks."

"How did you survive?"

"Survival was not a problem. Getting that colonel was a hell of a lucky break." Charity enjoyed the telling of this part of her story especially. "The colonel was really sly about handling black folks. The Pentagon kept stats. If he promoted too few blacks or disciplined too many, they asked questions. So he hammered the hell out of the weakest of his black soldiers—no second chance, no retraining, no probation. He drove them out of the service. He got rid of people like me by offering good transfers. He got me into officer candidate school. A hell of a deal."

I knew the kind of man she was talking about. "Did you ever talk to this commander?"

"I never got within ten feet of the man. But he's the reason I commanded a maintenance platoon for the engineering corps. I liked the people. I had some close friends." She squinted, thinking. This last fact seemed to surprise her.

"What happened? Why'd you leave?"

"Well, I woke up one day and found I was just like Reverend James and, believe me, no one should be like Reverend James."

"Reverend James?"

"My other uncle, my Mama's brother."

One very hot twilight in South Carolina—one of a long streak of ultrahot nights—six soldiers in Charity's platoon, crazed by heat and the smell of gasoline, staged a forklift race. They laid out two slalom courses on a concrete tarmac and put stacked pallets at one end of each course. The object was to race an empty forklift through the course, pick up the pallet, and race the fully loaded forklift back through the course. The racers drank beer and made bets. Charity caught them in the act, just in time to see a loaded forklift tip over, cracking the skull of its driver on the concrete. Until she talked about the forklift race she had sat, ramrod straight. Now she leaned forward, as if she had chosen only me to hear this story, Trimble forgotten beside her.

"The general was understanding. 'Troops get drunk, they do

things,' he said. 'Their commanders deal with it so it doesn't happen again. You do that, Lieutenant, and everything will be just fine. Just so nothing else happens on your watch.' So I changed. I leaned on them. The troops thought I never slept. My unit performance ratings skyrocketed. I made first lieutenant after minimum time in grade. It all bided with me until one week I realized I was looking at faces like the faces of the scared kids in Uncle Reverend James's Bible camp. I softened up a little bit, but the troops' faces stayed the same. I decided not to reenlist and took my commission to the reserves." She spoke crisply and quickly.

I wondered if she would have found Mater Dei was like Bible camp. "You regret leaving?"

"No. It finally got the Reverend James out of me. When he was gone, I didn't need that twenty-four-hour-a-day structure in the military."

"And you could come home because this man didn't matter anymore," I said.

"Well, I came home. I got work at the Federal Reserve Bank; got another college degree part-time at the U of I–Circle. The government preferences work for me; I'm black, female, and a veteran. The human-resources guy said I would go far with my intelligence, skills, and ambition. He knew every time I got promoted he would get credit for upping a black and a woman. I liked the bank."

"And you got yourself your own life." I took care in looking at her and I saw both daring and discipline in her face.

"I took a subscription to *Vogue*."

"You keep it on the same shelf as your *Road and Track*?"

She smiled, genial for a moment. "I had about a year and a half of fun. I was fine, I think I must have softened up a bit, because if I hadn't, Trimble would never have got up the nerve to ask me out." She smiled again and turned her face to her husband.

Our talk stopped then because the papers were ready. The lawyer for the Fed wanted me to explain the terms to both Charity and Trimble and to do so in open court. They knew the terms as well as the Fed lawyer, but the Fed wanted it all on the record. I obliged. "You understand that you have to stay apart, barring a life-threatening emergency, at all times while you are on duty at the Fed. If you do not obey this order, then either one or both of you will lose your jobs and you will not be able to come to court to get them back. The only appeal available to you will be an administrative hearing within the agency."

"I understand, Your Honor," Charity answered. Trimble said the same words. As she turned to leave, she moved her lips inaudibly forming the words "thank you." I was thinking how much I would thank her if she agreed to help me at the Fed.

At four that afternoon, I called Dave. "Can you meet me tonight? It could matter," I said.

"Has to be tonight?" he asked.

"Not absolutely. As long as it's soon."

"Tomorrow night, Paulie. I have something else tonight. It's the only night of the week that I can do it, and it'll take a full two hours, so let's meet tomorrow."

"I hope you'll be free tomorrow, Dave."

"I will be if you need me, Paulie."

Dave picked me up at Post Place, a stub of a street on the north edge of the Loop and well away from my usual haunts in South Loop. It runs into lower Wacker Drive, part of a complex of multidecked streets. Dave never asked me why I wanted him to do something; he just said yes or no.

He drove a Ford Crown Victoria, an old man's car. His father ran a Ford dealership, and Dave was loyal. His second car was a white Mustang convertible, which he used to cart around his endless line of women. I waited for him midway down the ramp. It was the beginning of a perfect night, the air soft and cool. I wore a reversed sweatshirt, nondescript pants, and an old pair of running shoes. I like to be noticed for my clothes, but that night I didn't want to be noticed at all.

Dave drove around the covered drive to find someplace where we could talk quietly.

Lower Wacker Drive is beneath Upper Wacker Drive. Both run along the Chicago River. Even the lower drive is built above the ground. As one drives south from the river, turning on Columbus Drive, there is still another lower level, this one resting on the bare earth. Because Chicago lies on low land near a big lake, the early buildings downtown were literally raised several feet above the ground. Men made fortunes from knowing how to lift a six-story building using jacks and timbers without cracking the plaster or breaking a window. The space left under raised buildings they used for tunnels, rail spurs, and the like—for the hard machinery of the city. Down here people could park cars with bodies in the trunks, knowing it would be quite a while before anyone took notice.

Dave stopped when he reached the darkest part of the lowest level, the police auto pound, now closed for the night. He let the engine idle and gave me an indulgent look. "Nobody is following us."

"That's a fine thing."

"So, Paulie, you gonna tell me why we're here?"

"I have a job especially for you, for us."

"What kind?"

"You're not going to kill anybody," I told him.

Dave laughed quietly. "Good. I was worried."

"It's a theft."

Dave stifled his grin. He knew that even simple jokes were beyond me. "What do you want to steal?"

"Paper money."

Dave put both hands on the steering wheel and breathed deeply. "Now, Paulie, I think that's tough to do, what with all the plastic and the checks and the wire transfers. Nobody keeps much of it around anymore, just armored cars and banks. Big risks there." Dave looked straight ahead for quite a while. I waited and looked straight ahead, too. It was too dark to see each other's faces clearly and, anyway, it was rude to stare at your oldest friend.

Dave could not be hurried. He had been the same way since high school. He even looked pretty much the same, memorable but not as exotic as Charity and Trimble. A couple of minutes passed before he said, "How much you thinking of stealing?"

"Depends on how much we can carry. Fifty million—maybe a hundred million dollars."

Dave whistled, and I think he felt silly for doing it. This was the effect of the enormity of my notion. He finally turned his face toward me. "You're crazy. Nuts," Dave said, but he said it half-heartedly.

I just shook my head no. Dave's fingers played on the steering wheel; it calmed him. "Paulie, even if we could grab that much money—the heat on us. It's just too hot. They'll have a thousand cops on just that one case."

"There'll be no heat at all, because—they'll never even miss it. They won't care."

"Never miss a hundred million." His voice was dismissively even.

"Not for a moment. Have faith, Dave."

"Who wouldn't miss a hundred million?"

Dave put the car in motion, moving east to the Lake Michigan yacht clubs. Above us lay one of the liveliest parts of Chicago and in the muted world below, I heard the syncopation of the city. He nosed the sedan to the ramp on the far east side of the covered streets. The lake was all we could see now, and on it sat a two-hundred-foot yacht, lit up like a Christmas tree. Four couples danced on an afterdeck. Both of us gazed at the boat.

"You could have a boat like that yourself," I said. "You could give up your off-duty jobs."

Dave looked down, his teeth worrying at his lower lip. Finally, he gave me a skeptical smile. "Too garish. I'd buy something smaller." He turned the car onto the open road and drove up to Lake Shore Drive. After a few moments, he asked, "Why this, Paulie?"

"As the fellow who climbed Mount Everest said, 'because it's there.'"

"First I ever heard that this was the guiding philosophy of your life."

I shrugged in the dark. "All right," I said, "there is this: I want to strike a blow against the system."

It did not get the laugh I expected. "You could explain that, Paulie," Dave said.

"It's not just the things I've told you before, the cases you have to decide the wrong way because the law is foolish or because it gets taken to extremes..."

"Those the ones you call 'doing injustice under law'? Hail

Mary, full of grace, Paulie Devine is an antigovernment protestor. You going to start chaining yourself to post office doors, throw paint on our congresswoman? Where do I sign on?"

"Yes, it's funny but when I was a federal prosecutor, I cared that I was right." I turned to face him across the car seat. "I never pursued a case just because I could win it and, you know, I could make a case made out of soap bubbles look built out of granite. When I was in the office there was a joke: 'Any decent lawyer can secure the conviction of a guilty man; it takes real skill to convict an innocent one.' We all knew that was a joke. I think some of the guys today don't know it's a joke; they think it is a standard to live by."

"How is stealing a ton of money going to make that any better?" Dave asked.

"I don't know. Maybe it's just the guy at the Fed. I'm angry at him."

I told Dave about Mrs. Blaskow and Redding Prindiville. The case had gnawed at me for months and was one of the lesser reasons why whenever I saw Prindiville, my stomach clenched like a fist. This lady—a late-middle-aged widow who was the sort of person who referred to herself as a lady—had lost her home to a foreclosure. Facing temporary financial difficulties, she was unwilling to cash in any asset her husband left her. He had told her never to touch her capital, just live off the income. She knew that it would take a long time to foreclose on her house, and so she paid every bill but the mortgage. Then after the foreclosure, she knew she had several weeks to redeem her house. She had a Treasury bill she could cash on maturity to do this. But she did not want to cash it even a day early because she was unwilling to pay the penalty. That was her husband's rule, and she was going to follow it.

On the day of maturity she took the bus to the Federal Reserve Bank of Chicago—only to discover that the teller windows were closed. They had closed down at 2:00 instead of 2:30 in order to celebrate a supervisor's birthday. She was sure she had missed her chance to save her house with the T-bill. For weeks she was so demoralized that she did nothing, and her neighborhood bank simply sold the house out from under her. Eventually she became angry with the Fed and sued.

She had no claim. The Fed was immune from lawsuits like hers. And, even if it was not immune, she had no real damages. There were lots of ways around her problem but she froze and didn't use a one of them. By the time I saw her, she knew this. She told me she wanted an apology and hoped for a voluntary payment from the Fed. I hoped that the Fed would say it was sorry and give her a little compensation, after which I would tell her to put the past away and live a new life beginning today. This works at times.

I never expected that Prindiville would appear for this trivial matter, but it was a public-relations dilemma and he was the new general counsel in Washington, D.C. I don't know if he knew that Ellen was my wife; she used her maiden name when she was at the bank. He would have found out soon enough when he started going to the national corporate counsel association meetings. Mrs. Blaskow told him outright that first she wanted an apology. The Fed public-relations strategy was to place the blame on Mrs. Blaskow, using her own mistakes against her.

"I do sympathize with you, madam, but you know the loss of the house was your fault, not ours," Prindiville declared with a showy gentleness. "The Treasury bill was good. We paid you when you came in with it a couple of months later. You know, you could have gotten a loan from a bank and used the Treasury bill as collateral, don't you?"

"Yes," she answered, "but—"

"There is no 'but' about it. You could have turned the bill in early. It would have cost you a few dollars but you would still have your house. That is right, isn't it?" He looked like a dentist who would conveniently forget to use anesthesia.

"I suppose."

"You could have gone to the judge in state court and asked him to extend the payment deadline. You could have gone to the mortgage company and asked them to wait one more day. You didn't do any of those things."

"No." The woman's voice was smaller now.

The old lady started to stare at my conference table, and her face reddened. "Yes, Mr. Prindiville," I interjected, "but perhaps she had a right to count on your office staying open until it is supposed to close."

Prindiville agreed this was "all a regrettable but avoidable misfortune," but his tone told me that he would never apologize for anything. He was Prindiville and he was the Fed, above legal error and above the moral duty to apologize just as he was at the Office of the Comptroller of the Currency. So I apologized for him and dismissed the lady and her lawsuit as gently as I could.

"That is one fine tale. But, Paulie, robbing a bank because the president's a mean lawyer? You going to rob the houses of all the jerk lawyers in Chicago? The work would never end. There's something else there, Paulie."

I was silent there for a few moments. Then I said. "Prindiville is the man who laid the brick on Ellen when she was at the bank."

"Oh, that guy."

"That guy."

"But didn't it work out okay in the end?" Dave asked.

"Ellen wanted to move up in the world, to be general counsel somewhere. She wasn't planning on staying on as assistant corporate counsel at a big national bank. When Prindiville accused her of violating the trust duties of the bank, she was lucky not to get fired."

"What was it that they said she did? I remember neither of you was giving me much in the way of details back then."

"There was a real estate investment trust at the bank, designed for pension funds that put in a minimum of two million each. Real estate values took a dive. Some of the fund investors got nervous and demanded their share of the portfolio to be paid to them in cash. Their deal with the bank said they had the right to do this, but the bank couldn't give out cash without selling a lot of real estate at depressed prices and this hurt all the remaining investors, most of whom wanted to leave their money in figuring that real estate always goes up in the end. This is what the bank had to choose between—break up the portfolio and lose money for everybody or keep the portfolio and refuse to give some of the investors the cash they demanded. Honor the contract and screw most of the investors or do what is best for the majority and dishonor the contract. A lawyer's nightmare."

"And Ellen decided what?" asked Dave.

"Dishonor the contract. If anyone wanted out, the bank could just give them individual pieces of property from the portfolio and let the investor do what he wanted with them."

"That's an abuse of trust?"

"No. It was her honest opinion—might be legally wrong, but she was trying to do the most good for the most people. Her problem was that the investors that wanted out included a few public employee pension funds and those funds had friends in Washington who decided to lean on the bank, hoping that the bank would throw some of its own money at the public employee funds and make the problem go away. When the bank went to the comptroller of the currency to get approval for its plan, the funds thought they had it wired for the comptroller to say no. But the comptroller didn't simply say no. In the person of Redding Prindiville, senior official in the office, the comptroller said the bank's entire course of conduct was a breach of trust and had one Ellen Doherty done right, all these bad things would not have happened. Bad enough, but then he suggested that she had given her legal advice knowing it was wrong and did so because she was ambitious and decided to tell the bank officers what it was they wanted to hear rather than tell them what was right."

"Jesus, Paulie."

"Yes, 'Jesus.' The public pension fund guys who caused the whole mess called Ellen and apologized. They said they believed that she was wrong but never believed she was acting in bad faith. These same guys said the same things to Prindiville, but he refused to back off. The comptroller had spoken and if the bank or Ellen disagreed, they could have a hearing. There was no chance that anyone was going to hire her for a high-visibility position in a serious company until that cloud over her head was gone."

"And it took a long time, didn't it, Paulie?"

"It took four years for the comptroller of the currency to say there was no mismanaging of trusts, no violation of law. Four goddamn years of administrative trials and court hearings and her having to live with the accusations of dishonesty. He was brutal for her. She could be tough to live with then."

"Paulie, it's hard to believe that Ellen could be tough on you. She adored you."

I looked away for a while.

"Of course," Dave said, "I can't imagine she would ever have spoiled you by saying that she adored you."

"I know," I said, "Ellen tried to be the same as she always was. With me, she failed. Everybody else saw her calm face; I saw her demons. She knew it, she was sorry, but we were both unhappy, often unhappy. I couldn't blame her, I couldn't help her, and I couldn't leave her. You never get back that lost time if you're trying for a big-time legal career, especially not when you're a woman. We never had reparations for those bad years of marriage either."

"I have a question, Paulie. How do you get even with this guy when he won't know that he has been hit? You said he wouldn't know."

"I'll know," I answered.

"Won't be enough."

"Probably not. But I plan to tell him after the statute of limitations expires and we can't be prosecuted."

So we sat silently some more until Dave said, "I am hoping you have a hell of a plan. I hope nothing goes wrong."

"If we're very, very careful, nothing will go wrong," I told him.

"Will you be wearing your robe during our robbery or will you be incognito?"

We drove out of the underground on to Lake Shore Drive, and I directed Dave nine miles to the north where we stopped at a steak house in Evanston near Northwestern University. You could eat the food there. Most people did not come for the good jazz.

"I'm with you, Paulie, whatever your crazy reasons," Dave said during a break for John Campbell and his trio. "You want to know why?"

"Yes."

"It's the way you handled school, the way you handled everything. You figured out how to get your way and then you executed your plans. I still don't know how you got them to let you out of high school after lunch."

"You know how. I always got an A. And I never challenged the teachers on anything—that way they would trust me. You, on the other hand, lived by your own rules."

"Paulie, you were going to movies in the Loop and hanging around Rush Street every afternoon."

"And talking to bartenders and call girls while they were having breakfast." I grinned at my friend. "But I was also in the Crerar Library and the Newberry Library reading books and writing papers. It was a trade-off with school, just like you had a trade-off. They put up with you because you were a four-sport all-state athlete."

"You're forgetting that my father gave them a new station wagon every year."

"You've always made it work, Dave, and so have I."

"Right, like your idea that we should forget about Catholic girls," Dave said.

"It worked, didn't it?"

My greatest early feat as a thinker was to deduce, from the bragging of the boys in the baseball leagues, the reason why we couldn't get laid, despite Dave's all-star athletic status and my own as a decent consolation prize for the girl who didn't get Dave. No girls, I declared, got it on with boys of their own religion. In those days the Jews said Catholics girls were great. The Catholics said Jewish girls were hot. The WASPs scored with both Jews and Catholics. Girls, I had reasoned, must start thinking about marriage years earlier than boys did and decide to surrender nothing to a boy they might marry.

I had failed with my dream girl, Nancy Leary, with a face like an oval jewel, accented with black eyes and framed by straight ebony hair. She, of a good Catholic family, admired me for being first in my class.

"Paulie, we had to work pretty hard to get invited to that youth group in the Fourth Presbyterian Church," Dave reminded me.

"But it was good for our character, hobnobbing with the impossibly elite Presbyterians on the best part of North Michigan Avenue, and you finally figured out that you were going to lose your virginity with a girl who wasn't Catholic."

"Sometimes you were a little too scientific for me, Paulie. 'Warm weather is good because the girls wear less clothing,'" he said, mimicking my precise tone. "'Cold weather is good because girls wanted to hug for warmth. Ergo we have to have a date on a hot, dry evening and end up in a place where the air-conditioning is too intense.' You said those words."

"I was right about that, too."

"Sort of."

On just such a hot and cold evening, two girls, one Jewish and one Presbyterian, accepted our invitation to see us play against Gordon Tech and then go to a movie. Finest damn game I ever played. I drove in the winning run. Dave played his usual fine game and looked handsome. After a movie about love lost and found, we drove to my house. My parents were in New York at a wedding.

I made love, clumsily, on the precise terms dictated by Andrea Weiss. It was not all that I had thought—and, later, learned it would be—yet even so, I had lain with an unclothed girl and believed myself to be a man.

John Campbell started to play his piano again. A short, final set. When it was over Dave and I got into his car. I asked him then, "What did you mean before when you said 'sort of'? Are you telling me nothing happened for you that night?"

"No, not at all." Dave was smiling.

"Tell me what you meant."

"You know, it wasn't a race, Paulie. But you thought it was."

"You meant that night was *not* your first time and you didn't want to hurt my feelings."

"Right."

"Okay, thanks, but you said 'sort of' when I said that my hot-cold strategy worked."

"Yes, and it works now even with grown-up women." He grinned at me in the dark.

"I see. So was it a Catholic girl the first time?" I paused. "Who?"

"Paulie, it was Nancy Leary, and you better hope that you

are better at figuring out crime than you are at figuring out women."

When we said good-bye that night, Dave looked straight at my eyes and told me, "If you're going to do this, then do it; don't let it sit. Start now. This is the voice of experience."

·

4.

I HAD TO recruit Charity. I hesitated. There was one step I could take first. If I could not succeed with it, then the robbery wouldn't work and I could stop now before I ever got to Charity.

Dave and I had to break in to a fenced trash yard, in a desolate plain beside the worn-out factories of East Chicago, Indiana. We would dig out a small truckload of recycled cash, a hundred million dollars worth of sausages measured by volume. It was valuable only to us, but I did not want anyone to see us take it. A smart police officer might figure out our intentions.

Dave and I were in a pickup truck, its doors declaring VAN SCOYK SANITATION. There is no real Van Scoyk garbage company; I rented the truck and I made the signs myself, using a graphics program that Ellen had taught me. Ninety percent of Chicago garbage companies are run by Dutchmen, so the truck looked right. I pointed out this cleverness to Dave, who was irritated. "Who the hell cares if we rob a garbage dump?"

"We're here. We might as well be prepared."

The vehicle entrance to the landfill was fenced, but unguarded. The gate was locked with a simple padlock. We were partly shielded by brown, ugly berms and by the hills of trash beyond the fence. There was some moonlight and a lot of light pollution from the factories operating through the night.

Both of us were wearing heavy coveralls and rubber boots; we put on gloves and protective face masks and moved quickly to the gate. It was good that the night was cool and damp. I pulled out my set of lock picks. Dave asked, "Where the fuck you learn to do that?" while I fiddled with the locks.

"In the Army, serving our nation. I could pick any ordinary locks made in Russia or Eastern Europe. I was thinking they fabricate them the same way here, more or less, so I can pick..." The lock clicked open. "Hurry. We've got to find it fast."

"How do we look for it?"

"It's the stuff that doesn't smell, and a lot of it will be encased in plastic."

We stumbled around, marching through Saharan dunes of garbage with Dave cursing under his breath. He suddenly sank up to his chest in some slimy waste just as I came upon the pile of plastic sausages filled with shredded money.

"Just some fucking quicksand somebody tossed in the trash," Dave muttered as he started to pull himself out by grabbing a piece of plastic pipe. It snapped with a very loud crack, like a gunshot. Dave fell back. I ran over, grabbed Dave's arm, and pulled him out.

"Hey. I found the stuff."

In that instant, something struck the plastic pipe that Dave had broken. The small piece of pipe flew up into the air just as we heard a sharp report.

"That goddamn pipe. You need to watch where you step."

"I didn't step on the pipe, Paulie."

Then came another report, bigger and sharper with a little distinct reverberation at the end of it. It was rifle fire, no doubting it—the first sound had been a rifle, too, a smaller caliber. Instinct told us to go for cover, but we froze—I am a little too obsessive to flatten myself into slime.

The next bullet, this from the small-caliber weapon, changed my mind. It struck an outcropping of twisted steel a yard from my shoulder. I threw myself forward, angling away from the steel. Dave tumbled back into the muck. At the last second he grabbed at the metal leg of a discarded chair. The chair rocked back and forth, gave way, and Dave sank nearly to his neck. Two more shots then, both rifles at the same moment. The bullets came low over the ground where I had flattened myself. I crawled toward Dave. Neither of us wanted to make a sound. Some half-crazed security guard, a police officer wannabe, was grabbing his chance to kill a burglar and get rewarded for it.

Dave sank to his chin in the oily stuff; he did not yell. More shots skimmed along the surface, hitting stray pieces of solid trash; the ricocheted bullets kicked up the surface. My stomach seemed to have fallen down to my feet; my heart had flown up to my throat blocking my airway; I felt suffocated. Dave's eyes grew wild. For him I guess this was worse than the time the burning roof fell and trapped him in the drugstore. His face was impassive but his hand moved wildly, senselessly. I watched it slide past a solid-looking piece of steel pipe, but his fingers never found it.

Dave grimaced when his hand pounded into my outstretched arm. I pressed hard on his palm and whispered his name. He grew calm. Then, straining at my limits, I let myself roll down the slope of the garbage mound, using my body weight to drag Dave out. The rifle fire never stopped. As I pulled Dave free and his filthy body tumbled down over the lip of the pool of muck, finally, there was silence.

"Dave, you okay?" I asked three times before Dave nodded.

"Who the fuck is shooting at us? Paulie, who have you told about this idea?" He was panting, but he could see by my face that I had told no one. "Okay, okay. Maybe there are guards here; they guard this stuff. This is a big problem with the plan." Dave breathed. The sky was getting smokier and the scene was getting darker.

The rifle fire began again, but the bullets were hitting farther off, I started to move away from the green money tubes. Dave followed me until we saw a flashlight beam shoot up from behind a large trash mound. The motes and black specks that we could see floating in the light of the beam made me want to hold my breath. A voice from a loudspeaker boomed through the air. "I told you kids to stay away from the dump! This ain't no rifle target range! I hear one more shot, I call the cops! You hear me, assholes?"

We froze in place, then saw the torchlight moving away

from us. We heard footsteps, faint clicks, and then we waited in silence.

"We are standing on the local shooting range, Paulie," Dave whispered. "Is that right?"

I shrugged in the shadows. "They're gone. They won't be back soon. Let's go back and finish."

Within minutes, we were tossing what looked like green plastic sausage tubes over the fence. When the pile was high enough to fill the flatbed of the truck, we kicked the remaining sausages around to cover up the hole we had left.

"Okay, it's smooth enough. Let's go." Dave loped to the truck and pulled it up to the green pile. I relocked the gate behind him. We loaded the stolen treasure of garbage onto the truck and covered it with a tarp after tossing in our clothes, boots, and gloves. We left the masks on.

Once in the car, I asked Dave, "I suppose you had a more exciting evening planned?"

He wiped dirt from his forehead. "The Gold Star Sardine Bar. I was going to wear my best suit. Lysette is singing there tonight."

"That's the singer you've been going out with?"

"Sometimes."

"She's very good-looking."

"Yes, she is, but I won't be seeing her because I have you for my best friend."

I grunted.

"Is that indigestion or an apologetic grunt?"

"I concede that it's apologetic."

Driving in silence, we turned out of the short road between the berms and the landfill. The sky was slick and pink, and a half mile down we passed a group of six happy teenagers, all headed to the landfill. Two of them were carrying deer rifles at their sides. We looked at each other.

"You saw the rifles?"

I nodded.

"Maybe you want to give me another one of those grunts?"

* * *

An hour later, Dave pulled the truck to a stop in the rear of a small country cabin by a lake. A summer place, in the southeastern Michigan woods, basic shelter, nothing more, it was a relic of the time when people roughed it on weekends, grateful just to escape the heat of cities without air-conditioning.

"This is not your place, you don't have a weekend place, so where are we?" Dave asked.

"It belongs to an old lady, a widow. I knew her husband. She never visits. How close are we to the hole between those two oaks?"

"I'll back up a few feet."

After Dave came close to the hole, we took off our masks and pulled on the gloves, then quickly showered green sausages into a large hole in the ground that I had dug and then lined with thick plastic sheeting the previous weekend.

"Pretty impressive hole. You dig it yourself, Paulie?"

The barrage of sausages stopped. The hole was filled to within two feet of its top.

"Get the plywood."

Dave handed me a piece of plywood that neatly fit into the hole.

"Let's step on it. Tamp it down. I don't want the ground to be soft here."

Both of us jumped on to the wood and felt it give and then not give under us. I rolled plastic over the wood and then removed another plywood sheet from the truck and put it on top.

"A plastic sandwich. Help keep it dry." I was breathing harder now. "Time to shovel."

The hole disappeared slowly as we pitched the dirt in and pressed down on the earth. When done, we blanketed the earth with twigs, leaves, and tree branches. Each of us went to a door of the truck and stripped off the transparent "Van Scoyk Sanitation" sheets and burned them while I repeatedly drove the truck back and forth over the green sausage hole.

"What's across the lake?" Dave asked.

"A few houses. They're in better shape than this one, but they're all small. It's not like the big houses in Harbor Springs."

"That's not a house they have here; it's a wood shack. A fire starts and the whole place is ashes in an hour," Dave said. "What did he do up here with it, your friend?"

"I guess you fish up here in summer, hunt in the winter."

"But I bet the teenagers drive up here to get laid . . . so does this lady have any teenagers around?"

"Not a one."

"This is where we are going to hide the money?" Dave contemplated the house as if he were figuring how fast it could burn.

"Yes."

"Why not just leave the shredded stuff inside the house? Put it under the floor, if nobody's ever here?"

"The widow could sell the place, or she could die. Either way, some contractor would be sent out here to do an inspection. Besides, I want to stay away from the house as much as possible. Someone on the other side of the lake might get suspicious." I was sweating as we got into our truck. I did not cool down until we entered Interstate 94 and were headed south back to Chicago.

5.

CHARITY SCOTT WAS not entirely honest if she would be willing to steal, but she was upright, loyal, and good for the roughest ride. Even if she turned me in for broaching the idea of robbing her boss, she knew she wouldn't get anything worthwhile—a nice plaque and little bonus—and after the fanfare she would still be left at the Fed with the bigots and the guys with the grudges. Besides, nobody was going to take the word of a bank guard against a federal judge.

Trimble would say yes if she said yes. He was hers, body and soul. In my chambers he listened to every word she uttered, endorsed her thoughts, mimicked her attitude and facial expressions. Without his wife, he would be lost.

If you sit near Buckingham Fountain, where Charity and I sat, the sound of the water makes it difficult to overhear you. The fountain is huge, recently renovated, and as memorable as ever, a perfect way for Clarence Buckingham's sister to make sure that no one would forget her brother for a long time. The mist from the towering sprays was cooling on the broiling day that I chose. She wore a modest gray suit, and I wore dark trousers and a light blue windbreaker; we both were dressed too warmly for the stifling heat of the day.

"You know, I forgot to ask you something the last time. You went back to the Army after you started at the Fed. Why is that?"

"It wasn't voluntary." She grimaced. "My reserve unit was activated and sent to the Gulf War. I didn't know how to do it quickly any other way, so I used my Reverend James methods to hound everybody in my command. By the end of the run up to invasion, the ground vehicles were in perfect desert fighting condition everywhere in the division."

"Everyone in the platoon hate you?"

"The command liked the results."

"How did you know that the troops hated you?"

"It was damn clear. The night before we moved, someone put something in my coffee. I woke up in the early morning in the driver's cab on the top of the largest piece of earth-moving equipment in the Army. It was being trucked to the front. When it got there, I reported to the field commander. He told me to wait in the communications van until I could be transported back. I was too angry to sit and wait. I ran to the earthmover and climbed into the cab. I told the sergeant I would take over while he handled the radio." Charity stopped for a moment and took an apple out of her pocket. It was lunchtime. She took a bite. "I spent the day making trenches for American troops and filling in trenches dug by the Iraqis. Twice I pushed a mound of dirt to the rim of an Iraqi trench and began to close the trench while the Iraqi soldiers were in it. Just rolled the earth in on top of them. The Iraqis started to fire once they realized what was happening, but still they got crushed or buried alive."

Her tone both chilled and impressed me. "You might have been one of the first American women soldiers in combat," I said.

"I knew how I had gotten there. I told the relief operator that I was there to do a quick check under the hood and went to the rear in a supply truck. I said nothing about my absence; no one in my unit did either. I asked to be sent home early, and the Army agreed."

I nodded, watching the crowd thicken for the Taste of Chicago festival; local restaurants served a few of their specialties, and a couple of music stages offered rock, blues, and country all the day and night. By long-standing tradition, honored today, the weather was always terrible, either stifling heat or torrential rain. In the early years of the Taste, the fair was a means to promote some fine restaurants, which would rent space to show off their cuisine at reduced prices, all to generate business. Now, all the food is egg rolls, pizza, and barbecued turkey legs. The big seller is the beer, a lake of beer. The prices are no longer reduced. Fewer Chicagoans attend, and instead families and packs of teenagers from the outlying suburbs and towns crowd the place. The Art Institute put up temporary fences and security guards to preserve the sanctity of their air-conditioned galleries and protect their clean toilets from the crowds they call "the locusts."

"I'm a lieutenant. Congratulate me, sir. I've been promoted." Charity spoke quietly.

"They like you now?" I asked.

"Hell, no. They don't like my taste in men. You know that better than anyone."

"I suppose I do," I admitted.

"I'm their type, very military. Then I take up with a white guy."

"So, Charity, everything is fine after your grand victory?" Like a lawyer, I asked a question to which I knew the answer. I wanted to see how she said the words.

"Yes, sir. Straight on. They resent the court order, just like you knew they would. They have all these rules now about how Trimble and I can never be together at work." Charity's voice thinned into a bitter timbre.

"That's reasonable. You're supposed to be guarding against

employee theft, and Trimble is an employee," I said blandly, searching to see how angry she was.

"It is reasonable, but I violate a rule even if I wind up in the lunchroom with Trimble. Every time I ask to work a different shift, they refuse. You know why? They're setting me up, and sooner or later I'll make a mistake and they'll boot me."

"They promoted you, Charity, twice. Sergeant and then lieutenant."

"Sure, when they fire me and I sue them, they'll say, 'Hey, we're fair. Look, we even promoted her.'" Charity angled her head to catch some more of the spray from the fountain.

"You are right-on there," I acknowledged. "Let me tell you about the kind of man you have at the top of your chain of command."

Redding Prindiville, now well into his tenure as the board's general counsel, had been sitting in one of my red leather chairs at my very old, heavy conference table, which had just been refinished for the sixth time and gleamed. Unfortunately, the government used to buy the best furniture for its judges or had the federal prisons make it out of the best wood, and the stuff lasts so well that I cannot spend tax dollars to get a new table. This beautiful table bangs my knees every time I pull a chair close. Prindiville banged his knees, too. We are taller than they were in the 1930s.

This time he had come for *Federal Reserve Board of Chicago v. Klonik Color and Ink*. Klonik sold ink to the companies that did the Fed's printing. It was not a legally insignificant matter of a widow losing her home. The inspector general of the Fed thought they detected fraud.

Klonik had submitted invoices on an outdated form that gave Klonik a higher price than the new contracting regulations provided. Klonik used the forms because its owner, an old man, was too frugal to throw them away. The old man's son treated the invoices as order forms; he billed the government with a separate statement using the correct rate. A purchasing clerk at the Fed ignored the correct statements and paid the invoices. The Klonik bookkeeper deposited the too-large check, and neither Ted Klonik nor his son noticed the difference. The Fed was a small customer for them. A year and a half later, the Kloniks' own auditor discovered it and wrote a letter saying that they had been overpaid. The letter went unsent for a month because the Kloniks closed down every September to give their employees a nice long vacation. That September, a routine computer audit at the Fed also turned up the discrepancy.

The inspectors general often do their jobs poorly. They employ an odd assortment of investigators, those who want to go to the FBI, those who can't get a better job, and retired police who wanted to enhance their pensions. Federal prosecutors often distrust their work. In Klonik's case the IG ignored crucial facts. The correct amount due on the correct format, filed at the correct time—all of this was in the Fed records, and the clerk who mistakenly overpaid was well known for his carelessness. The investigators made one call to the Klonik offices, but no one picked up the phone because it was September.

One day after the fraud complaint was filed in court, the Kloniks refunded the money. They did not know of the unserved complaint, but the IG would never believe that the Kloniks honestly refunded the money because their own auditor told them to do it. The Kloniks, who decided the right thing was to return the money before they were asked for it, were now deemed by the government to have admitted the fraud by rushing to give the money back.

When I first read the papers, I thought it might be fraud, the cleverest kind of fraud, just a few thousand dollars with a nicely designed innocent explanation all set up in advance in case they got caught. But judges always hear one side of the case first, and good ones learn to suppress their first impressions.

In court and in chambers the Kloniks were so terrified by the lawsuit that they could barely speak in complete sentences. They just kept saying "We would never..." and "I just don't know what we..." and then would lapse into a morose silence. Their lawyer hired a forensic auditor who looked at all the Klonik government accounts and found that Klonik always used out-of-date forms to record orders and deliveries and always submitted correct billing data on separate papers. I had, incidentally, learned a lot about the ink used to print money. Klonik had many government subcontracts including a few with the United States mint.

By the time the lawyer showed that the Kloniks always delivered a little extra ink just to be sure it filled the order prop-

erly, I was convinced they had made a mistake and not committed a fraud. Nevertheless, people have to pay for their mistakes
as well as their frauds; and I held a conference to see if the matter could not be settled.

Redding Prindiville came to inflict pain. He sought to de-
pose everyone at Klonik, peer into all their government con-
tracts, including one where the Kloniks had been underpaid for
years because of a government mistake. He wanted to take
sworn statements from Klonik's big customers. Klonik's lawyer
pointed out the high cost and how it would damage Klonik's
reputation with its other customers and might drive them into
bankruptcy after they had been selling ink in Chicago for
ninety-five years.

In conference, Klonik offered the government an amount
double what it owed and agreed to provide the same amount in
free ink—in other words, three times the government's loss.

"I don't care if they offer us ten times the loss," Prindiville
declared. "Judge, let me be candid with you."

"Always a fine idea," I told him.

"You were a government lawyer, one of the very best." He
was both fawning and contemptuous, as some lawyers are with
judges. "You know it's not the money. The government always
has the money it needs—we print it! We want people terrified of
perpetrating a fraud on us. We want them to know it will cost a
fortune and, if we drive them into bankruptcy, so much the better." He leaned forward, urging me into his conspiracy. "Probably these people over at Klonik didn't commit any serious
offense, but then our message becomes even stronger. You
make even a small mistake against the government, they'll
drive you out of business. We need to send a strong message
here. You understand; I'm sure you do." Redding Prindiville
smiled a regretful but satisfied smile.

I kept a straight face, though I got ink on my hands from
breaking my pen. I used my mildest voice to say, "I don't think
it is the best policy in the courtroom. The best thing is to do
what is right in each particular case. Let the messages be sent
by the politicians, not by the lawyers and judges." Prindiville
nodded stiffly.

"So, Your Honor, what did you do about it?" Charity asked.

"In theory, I can order a lawyer to pay the other side's legal expenses if the lawyer knowingly brings a lawsuit without good-enough cause. In theory, I can even fine the lawyer but the government will be offended if I go after one of their counsel, so they'll just assign the case to someone else who will press it to the limits because the elected government of this country does not want to be pushed around by a single federal judge, elected by no one and appointed for life." My voice was getting tighter, higher. I could feel it in my throat. Charity must have heard it, too. "If that doesn't work, they'll just find some other thing to sue Klonik for, and that case will be in front of a different judge. In order to punish Prindiville I would have to reveal what it was that he said to me during the pretrial conference. If I do that, then a lot of lawyers will be afraid to be candid about their cases with me; they'll know that I cannot keep a confidence."

Charity was listening carefully; the Taste of Chicago going on behind her.

"I could have found some pretext to dismiss the case, some alleged legal error. The government would have appealed and won. The appeal would have cost Klonik more money and just gotten the government angrier.

"The only thing I could do to help Klonik was to preclude Prindiville's assistants from talking to any of Klonik's customers, and that is what I did. Prindiville could still claim credit for coming down hard on government fraud—just bringing the lawsuit was enough."

"That's something," Charity said.

"Not enough. Just as I did with your case is not enough." My voice turned stony.

"What happened after all this?"

"A new judge was appointed to our court, and the clerk's computer randomly selected cases to be assigned to her docket; Klonik's case went to her. She was too new to see what Prindiville was doing and, while the trial was pending, the older Klonik had a stroke. On the eve of trial, the Fed accepted the offer of double payment. Klonik withdrew the offer of free ink. One condition of settlement is that Klonik could never tell anybody that the Fed took less than Klonik had originally offered."

Ellen had tried to soothe me during the case. "You know you cannot make everything right by yourself," she told me as I sat lumpish on our sofa, having related to her my fury at Prindiville. "This is not a mystery to you, Paulie. What can you be thinking? Do what you can and trust the system. You have to put up with Prindiville. The alternative is worse." She was reaching to touch my hand. I turned my palm up and held her hand very tightly. I might have hurt her, but she did not pull away. For a moment the bitterness and loss of self-confidence that Prindiville had caused was gone and, with it, the pain in our marriage.

I took a long breath and gazed out at the locusts. "There is something for you to do, Charity, to even this out, really to come out ahead, very far ahead. It is an unusual proposal."

Charity turned sharply back to me. I could see her shock. She was very quick, even a little quicker than Ellen.

"You!" She blew the word out in a rush of air.

"Yes."

Charity looked at the water in the fountain and the people and the lake and the big buildings and then looked back at me. "Go on," she whispered.

I leaned toward her. "It is dangerous, this idea I have. If you're caught, you won't be out of jail until you're old and withered. Even if you don't get caught, you still have to wait five years before you see a dime."

"You wouldn't do something small."

"I wouldn't."

"It will be very hard to do."

"Truly."

"And it's the place where I work?"

"Absolutely."

Charity got up and walked slowly around the fountain as though she was savoring the fresh air and the fine mist. I kept quiet. She returned to her seat and announced, "I'm in."

"I'm glad of it. Still and all, we need your husband, too."

Charity faced back to the spray, then at me. "I guessed that. But I can't be certain that he'll do it. I love him, but he is not the person of . . . steel and daring that I am. . . ."

"Yes, you are a person of steel and daring," I said. I must have smiled despite myself.

"If I do talk to him, it's all secret, privileged like in a court of law, my husband, right?"

"It probably is, but no matter. If the both of you don't go along, nothing is going to happen."

"What do we take out of there, if we do it?"

"At best a hundred million dollars, at worst twenty-five million—we split four ways."

Charity abruptly laughed. "You're putting me on. Can't be done. And if it could, how we gonna spend it? Someone's gotta say, Charity, darling, how come you and Trimble got fifty million dollars?"

"We will have to make new lives, each one of us. We have to wait for a long time, and then no more Taste of Chicago."

The two of us sat for a while. Charity relaxed, I began to suspect, by concentrating on a single drop of water dangling from the petal of a stone flower. I waited, turning my eye now and then to watch the beauty of the woman. When the drop of water spilled down, Charity spoke. "Why you, of all people? Sir, you got a great job. I bet you've never been poor."

"I would be lying if I said I knew. Maybe I'm trying to make a point."

"A damn big point."

Why, anyway? There was some anger at the government, a kind of trigger. Unlike the idiots who hate all government except that of their own supreme leader of their own small group, I was angry because I knew the government could do much better. Yet anger is an acquisitive emotion, searching for other grievances and always finding them. So I was also angry that Ellen had died.

I was outraged at criminals and their intense stupidity. The ones I saw in court just seemed to hurt other people to no end but their own ruin. I thought I could improve on them.

And the Fed was there like Everest.

I was a little bored, and I was lonely without my wife. The crime would be exciting.

But I thought it was still Prindiville. When Ellen's troubles were over, she ran into Prindiville. He said he was glad she was exonerated. He told her he had just signed the report that accused her and that some staff investigator was her real accuser. Ellen did not think much of Prindiville, but she believed that this government lawyer may not have thought she was a crook. At least he was backing away from the accusation. A few years

later, my first law clerk went off to work for the new comptroller. I asked him to look at the old file, and it was clear that the
investigator recommended no action against Ellen. Prindiville
insisted on accusing her because he thought the case would get
more attention if they banged a lawyer on the head. I could not
bring myself to tell Ellen the truth and risk the return of dismay
in her and misery for us both.

Ellen went to bed in fine health and the next morning died
before her time. Prindiville has risen steadily from one position
of power to another and now plays some small role in guiding
our national economy.

I just said to Charity, "I used to shrug things off. Now I find
I take offense at too many things. I want to even the score a little."

"My old preacher uncle would say that's a little touched."
She was shaking her head at her own remark.

"There is this, too," I added. "Who could not use twenty-five
million dollars?"

Charity nodded. I nodded. She went home to talk to Trimble.

I once heard—rather I overheard—Trimble describe that
night. Charity told him what I had said, but she did not tell him
who I was. I had asked her not to. His response was to use every
large piece of furniture in the room as a place on which to make
love. Trimble told her that he would go wherever she went.

Part Two

Discovery

1

UNITED STATES V. *William Serena* was set to begin with jury selection at eleven on June 30. Three separate fraud charges garnered some colorful media coverage because Serena was an Eastern European Gypsy, or at least his parents were, and he was caught by Detective Tony Plymouth who, lo and behold, was himself a Gypsy.

Before the prospective jurors arrived, Rick Mason, the prosecutor, and Mitchell Lang for the defense walked up to the bench to tell me that they had reached an arrangement, a guilty plea that would leave Serena open to a sentence within a guideline of eight months at the bottom and fourteen months at the top. Serena himself appeared in a plain gray suit, a kind-uncle type of man displaying contrition with a furrowed brow and a downcast mien from which I would have to discern whether he was truly sorry for what he had done or merely very sorry that he had been caught at it.

That was fine. I had other things I could do with the week I had allocated to the trial. I could run tests about how much money I could stuff into the long metal boxes I was thinking I might use to take money from the bank. It is easy to calculate the weight of cash, but figuring the cubic volume of large quantities requires a day or two of experiment. Then, too, my parents were visiting Copenhagen. I could fly there. It was summer and there would not be much night there and no one sleeps. I love places where things never stop. So I listened to Mason tell me why I should accept a plea of guilty and fly to Denmark.

Mason, who could do a good job only in a strong case with no unusual problems, made a sad speech about the illness of a crucial witness in one fraud. In another, the witness Tony Plymouth did not see or hear enough to prove that Serena was a ringleader. Mason took five minutes to say this. It was for the two reporters and the courtroom artist sitting in the empty juror box that Mason explained why the prosecution was now being scaled back and that, despite this, justice was still being done.

"All right, counsel. I am going to release the jury. Some other judge might need them and, if not, they can go home early and get back to their lives." I said this on the record.

"We agree with that," Lang said.

Tony Plymouth was in court staring in disbelief at the prosecutor's back. Plymouth seemed very alert, an officer who cared about his case. He looked briefly at Serena, and his nose crinkled up as if he had caught a whiff of rotting fish. Then I remembered my annoyance with Massachusetts Slim and that plea deal. I suddenly felt Copenhagen slipping from my grasp.

"Three things to do: Get custody of the currency, get the currency out of the bank, and conceal the fact that we have done this." I was whispering because Dave and I were jogging on a broiling day, moving toward our cars in the lot south of the Lincoln Park Tennis Club. No one was within fifty yards of us, but I had barely enough breath for the whisper.

"I'm glad to hear you are so far along in the planning, Paulie," Dave said, his breath full. "When are you going to tell me how we do these three things?"

"Two ideas, one simple, one more complicated." I stopped running, which made Dave stop too. "How can we get underneath LaSalle Street without being noticed?"

"The sewers run under the center of the street. The telephone runs under the sidewalk."

"Right, but they come together when they enter a building. I want to follow the underground pipes underneath the Fed."

"We can enter through one of the manholes in the alley between Adams and Jackson Street," Dave said, as if pondering a quarterback sweep left. "But you told me there's no way to dig into the vault. The closest we can come is ten feet away. Have I got that wrong?"

"We don't get into the vault. Trimble and Charity get the

money out of the vault area. They deliver it to a hiding place we carve out behind the retaining wall. We pick up the money whenever it looks safe." I buried my face in a towel. Adrenaline was starting to burst through my insides, killing the fatigue. I felt powerful.

"What about the surveillance cameras in the hallway next to the wall? We have to disable it. Who's going to miss that?"

"We can pop something in front of the camera that will look like an empty hallway. The surveillance screen will go dark for ten seconds tops. We can figure this out if we know we can get into the retaining wall."

"Paulie, don't they have vibration detectors around the vault? If we start digging, won't we be setting off alarms?" Dave began stretching himself against my front fender. I had stripped the rear interior of the Jeep to see how much stuff I could fit inside it without having anything show through the windows. Dave groaned a little when he stretched, but he was as supple as he had been on every athletic field at Mater Dei.

"Charity says they do have them, but only on the vault walls themselves and on the conduits carrying the cables into the building. We stay away from the conduit and, if we can crack the retaining wall without making much noise, this can work."

"Okay, it's worth a look, Paulie. Let's do some wind sprints on the gravel path," Dave said. He left sweaty palm prints on the left rear fender.

"You know I can't say no to a challenge." The adrenaline spoke.

"You going to throw up if we do them, Paulie?"

"That's right."

"I withdraw my challenge."

2

I WOKE UP the next morning thinking about William Serena and of what he was guilty. Later, inside my chambers, I slouched down until my head was resting in one of the cushioned corners of the red-and-white love seat. To my secretary and law clerks, I knew, I appeared to be comatose.

I was the judge, not the prosecutor, not the defense lawyer. I should let the lawyers do their job, let Serena plead and then send him away for his little spasm of a sentence. These are the rules, and I should follow them. That was Ellen's good answer to my complaints about pleas, prosecutors, and defendants and their counsel. Here the rules gave me some power to force a result upon the lawyers. Ellen might approve.

Defense lawyers who become judges often achieve fame as great friends of the prosecution. One of them sits on my court and has told me, "You were a prosecutor, so you might have entertained some doubt about the guilt of the defendant. As a defense lawyer, I had no doubt at all. You may have wondered whether he was a really bad guy. I usually knew he was worse than you could imagine." Prosecutors who become judges sometimes become the bane of their breed; the judge recalls his own days as a giant in the courtroom and resents the pygmy that now stands in his former place. If the prosecutor does not tow the judge's line, the judge may start ruling against the prosecutor just to show him who is the boss. A judge who is angry enough can kill a prosecutor's case by ignoring the law. Our constitution does not let the prosecutor appeal a wrongful acquittal. I did not want to be either kind of judge.

Yet the guilty-plea game is different from the trial game; its rules are special. The judge can say, "No, I will not accept the plea agreement."

I was going to see if I was right about what I saw in the faces of Serena himself and Tony Plymouth.

I value what I see in people's eyes in my courtroom. Judge Ben Golden, who presided over my first trials as a prosecutor, once told me that when he had sat as a judge in state court he had had to decide whether a man had murdered or committed voluntary manslaughter. The victim had been sitting in the front passenger side of a two-door car. He was shot through the head with the entry wound at the left temple. According to the defendant, the two men had been arguing and the victim, who the defendant wrongly believed was carrying a gun, turned toward the defendant, who was standing outside the car, and started to reach down to his waist. The defendant said that he then drew his own gun. The victim used one hand to grab the defendant's gun hand and while the two men struggled, the defendant said he believed the victim was using his free hand to retrieve his own weapon. So the defendant took the first opportunity he saw to pull his trigger when the muzzle was pointed at the victim. The defendant never saw the victim's gun, the police never found one, and the defendant was apparently the only person in the world who believed that the victim carried a gun. However, if the defendant had a sincere but unreasonable belief that he was acting in self-defense, then he would be guilty only of manslaughter.

The prosecutor argued that the killing was a simple assassination motivated by personal dislike. That meant Ben Golden had to believe that the defendant had somehow used his left hand, his weaker hand, to take the gun from his own right hand and with his left maneuver the gun behind the victim's head and then pull the trigger against the victim's left temple. If the defendant were out to kill the victim, why didn't he just take his gun in his right hand or use both hands and put it to the right temple and shoot right then, rather than snaking his hand in the narrow space behind the headrest of a tilted front seat? Ben spoke his mind about how he had looked at the case and then found the defendant guilty of manslaughter.

When Ben uttered the word "manslaughter," he glanced at the face of the defendant and saw a faint gleam in his eye and the barest trace of a smile, which told him that he, Judge Golden, had been had. Somehow the defendant had indeed put his hand around the head of the victim and murdered him in cold blood. "Paulie, this was over thirty years ago," Golden told me, "but it burns my butt even today."

"Counsel," I intoned in my courtroom at ten twenty-two A.M., "I am not inclined to take this plea of guilty. Maybe the sick witness will recover. We will put the case over for a while."

Now I could pursue justice *and* take my flight to Denmark.

3.

THERE WERE THREE ways, I decided, to rob the Federal Reserve. One would be to take the cash when the bank lets it leave the building, in armored cars destined for other banks. I simply did not think we would get enough money using that method, and it meant coming up with an armored car for us to drive into the Fed's loading dock. Armored cars cannot be easily bought at Larry and Leo's Like-New Truck and Van World. Another method was to steal the money and store it hidden inside the Fed until we could take it out. That two-part process doubled the risk of a screwup. A final method was to go in, grab a huge amount of money, and take it all out in one fell swoop. Each method would require different things of Trimble Young. In one of them he would have to play an enormous and difficult role. I did not know him, but Charity thought he could do it, and that assurance might have to be enough.

Dave chose for me. "I've been given a deal on a warehouse-garage," he said, even before he threw his paramedic uniform jacket on the antique ladder-back chair Ellen had bought for the foyer. "The place is filled with heavy equipment including backhoes, old Prevost tour buses—and an armored car. It's supposed to be a wipe-out explosion. So, should we use the armored car, Paulie?"

"I want to go to Copenhagen this week."

"You want to call off our plan?"

"No. I just want to do something else this week."

Dave's brow lowered. He was next to me, blocking the doorway to the living room, one thick forearm on either side of the jamb. "Let me tell you this about crime, Paulie. Take the shot when you have it. If you don't, you always find that somebody changed the locks or installed a new alarm while you were dicking around. I know these things. It's not 'when the spirit moves you,' Paulie, it's when somebody accidentally leaves the back door open."

Dave used his keys to the warehouse and we walked in at two A.M.

Armored cars are tricky. They have special keys for everything except the ignition. There was nothing in print about their locks. I tried and failed to pick open the door. Armored-car locks were not covered by my military training.

We rummaged through the warehouse offices, one of which sported a rack of keys that included one like no other key I had ever seen. It popped the locks on the truck. The ignition key dangled on a rubber cord on the steering column.

If you turned a key in the ignition, the doors automatically locked. If you opened the driver's door, the back doors locked. There were no buttons that unlocked a door. If the doors were unlocked, then the wheels locked. There was no way to glide into the Fed loading dock, pop the doors, load the truck, and race off. We would have to pull in, come to a complete stop, and manually unlock the safety doors. When we left, we would have to close and lock the doors before we could move the car out.

"Where the hell are you going to hide this truck?" Dave asked. "I can't see myself parking it in my driveway in Bucktown."

"I can rent space in Boujee's. He doesn't ask questions, and he doesn't know who I am. I was one of the few prosecutors who never hailed him before a grand jury on fencing charges. You just pull up, honk twice. He opens the gate, points to a parking spot, and waits for you to come back to the gate. He takes cash, gives you a ticket, and never looks at anything but your hands. Open all night, too."

"How would we get in the bank?" Dave asked.

"We paint it like the regular trucks that call on the Fed, then we stop the regular car from reaching the bank and cruise into the bank in its place." Charity could tell us when the trucks were due. The problem was that the real armored-truck drivers would know there had been a robbery and we were going to be easy to find driving a big gray-and-blue armored truck around Chicago. Maybe I could solve that problem.

"So, we stop the real armored car. Armed robbery."

"Maybe we could just ask nicely," I suggested.

I climbed into the armored car, started the engine, and drove it out on the street. Dave followed me to Boujee's, west of downtown, just off the Eisenhower Expressway. I had to stop to fill up the gas tank. The only gas station was in a neighborhood shrouded in darkness because the residents had shot out the streetlights; I was very happy to be in an armored car.

True to his reputation, Boujee seemed never to look at my face as he took my money. He didn't do any paperwork, just handed me a yellow piece of construction paper with the number 82 written on it in purple crayon. Eighty-two was the number on the steel post in the slot where I put the car. "Just you give that paper there to me when you want that thing," he murmured. I strained to hear him; his face was nearly parallel to the ground. He was very short, with pale fuzzy hair, and I thought he was aiming his voice at my shoes. He did raise his voice to say "Rent runs out, you don't come by here, I scrap the thing or whatever, it's mine. 'Course, if it's still here I might let you have it for the rent due or I might not. Got it?"

"Got it," I said. Boujee slid off in the darkness. I walked out. Dave had parked far enough away so that you could not see the license plate on his Ford. I ran over to his car and we drove out of that neighborhood, all awash in dim yellow light, the deserted industrial buildings and full-up truck depots all scheduled for urban renewal some day, some year.

4.

"NINETY-NINE C-R FOUR twenty-two, *United States v. Wriston,* charge of bank robbery, eight counts," the clerk called out. Two lawyers and a bedraggled-looking white man came to the lectern.

"Your Honor, we are here to change my client's plea from not guilty to guilty. An agreed recommended sentence of ten years."

The hapless defendant leaned on the lectern. He was a stoop-shouldered man in a dull brown suit that matched his eyes. Did this bank robber know he shared a surname with one of America's famous bankers? I glanced at the papers to make sure the defendant's first name was not Walter.

The procedure was rote, but I worked hard to disguise this from the defendant. For most defendants, this is a novel experience; even the repeat felony offender doesn't plead guilty often enough to get bored. To me, it was actor's work, sounding fresh in the thousandth performance.

"Mr. Wriston, I'm going to find out now whether you understand what is happening here."

I nodded at Wriston, as I nodded at every defendant at this precise moment. Wriston kept his eyes lowered. He shivered a little. The courtroom was not crowded, but the air-conditioning was set for a large crowd of overheated spectators. In the winter, it is heated like a teakettle.

The plea of guilty is a twelve-minute play. The judge has all the real lines and the defendant spends most of his time saying "yes," "no," or "guilty." When I sentence, I have a probation officer's report. If you are the ordinary man or woman of the world, the only way you will ever have your biography written is to run afoul of the law so that a probation officer can put your life on paper. Some of them write very well.

Dave Brody walked into the courtroom. I started to feel the thick wheel of the armored car against my palms.

"Mr. Wriston, you have to tell the truth; if you don't, it is perjury and could get you an additional sentence, more time in jail. You understand this?"

"Oh, the answer is yes, Judge." Wriston spoke like a man being slowly strangled.

A worn-out woman was sitting in the courtroom with two worn-out-looking kids, maybe eight and ten years old. A point in Wriston's favor, and his family looked upset that he was going away. Sometimes family members went to sentencing to make sure they were going to be rid of the defendant for a while, like the people going to an enemy's funeral to make sure he was really dead. I went on with my questions.

When I said "This is bank robbery, one of the most serious crimes. You understand this, do you?" Wriston, for the first time, looked right back at me.

"Yes, sir, I do." It startled me. Why did Wriston pick that moment to look up?

Five minutes later, he pleaded guilty.

"All I can say, Judge, is that I'm very, very sorry for the bad things I've done." Wriston said this while shifting some of his weight from one foot to the other and back.

"Norman Wriston, on eight separate days you walked into banks and handed tellers a note saying 'I have a gun. Give me the cash in the drawer or I'll shoot you.' It took you a month and a half to do this, you averaged about four thousand a bank, and you scared the devil out of the tellers, some of whom probably still have nightmares. The only good part of this was you didn't have a gun, just the note. And this is your second conviction for bank robbery. Mr. Wriston, ten years in prison, three years supervised release, and restitution. You are to surrender forthwith." I spoke in a very formal voice. I intone sentence.

No one moved. I glanced at the two U.S. marshals, shrugged under my robe, reminded myself to avoid obsolete legal words in the future, and then repeated, *"Forthwith*. I said 'forthwith.' That means right now."

The marshals came out of their semitrance, and I watched as they took Wriston into custody.

"Certain quality of irony there," Dave remarked as we drove out for a practice run of our armored-car scheme.

"What?"

"This afternoon a ten-year sentence for bank robbery, just before we start on the road to rob the Federal Reserve."

"Dave, up there I was pondering the luck of the Irish."

Dave whistled the first few notes of an Irish jig.

We had bought a scanner and set it to the radio frequencies that the Fed and the armored-car company used. Parked at Wells and Van Buren, I sat in the car with the scanner, a few blocks from the bank and directly on the regular armored-car route. Dave was going to stop the truck. He didn't tell me in advance what he was going to do, but I saw how he did it.

When the armored car came into view, he walked up to a Ford van parked on Wells and broke the driver's-side window with a hammer, which he then smashed down on the steering column demolishing the ignition lock and exposing the starter rod. He started the van by pushing the rod down. Then he pulled out in the armored-car's lane, backed right into the front of the armored vehicle, got out, and ran away.

On my elegant little chrome scanner I heard the armored-car driver radio his office and get instructions to stay in the truck while headquarters notified the police, because it might be a holdup. Nothing happened. The armored-car people guessed it was just a car thief who had accidentally crashed the van and run away. The van remained stuck at the accident scene for twenty minutes—more time than we would need to take the car's place in the loading vaults of the Fed, grab the money, and leave.

As it turned out, we would not have twenty minutes for our armored-car impersonation—we would have just two, which Charity told us was how long it took before the armored-car headquarters used the telephone to tell the Fed that they were running late. Then headquarters got on the radio notifying everyone on the route that the truck would be late and promising to call each scheduled stop to tell them when the truck was about to arrive.

So much for my armored car. We could radio ahead and impersonate the armored car company, telling the Fed that the truck was ahead of schedule and then drive into the Fed. There was no way we could stop the armored-car headquarters from telling the Fed when its truck was on the way. The real armored car could run ahead of schedule, too. If the Fed got two messages and two trucks showed up, we would be sunk.

"What the hell are we going to do with the armored car, Paulie?" Dave asked as we sat eating corned beef at Manny's.

"We can put it back where it came from. You still have the keys to that place, don't you?"

"Why would you think that? You didn't want me to blow up that building, so I gave the keys back." Dave was joking. He burned and blew up buildings no matter what I said or didn't say.

"Then we can break in and return the armored car."

"Won't have to break in, Paulie. There's just a pile of bricks and burned up timber there."

"Someone else did it?" I don't know why I asked. I know he must have done it.

"A fine job, done just the way someone like me would do it."

Lawyers sometimes call this kind of answer "nice"—neither truth nor lie.

"Listen, Paulie, nobody will miss the armored car. Your friend Boujee, what's with that?"

I told Dave that Boujee would just scrap the armored car after the six months I paid him for.

So we took our shot at something that didn't work, but, through our experiment, we started the journey, a fact of legal moment. The law declares that we were already guilty of conspiracy to rob the Federal Reserve. Not to mention car theft and criminal damage to property.

We had carried out the first indisputable overt act to consummate the crime. An overt act is a big part of the law of traditional criminal conspiracy. A group can agree together to commit a crime, but they were usually not guilty until one of them undertook a single overt act to help achieve the criminal goal. I suppose we committed an overt act when we stole the green money sausages from the landfill, but that one we could say was an innocent prank, not very exciting. Crashing a van into an armored car and running away is not an innocent stunt.

5.

RICK MASON'S SPARE opening in *United States v. Serena* emphasized the fact that Lois Kreutz had been bilked out of her entire modest estate, which had been just enough to enable her to keep her house and live decently in her golden years. Given forged securities, she was defrauded by William Serena, a smooth-talking con man. Lang, for the defense, agreed that Lois Kreutz had been cruelly defrauded but declared that she was sickly and badly confused about who had done it to her and that person was not his client, the upstanding William Serena, whose only connection with Mrs. Kreutz had been to provide her spiritual advice. The culprit, said Lang, was one Arthur J. Merrill, with whom the elderly Mrs. Kreutz had confused his innocent client.

Mason was saving Mrs. Kreutz's appearance on the stand for the end of his case. She was his key witness. I had been told she was still recovering from a variety of colds, flus, and fevers. He wanted to give her as much time as he could. Tony Plymouth, the detective, was calling on her each day to boost her spirits. When he wasn't with her, he was in my courtroom. His broad face gave nothing away, yet he seemed intense, nearly wise. I found myself looking at him as much as I looked at the witnesses and at Serena himself.

The first witness, a banker, testified that Lois Kreutz had withdrawn money from her money-market account on a certain date. Then, a stockbroker testified that she had sold many of her mutual-fund investments and withdrawn the cash. The date of that withdrawal was the same as the day of the bank withdrawal.

A friend of Serena's, a chunky, black-haired man in his middle years, speaking in a reluctant whisper, told the jury that the phone listed in his own name was, in fact, Serena's phone. It was something Serena had asked him to do, a favor for a friend to the tune of twenty dollars a month. I raised the volume on the witness-stand microphone; even so, I had to have the court reporter repeat some of his answers in a clear, audible voice. After this witness, there came a woman from the telephone company with records showing a few phone calls from Serena's number to Lois Kreutz's number.

All day long Serena sat calm, and the jury seemed unimpressed with the case against him. I wondered only briefly if I had guessed wrong about this case, because I had a busy night ahead.

The City of Chicago has a little agency called the Bureau of Underground. Its boss is dubbed "Satan" by some of his employees. A firefighter can examine Satan's records, plats, and diagrams at any time. Dave took a good look for the half block occupied by the Fed.

It took us no time at all to raise a manhole in the alley between Wells and LaSalle Streets, a little north of the Fed. In ten minutes we were at the outer surface of the wall we wanted to crack open. It was a dark, revolting place with conduits crossing in and out of the low, damp space. Amid rats and crawling insects, we had to wend our way through pipes the way a hand surgeon snakes around a nest of tendons. Here everything came into the building—power, telephone, television cable, sewer, and water. According to Charity's diagram of the vault area, matched up against the records of the Bureau of Underground, we would have to dig a tunnel of our own for ten feet to the right of the open shaft we had crawled through.

With folding spades we tested the earth and we pushed in about five feet. So we knew we could do it. When we came back, we would have to bring plastic braces and plates to stabilize our own tunnel. This could be a way in—if we could figure out how to chip away without making noise, using tools for which we had to supply our own electrical power, and if we could figure out how to fool the surveillance cameras.

We were covered with dirt by the end of the final foray. Dave laughed. "Can you imagine Ellen watching this, laughing her ass off, not able to get a word out?"

"You were the only one who could make her laugh like that, Dave." My eyes were stinging with soil grains.

"I think I miss her nearly as much as you do, Paulie."

He did, I know; and he was my company in that misery. Tired, stinking of the underground, we each found our way home.

6.

THE PROSECUTOR WAS using Tony Plymouth to deliver as much of Lois Kreutz's story as possible, to lighten the sick old woman's workload on the witness stand. I listened as Plymouth kept his facts in order without prompting from Mason. He was assured, matter-of-fact, without the odd jargon that infects so much police testimony.

Lois Kreutz had called for law-enforcement assistance and Tony Plymouth was dispatched to her house on Cullom Street, in a neighborhood of two- and three-bedroom houses near Graceland Cemetery on the north side. I knew, as the jury did not, that she had called because she had seen a picture of Serena in the news when he was indicted on his other fraud cases, and that she was anxious and on the brink of heartbreak.

Mrs. Kruetz's neighborhood, about three miles north of the Loop, not far from Wrigley Field, in Our Lady of Lourdes Parish, was turning younger and richer. I remembered the east end of Cullom had always been nice. As I concentrated on Plymouth's words, I could see Mrs. Kreutz and the detective sitting on her porch within sight of the cemetery wall. "She told me she was a docent at Graceland Cemetery," Plymouth reported. "You know, I didn't know what she was talking about, so she explains she gives tours in the graveyard. She asked me if I wanted a tour. I decided why not and we walked over there. She was telling me about the cemetery and I was asking her questions about her call to our office."

Graceland Cemetery, the defining feature of the area, is home to Chicago's most famous graves: the architects Daniel Burnham and Louis Sullivan; George Pullman of railroad-car fame; Marshall Field and Potter Palmer, whose names are still seen on display in the Loop; Chief Justice Fuller of the United States Supreme Court; Alan Pinkerton, and various mayors, governors, senators, and representatives. Philip Armour, the meat packer; Cyrus McCormick, the reaper king; and Jack Johnson, former heavyweight champion of the world.

When her husband died, Lois Kreutz told the detective, he left her the house and four hundred thousand dollars. The two children had gotten jobs on the West Coast. She was alone in the house they had bought in the 1950s. But she needed to increase her income, she told Plymouth; she wanted to travel more, to visit her children, to see the world. Lang could have objected to this, but he let it go.

Mrs. Kreutz found Arthur J. Merrill to give her financial advice. He advised her to buy preferred stocks with guaranteed returns. He would buy the stocks at the best price, but she would not have to pay him until he delivered the stocks to her. She would meet him at her bank, give him a check, and then put the stock he would give her into her safe-deposit box. After four months, she had paid him $270,000. She had the stock certificates, and they were all well-known companies. The dividends were supposed to start coming in the next two weeks. She hadn't heard from Mr. Merrill for a while; she was upset, and she wondered if the police could assist her in finding him. Plymouth said that her hands began to tremble as she spoke about Merrill. I let the jury hear this not, as the lawyers say, for the truth of what she said, but in order to explain what happened next—which was that Tony Plymouth took her to the bank where she opened her safe-deposit box and allowed the detective to take the certificates out and examine them.

In court Mason asked, "Tell us about the certificates, Detective."

"They gave the superficial appearance of legitimate corporate shares, sir, but . . ."

"But what, Detective Plymouth?"

"Anyone can buy these kinds of certificates. They come with the incorporation kits that are sold in business-supply stores. I went out before court today and bought one."

Lang stood up and said, "Objection, this is . . ." I stopped him by saying "Whatever it is, your objection is overruled."

Plymouth held up a kit and, at Mason's request, opened it and removed blank stock certificates with a pattern that, as it turned out, exactly matched the phony General Electric shares Mrs. Kreutz had kept in her box. Someone had used a word processor with a very high quality printer. The company names appeared to be embossed. Plymouth believed, when he saw them, that they were forgeries.

He testified that the certificates were processed for fingerprints, and the only prints found matched those of Lois Kreutz. In cross-examination, Lang made the minor mistake of emphasizing the absence of fingerprints of Bill Serena, to which Plymouth quietly replied, "Well, if Mr. Serena were the forger, I'm pretty sure he would be careful not to leave fingerprints." I hid my smile behind my hand; the cop knew how to testify. I felt relieved that I'd pushed the case to trial.

His testimony gave me my first close look at him; a witness passes within feet of me on the path to the stand and then sits about ten feet away. Plymouth was neither tall nor short, about five ten and a little pudgy. His very dark hair was so tightly curled by nature that it was probably never out of place above thick and mobile eyebrows; his nose was rounded and a little long, and it seemed he could wrinkle it at will. His eyes were so deep a brown that they looked black. If he kept his face still, then he would give away nothing. I wondered, if he could keep his face still, whether he had truly chosen to signal me to refuse the negotiated plea bargain in Serena's case.

After Plymouth, we all heard from a questioned-document examiner employed by the Secret Service, who pronounced the stock certificates to be forgeries made up on engraved sheets from over-the-counter incorporation kits. By letting the jury hear all this evidence without objection or complaint, Lang was emphasizing his contention to the jury that the issue was not whether there was fraud, just whether Serena was the villain. I wondered about it myself. In spite of Plymouth's assurance, the jury looked unconvinced. Serena was sporting the beginning of a little smile whenever the jury was out of the room. If the case was to be saved, Lois Kreutz would have to do it. If she did not, then I had made a serious error of judgment about Serena and Plymouth.

Early that Thursday evening Charity sank into one of my patterned love seats. Here in my chambers where I had helped her and Trimble, she thanked me again.

"It was not a favor," I told her. "I only help the deserving. That's why I helped you."

"You're a doll," she interjected.

"A doll?" I laughed but I was a little abashed.

She turned her face to the ceiling and whispered loudly, "He's a doll."

She was cool and she waited for me to lead. "You sure you want to go on with this?" I asked.

"Oh, yes, I do," she answered. She seemed more certain now than when she was at Buckingham Fountain, and I was less confident.

"And Trimble's willing to go along even though he doesn't know who else is involved?"

"He is, sir."

She gazed at me with her chin canted to one side as Ellen used to do, her classic head framed in the twilight window, where the north side of Chicago was beginning to light up and the lake sky to the east was showing several shades of blue.

There are as many shades of blue in Chicago as there are shades of green in Ireland.

My intercom chimed. I looked at the monitor, which showed me who was standing outside my chambers door, then I released the lock. Dave Brody walked in, still in uniform. There was a patch of blood on his shirt. Charity rose to shake his hand, and they traded names.

"The blood?" I asked. Dave's face was drawn. He almost looked his age.

"An eight-year-old girl, drive-by gunshot wound. Couldn't stop the bleeding. Hell of a day-ender."

Charity was taken aback, words lost to her.

No one said another word until Dave pointed to a small Bang & Olufsen set on my credenza and asked, "Is that new?"

I listened to the CDs that Dave Brody told me to buy. Today it was Marcus Roberts and his piano. "Yes, it is new," I told him.

"Need to do justice to the sound of the jazz, right?" he said and smiled briefly before he began to pace. Neither Charity nor I spoke.

"This is it," he said, less asking than stating. "The three of us and her husband; four people are going to do it?"

"I'd like to talk about that," I said. "The two who work there are going to remove cash slated to be destroyed. They are going to substitute the shredded money that we took from the dump. The weight of the shredded money will equal the amount they remove. They will store the money under the raised floor of the vault until we have reached the goal. Then Trimble is going to take a pair of pills that will slow his heart rate and drop his blood pressure. I have some of my mother's heart pills to do the trick." My parents had passed through Chicago last week and we'd had dinner at their favorite place, the no-longer-fashionable, but still good, Cape Cod Room at the Drake Hotel.

"The paramedics are called and you respond and take out Trimble. We will then use the confusion to distract security while we put the money in a place where we can reach it from outside the building. That's why we are talking about tunneling into that wall we looked at last night." Charity looked up, a sharp move of her head; this was her first real indication that we all weren't just chatting about the crime. "If that won't work, we can take a lot of cash out on the gurney with Trimble as we wheel him out." I turned to my paramedic friend. "I've thought about this other way, and if we use it, I'd like to have another set of hands. It will be heavy and I don't know if we can be sure they will let Charity help you. You want to recruit your partner, Dave?"

"No," Dave said without hesitation. "He's a kid, he loves the sirens, the excitement, the flashing lights. Rather be a paramedic than be a billionaire. Myself, I think he gets hard every time we go on a run. 'Course, at his age, you get a hard-on every thirty-two minutes or so." He stopped and started to blush. It might have been one of his secret weapons with women; not many grown-up men blush. "Excuse me, ma'am," he said to Charity.

"Forget it, honey," she replied. "I been out after dark."

I had to smile. I said, "I'll have to think some more about getting the money on the gurney. Maybe we take less."

Charity rocked forward, glanced at Dave, then placed her cool dark eyes on mine. "Why did you think Trimble and I would do this?"

She deserved to know. "The case, your case. It taught me about you—not just what you said, what the bosses said, and the reports I read. Trimble goes against the grain; maybe he's the best electrician there, but every supervisor has had disputes with him. He does it his own way and can't be loyal to his bosses." I looked squarely at her. "And you had your career nearly ruined by them and they are not done with you yet. This is one way, the only way, for you to end up ahead of the game. If you're asking about Dave, he's my oldest friend. You get all this, don't you?"

"Sure." Charity leaned back against the love seat, completely calm.

"We now have to belong to one another, because we have the power to destroy one another. We have to trust one another fully and respect my judgment that we can succeed."

"All for one," Charity said.

I told her about the tunnel plan and asked her if the Fed had vibration sensors on the outer walls.

She knew the answer off the top of her head. "Yes, they have some, but they are not set for high sensitivity. The El passes close by the building, and those trains would be setting them off every five minutes. I don't know if a little digging or hammering would trigger them."

"Can you check the logs tomorrow? Dave and I are going to start work tonight."

"Absolutely."

Charity stood up, took a step, and stopped.

"There's one thing I got to have, when we do this." Charity spoke so quickly that it took effort to understand her.

"And what would that be?" Dave asked.

"When we do it, we do it on that Wheezer's shift. We do it under that fucker's nose."

Dave was puzzled.

"Perfect." I said. Charity gave us a little wave and, as we stood, walked out.

Before Dave left I said, "You know, if we had to, I could go in the Fed with you. I could handle twenty, thirty million myself."

"You could?" Dave raised his eyebrows, but I ignored his little jibe.

I was going to make a series of plastic barrels to hide the currency within the Fed. On take-out day, we would push the barrels one at a time into the tunnel through a hole in the outer wall of the vault corridor. We would then seal the hole in the wall by using epoxy to attach a plastic plate covered with drywall, to match the wall we had cut. We would use a little vacuum device to clean the floor inside the bank. Our repair would not fool anyone who looked for very long, but since no one would know that a robbery had occurred, no one was likely to look that carefully at the wall for years.

That night as we dug we put a shallow trough in the bottom of our tunnel so that we could slide the money barrels easily. We needed space for six barrels. Cracking the wall in the corridor outside the vault was much harder to do. In the end, we used a high-speed, low-noise drill to make a circle about twenty inches in diameter, just big enough to push the money into the tunnel.

We carried a dozen batteries for the drill. We choked on the dust, but in four hours we had made the circle. What was left was to chip away the wall within the circle. The only way to do it was with hammer and chisel with both the hammer and the flat end of the chisel covered with cloth to cut the noise. According to Charity's check of the logs, the vibration sensors in the Fed security perimeter detected nothing.

Dave and I could not fit into the tunnel at the same time, so we alternated. The dust from the work was thick enough to choke us and sear our eyes; we wore goggles and masks that fit so tightly we could not speak. When we took off the masks, little rivers of sweat flowed out of them.

We managed five-hour shifts over the next three nights. The rats stayed away, but I felt worse every hour that I was in the hole. The first hour on Saturday night was worse than the last hour on Friday night. On Sunday night, I felt like throwing up from the first minute and could barely stop myself. When Dave and I got to the surface, I tore my mask away and leaned against the wall ready to vomit, but nothing came up.

On Saturday afternoon, knowing now that we could breach the wall, I bought a video camera. I have no interest in cameras. If Ellen and I had had children, our babies would have been the least photographed children on earth, but I needed it to test out a screen I would put in front of the surveillance camera outside the vault. On Sunday, I pasted three pieces of cardboard together to make three sides of a square. I painted and repainted the inside of the cardboard and then put it in front of the camera at a distance of two feet. Finally, I produced a picture that looked like the empty vault hallway, just a little out of focus. It could work for the couple of minutes we needed. I put several sheets of plastic on the outside of the cardboard to stiffen it, and I attached this to a retractable aluminum pole tall enough to reach the surveillance camera. I covered the whole thing with a plastic bag to keep it clean. Dave and I would leave it in the tunnel by the wall until it came time to use it. I finished the project just as Dave came by to pick me up for more hideous night work in the tunnel.

7.

ON MONDAY MORNING, the day that Serena would face his accuser, Lois Kreutz, I still felt terrible. I felt worse when Mason told me that Lois Kreutz had committed suicide the night before. Mason wanted to reinstate the plea agreement that I had rejected.

"My client is distraught over the death of Lois Kreutz." Mitchell Lang said.

He did not look at all distraught to my eye. Plymouth was the one with his head down and his shoulders slumped.

I had to think. I sat silent; it is my judicial prerogative to be silent for as long as I want, unlike the trial lawyer who does not have that luxury. I saw the display on my computer screen gyrate. Underneath the bench my feet had unconsciously crushed the flimsy network connection box by pushing it against the bulletproof panel. There was a tear in my shoe leather. My mind was raging, full of incoherent thoughts—Plymouth may have felt the same way. I forgot to breathe. It was hard to talk because I was winded.

"Mr. Mason, did the witness leave a suicide note?"

"Your Honor, she did."

"Have you read it, Mr. Mason? And you, Mr. Lang?"

Both of them nodded and then Mason said, "It was a very brief look, Judge. The suicide was discovered this morning, and the note was brought here by Detective Plymouth in the last few minutes. We still have only the original."

"Hand it to my clerk. I should read it."

I took the pale gray paper from my clerk. There was a printed monogram at the top. On it Lois Kreutz wrote:

I was tricked out of the savings my beloved Albert left. I was an old fool and that Bill Serena knew it. I know I will never get my money back from Mr. Serena. I will lose my precious home and my precious memories that this home brings to me every day. I will be a burden to my children. I can't live with these feelings anymore. I miss my beloved and I want to join him.

A couple of inches below the writing, she had started a second paragraph with the pen wandering over the paper, and the lettering irregular.

I have taken all the sleeping pills I have. I thought I would be gone by now. I almost threw up, but I kept it down. I am sleepy. Bill Serena—I see his face now. He did this to me. God will judge him. I feel better now. It is hard to write. I love...

Abruptly, I recessed and went back to my chambers. There I wept. I have cried more than once in my life. It is an Irish trait, I have always assumed, though I know few Irish-American men who admit doing it when they are sober. I was crying because she knew she was on the brink of death, knew she was never going to write any more words after these, and because she died thinking she was a fool. I wept and felt in my chest the foul tunnel air of the last few nights. What the hell could I do now?

In my bathroom, I looked in the mirror and, seeing myself, also saw a way to buy time. I looked quite as terrible as I felt, so I showed my face to the jury and sent them home because I was terribly sick.

On the fifth night, Tuesday, the nausea was slow to come. I had eaten no solid food for a day and a half. Suddenly the chills hit, and I had to force myself to breathe. They went away the more I hammered at the wall. I was going slowly now, since Dave and I were almost all the way through and we did not want to damage the inner surface of the wall. In place of the chills I felt ants crawling on my legs. I would slap at my thighs and the crawling would stop. When we stopped for a break, I rolled up my pants and was surprised to find not a single dead insect. I felt the crawling start again even as I looked at my exposed leg and saw nothing on my skin.

Dave finished most of the rest of the work. In the last few minutes when I was destroying the wall, I felt the crawlers all over my body and the nausea twisted in me harder than ever. Something in the air here was poisoning me. I could barely endure waiting among the conduits for Dave to finish.

I waited until we were in the alley before I tore off my mask and jammed my finger down my throat, trying to force myself to vomit—anything to relieve the nausea. Some acid, bile, something tasting awful came up and I did feel better. Dave pulled me along. "We don't want to be spending too much time in this alley, Paulie," he said gently.

I forced myself to walk fast. When we got to my Jeep, I gave Dave the keys and lay down in the backseat, only to notice the nausea was gone. Dave had turned twice and now was headed north on Franklin Street. I opened a window and then I felt a smidgen better.

"So now tomorrow or Wednesday, your pals Charity and Trimble will—"

"There was something in the air, Dave. I have never been so sick. Maybe we ought to see our doctors." I was talking much faster than I meant to. "I didn't want to say anything, but I kept getting worse every minute I was down there and this has been happening from the beginning; it's some kind of cumulative effect, or some allergy maybe. God, I feel great right now. I wonder if—"

"Paulie, just sit there a minute." Dave cut me off. "It's not the air, not an allergy, Paulie—it's claustrophobia."

"No. No, it isn't. I'm not claustrophobic." Not Perfect Paulie.

"Really? You spent a lot of time in your life in underground tunnels? No, of course not, and you figure you can handle elevators and airplane bathrooms, you're okay. A firefighter spends a lot of time crawling in the dark and inside collapsed buildings, and a lot of cadets flunk out of the fire academy because they find out they can't handle it. The first time they do it, they feel a little bad and each time they do it, it gets worse." Dave pulled the car over to the curb and turned to look at me.

"It's like a little message you send yourself. Then you do it again and the guy inside you says, what the hell, you didn't hear me the last time, see how you like puking every five minutes. The last message you get is crushing chest pain. Okay?"

"Right."

"Good."

"Dave, do you think I can go down there again when we have to pull out the money?"

"Probably you could do another hour for a hundred million."

8.

IN THE MORNING, I forced myself to eat waffles I made in a toaster and then drowned in syrup. All that was left of my illness was a lingering headache and the knowledge that I was not immune to ambush from my own psyche. In the Serena case I had no answer on how to proceed. The key witness was dead, the prosecutor wanted to give up, and I would have to take a plea of guilty and impose a sentence that was so small that it would be an insult to justice. In chambers, I was doing a lot of pacing and fiddling, cleaning out desk drawers, skimming law books, finding nothing, until my headache went away and, in its place, came the thought of a move, a neat tactic.

I reconvened court in Serena's case. Reading slowly and clearly, I put the last words of Lois Kreutz into the record. I read slowly so that I could gaze at Bill Serena. His face was a marble mask and heartless. He had not known that Kreutz could accuse him today, in the presence of his jury, even though she was gone from this earth.

"Your Honor, I too was moved by the suicide note, but that charge cannot be tried." Mason spoke very quietly. Then Lang added, "And Mr. Serena should not be punished for an offense on which he cannot be tried." But I get the last word in court.

"Counsel, I don't understand what you are saying to me. Look at the note. When she accuses Mr. Serena, she has already taken a fatal dose of barbiturates. She knows she is going to die. We know that she believes in an afterlife, she wants to join her husband. We know she believes in the judgment of God. This, Mr. Mason, seems to me to be a classic case of an admissible dying declaration; the law trusts the deathbed statements of those who believe they are soon to be judged by their maker. And, Mr. Mason, if the dying declaration is admissible, so, too, may be Mrs. Kreutz's sworn testimony before the grand jury, which is now corroborated by the dying declaration."

Mason opened his mouth but thought better of interrupting me.

"I understand the emotional effect of that note," I continued. "It had an impact on me. Perhaps you were so moved you over-looked its admissibility to prove your case. Now I am sure you want to consider it and consult with your supervisors."

"I suppose I do," replied Mason.

Lang was angry. "I must protest, Judge. I feel you are be-coming the prosecutor now, not a judge at all. Excuse me, but I have to say this . . ." I raised my hand to cut him off.

"Mr. Lang, ordinarily, I would never do what I have done here. But, you came before me with a plea agreement and you and the prosecutor asked me to accept it. The law says that I can decide not to accept it if it is against the interest of justice. How can I tell whether the plea is in the interest of justice if I cannot assess the strength of the prosecution's case? I did that, and the case is too strong for this plea. I will not accept the plea agree-ment. Mr. Lang, the bottom line is that I will not agree to limit the sentence to eight to fourteen months."

"Your Honor, I protest."

"The record will show your protest. But, Mr. Lang, if the ev-idence is as troubled as Mr. Mason says, maybe it's best for Mr. Serena to continue with trial and be found not guilty."

In a flat voice Mason said, "Your Honor, the government is ready to continue with trial."

"The very word, ready to proceed."

Neither lawyer looked pleased; I had interfered with their

expectations. Judges do that to lawyers and vice versa. The relationship of judge to lawyer is inherently crabby.

Tony Plymouth raised his head. His brown eyes were blank, but I could see he was biting his lip to keep from smiling.

I had to have a hearing about this dying declaration before the jury could see it. While I listened to evidence and arguments about why Mrs. Kreutz's note was reliable enough to be heard by a jury, Trimble Young went to the counting room by arrangement with Charity. He walked quickly away from the electrical panel where he was standing and crossed the huge white counting room. He carried a small green money sausage. He neared a large machine, opened a metal door, tossed the sausage inside, and moved quickly back to the electrical panel.

We were trying to figure out if he could plant previously destroyed money on the conveyer belt leading to the massive shredder and then extract undestroyed currency from it. Between his work and Charity's own tours of these rooms, they would be able to take millions without the cameras catching it. It seemed too simple to work, but who knew?

Over time, Trimble or Charity would put cash into easy-loading containers and store them in the areas where Trimble labored—behind electrical panels, under the raised floors among the electrical conduits. No one would take notice of the missing money because the weight of the stolen money would be matched by the weight of the shredded cash we added. In time, Dave and I would execute our emergency entry through the hideous tunnel, load the prepackaged money, and take it out fast. While we were inside, Charity would be in the surveillance room controlling the cameras and monitors so that the loading of the cash would not be seen.

The first step was to do the work at the conveyer belt without detection. Charity had told her security team that she was going to run an experiment to see if they could watch Trimble as he wandered around. She did not tell them what he was going to do. If they weren't able to see him, she would never tell them what he had done. If they did see him, she would say it was all part of the test.

I had miscalculated the angles and the clarity of the picture resolution on the monitoring system. Charity Scott saw every bit of what Trimble did on the television monitor. She turned to another security officer. "Rerun it."

He did, and both officers saw Trimble's exploit all over again. So, too, she realized, did the short, feral Ernest "Wheezer" Corman, chief of security at the Federal Reserve Bank of Chicago, who was standing half concealed at the far end of the room. He watched intently as the security officer at the console stopped the tape.

"I saw it. See what he did? I saw it the first time," said an officer watching the screens.

Charity suffocated her disappointment, picked up a phone, and punched buttons. On another monitor she saw Trimble pick up the phone. "We saw it," Charity said into her receiver. "Thanks for helping out, Trimble."

The security officer smiled. "That was a hell of an idea, Lieutenant."

"Yes, a good idea, Lieutenant," Wheezer said. Charity winced. "But you shouldn't have used Trimble as your guinea pig. You two aren't supposed to have any contact on the job. It's part of the court decree."

"That's face-to-face contact, Chief Corman."

"I think it covers all contact, Lieutenant Scott," he replied sharply.

The security officer at the console tried to shrink into invisibility, so as not to get caught between two supervisors.

"Go file some paper on me, if you feel that way," Charity told him.

"Not on this one, Scott. You got lucky here, but you'll fuck up someday, and I'll get both your ass and Trimble's out of here." The Wheezer's voice, she said, was angry, and he glared at her and backed slowly out of the room.

"I don't know why he backed out of the room," she said to me later. "Was he afraid I would attack him right there?"

9.

THE PROSECUTION OF Bill Serena would be based on a legal artifact from an age of faith when nearly all people believed they had immortal souls that were going to be judged by God, who would be celestially annoyed if they had falsely accused someone during their last moments on earth.

I would bet that Mason and Lang had thought about dying declarations in this case. Lang probably agreed to the plea deal because there was a chance the evidence would come in. Mason agreed because he was afraid to take the chance that it wouldn't get admitted.

Mason was right to be concerned. Usually a doctor testifies that he told the declarant that the end was near and a cop testifies that he asked the declarant about his religious beliefs. Then the declaration is made. Some police officers used to tell anyone with a bad-looking wound that he was dying and then ask if he wanted to say anything while he could still speak, realizing he would go to hell if he lied. This callous move could be effective. It did not matter if the witness died or not. The declaration is admitted as long as the witness believed he was dying.

A spontaneous dying declaration, like Mrs. Kreutz's, is a rare thing. My comments in open court signaled Mason that he could get this evidence admitted. That and my refusal to take the plea gave him the heart to go ahead.

Today's courts are skeptical of dying declarations of any kind. So I was required to have a hearing where I had to consider the whole story and decide if it was reliable myself. Only then could I let the jury know of it.

Tony Plymouth was the witness who was going to tell me the whole story of Lois Kreutz.

It came out in cross-examination that it was Tony Plymouth who wanted the federal prosecutor to indict Serena with some fanfare and photographs in the hope that some other victims would come forward. I wondered if he had more than a moment's trouble persuading the United States attorney to do a big roll-out of an indictment about a Gypsy thief caught by a Gypsy cop.

I sat through the hearing looking at a family album that had been opened and resting on Mrs. Kreutz's lap when she was found dead in her parlor. Judging from her picture, she was a pleasant-faced widow in her sixties. Mason needed to establish more than the fact that Mrs. Kreutz was kind and family oriented and a victim. He needed to show that the woman was rational. Plymouth declared she was clear and logical when she spoke. The only pauses and interruptions came whenever the neighborhood children came by. "Except for those interruptions, Detective Plymouth, did she tell you the facts in a coherent fashion?" Mason asked.

"Yes," he answered, and Mason told him to "relate" to Judge Devine the facts Mrs. Kreutz reported about Mr. Serena and "You can leave out the interruptions by the children."

I did not know what Mason might be leaving out here, so I interrupted him and took over his job. "Just a moment, Mr. Mason. I want to ask about the children you mentioned. What were they doing?"

"Some kids' game, like tag or hide-and-seek," answered Plymouth. "They were running up and down the streets, and the yards and the houses. Wild, loud stuff like little kids do."

"How would that interrupt your talk with the witness, Mr. Plymouth?"

"Judge, the kids were running across the porch, hanging on the railings, yelling every other second. I saw one hide under her porch."

"What did Mrs. Kreutz do?"

"Well, some of these kids would yell at her, Hi, Miz Krootz, stuff like that. She would say, 'Be careful, Jimmy or Johnny'— whatever. She knew their names."

"Did she do anything else?"

"The kid who was under the porch—she told him not to stay there because it was so dirty. But the kid didn't move. It was a good hiding place, I personally thought."

"Did she become angry with the child?"

"No, she just told him that if he was going to stay, that he should be careful not to step on the snakes that lived under the porch."

"What happened?"

"The boy left, and she gave me a little smile and said, 'They always go when I talk about the snakes.'"

Damn, this was good. Plymouth was doing well. Mrs. Kreutz came alive—rational, capable, the wise mother—and I was relieved. The questions and answers showed the victim to be a decent, tolerant person who would give a reliable dying declaration. They showed the detective as sympathetic to the concerns of children. It is the kind of detail I had always looked for as a prosecutor.

I had shown Mason an arsenal of weapons. Plymouth himself understood what I was after—I was sure of that when he put in that final detail—"She gave me a little smile." To use these details effectively is the highest example of the trial lawyer's craft. In this case, it was the witness who practiced the craft. Detective Plymouth clearly knew how to make justice work.

I gave the witness back to Mason.

Lois Kreutz had told Plymouth that she called the U.S. attorney after reading the newspaper article because Mr. Merrill, her advisor, looked exactly like the man who had been indicted. "I am not worried, because I have the stocks, but I thought I should talk to someone," she had said to the detective.

Mason apparently got my point because, as he continued, he brought out the fact that she told her story in a light, untroubled voice, and that Tony Plymouth thought she watched his face hopefully when she was done. Mason might have a little trouble getting these last facts into evidence. The detective may not have known Mrs. Kreutz well enough to say that her voice was untroubled or that she had a hopeful look, but at least Mason was on the right track.

The detective asked her if she would be willing to go to the bank now so he could look at the certificates. Then, I think, he lied to her, saying, "It may be that everything is all right." The jury would understand why he would lie in this way. They would respect him for it. She had lied to him, too, I thought, when she said she wasn't worried.

Plymouth did not hold back the truth when they opened her safe-deposit box. He took her out for a cup of coffee. Her apparent placidity was fading. She said she didn't want to tell her children. They had full lives and problems of their own. "I was a fool," she said.

During trial preparation Tony Plymouth went to her house a few times and found her to be morose, barely responding to anything he said. She mumbled at times, and he could hear the word "ruined" repeated over and over. He thought to give her comfort by explaining that if Serena were convicted, the government could seize all his assets and make some restitution to her. When he said this, she turned to him and told him, in her normal voice, that she would lose her house if she didn't get her money back. Another widow losing a house, I thought.

Plymouth called on her once a week and then more often as trial approached. She was becoming upset at how long it was taking to figure out where Bill Serena had put her money.

Just before noon, as I wondered how Charity and Trimble had made out in their trial run with the shredded money, I ruled that Lois Kreutz's suicide note was, in fact, a dying declaration reliable enough to be heard by the jury, which would decide, finally, if it was the truth. That afternoon the jury did hear it, all of them stone-faced. I could not read the jury. After they heard the circumstances of the suicide note and the note itself was read, Serena's lawyer stood up to declare that he did have some important questions to ask but since Mrs. Kreutz was, he deeply regretted, no longer with us, we would never have the answers to these important questions. A couple of jurors nodded. I adjourned court, distressed, the dead woman's face shadowing me as I retreated to chambers to change, so I could join Dave at a diner to debrief our co-conspirator Charity Scott.

* * *

The garish magenta diner survived as a going concern because it was the only place in the neighborhood west of the Loop that was open twenty-four hours a day. Cops and night workers who had no other place to go between midnight and six A.M. ate the greasy food on cracked tabletops and looked at the street through unwashed windows. In the early evening, it was the ideal place for privacy.

The problems with the surveillance cameras were bad enough and so was the fight with Corman—but there was more trouble for Charity. An hour or so after the camera test, she was called into the Fed chief's office, Wheezer Corman at Prindiville's right hand. Prindiville was very curt, one of his three tones along with sarcasm and contempt. "Chief Corman reported on your experiment. I do not want you thinking, even for one second, that our right to give you orders is limited by court decrees. You do what you are told. Judge Devine does not rule here. I rule here, and when Chief Corman speaks, it is just the same as me speaking. Is this clear?"

Charity was still steaming when she reported all this to me. I thought this incident meant we had to steal the money as quickly as we could, before Charity was suspended or fired. I confess that I also thought that Charity would never back out now or break ranks with Dave and me, and this was good.

"If we cannot collect the money bit by bit over a few weeks and have it stored and ready before the day we take it out, then the tunnel does us no good," I said to them. "And if we can't have it stored and ready, we can't use the barrels.

"It will take all four of us to load the money if we grab it all at the same time. We won't have the time to stop on the way out to unload it and shove it into the hole in the wall. If we could have gotten the money slowly over time, we could have stored the barrels near the hole. Charity could then have stayed by the barrels, I could have come through the wall, and Charity and I would have fooled the camera and gotten the money into the tunnel while Dave and Trimble created a little diversion. Even the alternate plan of taking the money out with Trimble depended on having the money suitably prepacked and ready to go. The only good thing about this nonworking plan is that I don't have to go into that tunnel again," I said.

Dave and Charity each gave me a small, bored nod. They were interested in hearing what would work.

I was trying to appear to be confident. "The goal is to be ready as rapidly as possible...then our goal is to wait for the perfect day when everything comes together...then after it is done, our goal is to do nothing for a long time."

"The Rule of Saint Paulie the Devine," Dave said with a small grin.

Charity was idly staring out the window. Dave kept squeezing a rubber bag filled with silicate grains, a device for rock climbers to strengthen their grips. Exercise like this was new to Dave, the only sign of aging I saw in a man whose face was unwrinkled except around his eyes.

I was not inspiring them or myself. "Let's meet next week. I'll have something then," I said, as I prayed that would become true. We parted in silence.

10.

THE SERENA TRIAL moved quickly. Mason was efficient now.

"Detective Plymouth, when you first interviewed Mrs. Kreutz, did she have any occasion to show something to you?" The prosecutor asked.

"Yes."

"What was that?"

"A picture cut out of the *Chicago Tribune*."

"If you know, tell us whose picture it was?"

"William Serena."

"Had you seen that picture before?"

"Yes. It was a photograph of Mr. Serena that I took when I arrested him."

"Do you have that newspaper clipping with you?"

"Right. Here it is."

The detective pulled it from a folder; it was encased in plastic.

"Did I ask you, recently, to search Mrs. Kreutz's home for anything?"

"Right, her scissors."

"Did you find any?"

"These, in her desk."

The detective produced the pair of scissors in another plastic bag.

Mason put on a document examiner from the Postal Inspection Service, who told the jury that the irregular edges of the newspaper clipping matched the irregularities in the blades of the scissors found in Lois Kreutz's desk. The picture was admitted to show why she had used the name Serena rather than Merrill in her suicide note.

Mason asked to have the suicide note read again. Lang objected. I overruled him. "What harm can another reading do? It's a short note." Lang did not bother to tell me what harm it would do. I knew as well as he did, and that's why I was letting it be read again. The jury reheard the dying declaration.

Lang could do nothing. No lawyer can cross-examine a dying declaration.

Throughout the day Serena sat, round and placid, sweet faced, looking like the character in Gilbert and Sullivan, innocent as a new-laid egg. A pretty fine performance—good enough that a jury might believe it, and when I realized this I felt as sick as I had on my last night in the tunnel under the Fed.

The jury retired to deliberate. They deliberated for the rest of the day. Then they asked to go home and come back the next day.

I turned down the lights in my chambers and tried to sit quietly in the love seat, but my mind whirled around on its own axis.

While I waited for the jury and then after I went home, I planned and replanned the robbery.

The failure of my initial plans was not a complete surprise. I always knew that the surveillance camera array might be too well designed. Still, it was a serious setback. The problem had become much more difficult. There would have to be a way to steal anything, no matter how tightly it was guarded, if your fellow thieves were the guards.

We had to take the money and get it out on the same day. If Dave and I went in as paramedics, we would need Charity to help us take and load because we could not store the stolen money in advance in boxes that could be loaded quickly on the gurney. If she were to do that she could not protect us in the surveillance room. We would have to disable the surveillance system, but then there was the really high risk that someone would close the building to prevent any exit. Given the necessity of grabbing all the cash in one fell swoop, we could get away with the crime—if we could create a diversion to give us the time we needed to do it all without being seen. But what diversion would be perfect?

I remembered all that discussion of the chemicals that made up the ink that Klonik sold to the Federal Reserve. To engineer taking and packing one hundred million dollars, undetected, required better crime through chemistry—the chemicals already in the bank and the chemicals we might be able to bring with us. If we did it right, then they would not be able to see us with their cameras when we took the cash and, when we were out of there, they would do the best inventory they could of all the cash and they would satisfactorily account for all the paper money that was supposed to be there. Dave would know exactly what we needed.

I had been through the plans so often that when I finally had the insight I needed, the whole thing appeared to me more or less in final form. It would work. I wished I'd had the true plan before I'd recruited everybody and not after.

There was just one wrinkle that could not be ironed out. Our robbery would get us a lot of old-style hundreds. The old bills would be good for a long time, but not long enough for us. By the time we were done waiting, virtually all the bills in circulation in the United States would be the new hundreds and the only place we could exchange the old bills in America would be at the Federal Reserve Banks, which would tempt fate. That meant much of the money would have to be used overseas. If we got mostly old bills, then to enjoy the money we might have to surrender our homeland for the kind of countries where no one asks questions about people who spend millions in bills that should have been out of circulation years ago.

11.

WEDNESDAY, THE JURY reached a verdict and trooped back into the courtroom. Most of the jurors looked directly at Serena which, in the folklore of lawyers, is a good omen for the defendant. I dreaded seeing the verdict. The foreperson of the jury, a convicted armed robber who had been a good citizen for the last twenty years, was very proud that he was deemed worthy of jury service and walked with his head held high. He stumbled against the riser leading to the jury box. He caught himself on the rail, but his paper went flying. The paper verdict is the sacred host of the courtroom, its contents a mystery to all but the jurors, and before it can be revealed to the world, the foreperson gives it to a United States marshal who, without reading it, hands it up to the bench.

When Serena's verdict floated to the floor, it landed well in front of the jury box. Everyone froze; the lawyers were afraid to touch it. Everyone looked at me, a part of the job I enjoy, being looked at, at least when I know what to do next. I told the marshal to pick up the verdict and give it to me. I opened the folded verdict to read "Not Guilty," and my face felt hot until I saw it was unsigned. Then I realized I held two verdict forms stuck together. The ink on the bottom form had not quite dried when they were folded together. They had handed me both forms I had given them. The bottom sheet of paper was signed by all twelve jurors and it said, "We, the jury, find the defendant, William Serena, guilty as charged in the indictment."

I was transfigured in a second, a cool intense joy in every cell that I had not felt since Ellen was alive. I counted the signatures to see that there were twelve, folded the verdict, and had it returned to the foreperson. He recited it from memory while looking squarely in Serena's eye. It was the only time I had ever seen that done.

Afterward, I sat in chambers reading through piles of paper and deciding whether certain cases should be tried. I was still very high.

The next days, when I was calmer, I began preparing for the great crime. I had to build trays for the cash and I had to construct a gurney to hold the massive weight of the money. Thanks to the U.S. Army, the only true construction skill I possessed was the ability to weld. In my day, we were always planning tunnels and such under the Berlin Wall. None of them were built, but the Army wanted to be sure that, if they were built, it would be trusted intelligence personnel who would do the building, and, as a young man bound for law school, I was exactly that.

I bought welding equipment. Welding is, to my surprise, a perishable skill. My first welds were so terrible that I spent nights relearning the work and how unpleasant it is to weld, as well as how easy it is to set your house on fire with a welding torch.

I presided over a weeklong trial of a man found with a private warehouse full of marijuana. It was the kind of case where one side had no chance to win, but under the Constitution I could not refuse to permit a defendant in a criminal case the right to offer a ridiculous defense. The defendant was pushing the case to the limit because he had a beautiful four-year-old daughter who was brought to court a couple of times by her mother. He melted when he saw them. At times I could hear the voice of the little girl playing outside the courtroom door. I wished I had the power to erase his crime for him. Having children is a good reason not to commit a crime.

*   *   *

A few days after the verdict, Tony Plymouth called to see if I would be willing to talk to him. I so admired his work that I would have paid him to come to talk to me. The judge never knows all the backstories of his cases and doesn't need to any more than the emergency-room doctor needs to know your life story before he stops the internal bleeding so that you can begin the next chapter. Nonetheless, I had developed a personal stake in what happened to Serena.

We sat on separate love seats, facing each other across a low glass table. "Wanted to thank you for the way you handled the case with Mrs. Kreutz. It wasn't going anywhere until you spoke up." A funny look crossed Plymouth's face, as though he was tempted to look over his shoulder. "Christ, excuse me, Judge, but maybe I shouldn't be here. His other case isn't over yet."

"Stay where you are. I've been told there is going to be a guilty plea. Serena has taken a fall on the biggest charge, so he is going to plead. The case is over," I said.

"Anyway, I really said what I came to say. I never saw a judge do what you did. I knew it was going all wrong, you see." Then he stood up.

"Oh, sit down, Detective," I said. I wasn't done yet with this sharp cop. "If you have the time, I'd like to know a few things about that case, the things that don't come into the record. You have some time?"

Tony Plymouth sat back down. I knew he had come here to say something to me other than thanks. I assessed him. He wore a dark gray suit, not expensive, but perfectly clean and pressed, a white shirt that looked new, and a solid dark blue tie—the kind of talking clothes a smart cop wears when he expects to be telling things to a judge.

"Give me Serena's story. Just between us, I like the tale of the hunt," I told him.

It was just what he wanted to do. He leaned forward and spoke without focusing on my face except every now and then when he would look to my eyes for some acknowledgment that I understood what he had to say.

"I'm after Serena for two goddamn years, off and on. His name—all over our intelligence files, one very bad Gypsy. You deal much with Gypsies, Judge?"

I shook my head no.

"You know some places in Europe Gypsies were honest tin-smiths, craftsmen who just stuck to themselves. Other places—outlaws, con artists, thieves with a bad image. A Gypsy lives with his company, like a family. They stay someplace for a while and then move together to some other place—no friend-ships, no ties to non-Gypsies. My grandparents left their company in California. They wanted to settle down. In their hearts they were always a little sorry. But my ma and pa wanted no part of being Gypsies, not the way of life, not the reputation. They moved to Chicago and never said a word about where they came from. It was my grandmother who told me I was a Gypsy, taught me a few words and a curse or two when Pa wasn't watching. Now I see Gypsy cops, lawyers, doctors, Americans—but I also got the Serenas." The detective stopped, the same way that Italian prosecutors stop in the middle of sto-ries about the mob.

"Have some coffee, Detective, or a soft drink, bottled wa-ter?" I asked.

He took the water and started where he had left off. "Serena has a wife and kids—I can't find him at home—he uses secret sublets, telephones under phony names. Well, finding him was one long pain in the neck, but I did it." When he paused to take a breath, he raised his right hand to the level of his shoulder, pointed his finger a little off to my left side, and made little cir-cles in the air. I understood the gesture to mean that there were things that he would leave unsaid because his listener could fig-ure them out for himself.

"He used his own kids. He exposed them to injury." Tony Plymouth shook his head in open disgust—it was a shame for Gypsies: honorable thieves don't put their children at risk. "Years ago his son got badly hurt in an accident. Serena delayed his medical treatment so he could set up an insurance fraud. He had his daughter, Ruta, jump in front of a slow-moving car, slam her hand down on the hood, scream, and flip herself across the hood. Lucky for her, she did it right and didn't get hurt. He got eight grand direct from the driver. That incident was part of the charges, but he paid the money back and the driver won't testify." He stopped for a moment.

"Detective, you want to have some lunch here with me?"

"Yes, sir, I could eat."

We ordered from the Corner Bakery. Tony Plymouth started to look around my office at my art and my professional mementos and he paused at the photographs of Ellen, one from a college drama where she stood in a bra and panties in a scene from *Butterflies Are Free,* another from our wedding, and a third from a trip we took to the Caribbean, years later, right before she died. The photographs stop everyone in their tracks. Ellen, Ellen—Christ, what she would have thought of my pointless welding of pipes in the garage? She would have seen through all my possible lies, that I was taking up constructive art, making sculpture from scrap metal. I could never have told her the truth—she would have thought me to be bad and, maybe just as bad, she would have found me ridiculous. Yet with Ellen reduced to photographs, and even with Detective Plymouth in the room, I could not stop myself from visualizing a series of double support rods to brace a gurney so I could roll a million one-hundred-dollar bills out of the Fed.

While we ate, the detective asked me about my own past. That was daring of him, given the difference between our positions. The first time Plymouth saw me he had to rise to his feet when I entered the room.

"I started as a prosecutor."

"Yes, I heard."

"You heard about the Boss?"

"Bosses was a street gang?"

"The Boss. The head Boss once shot a fifteen-year-old because the boy used to shout, 'We are the Bosses' at the meetings. I was the most junior guy on the team going after the Boss. My little piece of the case was a murder of a rival gang drug dealer. A detective, Aaron Pinkney, walked in, said, 'Hello, kid. I hear you gonna indict the Tree boys for killin' Little. Believe me, you don't wanna do that.' Pinkney's a good detective and I was a kid, so I asked him why not indict. He said, 'Because the Tree boys can't shoot worth shit. You got four eyeballs say the Trees leaning out a movin' car and shooting revolvers and hitting Little, the medical examiner says five times. Trees can't do that, be lucky to hit him once. Your witnesses are lyin'.' All right, how the hell was I going to verify that?"

My story stopped for a moment. I covered my silence with

Tony Plymouth by taking several bites from my sandwich. The double bracing rods on the gurney were intruding on my thoughts. They would not work. Doubling the braces would not double the strength of the gurney's structure. The extra welds would weaken the struts. I would need a single bracing rod and I would double its size. And I could not even get through the sacred story of the creation of the great me, not without plotting my crime. I diverted my mind back to the Boss.

"I talked to every witness and went over and over their story until I knew every detail of it. I wanted the biography of all the players. This took a lot of time. I borrowed the method from the military historian S. L. A. Marshall, who figured out what happened in battle by interviewing every survivor in great detail."

I didn't tell him it was the method I was using with Dave and Charity to discover how the Fed worked and the paramedics, too, and how to make money trays and everything else that went into the robbery.

"My witnesses against the Trees could not have seen the shooting—they were with their connect, getting paid for the drugs they'd sold. The connect was available only once every day, and his dealers would not be out and about when the connect was around. Little's own gang killed him because they didn't like him and then they pinned it on the Trees because the Trees were the ones who got cocaine from South America for the Boss. With the Trees in jail, the Boss lost its cocaine connect and all its cocaine business to the other gangs—it wasn't personal; it was just business."

The detective shifted in his chair and leaned toward me.

"Some prosecutors thought I was a rookie with an overheated imagination, but we dropped Little from the case; we didn't need it. My reputation was made about six months later when a wiretap on the King headquarters recorded a conversation in which the King admitted killing Little and framing the Trees. I was put on big cases for the rest of my career because someone told me I was wrong and I listened to him. God bless Detective Pinkney."

I could tell that Plymouth appreciated the story. If you are going to be good in the law-enforcement business, you must learn to listen to somebody other than your bosses; you must learn to be exactingly thorough, and you have to stand up for the truth even if the truth seems a little fishy.

"I know Pinkney, Judge. He was on the job when I first made detective. He was good," Plymouth said. "He tried to look stupid so that the suspects would underestimate him."

"And it works, doesn't it?"

"With the wise asses of the world, it does, Judge."

We balled up our papers and wrapping from the Mediterranean turkey sandwiches and the black-and-white brownies.

"Detective, I can see why the Florida thing is going nowhere. But what about the other phony accident?"

Plymouth looked down at his palm before he spoke. I wonder if he was reading it. "I'd go to his hiding place, about twice a week. This was near where I live in Wrigleyville. I see him meet up, five other guys, three of them black, two cars between them. Serena has these cement blocks stuck in the trunk of his car. He drove off, and the five men piled into two old beaters. There's this caravan out west of the Loop, where they pull into this old garage building. Half the lots around it are rubble. I park a block away. I called in my location, just in case, and I hustle on to the garage. I'm breathing so hard they could have heard me."

"Well, explosive bursts of speed are not part of life as a fraud/theft investigator," I remarked.

"And I don't work out much," he admitted. He patted what looked like a mostly hard gut.

"Were you able to see anything?"

"No. I start circling around the building, looking for something that's open. Halfway around I get a faceful of spider webs. I can't stand spiders. I'm slapping myself and dancing around. Then I saw a window rusted open about three inches. I got down and crawled to it, couldn't see in but I heard them. It was easy to figure. Doubleten, a guy who's been doing phony accidents for years, brings in Wilson and Richards, two street mopes who agreed to having a leg or an arm broken. Then they got into Doubleten's car. Doubleten's supposed to take the Dan Ryan and pull in front of an expensive-looking truck—Serena told him an orange Schneider."

"I assume, Detective, that Doubleten stands on his brake as hard as he can to make sure there is a crash. And the phony lawsuit is good as gold because there are real broken bones."

"Right, Judge. Serena told them he was paying two grand for the arm and thirty-five hundred for the leg, and the idiots Wilson and Richards are laughing when he asks which one wants the leg. Next I hear someone say "Heads." Then I hear some scraping and clanking and a yell. One of the idiots says he's outta there and the second idiot says, 'Man, see my arm, man, see it. You don't get that fuckin' leg up, I gonna use my good arm and bust yo head.' I hear a loud bone crack and roar of pain." Plymouth winced at the memory. "Then moaning and heavy breathing and a lot of shuffling—a guy says 'I pissed my pants.' Then the cars start. Later on I learn that Serena put the arm and the leg on the cement blocks and broke the bones with an axle."

"You didn't have time to set up a surveillance on the accident, did you?" I asked.

"No, and even if I did, I don't think I'd get the help. We don't assign a lot of cops to property crimes. I get to my car without losing them. The three cars stop at the top of the north-bound entrance ramp, and Serena gets out to stand on the overpass. He's looking for the right truck." The detective was clearly rapt with his own story. "I go two blocks south and enter the Ryan going north, and I pull to a stop on the shoulder underneath the overpass. I sit and wait. About fifteen minutes later I see an orange truck in the rearview, and then I see Doubleten's car come down the ramp followed by Serena's two white guys in their car. Now I figure out that these two guys are going to be the impartial witnesses to the crash."

"That's a nice touch, two white witnesses coming forward to back up the black driver," I observed. "The traffic officers wouldn't think of collusion." Tony Plymouth made one of his finger circles in the air in front of him. I wondered how Wilson and Richards had passed the time with the pain. Serena was thinking of his seventy-five percent of the insurance settlement.

"And Serena..."

"He drove down the ramp, couple seconds later. I pulled out after I saw him. I just followed along. The orange truck was in the middle lane. Doubleten was cruising thirty feet in front of the truck. Serena accelerated. When he was past Doubleten, Serena jumps into the center lane, cutting off Doubleten, who does it like he was supposed to. Serena kept on going. The truck driver tried to stop, but he had too little space and the car in front of him just wouldn't come off the brake. The entire trunk of Doubleten's old Monte Carlo was crushed by the truck. Of course an accident investigator is going to see that the tire marks were very unusual. When a braking vehicle is hit from behind, the driver of the struck vehicle almost always comes off the brake, trying to get away from the vehicle that seems to want to drive over his back. Doubleten never let up, and there's this very long rubber track on the highway. But you can't make a case of fraud out of that one detail."

Suddenly, I found the story less pleasing. What happened to Serena could happen to Dave and to me. Some cop could see something that piqued his curiosity, because there were some odd sights to be had when we robbed the Fed—the way that Dave and I would go into the bank separately, the way I had to hang around the bank waiting for something to happen, the way I would go my own way at the hospital. All the cop would have to do is to follow us around and he would stumble on a man wheeling around a hundred million in cash. "And the case against Serena?"

"The two idiots and the lawyer who will say that Serena hired him. The U.S. marshals can't find Doubleten."

"This is good work," I told him.

I walked him around the rest of my chambers, showed him the souvenirs he had not seen. The intergalactic ray gun toys from a patent suit, a defused hand grenade from the Boss case, a counterfeit IBM ThinkPad, a spoke from the wheel of a ship that collided with a barge near the Port of Chicago, and a wall of pictures of me in my present and former glory. He admired my toys and said all the appropriate things, so I decided to talk a little more about Serena.

"I have to tell you something, if it can stay between us," I said, and the detective nodded. "I thought that Serena is the equivalent of a murderer. He murdered Lois Kreutz. Then I thought maybe not, that he's just a con man who picked the wrong victim. Now I think I might have been right the first time. Breaking bones with that axle, doing it with his own hands, that seems to go beyond the ordinary con game. This man may not shoot you, but he sure doesn't care if you die as a result of what he does to you. Am I right?"

Plymouth looked at me so openly, so unlike an officer on duty, that I knew he liked me. "More than you know, Judge. He'd be killing people left and right if he could figure out how to make a dead man write a check." The detective did not smile when he said this.

"I could give him a higher sentence if the case with the orange Schneider went to trial and he was convicted."

"Mason's afraid that the two idiots will get bought off and say that it was Doubleten's plan and not Serena's, so he might lose, and I don't think he likes to take a chance."

Now I could give Plymouth a gift. "I can tell you how to make him take it to trial, if that wouldn't make you uncomfortable."

"No," said the detective, "if I could get Mason to show a little backbone."

"You're a Chicago police officer, not a federal agent. Mason has very limited control over you. Tell him you're going to hold a press conference. Remember, you're the story here, the only Gypsy police officer..."

"There are others, sir."

"I'm sure there are but you, Detective, are the only famous one, and the media has been paying attention to you and the media loves criticism and dispute. Just tell Mason that if he loses, you'll take the blame and if he wins you'll give him all the credit. He'll take that deal in a minute, especially if the alternative is the hostile Gypsy hero on the ten-o'clock news."

The detective started to grin about halfway through this. I suppose I could have stopped and just made a circle in the air with my finger.

"Good idea, Judge. I can tell you a thing about Serena from another investigation—prove what kind of creep he is." The detective said this and paused, but I could not spend any more time with him that day. I had to go to meet Charity and Dave. They were beginning to doubt me and my plan.

"I want to hear it. But it will have to be another day."

"I'm looking forward to it, Judge."

"It won't work," Charity said, in a "this is final" tone of voice that I had come to recognize. "We can't do a substitution. If it worked, we could have taken a few million a day."

"So we go back to square one?" Dave asked.

"Uh, I guess." Charity sounded tentative. Dave looked uneasy. He and I were in the magenta diner, seated back-to-back to her at the next table over. It was a three-way conversation that I hoped didn't look like one. Maybe this back-to-back move was a little over-the-top, but Tony Plymouth's tale of how he had stumbled on Serena's auto accident scam had unnerved me.

Dave and Charity were glum. They did not know I was ready with a new plan.

I told them the details, and I sounded cadenced, judicial, reassuring. I pretended to know exactly what I was doing, and I hoped and expected they would pretend to believe me.

Charity said, "It can work, yes, but will you have enough time to get a hundred million? I don't think so."

"Then we'll stop at fifty or sixty million," I said.

"You may have less time than you think, going in that way." Dave said. "This is in the Loop—the response time in the Loop is under four minutes, three at most. It's going to crowd up real fast."

"How fast?" I asked.

"Well, they don't all rush in at once. They send in two or three to reconnoiter—the rookies first."

"Then maybe we'll stop at forty million. It still works."

12.

MASON DID NOT look particularly pleased to be in the courtroom for the second Serena trial—that fear of losing sometimes spooks you. The evidence was simple enough. Plymouth testified. An expert said the skid marks were consistent with an intentionally created accident. The lawyer testified that Serena had hired him to represent Wilson and Richards. A professor of medicine and an accident reconstructionist both said that the clean break in the leg was highly unlikely to have occurred as a result of the automobile accident if the victim had been sitting in the backseat as he had claimed.

After the prosecution rested its case my jury went home, but I had more to hear from the lawyers. The defense was going to call Wilson and Richards to say that Doubleten was the mastermind and Serena came in at the last minute. The government wanted to use the things the two had said to the grand jury about Serena. Lang said these earlier statements were coerced by Tony Plymouth and, for this reason, unreliable. Plymouth climbed back into the witness chair.

After the lawsuits were filed, he told us, Tony Plymouth looked for Wilson and Richards. He found them drinking together, washing their pills down with bourbon and arguing about why the leg should be worth more than the arm. The argument was just crossing the line into the unfriendly when Tony Plymouth introduced himself and told them they were both going to jail. The detective just wanted to know why they would let themselves be hurt so badly for $6,000, considering that the guys in charge were going to get $900,000.

The $900,000 figure was overstating the case. The lawsuit might settle for $200,000, maybe $300,000. But the complaint filed by the lawyer asked for $900,000, and Tony Plymouth had a copy of it to show Wilson and Richards. Apparently, he did not have to tell them about overhearing the whole conspiracy or to lie to them that some other guy had ratted them out. The disparity between $6,000 and $900,000 was enough to start them talking.

The trio then visited the lawyer's office. The lawyer said, "Even if what you say is true, I never knew any of this. I mailed the summons out and some demand letters. I wouldn't get myself involved in a federal mail fraud.".

When the detective brought Wilson and Richards to the grand jury, the two men were so upset about not getting lunch from the federal government that Plymouth gave them money for a big meal. Lang tried to make the case that the lunch was a bribe. I was unpersuaded, and Lang was hardly surprised at my ruling. He was contending with a cop who had heard the conspiracy in the making. The government could use the grand jury testimony of Wilson and Richards if and when they testified to the contrary.

The trial took another day. The jury heard the laughable story of Plymouth's alleged dinner bribe. The jury too was unpersuaded by Lang, and again Lang was not surprised by the guilty verdict. Serena dropped his mask after the verdict, showing how contrite he was. He looked squarely at me and said something I could not hear—maybe a curse; he spit on the courtroom carpet after he finished.

Serena had no conscience and was, morally, a murderer and, unjustly, he would not be sentenced for murder. Despite the verdicts I felt a little empty.

"We need the exact dimensions of the money carts and the cash trays, Charity." I spoke into the phone in our dusty headquarters, a small office that Dave Brody had sublet from a failing insurance firm. Brody paid in cash for the office and the phone. It would have been easier and better if we could have all used pay phones, as Charity was doing now. But that was no longer possible: the phone company was doing its part for the good guys in the drug war, so you could no longer receive a call at a pay phone in Chicago.

"That shouldn't be hard to get. They put bids out for those," Charity said. I visualized her holding the pay phone away from her ear. She had told me she was never eager to touch the handset, as it carried the residue of somebody else's body oils.

"But we don't want to write a letter and ask for them, or file a Freedom of Information Act request either, do we?"

"Or maybe a lawsuit? Very funny, Judge. No, I got to get them myself."

"I don't see another way. Is that going to be difficult?"

"I hope not."

I left the office. The building held some charm for me. This lower-middle-class sector of the Loop was populated by jewelers, insurance agents, opticians, and a lot of one-of-a-kind repair shops. If you wanted to repair, rather than replace, fountain pens, electric staplers, or coffeemakers, you came here. Someone in the building could even repair a Lava lamp. There were no lawyers in the building, no one who would know me.

The next day Lieutenant Charity Scott ordered a special security review of all Fed equipment and consumables. The Wheezer confronted her. "What the hell are you trying to pull, Scott?"

"God love you, Corman, nothing special. Last I read in the books, we are about protecting all the Fed property, not just the money. We need to take a look at what we have—unless you want to order me to stop." Charity did not try to keep all the challenge out of her voice.

"Yeah, right," mumbled Corman as he turned on his heel.

The inventory papers listed the money carts and their general dimensions. I needed exact dimensions. Charity went to Files. "Just checking equipment, honey," she told the clerk, who then went to lunch and left Charity alone in a room where she had no real business being.

Finding the right file drawer, she jammed the cart specification sheet into her uniform blouse. She had to make a copy and get it back into the file right then. A second visit on another day would be too unusual, too much like lurking to escape notice. She heard a little soft squeak, once, twice, a third time. She dove behind a desk and wedged herself into its well just as Corman popped his ferretlike head around the corner. He walked into the room, from one end to the other. Crouched under the desk, Charity started to sweat. She'd made a mistake. It was no huge deal for Corman to see her in this room—unusual, but not wrong. Hiding under a desk was very wrong. Corman passed within a foot of her. He literally sniffed as he walked, but he kept on going and left the room.

Charity told me she stopped to thank the Lord that she was allergic to perfume. She emerged, forcing herself to walk confidently to the copier room. She made a single copy of the specs and raced back to the first file room and replaced the originals. She started toward the security office, but saw Corman skulking in the lobby outside the file section door. In a thousand years some cultural archeologist is going to think that we Americans worshiped two gods named "shit" and "fuck," since we always seemed to invoke their names when we saw trouble coming, but Charity was not that sort of woman. *Jesus, baby, save me,* she thought.

Charity waited in the hall until the clerks came back from lunch. She asked for and was given a copy of the security monitor specs and the tape deck specs, documents that a security officer might reasonably want to see.

Minutes later, Charity walked from the file section door past Corman.

"More work for our limited security force, Lieutenant?" the Wheezer snapped.

"Yes, it is. Why don't you have one of your team check compliance with these specs?" Charity thrust the monitor and tape deck specs toward him. As he leafed through the papers, Charity thanked him for his help and walked away with the money cart specifications hidden under her blouse.

13.

I WROTE A letter to the superintendent of the Chicago Police Department praising Tony Plymouth. It might do him some good, and he deserved it. I was proud of my own work. Tony Plymouth and I had put a bad guy away.

I worked on my plans to build the gurney and the money trays I would need. I put tape on the floor to mark out the several spaces in which we would have to work, and I built a small wooden frame three feet high, six feet wide, and nine feet long—a reproduction of the raised floor in the security camera room. We would rehearse our movements in the marked-out floor spaces.

Sweating in the basement, tracing the steps to be taken in the Fed vault in my complicated dance with Dave, Trimble, Charity, and the gurney, I wondered what Ellen would have thought of my behavior in the Serena case. I had done something like it before when she was still with me.

The defendant, Younkass, had killed Irene Projcha, a civilian secretary up at Great Lakes. He had pushed a kitchen knife into her throat. His defense was temporary insanity, a blackout, and he had a history of stays in mental hospitals to back it up. The blackout story was dented a little when he told the police about the dress she was wearing, the blond tips in her hair, and the two women who shared her office. What would destroy his defense was evidence of motive, and the prosecutor had a series of increasingly angry letters Younkass had written about how Projcha had had him fired from his job at Great Lakes. The prosecutor did not know how to get them into evidence, and his endless and useless pausing to think of what questions to ask was turning the jury off. I interrupted him and put the letter into evidence with four questions: Younkass gave you a letter one day at lunch? Yes. Did you read it then? Sure. You kept it until the police asked about it? Right. Is Exhibit Six the very same letter that Younkass gave you? Yes. I helped the inept prosecutor three more times in the trial.

I came home and eagerly called Ellen in Singapore to tell her what had happened. Ellen's company, Choctaw Chip, was acquiring a Singapore chip maker for just over a billion dollars. This usually meant a lot of work for the general counsel, but I never remember her saying anything on the subject. We talked about it again when she came back from Singapore the day before the trial's closing argument.

She must have seen how satisfied I was. "Paulie, dear, you probably went further than ninety-nine out of a hundred judges would have gone, but you didn't cross the line. The government still had to prove the cases; you can ask a few questions as long as you don't take over the case."

I appreciated her opinion because she had been as good a prosecutor as I had been. "But I went right to the edge of the line."

"All you have to do is ask yourself honestly, is this a judge's action or is it the act of someone who is above it all?" She said it in a dull voice and sat silently for a bit. Then she said, very harshly, "Now I'm going to take off your clothes and mine too."

Ellen pushed me into the huge blue-tiled bathroom next to our bedroom. She closed the door and, in darkness, stripped both of us. She bit me on the shoulder and went down my body, biting and pinching. She pulled me to the very hard floor, startling me, and mounted me. She leaned on my chest with her hands. I was crushed against the floor, and I could barely breathe. She finished before I did and pulled away. I started to get up and she pushed me back down. This was not Ellen, these acts, and it was not like me to yield. So I forced myself up against her pressure and, when we both stood, I pulled her arms behind her back and held them there. I turned up the dim accent lights behind a set of display shelves, and I could see ferocity in her face. She was angry, angry at me, I thought. What the hell had I done to cause this fury? I forced her to the shower, took the handheld spray and aimed the hard stream of water between her legs. She grew rigid. I would not let her go. Then she pushed her legs open for the spray. When she finally tried to avoid the stream of water, I turned it off. I put her on her back on the rug in the bathroom and held her arms against the floor and stared at her. In a moment she pushed herself against me, and I let go of her arms. It did not take long. Her skin was still soaked when we were done. We did not speak until the morning, but she finally put her hand in mine before we fell asleep.

When the guilty verdict came in for Younkass after a long deliberation by the jury, we had a celebration dinner at the Everest Room, a very expensive place: everything is very soft there—colors, fabrics—and you can push a finger half an inch into the cloth on the walls. For a temple of haute cuisine, the service was friendly as well as efficient.

"So, Paulie, these two weeks with the Younkass case, they were good for you?" She began as we finished dessert.

"Very good."

"And was I helpful, our talks and all?"

"I would have been nothing without you," I replied, hoping that I sounded grateful and contrite, even though I wasn't sure what I should be contrite about.

"Paulie, dear, I really hope that is not true, because that was the one and only time you will ever see me act like a motherfucking Stepford wife."

Ellen never used foul language. There was no place to run and hide. I was bewildered, tumbling with Ellen into a space that had never before existed for us.

"I was in Singapore. Did you really notice? I spent every day dealing with the trusting children who are my bosses. All they wanted was to do a billion-dollar deal even if it meant they would lose effective control of the company. Every other day I confronted a group of overseas Chinese, only one of whom was decent to me. The rest were revolted by the thought of negotiating with a woman. If their grandfathers had met me ninety years ago, I would have been taken captive and sold into slavery. Every time I said no to them, they got up and left the conference room, and my bosses always wanted to beg them to come back. My career was up for grabs. I forced the deal, and on good terms. Right now I have a sophisticated Chinese director on the corporate board and, with the benefit of several thousand years of mercantile blood flowing in his veins, he is very close to talking my gullible young techies into giving away all the things I won for them. This, Paulie dear, is bigger than your Younkass case, more significant than your judicial woes. You have never asked me what was happening. I tried to tell you once and you interrupted me, to tell me what the Supreme Court of Upper Volta, whatever, had to say about direct identification...."

"I'm..." I started.

"Sorry, very sorry, never do it again, all that. And something else—I think you did cross the line with Younkass. I gave you all that encouragement because I thought you needed it to get through the damn case, but you did become a prosecutor. Don't do it again. Jesus, Paulie, if you can't sit still and be a judge, quit the job."

I sat there, I thought I was seeing stars, as if I had been hit in the head by a baseball. Ellen began to sip her espresso. She would glance at me as I roiled inside, knowing she was right about my being a bad husband and a bad partner, and not sure that I did right in the Younkass case. I began to I think I had lost her. The silence went on forever.

"Paulie, dear, why don't you finish my dessert? It's very good." She picked up her plate and smiled at me. I have never had a better gift than that smile, and I will never have it again.

14.

I DROVE SOUTH to Pontiac to buy a heavy-duty glass cutter. The store was halfway between Springfield and Chicago. I stopped at a café that I visit every year on my two-day excursion to the state fair, where I would meet up with the federal judge in Springfield whom I knew from our prosecutor days. We had the clout to go anywhere at the fair we wanted. We stood backstage for the nightly rock concert, toured the carny, and watched the crowd devolve from farmers and families at noon to the nighttime low-rent corps of high-school dropouts who were goaded by a vicious-tongued bozo into blowing their cash on a chance to knock him off his stool into his water tank. *America's future,* I used to think in one of my worst moods, but few of those losers would wind up robbing banks like Perfect Paulie.

By contrast, there was the very helpful kid at Pontiac Hardware who gave me good advice on glass cutting and who wasn't taken aback when I paid cash. I suppose the local farmers also paid in cash.

I spent hours at my desk at home, working to make trays that looked like the glass trays the Fed used for cash, based on the plans Charity had copied at the Fed. My trays were to be slightly smaller; they had to fit precisely within the Fed trays.

Then we would tip the Fed trays over and the cash would settle into ours. Our trays also had to fit neatly into our carrying box on the gurney.

I drew multicolored lines on a computer and then manipulated them around the screen until a series of rectangular plates came together in the shape of trays. Around a graphic outline of trays, I drew and moved bars, corner pieces, and cross braces, until they fit neatly around the trays. I saved a few to a computer file, then added four meaningless table legs to the corners. If someone were to find them, the drawing would appear to be an odd-looking worktable. I decided it would work and printed each of the drawings that had been saved. Then I deleted each drawing from the computer memory. I removed the set of drawings from the printer, but not before I put on a pair of rubber gloves. This was my plan for the gurney.

In the typewriter well of her side of the partners desk, Ellen had kept a modeling kit of multicolored plastic pieces—like enough extra-large Legos to build a Sears Tower—that could be fit together to make anything. She liked to make things with her hands, and I could never redirect her into something useful like carpentry. Upstairs in the library I kept a small album of photos of the things she built, fantasy structures like Gaudí's absurd Barcelona cathedral.

I built models of the Fed vault and models of the halls and rooms we would travel through on the way out. I used Ellen's camera to take Polaroids to show to Charity. She would mark corrections on the photos, and I would make new models and new photos until they were perfect.

After three weeks I was ready to make the gurney, to make the trays, and to build whatever mock-ups we needed to rehearse our movements.

I was a very good judge during these weeks. Mental effort has its own momentum and I was a solver and unraveler of the first order, attending to crime at night and justice in the day.

After I had choreographed the theft, I phoned Dave to tell him to get the glass I needed. "Pay in cash," I instructed him.

"Good thing you told me that, Paulie," Dave said. "I was planning to use my personal Discover card, and was going to write 'bank robbery' on the receipt so I wouldn't forget to deduct the cost of the glass as a business expense on my tax return."

When we had the glass, I showed Dave how the glass cutter worked. "Okay. Let's go," he said. He liked tasks like this. He would have loved shop class if Mater Dei had offered something so practical.

For several hours, we measured and cut glass. Our first attempt resulted in a fine-looking glass tray that was two centimeters too large.

"Goddamn it!" I said. Then I took a hammer and smashed the tray to pieces. When I finished, Dave remarked, "Excellent judicial demeanor."

I did not laugh.

"We'll get better at this, Paulie."

Somewhat restored from my frustration, I took a broom and cleared the glass from my basement floor.

Dave brought a new sheet of glass to the measuring table and we started over. Halfway through the cutting, I shared truth with Dave. "You know, smashing that tray . . ."

"Yes."

"All in all, nearly as good as sex," I confessed.

Two days later, we had one perfect tray and the glass pieces to make six more trays. The perfect tray was a simple rectangle, about three feet by two feet, and eight inches deep. The precise measurements were in millimeters. It consisted of one large bottom plate and four side plates, glued together. Gluing glass is very difficult to do, and Trimble would have to do the gluing in the Fed. We could not sneak completed trays into the bank.

"What do you plan to do with your fortune, Dave?" I asked one evening, my reading glasses sweating down my nose as I pressed glass plates tightly together, testing a new glue.

"Let me tell you, Paulie." Dave was intently squeezing another layer of glue between two pieces of glass. "I'll live in Geneva and various ski resorts. I will speak fluent French and I will ski beautifully. I will be pursued by women of wealth and nobility. I will marry one of them. Thin, raven haired, and pretty. She'll be a real princess and have a name like Hohenzollern. Her family will be thrilled because of my money and because I will be willing to change my name to Hohenzollern.

Maybe, I'll be a baron." Dave looked up and began to imitate the queen of England waving to the masses, a tube of oozing glue in his hand.

"You going to ask Bridget and her father to the wedding?"

"It would be rude not to." Dave gave me a princely smile.

For respite, we went out for music. This time we did the Green Mill; there was a quartet with an organ and the guy knew how to swing and the room was pulsing—it empties the mind nicely. Walking on Broadway, deserted and decrepit this far north, I found my mind filling up again.

"I'm thinking about doing more to take some of the attention away from us when we carry the money from the vault to the sidewalk," I told Dave.

"You don't think that a lot of people running for their lives will be enough of a distraction?"

"I don't think the security people and the emergency personnel are going to be losing their cool. I'd like to give them something else to do. And there are going to be a lot of firefighters pouring in. I'd like to run up against fewer of them."

"You know, Paulie, I'm thinking about my Hohenzollern bride. I like thinking about her. In case I can't find one, what's my backup?"

"Be serious."

"I am serious. Give me some help here." He stopped to put his hand to his head, Rodin's *Thinker* pose.

"Anyone from France named de Bourbon—royalty," I suggested.

"Very helpful, Paulie. Now what did you want to talk about?"

"Staging an unsuccessful robbery attempt—very loud, garish even. I want to blow up the door at the armored-car port and then make a lot of noise with fireworks and then I want them to find that armored car—the one we stole—abandoned in an alley a couple of blocks away."

"It doesn't take that much planning," Dave said. "We can get commercial explosives to blow the door apart; we'll need sixty-percent dynamite. We need primacord, explosive rope, to string the dynamite together, and a small electric timer to trigger the detonation. Makes a nice package we can plant outside the door the night before we go."

"How about plastic explosive?" I asked. Our footfalls seemed loud on the deserted Broadway sidewalk.

"Absolutely the best, except one thing: The only place it's easy to get the stuff is in the movies. I'd need to ask around for it, so even if I did get it . . ."

"There would be a lot of people who knew you were in the market for semtex, and one of them might tell the police," I finished his line for him.

15.

SENTENCING SERENA WOULD not be as simple as it had been with a character like Wriston, the useless bank robber. The prosecution also wanted to prove the incident with Serena's daughter Ruta so that I could consider it when I passed sentence. Proving it meant witnesses and a hearing. Serena's two convictions had apparently convinced the driver whom he had defrauded that she had to testify.

Around this time, I was about to follow Serena's splendid example of perpetrating multiple criminal acts. Neither Dave nor I had a blasting permit and neither of us was a good forger. Charity said she was terrible doing anything with paper. So, we could not easily buy the dynamite. We planned a nice theft, a breaking and entering, at Collins Construction Supplies in DeKalb, Illinois.

DeKalb isn't that close to Chicago. Charity ventured out on a weekend and drew a plan of the interior of the store. The next Saturday, Dave and I drove more than an hour west of Chicago. The place was open a half day on Saturday; we'd look around, wait until closing, and then hit the back door. Dave brought a large tool, a door breaker, that the fire department uses.

I went inside myself to check the accuracy of our plan of the building. Charity's drawing was perfect. Then I acted like a little boy who loses his nerve when his buddies dare him to shoplift a baseball. Only it wasn't nerve; I couldn't steal from Collins and make trouble for him with federal inspectors. It had been a stupid idea. We were lucky we weren't caught when we did the armored-car crash test. Explosives were out of the picture.

As I left the store, I saw a very big man with a dumb look on his face loading dynamite onto his truck. He seemed to be concentrating very hard on what he was doing, which, I suppose, is not so dumb a thing to do when you're handling dynamite. But he was not paying attention to his blasting permit, which he had shown to the dealer in order to buy the dynamite. It still sat on the loading dock counter, flapping in the breeze, held in place by a brick. When the man's back was turned, I walked past the counter and took both the permit and the brick.

Dave had a phony identification—several of them, actually—so back home in Chicago all I had to do was make up some more signs for truck doors. This time I used the name of the company that had the blasting permit, and the next day we bought our dynamite and primacord at a construction supply house in nearby Cicero.

We bought much more dynamite than we needed, so we could run tests.

Over the next two weeks Dave and I cruised through the unused industrial areas around town—the Tenth Ward and environs—looking for abandoned buildings with rolling overhead doors like those used by the Fed at the armored-car port. We blew up three of these doors until we found the right combination, meaning the smallest amount of dynamite that could shatter the door. I discovered that blowing things up is fun. Of course, there were investigations of these blasts, and law enforcement would be able to use the markers in the dynamite to trace it back to the places that might have sold it, and I am sure somebody from the Federal Bureau of Alcohol, Tobacco and Firearms paid a visit to the store in Cicero, but it would lead nowhere. So far we were still perfect.

Every time we blew up a door, Dave and I would run inside and look quickly at the interior walls, to see pieces of the door blown into them. We wanted the door to shatter and its pieces to slam up into the ceiling. We never quite got all of it to fly up. That meant that someone inside the armored-car port could be killed when we blew up the door. Dave and I didn't talk it over; we just worked as hard as we could to direct the explosion, and we were upset when we failed. I was not going to be a Serena and kill someone, even inadvertently. Ellen would have hated that, and my new friend Tony Plymouth wouldn't approve either.

We could not put the explosive outside the door at the Fed. The dynamite had to be planted inside the port so that the door parts would blow out and up against the solid brick wall of the office building across the alley.

16.

HAVING DECLINED TO burglarize the construction supply store, purchased, semi-honestly, all the dynamite we needed, and destroyed only abandoned property, I did not feel awkward when I sentenced William Serena.

Ruta Serena testified that the idea of throwing herself in front of the car was hers. I admired her for trying to help her father. Although she looked sincere as hell, I could not believe her and no one else listening to her and watching her did either. Mason deserved credit for leaving her alone on cross-examination; he knew that her story was utterly incredible and there was no reason to make her look like an idiot in open court.

The maximum sentence I could give the murder of Lois Kreutz was thirty years. Five counts of wire fraud in Kreutz and one count in the auto accident case meant five years maximum for each count; I could string them together, but only in theory.

I was not fully free to do that. Federal sentencing guidelines said the sentence should fall within thirty to thirty-seven months. You could argue that the guideline should be higher or lower, but in my view no guideline provided for an adequate sentence for Serena. I would have to depart from the guidelines—which I could do if certain circumstances applied.

Mason did a really good job. He knew now that he would not lose. He would give me all I needed to do what I needed to do.

Bill Serena did not say he was sorry; he said he was innocent and would appeal as long as "I got the breath in my lungs, Judge." I could barely look at his self-righteous face.

Then it was my turn. The courtroom went quiet; Serena shifted his weight from foot to foot. He looked up at me and then at Mason. His eyes narrowed, and his face thrust forward as he looked at Lang; it was a glower, very angry, but this was par for the course. The defendant rarely resents the prosecutor and the judge, who are just doing their jobs—the defendant blames his own lawyer, whose job, as the defendant sees it, is to get him off the hook. Few defendants buy the argument that the job of the defense lawyer is just to see that there is a fair trial. I waited until Serena was done staring daggers at Lang. Then I sentenced Serena.

"I am persuaded by the argument of the prosecutor and I grant his motion for upward departure on these grounds: Section 5K2.1 Death—here because the fraud guidelines do not reflect an allowance for the risk of death to the victim, Lois Kreutz. Section 5K2.2 Physical Injury—here because of the intentional injuries to Wilson and Richards. Section 5K2.3 Extreme Psychological Injury—here inflicted on Lois Kreutz. The conduct of the defendant shows utter indifference to the fate of those he uses and those he targets as victims. The use of his own daughter, exposing her to serious risk of injury—think, Mr. Serena, of what might have happened if the driver of the car had not stopped or had reached for the brake and hit the gas pedal. You are prepared, indeed eager, to initiate schemes that can injure or kill, even your own child. I regard what you did to Mrs. Kreutz as the moral equivalent of murder and I sentence you to three hundred months in prison, to be followed by three years of supervised release, a fine of fifty thousand dollars, and restitution to the estate of Lois Kreutz.

"You have the right to appeal your conviction and your sentence. If you wish to do so, ask Mr. Lang and he will tell you how to go about doing it.

"Bail pending appeal is denied. Court is adjourned."

Tony Plymouth, my new pal, patted his hands together, silent applause for me as I departed my courtroom. The sentence was twenty-five years. Under the law, Serena would serve at least twenty-one of those years in prison. Neither the fine nor the restitution would be paid, of course; no one would ever find Serena's ill-gotten money. Still, I was pleased with the hearing. A reasonable approximation of justice was done in the courtroom, and I was the proud perpetrator.

Charity called me Monday, Wednesday, and Friday using different pay phones. After I filled her in about the glass trays, I shipped them to her through a mailbox service.

Trimble brought the side pieces into the Fed hidden in his pant leg, one at a time. The bottoms of the trays he fitted into cardboard cases with electrical equipment markings and delivered them one at a time. It took nearly a month and a half. He hid them in open view in an equipment storage room. Glass shelving was common in money storage rooms and in counting rooms. The Fed kept a supply. The storage area was outside the highest security perimeter. Charity reported that Trimble was steady and cool every day. I think they were very happy together. Our plot gave them something to do outside the bedroom. Doing crime together creates and renews intimacy, I think, and this conspiracy lessened the bitterness they felt toward Wheezer Corman and the men who ran the Fed.

Trimble assembled the trays in his equipment room. He had to do his work in areas not routinely covered by surveillance cameras. Even so, he did it during lunch hour when few people were in his area, and he had to move like a dervish doing the work of gluing the trays together. This was tough work; Dave and I had not found an easy way to do it. According to plan, Trimble put sticky brown paper tape on the side of the tray and put the tray on one shelf of his cart. He piled the tools into the tray and around the outside of the tray, which thoroughly disguised it. He had started on the second tray when he heard his boss calling his name.

Trimble thought to hide himself and crouched down behind the steel tool shelves. It seemed he was clumsy under stress, from what Charity reported, though she would not have admitted that, in so many words, to Dave or me. When Trimble pulled on a corner post to hide himself a little better, he toppled the stack. It made a sustained racket. He told Charity he thought he was going to get caught. She would tell him he would never get into trouble just because he had glass trays.

"Jesus, Trimble, you got some broad in there with you?" asked his foreman who stuck his head through the door and saw Trimble on the floor along with dozens of tools and pieces of electrical hardware.

"You all right?"

"Yes, sir."

"We need you to check the fixtures in the president's office. His ceiling lights are flickering."

"But, this—"

"Clean it up later."

Trimble felt desperate and hoped it didn't show. He told Charity he had been frightened.

"And lock this room up. I don't want anyone coming in here and making it worse."

The boss started to leave, and Trimble saw him turn to stare at the floor and at the glass shelving. Trimble told Charity that his mind went blank, but the boss turned away without asking a question. "Goddamn, Trimble. I hope you didn't break any of the glass" were his parting words.

He walked out. Trimble grabbed his tool belt and followed him, locking the equipment room door.

When he came back he pasted a handwritten sign on the equipment room door: CLOSED TEMPORARILY FOR CLEANING.

Trimble finished making all the trays and taping them. Now he had to wait for a reason to go to the vault.

Trimble complained to Charity about the trays. "I don't know if these people know what they're doing," he said to her, and she said to him,

"What say, baby?"

"It took forever to glue those trays together, and I did it as fast as it can be done. I could have gotten caught, I almost did, through no fault of mine," Trimble said.

"Why was it so hard?"

"It's glass; it's hard to glue. We should have used plastic; that would take no time at all."

"You're right about that, baby," Charity spoke slowly and calmly, "but we don't use plastic much around the bank. Anybody finds it, and they know right there it doesn't belong; we have to use glass. Our partners must have figured you were good enough to get it done, and you were."

Trimble relaxed.

"What can we do to get you in the vault?" Charity asked.

"We have to create a power surge in one particular place on the line. It has to be enough to trip the breaker."

"Can you do it, baby?"

"It's easy to do but if I try it, Charity, I can only do it in areas I have access to."

"Can I get it done?"

"Yeah and there is something else you can do," he answered. They went to the bedroom.

I thought I needed to know everything that Trimble and Charity did and what happened when they did it. Charity, who knew how to reconstruct battles from people's memories just as I did, went over the details with Trimble time and again and I went over the details of what Trimble said and over the details of her story with her just as often to the point where she was exhausted enough to let this last scene from her marriage slip out. Then we just let it go and sipped a little coffee together in the diner.

Charity brought the dynamite in, two sticks at a time, hiding them on the shelf of a supply closet. Dave had wrapped them in as airtight a package as he could make. The primacord was in the last package. Trimble assembled the detonating device from a couple of timers he bought at Radio Shack; he also made the box that would hold our little bomb. On the outside it looked like a standard tool-and-parts box found around the Fed, but the inside had heavy metal plates designed to direct the force of the explosion.

Trimble waited until he was called to do some routine work in the armored-car port, and he took a regular tool and parts box with him. He had very clear instructions from Dave, via Charity, about where he was to leave the box. He left it with no trouble at all. He retrieved it twenty-four hours after he had left it in place, and no one ever noticed. The bomb would work. Charity could trigger the timer by remote control, and since she was going to control the timing of the theft, we would have no missed signals. Our bomb would explode when it was supposed to explode.

"Is the box ready, the diversion?" I asked Charity, speaking now face-to-face in our magenta diner. The plan was progressing so well, I had relaxed a bit about the Tony Plymouths of the world pricking up their ears from across the room.

"Yes, I can put it together in a few minutes. It's just that I have to put it in place myself. I can't count on Trimble being called to the port. I go there every day. I don't think they'll notice me with the box. But it won't be right away. I won't be in the bank the next three days; I'm stuck at home." Charity said.

"How come?" I asked.

"I'm reporting in sick. I have to get out of a week of supervisory training at FLETC in Georgia."

"You could go to Georgia. We'd put stuff on hold for a week. It might be less suspicious if you did go down there."

"That's so," Charity said, "but Trimble has a problem spending even one night without me and a week would drive him crazy. Usually he won't fall asleep unless I'm holding his hand. Last time I did this, he took leave to go with me. Now he's used up all his leave time."

At Radio Shack Trimble Young bought a lamp dimmer module, a lamp remote control set, and an eight-outlet adapter. At home with Charity, he broke the circuit board and its wires from the lamp dimmer. The circuit board went into the outlet adapter. Soon he would install the adapter in the vault room. It would replace an existing adapter, and he would plug the vault equipment back into the modified one. On the day of the robbery, he would plug the remote controller into another outlet running off the vault transformer. He would make the current surge and blow out some equipment—and he would be called to fix it. Before he left the vault room, he would replace the altered adapter with an ordinary one and slip the doctored adapter into his pocket so that it would not be found. Trimble was in his element, Charity said, when he was using his hands to create something special.

A few days later, Charity sped to a spot in the wall adjoining the back part of the vault. She knew she had exactly thirty seconds before the camera would pick her up. She ran an electrical pulse detector along the wall. When a needle moved up the gauge, she made a tiny mark with a green pen where she had found a power line. She ran back down the corridor. She was a little breathless and damp by the time it was over.

On her next shift, she began examining a computer printout and looked carefully at the computer clocks. She had to mark the start of a cycle where the surveillance cameras covering the outer vault walls would change targets. When the number hit 14:38:26 she had fifteen seconds to get to the corridor to start her run to the wall. She left the room. In the hall she looked around, and seeing no one, sped back to the wall with the green mark.

Now came a hard part. I knew, from an investigation of bribes paid to city inspectors, that nearly all buildings in Chicago use "Thinwall" conduit to carry wiring, a round pipe one-half to one inch in diameter. There was no way to tell the exact location of the conduit, so if you drill into the wall you might not hit the center of the pipe. If you don't hit the pipe dead center, then the drill bit will likely slip off. So Charity had to use a small hand compression drill to put a hole into the wall. It was hard work, but she could feel if the drill bit slipped. She got the center of the conduit on her fourth try. Trimble had to rig the circuit breaker panel to prevent any contact with the wires, causing a dead short or a melting of the insulation. Still Charity ran the risk of running the bit into hot 120v/240v lines—and that is what she did. She nearly screamed at the heat of the shock that shot through her hand. Fighting through the pain, she put a small wire into the hole, pushed it in with a pencil, and then inserted a white plaster-colored plug into the hole. She ran back around the corner and looked at her watch.

She was out of time, but at least she was in the cross hall between the vault and the outside wall when she was caught on camera. Putting on a game face, she started to inspect the corridor for the benefit of the monitors.

That night, Trimble told her the risk she had taken had paid off. There was now a permanent anomaly in the electrical readings at the vault's electrical panel. Trimble was assigned to repair it in the morning—which meant he could repair it so that he could set it off again whenever he needed it to do so. "I take Trimble in my arms and hold him very tightly," Charity would tell me. "It's my way of making sure he listens to what I say."

Here is one vital thing she told him: "Trimble, when you do go into the vault room, I want you to refuse to go in there unless they move the money carts to the inner vault, so that they are safer. You don't want to be so close to so much money, right? It's the only way they will let you work without a guard watching you."

Trimble spent the day in the vault. He was nearly always on the surveillance screens, all he appeared to do was fix the panel. He concealed his work by shielding it with his body and his arms and his hands. The panel worked perfectly. An expert would have to take it apart to realize the safety systems had been compromised.

I built a mock-up of the raised floor so that Charity could rehearse. Before the robbery she would have to bring things that we needed into the Fed, and she would hide them beneath the raised floor. She would have to be exceptionally quick about it.

Dave drove Charity to my house. A couple of blocks before he turned onto my street, Charity ducked down so she could not be seen. I gave her a quick tour of the house while Dave set up in the basement. She looked at a picture of Ellen and smiled. She turned her smile to me and touched my arm. "She made such a beautiful place for the two of you," she said in a very soft voice. After a couple of seconds, I managed to say, "Thank you." We went downstairs.

Dave and I watched her rehearse; she was very fast in the beginning and became even faster. This first time she tried it she wore workout clothes, thigh pants and a loose shirt. Dave did not stop looking at her when she repeated her moves. I know what he felt like; I felt it myself each time I saw her navel. She pushed herself quickly under the floor and lifted herself out with the same haste, and I understood why Trimble did what she told him to do.

After she mastered her moves, I sent Dave to Charity's house while she and Trimble were at work. On the floor, he chalked a full-size diagram of the target area of the vault. He left the key to her house in a magnetic key safe attached to a rain spout. Charity and Trimble were expecting the delivery, and they used the diagram to rehearse their moves and made a videotape of it so that I could see what they had done. They wore ski masks for the taping. My two partners in crime were doing fine.

We demolished the mock-up of the raised Fed floor system. We destroyed a circuit Trimble had constructed on a bread board so Charity could demonstrate his electrical scheme. There were holes to be filled in the walls where Charity had practiced drilling into the conduit. Then we had a complicated job building two large, hollow rectangular containers large enough to hold several glass money trays. One was made of plastic, and a larger one was made of metal sheeting. And next we had to sew a fabric sheath for the plastic container. The container was supposed to look like a cushioned pad resting on top of the gurney.

The last couple of days before committing the crime became possible I spent welding aluminum pipes in a complicated pattern to the gurneys with the telescoping legs. I had to use a cutting torch to make room for some struts. After that, I could start with the welding torch. To get the raw materials, I had to buy gurneys from three separate medical supply houses. The medical supply house called them cots to distinguish them from the movable carts they use to transport corpses in the morgue. I had to drive to Benton Harbor, Michigan, to acquire the last of them. I crossed two state lines to do it, thus adding another violation of federal law to my life's criminal record as kept by the All Seeing. The construction was slow work. I made metal braces to hold the metal container on the underside of the platform on which the cushioned pad would rest. When the gurney was ready, we could use it to wheel an oh-so-injured Trimble out of the Fed along with a hundred million dollars. The guards would see Trimble but not the money.

"I didn't know you knew how to weld," Dave remarked.

"Another military specialty."

"Why did I think you were a lawyer in the Army?"

"I wasn't a lawyer then. I even wanted to go to Vietnam, but the desire seldom lasted more than a few seconds."

"You wanted to go!"

"It seemed exciting at the time, a good way to prove my manhood," I said, the welding torch alive in my right hand.

"You were crazy."

"I was eighteen when I thought that, so I was crazy. Anyway, I changed my mind and waited for the draft. By then I had learned Russian and German in college to keep me out of Southeast Asia and the war was over anyway."

Dave shrugged at this. I rarely even thought of it anymore.

"Is this going to fit for sure?" Dave asked after the work was partly done.

"It'll fit if you can get it in the ambulance, Dave."

"Yeah, I can. But it's going to look extra-large." He eyed the gurney critically.

I lit the torch again and turned to the steel pipes. This thing had to be strong enough to hold up to a million hundred-dollar bills and yet be easy rolling so that no one would see us obviously straining when we moved it, fully loaded, out of the bank. My skills had improved; I made nice utilitarian welds and never once came close to setting anything on fire.

The device looked a lot like an ambulance gurney, used to wheel around the sick and the injured. I had the blueprints for this device and for the glass tray in a little false-bottom drawer that came with the partners desk. The hidden drawer was on one side of the desk, but there was not one on the other side. Ellen once wondered if one of the original partners, the ones who had the desk built, was cheating the other partner and hiding papers from him.

17

WORKING IN A space about the size we would have in the vault, we lifted glass trays filled with heavy bond paper, about the same weight as cash. After hefting them, we hauled them to my gurney and pushed them as quickly as we could into hidden compartments under the metal frame and beneath the false mattress pad. All three of us were breathing very hard. I didn't expect this to take so much effort. We knew Trimble would not be likely to give us much help; he had another role to play.

The gurney creaked under the weight, but it did not break or crack. My arms began to shake during the second run-through. There was some spare room for loose cash in the compartment, and my hands were trembling so badly that I dropped more test paper than I loaded. Dave and Charity both did better, but we were sopping wet—not a surprise if you load tens of millions of dollars in less than four minutes. When we all took off our jackets, I saw that Charity's back had the definition of a body-builder's. She looked every bit as strong as Dave, who was keeping his mind on the business at hand by keeping his eyes on her hands and arms. She was a wonder when she was in rapid-fire motion. Presiding over the whole exercise was the only good color portrait photograph of my wife, which I had placed in a niche on a sunless wall. I kept my eyes away from Ellen's face.

Afterward I said to Charity, "Now I want you to meet Dave at the Bop Shop on Thursday."

"Where's that?" she asked.

"Look it up in the phone book. Go after ten, and don't dress too well. No one notices anyone else. Wear black." I was a confident Paulie now, leader and master criminal. What they were to do in the Bop Shop they could have done in my basement, but then they might have left traces of chemicals in my house. These were chemicals that should not be found in any of our houses. It was also a trial run of our ability to operate out in the open.

On Thursday, the Bop Shop was crowded with people under thirty, attracted to the bad neighborhood by cheap drinks and straight-ahead bop. A lot of the crowd were white kids wishing they were black musicians. They all smoked, and Charity coughed after her first breath of Bop Shop air. I sat in the darkest corner and stood lookout.

Charity bought a beer and surfed through the bar into the music room. The floor looked filthy and the patrons dressed and looked as if they should smell bad, but they were clean. She found Dave sitting high up on a two-level platform at the back of the room. Dave was ten feet in front of me, but I was not all that visible.

She sat near Dave but not really with him. When he leaned over, it would look like he was trying to pick her up, and he did lean over and speak.

"I have the plan of the room. Here's a diagram. You have to stick the wafers where I have marked the plan. Trimble will have to tell you where on each wall they go. Match the color on the wafers to the color on the wall, and save the green ones. You have to do this right before everything starts." Dave's voice had a very clear timbre, easily heard through the music.

"This is chemical, right?" she asked.

"Yes."

"Won't it leave traces?"

"Yes, but it's consistent with the paint and the ink in the money. Paulie has the chemical breakdown. If the investigators analyze the walls of the vault, all they will find is what they would expect to find, traces of ink and paper." Dave knew arson. "All that's in here is the same stuff that makes Kleenex, with a tiny bit of naphtha for the smell, some other stuff, and a nitrate compound to make it burn, but not too hot. The fire spray is triggered by heat, not smoke, and the later the spraying starts, the easier it is for us to work.

"It's the same thing the bookies use on flash paper betting records so they can burn their records before the police break down the door. There are some wafers with potassium chlorate, lactose, sal ammoniac, as well as naphtha—for smoke."

"Could they trace it back to where it came from, I mean, where I store it?"

"If they had the right equipment."

Charity paused to think about this. She turned away from Dave to think, then turned back and asked, "Do I have some extras?"

"Oh, yes, plenty."

"Okay. I'm ready."

I watched as Dave handed her a slip of paper folded very small and a plastic bag of wafers.

"Now," Charity whispered, "no one in this place is gonna think this is a pickup; they'll think I'm scoring coke."

"I'm going to touch you now, and you're going to get pissed off and walk away," said Dave.

"Be careful where you put your hand, white boy."

Dave touched her shoulder, the one closest to him. He looked like he meant it. Charity stood quickly, firmly pushing Dave's arm away. She glared at Dave. Dave shrugged.

There were no sharp-eyed Tony Plymouths in the room. Charity edged away from Dave and sat on a lower level for the rest of the set. She did not watch Dave leave.

The next day at the bank, Charity waited until the other officers turned their attention to a money shipment leaving the Fed for Milwaukee. On the screen, the carts were visible all the way from the time they were rolled out of the vaults and into the trucks. Charity would use the distraction to lift a floor panel in the video surveillance room. She stood behind a tape-recording tower, and then lowered herself into the five-foot-high crawl space and secreted her wafers behind a set of conduits. She then rose quickly and silently. I had seen her practice the procedure in my basement until she moved as gracefully as a ray swimming in the Caribbean. She would put the floor panel back in place with the small suction-cup handle she had used to raise it. She slid the handle back into its place on the shelf. She was sure she had not been seen. It was the Wheezer's day off.

"Everything is ready, except we haven't talked about the bomb box. Did they notice you when you brought it in?" I asked Charity when we met a final time at our office in the little jewelry repair building on the eastern border of the Loop.

"No. But I couldn't leave it exactly where you told me to leave it. There is a new electrical cable and junction box mounted on the floor next to the door. So when I put the box down, it ended up about half a foot farther from the door than Dave said it should be."

Dave scrambled to my desk for paper and pen. "Draw me a picture, Charity. Show me the door track and the wall and where the box is sitting now."

He stood over her while she drew; she seemed not to notice him leaning over her shoulder. When she completed the drawing, Dave said, "Fuck it."

We looked at him.

"If the bomb goes off from here," he said, pointing at the drawing, "it will drive some of the metal fragments into the side wall at the other side of the door frame. It will also drive some of the metal fragments of the door track into the near wall. And there will be bad angles on the fragments. We'll have a little shrapnel bouncing around the room. Not everything will be flying straight up."

We were all silent.

"There is not much chance of anyone getting hurt. Everybody will be paying attention to the alarms we have already set off. But there will be someone in the truck port, so . . ." Dave said.

"No bomb," Charity said, "not even if it were Corman in the room."

"No bomb for me either," I said, "not even if it were Prindiville in the room."

Dave smiled with relief, a smile I expected from him. He would never kill.

We lost our diversion—there would be no faux attack on the Fed—and cemented our bonds: we wanted everyone to live.

Part Three

Trial

1.

To implement our plan, Charity suggested a new security procedure within the Fed. A security officer was to tour the money rooms at least once every two hours. The officer would inspect the operation and, by his very presence, remind employees that security was tight. This would be a routine to be followed even in the absence of any problem or security breach. Wheezer Corman agreed to this. I suspected that he would try to manipulate the program to force Charity to do a tour when Trimble was in the money rooms, which would be a clear violation of my court order. Corman would have figured he could help it along by paging Trimble to come to the counting room when Charity was there. Charity predicted that this would be his first thought, and I believed her.

The new routine started, and the security people would inspect the rooms and the employees who worked in them. Charity never did the tour herself: she would wait until the arrival of what we started to call "The Day."

Charity had to pick The Day. She was the only one in a position to know when The Day arrived. Dave, Trimble, and I were in Charity's control and had to wait until she acted. Charity liked this part—she was the quarterback and she started play. It was, I knew, a rush for her. I knew it would reinforce her commitment to the plan and, in turn, Trimble's adherence.

The waiting was a major stressor, a drain on everybody's resolve. Usually one day out of every five at the Fed was a candidate for The Day, a time when the right amount of money was being moved and every one of us was available. Once in a while there would be two days in a week that would augur well and then fall through. The Fed tried to avoid patterns, so we could not count on any particular day of the week being the right one. Charity would be able to tell us on the evening before. When she said yes, we had to check whether Dave Brody would be on duty, and I had to be able to leave the courthouse quickly, which meant we could not use a day when some notorious case was on my docket. All this left us, on the average, two to four days in every month. Two winter months went by this way, with our adrenaline ramping up, surging with promise, then receding again.

On each one of the good days, Dave would drive his station wagon to my garage and wrestle into the car the very heavy gurney we had constructed in the basement. Then he had to go to the fire department ambulance port, arrive well ahead of his partner, and substitute the heavy gurney for one of the two his ambulance always carried. Charity had to take great care when strapping the device with the exploding powder squibs on her husband. I had to be sure, too, that I took with me the generic white lab coat with the hospital shoulder patch that Dave had stolen on one of his runs to the Northwestern Hospital emergency room. I bought a half dozen white dress shirts, one size too large so I could wear them over my disguise, which was the paramedic's uniform that Dave procured at Kale's on Roosevelt. I purchased a very clunky Ford Expedition with a very large storage space, and I started to drive it to court every day. It cost more than my Jeep and looked much worse.

Every four weeks Charity had to replace the chemical wafers that Dave had designed for us. He had never used anything like them, and he searched the fire department technical database to find what we needed. Dave had to make the wafers and Charity had to hide them. I was growing weary of wearing two shirts and driving a bad car. Trimble must have been sick of wearing the squibs that, if they were handled badly, could kill him, particularly since, like Charity, he had to carry a supply of incendiary chemical wafers in his pocket in order to be ready for The Day.

The Fed had its own gurney and some staff trained in first aid. I was not worried about the staff; I did not think they would be physically able to do anything to stop our plan if they did not have the gurney. But whenever there was a chance that we would try to carry off the robbery, Charity would have to disable the Fed gurney. I made a wheel for the gurney and weakened the insertion rod. Charity would have to replace a good wheel with the defective wheel. If anyone tried to use the gurney, the wheel would snap off. We had some luck here; the Fed stored its gurney in a small room adjacent to the security monitoring station. Charity stashed the defective wheel behind a grate covering an air duct in the storage room.

I did not think anymore about the bigger issues of why I was going ahead. I tried to talk to Dave about it and he, the voice of experience in crime, never said anything more than "Paulie, you are in, willing to do this, or you aren't. You can't think your way into it or out of it." Of course, a man like me wouldn't truly believe that for very long.

Charity had a pager, rented under a phony name.

Dave had a pager, rented under a phony name.

Trimble had a pager, rented under a phony name.

And so, too, did I.

Dave always used the phone first. Each day he paged Charity and left a message. "0" for no, "1" for yes, meaning that he was available that day. If, by some miracle, someone monitored these messages, it would seem to be nothing more than a vagrant digital code transmission.

If Charity received a "1," she would decide whether the time was right. If it was, she would page Dave and Trimble and leave both of them a "1." Charity didn't have to bother with the zero; it was one less message to track. She used a phone at the Fed that a dozen other people used as well.

The essential thing was the money. There had to be three carts with one-hundred-dollar bills, and they had to be in the vault adjacent to the counting room between eleven-thirty and twelve-thirty. Both the room and the vault were painted all white, floor to ceiling, so that it was easy to spot any cash that dropped to the floor. A thick glass wall on one side of the room and vault allows someone in the hallway outside the counting area to see what is happening inside. In the vault are the chrome carts with their glass money trays. On the day I first saw the vault there were so many carts pushed together in the vault that there was a three-foot hedge solidly constructed out of United States currency.

The hundreds were there one windy winter day as Charity set out to do her very first routine security tour of the money rooms. She notified her crew that she was starting her round, and she left the room. Wheezer had tried to make a habit of hanging around before the counting room tour was assigned. He wanted to know if Charity was going to do the tour herself.

This one day, when he saw Charity leave, he made a call on the internal line asking for an electrician to come to the counting room and was told, "We'll send someone." Corman knew the only someone to send was Trimble; he ran down to the counting room to wait for Trimble and Scott to wind up together in the same room. Corman would also have to tamper with an electrical panel so he could justify his call for an electrician.

Corman did not see Charity when he peeked into the barred door to the vault. She observed that the hundred-dollar-bill carts were being moved to the vault door. Turning on her heel she hurried back to the surveillance room. Trying to be nonchalant, she spoke slowly, "Where is the money going?"

"They notified us just after you left, Lieutenant. The armored car was early. They're moving now."

"Then I'll tour later."

Hiding her disappointment, she turned to the monitors in the surveillance room. In a few minutes, Trimble appeared on the screens. Charity used the remote controls to pan the cameras in the counting room. She saw whom she was looking for—Corman in a corner, quiet as a broken television, watching Trimble check the electrical panel. The Wheezer turned to the entry port through which he must have expected Charity to come at any moment.

"You're foul." Charity unwittingly said the words aloud as she noticed exactly where he had gone and surmised what he had done. No one seemed to hear. While everyone watched the movement of the money, she hid her incendiary tablets back under the floor.

Now we knew what the Wheezer might do on the day of the robbery, and we could take account of that in our plans. This first wrong day was not a total loss.

Everything was absolutely right one Wednesday. Each of us was in position and the money was in place. Except the carpenter unthinkingly took Trimble's equipment cart. Trimble hurried everywhere he could to look for the cart. "If he sees those trays, I can't explain it," Trimble said when he called Charity. He knew that once Charity did her tour, she would take some actions that couldn't be undone.

From what I gathered, Trimble rarely thought very much about anything; deliberation and planning were not the essence of Trimble Young. Charity did all the thinking for him. He must have been desperate to find his cart. Charity always said he did not react well to the unexpected. He put a call over the employee's communications system. "The electrician's cart is missing. Please notify maintenance if you see it." The cart did not appear, but Charity heard the message and stopped her money room tour before doing anything more than walking through the room. Trimble was rightly proud of the way his message had saved the day. When sometime later, the carpenter came and said he had mistaken Trimble's cart for his own, Trimble was smart enough to make a big issue out of it, which pleased me. I wanted him to have some confidence in himself. After all, how far could his worship of Charity take him?

A Monday in mid-August, the morning of the robbery, Dave picked up our custom-made gurney and put it in his ambulance. He had done this many times before. I heard him drive into my garage and went down to help him slide the fire department's regulation-issue gurney into my sport utility vehicle. Our gurney was quite heavy because we had loaded it with all the shredded money we had stolen from the waste dump on the night we were almost shot.

Trimble got dressed in his bedroom. He had to stand upright while Charity installed one of Dave's contraptions on him. I imagine with his pale appearance it looked as if the king of Sweden were being dressed by a Nigerian valet. Charity attached a series of small sacs with explosives to Trimble's body, one on his right thigh, one to his right upper arm, and finally one on his right lower arm. She connected all of them with a colored wire. Then she helped him dress. She looked at his long-sleeved white undershirt and asked, "Is this shirt okay?"

"Yeah, I'm sure it is." Charity remembered this answer.

"Hope it's today." He said this every time.

"Yeah."

I was at home dressing in my paramedic's uniform, putting my dress shirt over my uniform blouse. I selected a dark gray sport coat which did not look out of place with the uniform pants. Then, in my garage, I checked over the vehicle. The backseats were folded down, a standard-issue gurney in place under the canvas sheath. The lab coat was folded under the passenger seat, and there was a small belt pack with a Red Cross marking, festooned with a few rolls of adhesive tape for the appearance of legitimacy. The license plates were registered to my name. I would have preferred phony plates, but the security officers at the courthouse sometimes check plates on entry into the underground garage. If the plates did not match the numbers in their files, they would make a note and ask some questions.

If I received the signal that we were going ahead, that would mean I had thirty minutes to take the car out of the basement of the courthouse, drive to the Northwestern University Hospital, and park it. There was a chance I would find a legal space but, if not, there were two no parking–tow zone spaces that were never filled, not at the same time. I could leave the car in one of them, turn on the flashers, and rely on at least a couple of hour's delay before it was towed. I used my computer to create a windshield placard stating NORTHWESTERN MEDICAL FACULTY FOUNDA-TION/MEDICAL SUPPLY DELIVERY. I had a line for the date and the signature of the foundation director. I made an illegible scrawl for the signature and typed in a date. I guessed that no police officer would decide to write down my license plate number and put it into a police department computer. Even if someone did, the world would not end. The connection between my sport utility monster van and the robbery of the Fed would be too difficult to make.

After I parked the vehicle I would don the lab coat, grab the belt pack, take the ordinary gurney out of the car, and leave it at the automatic portal, then jog east half a block, get into one of the taxis always cruising on Fairbanks Court, and ride it to Adams and Wells, passing the courthouse on the way. Next I had to duck into the unattended lobby at 221 Wells and remove the face piece from the belt pack, replace it with the lab coat, and start to walk quietly toward the bank, waiting to hear the sirens.

2.

CHARITY WALKS BY the vault storage and looks in. She checks a shipping manifest. She peeks at her pager and sees the number "1." At a desk phone she taps out a number and listens. She fiddles with the phone and hangs it up, muttering about busy signals for anyone who cares to overhear. She goes to the storage closet near the surveillance room and sabotages the Fed's gurney.

Dave Brody's pager vibrates, and he sees the number "1."

I am on the bench when my pager starts to vibrate. I do not bother to look. If the pager is triggered at all, this is my signal.

At this moment a jury of eight is listening to an enormous person, so enormous it is hard to tell if the witness is a man or a woman. His is a tale of obesity as a disability unfairly keeping him from fulfilling his dream of being a police officer. The idea of this behemoth running after a fleeing felon is a comic vision, the kind of thing Chaplin would have put on film and maybe Chaplin did. Some jurors hide smiles but my courtroom face is as still as a visage on Mount Rushmore. I look at my watch. When there is a pause in the flow of words, I rap the bench with my knuckles.

"We'll break now. An hour and a half."

The witness looks dismayed; he was in full flight in the telling of the century's greatest grievance. The lawyers look relieved. All I do is rise from my chair. The case never should have been tried; to be a good police officer is to move, and this man had trouble getting from counsel table to the witness stand. I welcomed a case that I could interrupt while knowing that I was not ruining a good lawsuit.

I exit through one of the rear doors of the courtroom and enter my chambers through the private door, the one that bypasses my secretary and law clerks. When I wear the paramedic's uniform there is always the risk that someone would notice the odd fabric of the pants. The dress shirt covers the uniform blouse, the shoes are plain and black, the pants are clearly not dress slacks, and to disguise them I iron a crease into them every day I wear them. The best protection is to avoid contact with other people until I put my judicial robe on. Our chambers are designed to protect the judge's privacy, and this helps me.

I drape my robe over the rowing machine I keep behind the private door and don the gray blazer I left on the door hook. In less than a minute I am behind the wheel and driving up the ramp out the courthouse basement. The traffic in Chicago is beginning to resemble the traffic in New York, with the same sort of difficulties crossing east or west. I lose nearly five minutes moving a few hundred feet past State, Wabash, and Michigan. My pulse is steady; the rest of me feels as real as dreams, but I forget to breathe sometimes until I hear myself gasp. When I turn north on Columbus in the middle of Grant Park, I make up the time. The sun is very bright; the park shimmers, and so does the lake. It is a good day for sunglasses and I put on a pair with very large, dark lenses. At the stoplight at Ohio Street I tape a Breathe Right strip on my nose. This along with the lab coat is my disguise.

At Huron I turn left, and I have the very good luck to find a metered spot next to the surgery building where the emergency room is located. Behind the spot is a crosswalk, so no one is likely to park behind me. I put the delivery placard in the windshield well, take off the blazer and my extra-large white shirt and tie, leaving them folded on the front passenger seat. Then I slip on the lab coat and a surgical cap to cover my hair. Getting out of the vehicle, I feed the meter and then open the lift gate and remove the fire department gurney, which I wheel to the emergency room.

Inside the double doors where they roll in the nonambulatory patients is an alcove. Equipment is left there by paramedics; it is part of the exchange practice. I watch as a paramedic wheels in a badly injured man wearing the paramedic's cervical collar. The doctors are afraid to move the man—they keep the stretcher, the rolling gurney on which it rests, and the cervical collar. In exchange they replace these things from the hospital's supply. I leave my gurney in the alcove.

For the first time in recorded history, there are no cabs on Superior Street outside the hospital. I run madly for a block and a half to Chicago Avenue, where I find a dozen cabs are hiding. I am out of breath; my side hurts. I have forgotten to breathe since the moment I saw there were no cabs outside the hospital entrance.

I gasp out to the cab driver to take me west to Wells and then go south into the Loop. I decide I do not want to pass by the courthouse. Next, I am inside 221 Wells, a building close to the Fed. It is less than twenty-five minutes after I left my chambers. In an old-fashioned wooden phone booth, I do a very cheap imitation of Superman, removing the lab coat and the tape from my nose. The tape goes on the floor, the lab coat into the belt pack from which I have removed a half-mask respirator that will cover the lower half of my face. I put on the belt pack. I walk slowly out of the building and move south and then east, heading toward the Fed.

About the time I parked at the hospital, Charity takes a small vial of a smoke chemical out of her pocket and puts it on the floor of the surveillance room. She crushes it with her heel and waits.

Moments later, the two men at the television consoles start to sniff.

"Lieutenant, you smell something burning?"

"Yeah, I do."

"Smells like it's coming from below," adds one of the guards.

"Stay at the monitors. I'll check," Charity says.

She lifts a floor panel, climbing down smoothly and quickly into the space beneath the raised floor of the surveillance room where she hid the colored wafers. She moves to the conduits against the east wall and grabs the plastic bag filled with wafers of several different colors. She takes a small plastic bag out of her blouse, shakes a few wafers into it, and slides it back into her blouse. The rest of the wafers she empties into her pocket. She lifts herself out of the floor well.

"Nothing wrong under there."

"Yeah, Lieutenant, it seems all okay up here now, too."

"Just one thing or another, I think. Know what?" Charity says evenly. "I'll do the tour myself today. I need the walk."

She leaves the surveillance room. Wheezer Corman sees her leave and picks up a telephone, as is his habit in recent weeks.

Charity checks the vault room and hurries on through hallways down to the counting room. We are all pretty sure where the Wheezer is going and where he will stand in order to watch her. She has to do some of her work before he arrives. The rest of it she can complete outside his view even if he is in the same room with her.

In the counting room she walks about smartly, clicking the floor with her heels. She knows that employees will turn away from a security officer on an inspection tour. She takes Dave's custom-made wafers from her pocket and presses the first wafer against the wall as she passes one counting table. The color of the wafer matches the color of the wall and adheres to the wall. Charity repeats this at different places on the walls, once using a brown wafer on a brown part of the wall. She is careful where she plants them, with none on an open expanse. She presses the last one into place just as Corman enters the room and sneaks into one of the recesses between the counting tables where he can watch the door.

Charity pretends not to have seen Corman. Her pace slows. She does more inspecting and less pressing of wafers. Still she gets each wafer into its proper place. She saves two whites and six greens. She knows the Wheezer must be getting anxious. What he expected to happen hasn't happened. He had called for an electrician, but Trimble is dawdling in his workroom. Trimble is ignoring, for now, the fact that his boss told him to go to the counting room.

Charity strides out of the counting room and out of sight of the cameras for a few moments. She runs upstairs to the officers' locker room. As she exits on the stairwell, she hears running footsteps behind her. It has to be the Wheezer!

The hallway to the locker room is always eyed by a surveillance camera. She slows to a fast walk, an officer's walk, showing none of the panic that she feels, and moves into the locker room, where every officer has a storage locker. At the end of the room are three doors, one to the women's dressing room and showers, another to the men's, and the third leading to a large open area next to the storage vault.

Charity enters the locker room while pulling from her blouse the small plastic bag with the extra wafers. She darts to Corman's locker and presses a couple of the wafers onto the underside. She slips from the room through the vault area exit just as Corman starts to open the locker room door. Corman enters the empty room. He stares for a moment at the women's dressing room door. "Goddamn it." He moves to the door and opens it, simultaneously saying, "Jesus, excuse me, wrong door," while he looks around. A woman security guard, half dressed, turns, gives him a disgusted look. "Corman, get your butt out of here, you..." He closes the door; he will pick up a reprimand when the woman guard reports this to the Fed team investigating the incident that we are about to cause. He exits the locker room only to catch sight of Charity calmly checking the storage vault. She glances at him. "You need to see me about something, Chief Corman?"

Corman just walks past her, his wheeze audible. He does not hide his disgust.

Charity waits a full minute after he is gone. Then she starts to inspect the hallway behind the vault. She looks at her watch and turns the corner, then trots to the spot where, months earlier, she had drilled a hole in the wall and planted the wire along a power line. Using rubber-coated tweezers, she pulls out the plaster plug, twists and pulls part of the wire off the line, leaving part of the wire still attached to the line. Then she slaps the intact plug back on. She gets back into the first corridor before surveillance picks her up.

Extracting part of the wire changes the flow and resistance on one of the lines that eventually runs to a circuit breaker in the central panel in the counting room. The trivial change would not matter much if Trimble had not altered the circuits in the panel. This magnifies the change in the current, and some safety switches are tripped. Alert signals light up on some electrical system monitor boards. Back in the surveillance room, Charity waits for someone else to notice it and to call Trimble. She did not have to wait long; she had a fresh, well-trained crew.

They report that they have spotted the warning signals and called for the electrician.

"Is he on his way?" she asks.

"Yes, Lieutenant. Maintenance had actually sent him down before we called."

"Okay, then I'll stay here."

She sees Trimble cross the lens of surveillance cameras as he hurries to the counting room. Once there she sees him go to an electrical panel that was showing no evidence of a problem. She knew he was waiting for something quite specific. Eventually, Trimble's early handiwork would cause polarity breakdowns. When it did, there would be audible noises and a funny ozone smell and a burning smell, frightening even to electricians. The electric wiring in the walls would heat to a little more than 550 degrees Fahrenheit. The wafers would ignite at 450. It was not necessary for the paint on the walls to ignite, but there were chromate pigments and oils in the paint that might burn at 550.

SNAP.

"What was that?" asked someone.

SNAP.

SNAP.

SNAP.

SNAP.

"Jesus!"

CRACK.

The air wafts around the counting room next to the vault, carrying the smell of a just-passed electrical storm.

A few of the employees begin to edge one way or the other on their stools.

Trimble wanders over to the noisy electrical panel. He gingerly touches the door and then starts feeling along the wall. The places on the walls where Charity has placed the wafers are warm. He follows the warm path along the wall until he reaches the vault door. The door is open, but the inner barred gate is shut. He plugs his Radio Shack remote lamp control set into an outlet on the same circuit as an outlet he had previously modified. Using the remote controls, he blows out some of the equipment connected to the modified outlet. He then rushes over to that outlet, unplugs everything, and removes the outlet, replacing it with an unaltered one. On the monitor, Trimble looks worried. Other employees watch with growing dismay at the cluster of dead machinery. Trimble goes back to the vault entry.

A security guard arrives, the surveillance officers having picked up the agitation of the employees. The guard consults with Trimble.

"Frank, touch the panel door over there—just use your finger and wet it before, you know, before you...," Trimble instructs the guard.

"Right." Frank does what he is told.

"Very warm, Trimble," he says.

Trimble beckons. Frank moves to the vault and feels the wall where Trimble points.

"Should we get people out of here, Trimble?"

"No, but I'd be getting ready to, just in case. Meanwhile I have got to get into the vault to check the conduits under the floor."

Frank uses his radio to ask for permission. In the surveillance room, the officer who receives the request looks at Charity.

"It's your decision, Wally," she says. "I can't do anything. It's Trimble..."

"Let him in. Just keep an eye out," Wally tells Frank.

The barred doors open to Frank's key. Trimble and Frank walk into the vault and around several loaded money trays. The two men lift a floor panel and Trimble clambers into the floor well. Then he pulls himself out and tells Frank, "I need the electrical cart."

"Sure."

Trimble hustles out to the cart and wheels it quickly back to the vault room. Then he drops himself back down below the floor.

"What do you see, Trimble?"

"Can't tell. Nothing looks too bad so far," Charity and the others hear Trimble say.

Underneath the floor, Trimble takes a few of the colored

wafers from his pocket and presses them onto electrical conduits. Then he does nothing. He sits and waits. Once in a while he taps a pipe with a wrench to make a little noise. Mainly he looks at his watch.

Dave Brody and his young partner eat lunch every day at the same time. Dave picked a place near the Fed, the same place every day. His partner would grow tired of this except that the Loop is filled with beautiful girls, and many, many of them pass by the windows of Dave's regular booth at Morgan's. They don't have very long for the break.

On this day, Dave looks at his watch and orders a cup of coffee.

"You know," says his partner, "not a single call, never this quiet."

"Right."

"You sure it's on?"

Dave shows him the radio with its green light shining. He doesn't show him the piece Dave has removed from the back of the receiver, disabling it. If any more time passes Dave will have to call dispatch to advise them that his radio is out. If a call did come for them and they did not answer, a fire commander would start trying to find out why. Dave, Charity, Trimble, and I are operating with very tight windows of opportunity.

Trimble takes a last look at his watch. He knows this is it—exactly one half hour after the pager signals were given.

He scrapes a wooden match on the metal toe of his work boot, using it to melt a small hole in an electrical conduit, a piece of plastic tubing. He lights another match. He holds the flame close to one of the wafers he has pressed against a wall. The wafer starts to smoke.

He puts on goggles. Then he calls the maintenance supervisor on his hand radio.

"I have some trouble here. There's a little smoke," he reports.

"Trimble, should we evacuate?"

"Maybe, I don't think so, but I don't know, maybe just . . ."

Trimble stops talking long enough to put a small battery-powered device into the hole in the conduit. He stands as far away as he can and then throws a small switch. What he sees isn't much, but he hears a little sizzle.

The electrical surge he creates shoots instantly back along the conduit toward the electrical panels in the vault room and the counting room. The fairly small variation in voltage and amperage would have no effect if Trimble had not compromised the control panels. All the safety switches fail. Trimble set them up to do so like a formation of stacked dominoes. The circuits turn molten very quickly. The counting room wall begins to smoke. The heat along the wall activates the wafers.

The smoke thickens. Trimble removes the surge device from the conduit and puts it in his shirt pocket. In the surveillance room, smoke is now visible on the screens. A security officer at the console whips around to tell his partner. "Call Trimble and ask him what's up. Jesus, look at the smoke." Charity stares at the monitor, looking stunned.

In the counting room, the security officers react quickly; they start to evacuate the room. Before they are halfway finished, it is impossible for them to see through the smoke. The alarm buzzer sounds, piercing the air for one second out of every five. A very bright emergency light flashes over the exit door. First the Buzz, Buzz, Buzz. Then the Flash, Flash, Flash. The counting-room clerks respect their fear and surprise and scatter. On a security screen Charity sees a slim woman dart to the exit—she collides with a cart and knocks over a bunch of stacks of bills, her foot landing squarely on a stack of fifty-dollar bills. The stack slides like an ice skate until the paper band breaks and the bills squirt into the air. The young woman tumbles onto the conveyor belt that takes the old money to be shredded. Charity sees the woman's mouth open to a scream position and stay there until the woman realizes she is too big to fit into the shredder gate.

Her screams make other people scream, and the security officers do nothing more than pull people out of the room.

Outside the counting room, Corman commands the officers to sweep through the room on their hands and knees to see that the room is clear. In the surveillance room, none of the monitors for the counting room or the vault show anything other than smoke. Some of the smoke starts venting into the lunchroom.

"Lieutenant, look at the lunchroom. Some of them are beginning to panic," the guard at the monitor reports to Charity.

Charity looks quickly. "Yes, evacuate it. Tell Chief Corman we need him in the lunchroom. And turn on the sound monitors we have in the money rooms."

Inside the vault, Trimble, wearing his goggles and a disposable air filter mask, ignores the smoke. Very quickly he takes his glass trays out of the lower part of his equipment cart and puts them on the top shelf of the cart, then wheels the cart over to the money trays. On the top of a tray of hundred-dollar bills he puts one of the trays that Dave and I made. It fits neatly inside the tray in the cart. He repeats the process with other trays, trying to get as many done as he can before Charity arrives. One of them is troublesome. "Goddamn it. Get in there," Trimble swears audibly.

Charity hears Trimble's voice in the surveillance room, and her heart somersaults—she knows he must be having trouble with the trays. She prays no one tries to figure out what he is talking about.

Trimble jockeys the tray into place and peers at his watch. He pulls a small tab on his left sleeve. He holds the arm away from his face. The sleeve bursts into flames, but Trimble is not burned. He moves as close as he can to the surveillance camera and starts yelling into the lens.

At about this time, Dave puts his radio back into working order; he turns the volume down and holds it to his ear while he jogs off in the direction of the men's room. He'll wait there until the call from the Fed comes.

In the surveillance room, all the guards can see is Trimble's arm on fire and his face with his lips moving, the smoke obscuring everything in back of him. They activate the one audio monitor in the vault.

Trimble Young screams. He shrieks, "I'm on fire, I'm on fire." He yells, "Burning, burning." Then another high-pitched scream, and he gasps for breath. Trimble makes good work of this part.

The screams peal out of the surveillance-room speaker. Two uniformed guards go pale, frozen in place for a second. Charity wills her face into a mask of anguish. A guard darts for the phone; he keeps muttering, "Jesus, Jesus, Jesus." He yells into the phone, "Get paramedics, we've got injuries in the storage vault."

Charity bolts for the door. "I'm going down there," she shouts.

"Jesus, Lieutenant, that's against the rules."

"He's my husband. Fuck the rules."

As she flies out the door, Trimble Young screams again.

Corman starts to pull people out of the lunchroom. The air carries an aura of smoke, along with a few visible wisps.

He sees Charity fighting her way in the opposite direction. She is going down to the vault. Corman turns to her. He's moving along in tandem with her a few feet to her left. Charity yells at him, "Hurry, Trimble is on fire! He is burning. Please hurry—help me." Both of them, ten feet apart, are moving in the same direction until Corman is clobbered by the same woman who earlier tripped on the fifty-dollar bills. She moves in a mindless trot right onto Corman's feet and ankles, trying to climb over him. The two of them thud on the beige tile floor, and then the woman rolls to her feet, blindly agile in her panic.

Corman sees a raft of fifty-dollar bills stuck to her shirt. His instincts take over, and he grabs for her and the money. "You can't leave here with money!" he growls wheezing. She is unhearing, and she leaves. "You can't leave!" he screams. She doesn't stop. He doesn't know which way to go. He is trying to save the fifty-dollar bills, and yet he knows that a real emergency is under way in the vault. New fire alarms sound, painfully intense hooting from a horn near Corman's head. He goes after the woman, trying to grab the bills off her shirt, scrabbling after her like a crab on a beach of burning sand. Finally, he decides. Dropping the money he turns against the crowd to go down to the counting rooms. Charity, seeing and hearing his struggle, turns her head away to conceal her laugh.

* * *

Dave hears the call for paramedics at the Fed and runs to the ambulance door. He turns the volume up so his partner can hear it. He accepts the run and yells, "Hit it!" The ambulance careens up an alley to LaSalle Street. Its sirens sound and I hear it and begin to trot to the front entrance of the Fed.

When Corman gets to the counting room, the fire spray system has started to work. The floor is slick. The smoke has thickened. His visual field is about two feet, and his eyes are burning.

Charity has made it to the vault and she has the same tiny field of vision, but she can use her eyes because she wears swimmer's goggles. Trimble already had on his own goggles, and she helps him extinguish the smoldering on his sleeve. Seconds later the two of them have jammed all the rest of our custom trays upside down into the Fed's hundred-dollar-bill trays on the Fed's money carts. They flip the two trays over and the money now rests in our trays. They slide the Fed's trays back into the carts.

Dave and his partner leap from the ambulance in front of the Federal Reserve. Traffic is unperturbed, and no crowds are gathering, but a few people stop to watch when they pull up. "I'll get the gurney—you deal with security to get us in!" Dave yells at his young partner. I hear it because I am rounding the corner, sticking close to the building, keeping out of the way and largely out of sight behind the northernmost Corinthian column. The kid bolts into the building and comes out almost as quickly as he went in. With him is a gray-haired man speaking into his handheld radio. The kid shouts out, "It's all set!" Dave lets his partner come to the open rear of the ambulance and then he gives him the crucial message: "Get behind the wheel, Dooley. There'll be plenty of people to help me inside."

Dooley hesitates. He wants to go in; firefighters always want to go in. Dave talks fast, all decisive urgency. "It's going to take a long time to bring anyone out. They'll have a sally port. When I come out I want to roll right then, not a second of delay— sorry." The partner shrugs and hurries to the front of the ambulance.

Dave pulls my special gurney off the rear deck. The telescoping legs work fine, and Dave is able to conceal the extra effort he has to make with the heavy gurney. I pull the half-mask respirator down to cover the lower half of my face. I put on a dark blue cap with the *C.F.D.* logo, and then I move out. I reach the door at the same time as Dave does and join him with the gurney. We burst into the lobby of the Fed.

"Where? Where? Where? Somebody speak up," Dave shouts.

"Follow us," says one of the entryway security guards, who sets off running to a heavy door.

I wheel the gurney behind Dave. We shoot down corridors as fast as we can, as fast as our escorts can handle the keys, amid a ton of shouting and sweating. "Angle down to the right."

"Wait, I dropped the keys."

"Run ahead, get the first door."

"Hold it, hold it, hold it, okay—go, *go!*"

After we clear the first sally port, I see the Fed's broken gurney pushed off to the edge of the hallway.

The wheels of our gurney hum on the floor. There is a little squeak every time we have to stop. These sally ports would slow the incoming firefighters just as they are slowing us down. Our advantage might be that the four of us and our two guards can move as a group through the doors. More than ten fully equipped firefighters would have a tough time fitting in the space between the outer and inner door of each port.

We do not move that fast, but everybody is panting from anxiety that labors our breathing. There is a constant clicking of keys. Dave starts to take control.

"How many are hurt?" he yells.

"Don't know."

"What kind of injuries?" Dave yells.

"Burns, they said, burns." The guards, eyes tearing, head up toward the fire.

Dave grabs one of the two standard respirators from the gurney. I had not even noticed they were lying there. He signals me to take the other. We both slide them on. I leave my half mask dangling around my neck. Wearing a respirator was a signal to everyone around us that we were not in a safe place to be, all enacted to encourage them to leave. My respirator did a very good job of concealing my face behind the yellow inhalation valves and the red filter covers.

We go through the last door and the noise is overwhelming, worse than the smoke. I expect the smoke. A few people are still screaming. If they are not screaming, they are coughing. The sound is bouncing off the walls. The ventilation fans thump and whirr to pull out the smoke. Altogether it is a roar punctuated by clanks, thuds, and bangs from the running feet and wielding of equipment. Electronic alarm warnings add to the din—chirps, buzzes, hoots, and wails. Some ancient alarm bell is also clanging away in an irregular beat. I like this.

As alarms are activated both Fire and Police are notified. Our three to four minutes until firefighters respond had started to elapse. Dave said there would be at least two pieces of equipment. The firefighters would pile off the trucks and head for the same place we were going.

We dash up to the door to the counting room. Corman looks nearly blind with the smoke and he is in obvious pain. Dave raises his respirator and shouts for someone to take Corman out and flush his eyes with warm water. "Warm water, remember, *warm.*" Our guard-escorts are beginning to dab at their own eyes. The respirators protect us. I am getting used to the din, my ears are shutting down, I think.

"Go get some kind of mask," Dave yells at the guards. "Just point us in the right direction." Then he presses the respirator back against his face.

"There's a vault door, thirty feet to the right. I'll be back in a sec. Harry'll stay with you," the guard shouts back.

Inside the vault room, Charity hears the commotion of our arrival and then touches Trimble. "It's time, baby." She removes her swimmer's goggles. She does not want the other security guards to see them.

Trimble winces and pulls two more tabs inside his clothes and flames burst through his clothing. Now he is actually afire and he yells out in pain, this time for real. He writhes on the floor.

Unthinkingly, he pulls his right hand up, bringing his arm in contact with his head, a simple reflex. But then his sleeve ignites flaming yellow. His face and hair burn. This was not supposed to happen.

Charity feels a bolt of terror. She hollers for help. The two sounds meld into an awful keening that penetrates all the clamor. Outside the room, I think Charity and Trimble are just following the plan.

Dave and I wheel into the vault with the gurney. Trimble and Charity see us. She ceases her shout. I am jolted by the sight of Trimble's face and hair—cherry red skin and live flames in his hair. Dave quickly smothers the fire while I stand there uselessly.

Twisting around, Dave pulls at his face piece and shouts at the security officer poised at the vault door. "I forgot the inhalator. He may have inhaled flame. Go up to the ambulance. Get it now, get it back here as soon as you can." Dave pulls the surge device from Trimble's burned shirt and slides it into his own pocket.

Dave's voice is about the only thing anyone can hear over Trimble's high-pitched cries. The man obeys. Now the four of us thieves are the only people in the vault. The surveillance cameras are still useless because of the smoke.

Dave grabs Trimble's arm and injects him. "It'll kill the pain right now. Come on, let's finish this."

Charity stands frozen, staring at Trimble, the puckering red splash that was one side of his beautiful face.

Speaking softly to Charity, Dave urges, "Come on—you want him to go through this for nothing? Come on." He sees Charity's goggles in her hand, takes them, and puts them on her eyes. He takes a half-mask respirator from his belt pack and puts it on her face. This seems to bring her back to life. Trimble goes quiet. Everything else seems to have gone quiet, although I know this isn't true. I wonder if my hearing has been damaged.

The two of them pull the gurney's special rectangular compartments open. I open a flap in the side of the false cushioned pad resting on top. Yanking out all of the green sausage money, we toss it on the floor. The hidden compartments on the gurney are now empty. Dave opens a small canister and more smoke pours out.

We seize our glass trays full of one-hundred-dollar bills. We slide them into the gurney's disguised lower compartment and into the upper box hidden by the false pad. Trimble's screams are dying into moans. Dave and Charity snap the compartment panels shut on the gurney and I close the Velcro flap on the pad. The trays aren't visible. Neither are the extra packs of hundreds that we used to fill the few inches I had built in as a safety margin.

No one says a single word. We follow the script.

I look closely at the gurney, which is now filled with millions, and I am alarmed. The thing looks very odd. An ordinary gurney is just a frame of metal tubes, put together to make four telescoping legs with rubber wheels mounted on universal joints. My gurney has extra struts to support the weight, side panels to cover the secret compartments, and the mattress on top is many times thicker than normal. I had been sure that no one would notice these things in the crisis of the moment. Now I'm not sure, but I can't do a thing about it except play the plan to its end. It's not a hard choice, but I am dripping with sweat. My eyes are swimming in it, burning like hell; blinking doesn't do any good, and I don't want to remove the respirator. I start to close one eye at a time, and this works. As soon as the pain becomes too much, I close that eye and open the other one.

"Put him on the gurney," Dave says.

They help Trimble to his feet and lay him flat on the gurney. Trimble is aloft now in a warm morphine bliss. Charity whispers in his ear, "Darlin', you got to pretend more pain now, you got to scream a little now."

"I don't know . . ." He slurs his words.

My ears come back to life. A relief—I welcome the roar, but still it has lessened compared with the frenzy when we came in. The people have cleared out. No one is dropping equipment anymore. The big sound now is the fire alarm pulsating through a cycle of high and low tones. It must have been going on for a long time, but this is the first I notice it.

The footsteps of the men with the inhalation equipment are audible now—they come yelling, "We got it! We got it!"

Trimble manages not a scream but a croak, very loud, unnerving.

"Stay back," Dave shouts through the open door. "We got more fire in here."

Charity shovels the bags of shredded money onto the empty Fed carts as fast as she can. A few bags stay on the floor. I light one bag in each Fed cart. Flames erupt. Charity tosses her unused green wafers onto the pile. Smoke billows. All the shredded money on the Fed carts is aflame. Some of the burning paper floats down to the floor and ignites the shredded money on the floor just before I have a chance to ignite it. I set fire to some intact bills, because there have to be some charred hundreds left for the investigators; not every single bill would be totally consumed by flames.

Dave picks up his smoke canister, puts the cap on, and pockets it. Then he and I ram the gurney out the vault door, followed in close order by Charity and a cloud of pungent smoke. We are going to go out loud and strong, we will build momentum, we don't want to give anybody any time to imagine what we might be doing.

Dave lifts his respirator and shouts, "Coming out, coming out, make way, *make way, injured man!*"

As we burst out of the vault room, two guards give us an escort. Perfect.

"We don't know if his lungs are clear," Dave tells the guards, and then he slides the respirator back down. "We just got to get him to the burn unit."

The last of Trimble's electric trips ignites and fire breaks out again in walls and floors. Perfect. We propel our wheeled cargo through hallways and rooms as forcefully and as fast as we can. The first passages are empty of people. The buzzing, clanging, chirping, and beeping reverberate as loudly as before, and I think I feel the floor vibrating. I see wisps of smoke, which I cannot smell through the respirator mask. We catch up with all the employees who are fleeing the work areas and the lunchroom. I hear someone yelling as loudly as possible, "I have to go back to get my purse. Let me through. *Let me through!* I have to go back to get my purse. Let me through. Let me through." A few others are uttering words, but I can't understand what they are saying. There is an odd sound; the rooms seem to be breathing, but it is the collective panting of a hundred frightened people. It underscores the alarms. The wheels of the gurney are all squeaking sharply. Can they support the weight of millions of dollars? Nothing I can do about it if they cannot.

But that's wrong: I see one of the braces holding the lower container is starting to pull down away from the frame. The container is immensely heavy; it needs every bit of bracing. I slide my hand up to the loosening brace and try to hold it in place. It takes both hands. I am running along the side of the gurney while I pull it, with Dave pushing it from behind.

Charity runs with us. She barks out the same command to every guard she passes. "Cut the power to those rooms. Cut it!"

I see that the first person to obey is Wheezer Corman, who coughs into a phone as he tries to get it done.

Then I see the first real firefighters. As Dave had promised, they don't all rush into the building at once. We will not have to fight our way past thirty big people wearing helmets and thick coats and carrying fire axes. They have sent four men in to report back, younger, less senior guys. But I worried that they would stop us to get a report from Dave. We did not have the time to stop. I had told Dave that the worst thing would be if one of them tried to help us with the gurney; they would know the damn thing was much heavier than any gurney ought to be. "Paulie, this is the fire department," Dave said to me. "The firefighters won't be doing any paramedic work unless they have to. The fire department needs a lot more paramedics and a lot fewer firefighters. The real firemen aren't happy about that. We aren't real close to each other." The fire department advance team stream right past us.

My eyes are on fire. My leg muscles are burning with strain. The loose brace is sagging, and I am losing my grip. When we come to a stop at one of the sally ports, I look down. I see my hands wet with my blood. There is a deep cut in my left palm, ripping up from the heel of the hand to the bottom knuckle of my middle finger. I had brought some flexible, heavy-duty plastic cable ties to use for emergency repairs if the gurney started to break up. I pull them out with my right hand and thread them through a support bar and underneath a flange on the brace. It seems to work, but my hands are so slippery that I cannot pull the flex ties tight.

The first sally port door opens, and we move into the port. The first door closes. The second starts to open. I hear a creak from another brace on the other side of the gurney. I point it out to Charity and then I point to the flex ties I had put on my side. I hand her a couple of blood soaked ties. Dave sees my bloody hands, grabs them, and looks. He pulls a gauze pad from his belt pack and presses it into my hand. Charity ties off the loose brace on her side.

I put my hand back on the brace. The metal flange seems to be pushing the gauze pad right into the bone. I am full of adrenaline; I perceive the pain as intense and sweet.

The second door opens fully.

I see twenty more people in black rubber coats with reflector stripes and shiny helmets. We push forward, but they don't give us much room. Every time the gurney bumps against one of them, it clanks and the brace drops. I am bearing a lot of weight with my arms, which are beginning to pang. The weight of the money is shifting, and I feel the gurney start to lean. It is hard to keep it going in a straight line. The gurney is starting to clank even when we do not bump into a firefighter. Then I think we are through the crowd. Charity finally sees what is happening and signals Dave to look.

Before he can do anything, we are met by another twenty firefighters who run in from the north doors. Three of them cannot stop in time and plow into the gurney. It is tipping over, teetering, and we are going to be finished. I can taste my whole life in my mouth. The damn thing might not fall apart, but we could never get it back upright. Charity pushes up against it. I feel my bloody hand begin tearing against the brace. The pain is harder.

Then some firefighters from the group behind us fly to help keep the gurney erect. It is hard to believe how fast somebody can move wearing all that equipment. Five or six of them hit the gurney at the same moment and stop its fall. There are so damn many of them, they never feel the weight. We are at dead stop now. The three of us push and pull as hard as we can and try to act as though we are not killing ourselves. The pressure on my hand causes a pain so severe I can feel it from the back of my head down to my heels. I am not thinking. I am just there and happy when the wheels begin to turn and the clanking does not start again.

Dave lifts the bottom of his respirator and says, "Take it slow now." Then for the benefit of the guards who are with us, he adds, "This man on the stretcher has taken about as much bouncing around as he can."

In the lobby of the Federal Reserve, everyone peels away from the rescue parade. Dave and I move slowly, the braces making creaking sounds. My left hand is now in exquisite pain. The blood is overwhelming the gauze, and I see blood drops fall to the floor. I feel nausea. I cannot take off the respirator but if I throw up, I will drown in my own vomit unless I take off the respirator.

Someone says, "That's Trimble."

Someone else says, "He's bleeding."

Trimble is conscious enough to raise his head to find out where he is bleeding, but then it drops back.

The gurney seems to be moving one inch a minute. I am leaving evidence of my presence with every drop of blood and all the DNA that it contains. Another brace starts to sag. I cannot do anything about it except pray, and I don't do that. It seems to me that the container is riding a little lower and that an alert witness would see that it is not an ordinary gurney. If the container does fall to the ground, we will spend the rest of our lives in prison.

We reach the curb next to the ambulance. We cannot afford to let the gurney bounce on the curb as we lower it to the street. Dave and I lift as much weight as we can before we push it into the street, and it feels like a railroad spike has gone through my palm.

Charity slides into the ambulance. She moves all the way to the front wall behind the driver. She wants to block his view.

Dave and I use every bit of strength we have to get Trimble and the money into the ambulance. I feel the cramp in my right hamstring as I clamber into the back with Trimble, who has passed out from exhaustion and morphine. There is little noise now—the world has stopped. Dave pulls his respirator off and says in a normal tone of voice: "Push it. Go to Northwestern." Dave's partner shifts gears, and we move out fast.

In the back of the ambulance, the siren wails; it seems like such a puny sound to me now. Charity turns and whispers to

Dave, "What happened? His face wasn't supposed to burn. Look at him."

Dave doesn't look at him. Neither do I. "Something flammable in his shirt. He must have forgotten to be careful about the clothes?"

Charity put her face into her hands.

"It's not that bad, Charity. He'll get better. He'll have more pain than expected, but he'll recover."

In his peripheral field, Dave sees a car with flashing roof lights, a squad car. "Jesus, are they following us?" he blurts out.

A Federal Reserve security car is trailing the ambulance. I see it from my spot directly behind the driver's seat where I crouch to avoid being seen by Dave's partner. My hand, now removed from the gurney, is growing numb. I think the nerves might be damaged. When the pain in my hand lessens, I notice that the crouch is torturing my leg and I am drenched with sweat and beginning to shiver. I lie flat on the ambulance floor, and my leg relaxes. I realize then that I am still wearing my respirator over my face.

When I shove it off and breathe cool fresh air, I experience physical joy wildly out of line with my immediate circumstances. My heart stops pounding, my chest stops aching, and the pleasure of the moment is so intense I do nothing at all; I am useless.

Dave quickly checks the gurney to see that all the hidden compartments are closed up. He takes the flex ties from my pocket and uses all of them to bind the flanges of the braces to the support rod. I watch him and come out of my stupor.

"Charity, what's happening?" he asks, his tone insistent.

Charity looks at the car, dazed and silent. Dave taps her shoulder. She shudders in surprise, but then she bends back over Trimble and speaks to us. "No worry. They are supposed to do that. It's regulations. They have to inspect his clothes and effects and mine for hidden money. Employees have tried to grab a few bucks, then fake a heart attack."

Dave nods, although she is just reminding us of what we already knew. He grabs my left hand, leaves the bloody gauze in place, and slaps two more pads on it. This time he tapes them into place. He sticks a pill in my mouth.

"Vicodin. Swallow it. Tastes terrible."

I swallow it. Dave points at Trimble. We have something to do. There is a second gurney in the ambulance, and we must transfer Trimble to that gurney.

The mile and a half route to the hospital is simple. We turn left from LaSalle onto Jackson and head toward the lake. A few hundred feet before we hit the yacht club, we turn left onto Columbus Drive, which turns into Fairbanks Court, which runs through the hospital complex.

The turn onto Columbus is sharp. Dave's partner will be looking forward when he makes the turn, and we can use the centrifugal force of the turn to help us move Trimble to the ordinary gurney. I feel better. Our timing is good. We slide him easily. I scuttle back to my hiding place. When the ambulance is opened, I will be concealed behind the money gurney when they unload Trimble. The clambering is killing my leg again, but the Vicodin is still good for my hand. While I crouch down I take the lab coat out of my pack, put the sunglasses on, and stuff the half-mask respirator into the pack. I struggle with the lab coat until it is on. My leg pain becomes so intense that I bite down on the rubber face piece of the full respirator. I do not care if some forensic dentist matches the teeth marks to my dental print. I only care that I do not yell in pain.

The ambulance brakes at the emergency-room bay. Dave and Charity shove Trimble out before Dave's partner can get to the rear. Charity lets go of the gurney. Dave and his partner wheel Trimble into the emergency room. He is expected. The two Fed security guards are there by the time he is transferred from the gurney to an examining table. The guards watch Trimble until it is clear he is badly burned. Charity is an ashen charcoal. She keeps asking if Trimble will be all right. Dave's partner starts filling out their report while Dave asks a nurse for fresh supplies for the ambulance. The burn team of doctors and nurses swarm all over Trimble, pushing everyone else, including Charity, out of the way.

One of the Fed guards goes to the nurses' station to provide information, while the other hangs around the treatment station for Trimble's clothes as he is surrounded by doctors and nurses. The guard at the nurses' station then starts back to the ambulance, but he is too late. He will find nothing in the ambulance and will see nothing amiss when Dave brings the other gurney back from the emergency room. He will be distracted by Charity, who recovers enough of her composure to remind the guard that he should not forget to search her and her clothes. The two of them go off to find a female nurse to assist the search.

I wait no longer than it takes for the emergency room doors to close. I jump to the ground, ignore the shock of the renewed leg cramp, and seize the fire department gurney I had left in the hallway less than an hour earlier. I put that one back in the ambulance. Then I pull the money gurney out and wheel it as fast as I can to the corner of the building about forty feet away. After I turn the corner, I start moving slowly away from the scene. I look bored as I wheel it the few feet to Superior Street, turn it right on Fairbanks Court and then right again on Huron to my vehicle. It takes an enormous effort to make it look effortless when I load the gurney into the back. I cover it with canvas. I get in and drive away.

I travel west across Michigan Avenue, and then the urge to look is too strong.

I bring the car to a stop in a parking lane. I pivot in my seat, snap open a panel, and look at the edges of thousands and thousands of hundred-dollar bills. I wonder briefly if the volume of the shredded money we burned at the Fed is about the same as the volume of the money I have in my vehicle. The shredded money took up the same amount of space as the stolen money now does, but it sure did not weigh the same. It should not make any difference; it is very hard to predict how much material will be left after you burn paper, but I want to worry about something.

I put on my shirt and tie over the uniform blouse and drive back to the courthouse.

When I pull into the courthouse basement, some blood has seeped from my left hand onto the bottom of my tie.

I wave my right hand at the deputy U.S. marshal at the federal prisoners' sally port. I go back to chambers. In my bathroom, I remove the wrapping and look at my hand. I will have a wide, flat scar on my palm. I nearly faint from the sting of the antiseptic. I rebandage the hand. I put on my robe and pull the left sleeve down quite far. If I keep my left hand at my side, the bandage won't be visible.

I go back into the courtroom to hear the rest of the testimony of the would-be four-hundred-pound patrol officer. To get myself back in the case, I consciously try to summon the image of this rhinoceros of a man chasing a gazelle of a thief. This does not work. The comedown from the adrenaline high is irreversible. I am spent, and the Vicodin is pushing me under. I pretend to listen to the trial, but it does not matter if I do, because the jury will decide.

3.

THE NOW-SILENT VAULT room at the Federal Reserve was a charred mess. All the money in the Fed carts was immolated into ash. Eight hundred million dollars of United States currency was the rough estimate of loss. The fire was out, but the smell still remained strong, and now just two things were paramount to the bank: accounting and security.

I had put small metal ramps on the undercarriage of the gurney to ease the slide into my utility vehicle. That night in my garage, I pulled out half the money handful by handful and put it in the front of the car. I worked alone because I was not patient enough to wait. With the very heavy load lightened I pulled the gurney out fairly easily and emptied it, piling all the money onto the rear storage space of the vehicle. I wheeled the gurney and glass trays into the basement workroom. I could then take another pain pill, collapse into a soft chair, and stare at my handiwork.

When Dave Brody arrived a half hour later we spread two sheets on the floor, one on top of the other, the glass trays between them. We put goggles over our eyes, and with old baseball bats, we demolished the glass trays. We should have used metal bars, but we are Irish and nostalgic about our youth. Pieces of glass flew sideways and up; the air glittered with glass beads. Then I took my cutting torch and sliced the gurney to pieces. After the destruction came the careful cleanup of small pieces of glass and steel pipe. "Now, let's wrap the metal scraps in plastic, wipe them off," I told Dave. "We'll put them in the dump."

Next we sat in silence and counted the money. Each package was worth ten thousand dollars. I counted 3,607, and Dave counted 3,693. We had seventy-three million dollars. We had not gotten the hundred million. I had suspected there really was not enough space in the gurney. Certainly our gurney would have collapsed under the added weight. I was relieved we hadn't been too greedy.

I did not care that we had fallen short of the hundred-million mark. We were not going to seek recognition in the *Guinness Book of World Records*.

We left to bury the money. On the trip up to the deserted summer cabin, through the increasingly vacant countryside, Dave followed me at five miles an hour below the speed limit.

There was a little moonlight glinting off the lake when we arrived at the cabin. We would not have to use flashlights. No cars were parked at the two cabins we could see on the other side of the water. We could work faster without having to hide ourselves.

I asked, "What went wrong with Trimble?"

"His shirt was the wrong material. It ignited very quickly."

"But he had already burned the other sleeve just before that. He must have known it would flame."

"Before he burned the other sleeve, Paulie, he sprayed it with accelerant to make it burn faster and he had coated his arm so his skin wouldn't go up. This other sleeve was not supposed to burn at all, so he didn't coat his arm. Then when your skin is burning, you lose control. He pulled his arm up, and the collar caught fire and his hair. He kept flailing at his face with his burning arm."

"Christ. He was really in pain."

"It was his own fault and it won't kill him and he'll have a lot to console him." Dave sounded like his tough father.

We buried the money in the same hole we had used for the shredded money, and we covered the hole the same way we had before. Then we sat for a while on the cabin porch and looked through the trees. I was exhausted now.

"You remember we had a fight on the first day we met in high school?" Dave asked.

"It was the second day, practicing double plays. I think."

At Mater Dei, Dave and I were first thrown together because he was the shortstop and I was a second baseman. The coach assigned endless practices on turning double plays. We stopped only when both of us were ready to topple into the dirt from fatigue. Dave did not need the practice. On the double plays that he started, the ball always, always came to me at shoulder height and at the very instant I was ready to begin my pivot to throw to first. His touch left the ball softly suspended in front of my throwing hand.

When I started the double play, Dave had to handle my tosses off his shoelaces or over his head. Sometimes he was wound like a corkscrew trying to touch the base, dodge the oncoming runner, and make the throw. Finally he got tired of my throws and he said, "Hey, Perfect, just give it up."

I tackled him as hard as I could, putting us both down on the dirt. I swung at his face even though I was flat on the ground and yelled, "Screw you, Brody." He whacked the side of my skull with his gloved hand. Without the glove, I would have been hurt badly. The coaches came. Dave laughed. "You aren't going to quit, are you, Perfect?"

"Shove it," I cleverly replied.

"Okay," he said. "Let's do another ten plays." He was on his feet. I was sitting on the ground. "You can't play the infield sitting on your ass, Paulie. Get up."

A few days later Dave taught me how to throw the ball by

thinking only of how I wanted the ball to move and not to think about cocking the wrist or planting the foot. "If you concentrate on what you want the ball to do, your body will figure out how to make that happen."

I leaned against the fat pole that supported the overhang of the cabin roof, but I stood up quickly when I felt myself falling asleep. Dave was sipping a beer, gazing at the lake, maybe thinking of Monaco and marriageable princesses. I had told him if he found a German, he could become a *Grossherzog*— grand duke. A good title, he said.

"Dave, do you remember telling me just to think about where I wanted the ball to go when I threw it?'

"I could have said that—sounds great—but when I played ball, I didn't think about anything. I just did it."

I paced to stay awake—Dave stood up, too, ready to leave. "What now, Paulie?"

"We wait five years."

"What if somebody has a problem, something, whatever?"

"Call me or find me at the Palmer House. I eat lunch there every Friday."

"Paulie, you look great in the Expedition. My dad would sell it as a truly big car for a truly big man," Dave said with a grin.

"I'm donating it to charity as soon as I can." We got into separate vehicles. I rolled down the window to signal Dave. Dave lowered his window. I asked, "Well, *Grossherzog,* will you stop setting fires now?"

"Yes," Dave said.

"A fine thing," I told him.

He saluted me and drove off. I had to wait until I trapped the horsefly that had flown into my van, the kind of fly that never allows itself to be waved off. It just keeps trying to sting you until you kill it.

Part Four

Post-Trial Motions

THE ENORMOUS ROTUNDO who wanted to chase down alleys in pursuit of the assorted criminals of Chicago was back in court on the day after the robbery. Really, I should have taken the case from the jury, but I needed to stay busy. The jury advised the rotundo that he should try another line of work. He had a few days to appeal.

Dave came to the house to tell me that Trimble was still in the hospital, doing all right. "Those burns blow out a lot of nerves. It takes a while before things start to hurt."

"That was something yesterday," I said.

"A tribute to the skills we learned at Mater Dei."

We sat in the quiet of my kitchen, sipping very cold Harp.

"Were you an altar boy when Alderman Koski died?"

"My parents didn't want me to be an altar boy," I replied.

"Why the hell not?"

"They thought the process was corrupting. The altar boys got a day off from school if they worked a funeral, and they could sneak a drink if they worked a wedding."

"For Koski, we got lunch and dinner and a few bucks, more for the boys who worked the banks of candles at the sides of the altar," Dave said, his voice a little distant thanks to the mix of ale and memory. "We grabbed a little drink there, too. Weddings were overrated, just tips. Sometimes you could sneak into the storage cabinets for a few shots of the communion wine."

"And, Dave, how did you get to be an altar boy at Queen of All Saints?"

"Well, sucking up to the priests or mowing the mortician's lawn."

"That's what my parents knew," I said. "Now, of course, I guess altar boy skills carry over to crimes like ours. The best boys slide to and from the priest's side at the perfect moment, ring the bell on the dot, and prepare everything else with precision—cruets, hand towels, incense boats, and thuribles."

Dave reached for his bottle. "Father Cooney would be so pleased. Especially if he knew that this Prindiville is a Protestant—he is, isn't he, Paulie?"

I smiled. "I don't know. He's from Vermont, with kind of a French name. He might share our common faith, might have been an altar boy himself."

We sipped some more Harp.

"Well, I never saw much in the schools to foster my faith, Paulie. It was politics made it go. Jerome Keegan, man, he believed everything, and they were always on his ass about something and he wound up a fucking monk in Montana." Dave put his bottle down with an audible clink.

"And the monastery has a vow of silence, so nobody yells at him," I said. "How about Tommy Currie? He was second in our class. Royce had him down to be the first American pope. Remember his confession rule? Cop to the little ones, leave out the self-abuse—and for him that was leaving out a lot—and then the next confession he admits to lying, one lie for each time he jacked off. You know, he told me this twenty years after the fact at some alumni dinner where everyone was careful not to keep calling him Handy. He's a gynecologist with a huge practice."

"No doubt due to his winning bedside manner," Dave observed. He sipped some more and put his hands, palms down, flat on the marble top of the kitchen table, which I knew to be one of his signs that he was speaking without a trace of jest. "I mean, Paulie, what religion did Mater Dei teach? You had a bunch of rigid jerks, and the few cool guys weren't that religious."

Dave wanted to know. I rarely saw this in him. "The school wasn't trying to foster our faith," I said. "The faith comes into your life when you're much younger. Mater Dei was just trying to teach us the curriculum and to socialize us. The only real difference between it and the public schools was the way they kept most of us so busy we didn't have the spare time to commit all the sins that most of us were eager to try. They weren't hypocrites; they were realists."

"Good answer, Paulie. I think I like it."

After Dave left, I went downstairs to my desk. I looked at the legal papers I had brought home, writing notes to myself for the morning. I wasn't ready to sleep. I was woozy from lack of sleep, but the adrenal gland didn't know when to quit. I looked at Ellen's side of the desk.

When we bought our big, empty house, we knew we would have money to do things with it. In my new place at the law firm my work was just a little more interesting than high-school trigonometry—it was not so difficult to learn the technology and the business practices of dozens of companies. I met many interesting investment bankers. The bar associations ought to spend money publicizing investment bankers; they make lawyers look saintly. But I did not need the fortune I was making in high-stakes lawsuits. Ellen was paid well enough on her own, even when she was forced to stay at the bank while Prindiville's charges of illegal investment fund management were being investigated and tried.

We were very busy, the two of us, and our big house stayed very empty. We ate dinner at a small game table and, when we opened the windows on a breezy day, the place sounded like the cave of the winds. Between us we made a million dollars a year and, with desperation winning out over fear, we hired an interior designer. A slight old man, he dressed like Oscar Wilde and showed us a photograph of his wife and four children. He loved furniture and lamps and wallpaper and he had a way of making you love them too, at least when you were with him. We wound up with a lot of very good furniture.

She had many friends. We liked crowds at our house, and we could afford the catering bills. I liked her friends and Ellen liked Dave Brody.

A thing that kept us together when Ellen was under siege at the bank was our effort to conceive. When we knew it was a lost cause, Ellen's life outside our little family was back on track. Our inability to have children was a sharp pain that subsided to a dull ache, endurable because neither of us really expected a perfect existence, especially after our crisis.

On her side of the desk is a photograph, one thing I would like to put away but it sits where her hand put it. She brought it home from Charleston or Savannah, a business conference. It depicts a marble statue of two babies, a year old at most, asleep. One of the white marble babes sleeps on her back and the other on her side, nestled against her sister with her arm resting softly on the other's rounded belly. I suspect they are not asleep in this world. I told Ellen what I feared. "It's too moving," I said. It looks like a memorial to . . . I mean, something a parent would want if he had lost his babies."

"Don't be so Irish, Paulie. It could be a sculpture of two sleeping babies, a celebration of infants. Their faces are so sweet. My mother always said I was at my best when I was asleep."

Ellen spoke distinctly in a clear-water kind of voice, smooth and steady.

"My mother said the same about me, Ellen."

Ellen was finally able to leave the bank and spent a while at United Airlines restoring her faith in herself before she finally had her big chance and became general counsel of Choctaw Chip, a designer of computer chips and their manufacturing process. Its products were in wild demand. The very complex Potato Chip would soon be replaced by the phenomenally fast Chocolate Chip. The Wood Chip was a very few years away. The men who started the company were still very young. Despite the hundreds of millions that was their worth on paper, they were still more interested in the business than they were in the wealth. Ellen was older than all of them.

I became a United States District Judge for the Northern District of Illinois. Ellen said, "I love you and I am proud of you." A federal judge—a job for life, a life of power and prestige. The President of the United States nominates you, the United States Senate confirms you, and the President makes a formal appointment and sends you a fancy piece of paper, your commission, which you present to the judges of the court to which you have been appointed. A day is scheduled for your

oath of office. All the judges gather in the ceremonial courtroom. The chief judge asks you to raise your right hand, and
you swear this oath:

> *I, Paul Eamon Devine, do solemnly swear that I will admin-*
> *ister justice without respect to persons and do equal right to*
> *the poor and to the rich, and that I will faithfully and impar-*
> *tially discharge and perform all the duties incumbent upon*
> *me as a United States District Judge under the Constitution*
> *and laws of the United States. So help me God.*

After the oath, the chief judge says something like "Welcome to the court, and come up here with the rest of us and have
a seat." If the new judge has enough money, or his friends do,
he has a lavish reception after the ceremony. During mine,
which was very lavish, I held Ellen's hand whenever I could. I
was uncomfortable without her. I was very needy then. I was
thirty-eight years old when I took the oath, a little too young.

The important thing the new judge thinks is this: I have been
given extraordinary power over the lives of human beings and,
since I have a job for life, I can do the job exactly as I see fit because, short of conviction after trial before the United States
Senate on charges of impeachment by the United States House
of Representatives, no one can fire me. I was a new judge and I
thought of these things, judicial authority and judicial independence. It is, as my father said, "heady stuff."

It is a job, Ellen said, that appeals to the dangerously self-
obsessed.

When you are born into the world, all that is around you ex-
ists to serve your needs; you cry, and somebody magically
grants your wish. When you become a federal trial judge, you
are likely to recapture that delusion. Everyone stands when you
come into your courtroom. They rise for you. First thing in the
morning, there may be twenty lawyers each waiting to be heard
on some motion or to report on the status of their cases, speaking only to you. Everyone else in the courtroom is just a random eavesdropper. The other lawyers in the courtroom watch
you, trying to discern whether you are in a good mood or a bad
mood. When you say yes or no or not today, there are often pal-
pable consequences for the lawyers and their clients. Then you

proceed to whatever case is on trial. If there is a jury, the jurors look at you carefully to see if they can find a hint of what you are thinking about the case. When you return to your chambers, your court clerk, your secretary, your two law clerks are all there to serve you. You are the center of the universe.

Some of us never get over this, Ellen reminded me.

For most of us, the feeling goes away in a few weeks. It is not you who is the center of the universe, even the small one that consists of the docket of a single judge. The center is whoever walks in the room wearing a black robe. You are still a lawyer like all the others in the courtroom. A judge is a lawyer who has the last word in a particular courtroom on a particular day. If you forget you are just a lawyer with a robe and you think too hard about the godlike powers you have, it can freeze you in your tracks, leave you afraid to decide anything because you will be afraid to be wrong. A judge has the duty to say what the judge thinks, and that is often harsh. A lawyer who thinks her client is lying or has a losing case may advise against bringing the lawsuit and then soften the blow by saying "You're in the right, but you can't prove it" or "You've done nothing wrong but the law is unfair, or the courts are unfair." The judge has to say, "You have lied" or "You are wrong." We can vindicate too and tell people they are right and true, but that means the other guy is wrong and false.

Ellen, at home, contradicted me, educated me, challenged me, and once in a while agreed with me. She is there with me now on the bench.

The first anniversary of my becoming a judge, I came to Ellen looking as bad as I felt. "Jesus, Ellen, I just finished a terrible case."

She was sitting in her favorite chair, surrounded by chip papers, but she attended to me first.

"A salesman with a lot of clout at Chrysler," I told her, "he gets hired by a plastics company to sell plastic parts. He makes a quarter million a year, but the company cuts manufacturing costs and delivers bad plastic to Chrysler. His bosses won't fix it. He fears losing Chrysler as a client, so he starts his own company, subcontracts the manufacture of plastic parts to a reliable manufacturer, and sells that stuff to Chrysler at no profit; he just wants to keep Chrysler happy until his contract with the plastics company runs out. When it does, the company refuses to pay him a final commission, a few thousand. He sees a lawyer, but he does not tell the lawyer about his private deal with Chrysler. The lawyer sues for his client's commission. The company lawyers find out about that deal and countersue."

Ellen shook her hair from her eyes. "It's an easy case, Paulie. The salesman violated his obligation to the company. He stole business from them."

"Legally, yes. But if you were in court you would know that the salesman is a decent guy who was acting from desperation and not greed. You'd know the company executives were dim-witted, small-minded, and mean. They deserve to be bankrupt. Instead the salesman is going to be bankrupt. His five kids won't be going to college. I just celebrated my first year of judging by perpetrating injustice under the law."

"You want the law to say that the nicest person should win?"

"Why are you fighting me on this? We never fought before."

"We fought the first day we met, Paulie."

"That was different. We were on opposite sides. Why are you doing this?"

"Paulie, there is no perfect law, and if we don't follow the rules we have, then we aren't going to have justice; we are going to have chaos. Why don't you talk to Judge Golden about it?"

What the judge had to say in his elegant chambers, six floors above mine, was this: "Maximum angst, these cases. You can't blame yourself. You got the law and you got the facts right."

Law is made by man, Ben believed, and law is flawed like democracy, a dubious enterprise but better than any alternative. It was a fancier version of what Ellen had already told me.

"Yes," I said to Ben, "but what if that thought doesn't console me?"

"Well, Paulie, some people cannot stand being part of a flawed process, apart from their own imperfect lives. But you don't find a lot of them among the ranks of lawyers. You were a good lawyer." Ben Golden was my favorite judge when I was a trial lawyer. He has an enormous head, set on top of a large, strong body, and he grew a small snow-white beard. If you tried to contend with him, you felt you were dueling with God. He used his appearance to control the courtroom.

Ten years ago he went on the Court of Appeals for the Seventh Circuit. He retired just after I went on the bench. He still hears cases, even though he'd be paid the same if he just stayed home. It must be a fine job; people who have it are willing to work for nothing.

"Don't ignore the law," Ben told me. "If you can't perpetrate those errors that the law requires, then get off the bench."

A day or so after I spoke to Ben, Ellen asked me if I wanted to send the salesman a check for the money he had lost. "It is what, a hundred seventy-two thousand? I make a lot of money, I have stock options, we'll be wealthy. Even if you count what we have now, we could handle five or six cases like this before we would have to sell our house." She asked it with a lilt in her voice and a little smile on her face, and her freckled forehead was crinkled.

"Remember Judge Kelly?" I asked her. "He would find a defendant guilty of battery, but if he thought the man was provoked into throwing a punch, he'd fine the defendant one dollar and then pull a dollar out of his wallet and give it to the clerk to pay the fine. It was a hell of a gesture." Yes, it was, but Judge Kelly was a clown, a laughingstock among the bar, and she knew I knew it.

Recalling her felt comfortable until I also recalled, involuntarily, the morning I left her to take a run at my club. I heard her mumble good-bye. When I came back home, I found her in bed, completely still and cold. I stopped this memory reel.

2

"CHARITY WOULD LIKE to see you about Trimble. How about the diner?" Dave asked while we sat in the Plaza Tavern. It was ten days since the theft. The place offered good jazz, but one side of the room is a glass wall that looks out on the Bank One plaza with a huge fountain and a mosaic made by Chagall—too large, too well lit, and too straight for good jazz ambience.

"Not that diner. We ought to pick someplace new."

"How about O'Hare? Take the subway out, get lost in crowds."

"Right. The chapel at O'Hare. Set a time and call me, Dave."

Charity looked worn the next night. "The burns hurt much more than Trimble expected, and a lot of the pain won't go away. It looks like there's gonna be some scarring. Trimble goes crazy when he talks about his face being 'puckered red ugly.'"

"You talk to a plastic surgeon?"

Her profile was elegant as she sat in the next row of chairs. "Yes, and Trimble did too. One of them was not too damn optimistic. I have to spend every spare minute with Trimble. At least he understands that I've got to be at work, on the spot at the Fed in case of something."

"Can we do something to help?" Dave asked.

"Make me a day with an extra eight hours for me to sleep in."

Dave patted her arm.

At least we were in a calm place, the chapel at O'Hare Airport. Each of us had taken the subway Blue Line, forty minutes from the Loop. I can walk out of the courthouse, take a few steps, and enter the station. When flights are on schedule, the interdenominational chapel is usually deserted, particularly after the city started carting all the homeless off to the shelters. All I had to do was check to see that the weather was going to be clear and no white-knuckled traveler would be in here asking God to look after landing gear.

Charity leaned forward and turned her head to face us, side by side in the blond pew.

"Something funny happened at the hospital."

She had been standing outside his room because she knew that Trimble was being debrided, that it hurt, and that he preferred she not see him wincing and flinching. She could monitor most of it through the narrow space between the edge of the open door and the jamb.

Trimble lay tensed and grim while the nurse peeled the dead skin away. Her movements were quick and precise, and she kept talking to him to keep his mind occupied.

"You're really doing well," the nurse told him. "These burns on your arm and leg are very shallow. Just a little deeper on your face and head." She medicated his skin. "This is going to prevent infection."

Trimble tried to smile at her and then groaned.

"It hurts to smile, doesn't it? You'll get over that, too."

The nurse was good, treating him like a man and not just a patient. Trimble had mentioned this nurse, Bonnie, to Charity. She was a compact, pretty woman with very short dark hair, and now she lingered to smooth lotion on the skin around the burns. "Say, how did this happen?" Charity heard her ask.

"Electrical fire . . . bank," he grunted.

"You were the one in the fire where all the money got burned up?"

"Yeah."

"Wow! All that money. You ever take any, sneak out a few bills in your shoe?" the nurse joked.

Trimble scowled.

"I was just kidding, really. You're doing fine." She drew her hand gently across his unburned shoulder and let it rest on his upper arm. Charity had an intuition that this moment was wrong.

Bonnie the nurse took blood pressure, pulse, and temperature. She gave him Percodan to swallow, to dissolve the pain of debriding. Trimble gulped it down. Charity moved into the doorway. The nurse looked intermittently at her while she kept a hand on his forehead until the pill had some effect and Trimble dozed. As she left the room, she asked Charity, "Your husband?"

"Yes. How is he?"

"I'm Bonnie Owens, one of his nurses. He's coming along just fine. I hope the facial burns heal. He's one good-looking guy."

Charity just nodded and the nurse said, "It's a joke. I've got my own man."

Bonnie Owens walked out of the room. Charity followed her after a moment. She wanted to tell Bonnie Owens that she was grateful and not at all offended by the remark about Trimble being good-looking. Trimble needed a caring Bonnie Owens, and Charity had some sense that she should engage this woman. She saw the nurse turning down a hallway at the left end of the corridor.

As Charity turned the same corner, she heard Bonnie Owens's voice coming from a small meeting room where the nurses ate lunch. "I don't know, Detective. He didn't say anything to me."

Charity stopped and sat on a plastic chair someone had left outside. Once again she was an eavesdropper.

"It was worth a try," the detective said. "I called you because I know you like the chance for a little detective work."

"Why are you so interested?" Bonnie asked. "Is it about the money?"

"It's a police matter."

"That's all you're going to tell me?"

"I can't tell you anything else. It's a police matter."

"That's never stopped you from talking to me before about your exciting police career," Bonnie replied.

"I was trying to get you to come home with me," the detective said.

"And it would have worked, Tony, if I liked men."

"Don't remind me."

"Are you going to tell me your secrets or are you going to save it for some other vulnerable woman in this hospital?" Charity heard the woman's voice sharpen.

"Hey, I'm here a lot. It's business. Most of the women I meet are doctors and nurses."

"And you always leave your coat open so they can see your pistol," she responded.

"It's a calculated risk. Some of them don't like it." He started to laugh.

"So when you do tell me your secrets, it is just because I'm a lesbian."

"Sure. You're just one of the guys." The detective's voice lowered and Charity had to strain to hear it. "What I think is it's a scam. This guy wants to get the Fed to retire him on that workmen's compensation. A security guy at the bank tells me they were trying to fire him, so I think he rigged up his injury. Then it gets way out of hand, starts a fire, and does a ton of damage to the building. It's a good fraud case, has lots of color." The detective chuckled softly. "Now don't tell anybody what I just said."

"Yes, sir, Detective Plymouth, you big powerful man, you."

Charity stood up. She heard a cup clink down on a table. "What does the doc say?" the nurse asked.

"Doctor Lutz, the emergency medico, you know him. 'Lucky,' he said. The torso burns were pretty limited, reminded Lutz of the time a movie stuntman was burned by exploding squibs. 'Maybe,' I say, 'it's not lucky, it's strange.' 'What do you mean?' asks the doctor. 'Could these have been caused by squibs?' I ask. 'Sure, Detective, but this guy isn't a stuntman, he's an electrician, and electricians get burned too. They had an electrical fire.' 'But,' I protest. 'But nothing,' the doc says. 'The burns on his face were not caused by squibs. They had an electrical fire.' End of story."

"So why are you here?"

Detective Plymouth paused. "Do nurses always think doctors are right?"

"Doctors are gods. They all think so."

"Right. How bad are the burns?"

"They aren't terrible, but they're real burns, and he could get some scarring on his face. They don't know whether he's going to have nerve damage."

Charity turned and walked as silently as she could back to Trimble's room.

A little later Bonnie Owens returned to the room to check on Trimble. As she examined his burned skin, she asked Charity what she did for a living and what she had done before the bank. Then she reciprocated with an account of her own career. Just two professional women comparing notes. Charity thought it was a disguised interrogation.

Detective Tony Plymouth. It made sense, and it made my insides crumble.

"How does Trimble feel today, Charity?" I asked, keeping my voice even.

Charity stared darkly at the generic stained glass over the generic altar. "He's worried about his face. He doesn't say it, but every time they take the dressing off he looks at his face. He was really beautiful, Judge, and he likes being beautiful. He's been beautiful since he was a baby."

"Do you think he would say the wrong thing to the nurse?"

"No way. We have plans, Judge. He figures he can pay whatever it takes to get his face fixed up."

"In five years," Dave said. "Then he can pay."

"You don't speak out loud about this in the hospital?" I think I kept my anxiety out of my voice.

"No, sir," she said. "He just talks about plastic surgery and asks me to check the insurance policy. The man's not stupid."

I stood up and walked to the front of the chapel and turned to look at the pews. I felt priestly for a couple of seconds. "The question," I said, "is whether Trimble ought to file a claim of some kind against the Fed for his injury."

Dave shrugged. Charity said, "You're the judge—you tell us."

"I think no. It puts a crimp in this detective's theory, and if he does file a claim there might be some kind of further investigation. Why risk anything? So no."

I sat down again. The chapel is very bright and improbably quiet in the noise of O'Hare. I rested. Cool air was pushed through the room. Dave and Charity were as still as I. We might have stayed for a very long time, if a young, curly-haired priest had not walked in to retrieve his Mass kit. "You want me to say Mass?" he asked.

It was nice; there are so few priests today that they are always in a hurry. I said, "I took Communion this morning. Thank you very much, Father."

"God be with you," Dave said. Charity looked at us as if we had just donned Polynesian masks. We followed the priest out of the room and all the way to the subway.

3.

"MISS KRIZNY, HOW old were you at the time of this incident?"

"Nineteen, I think."

"You think?

"Wait a sec. Yeah, nineteen."

"How long had you been working as a teller at the Harris Bank branch?"

"Two weeks."

"This was not a permanent job for you?"

"No, I'm going to college, just a summer job."

"What are you studying?"

"Just required courses, but I'm going to be a clothes designer."

"Did you design that purple dress you are wearing?"

The prosecutor objected to this last question by defense counsel. It was irrelevant but I saw no harm, so I let her answer.

"Yes, and, like, my mom did the cutting and I sewed it."

Miss Krizny could pass for fifteen, and she smiled easily, prettily, a big grin showing lots of white teeth. She was comfortable on the witness stand, but her medium brown hair and sallow skin made the muddy purple the wrong color for her. The sewing looked fine, though.

"Now, when the man handed you the note that said he had a gun and wanted money, what did you do?"

"I said, like, are you serious?"

"What did he say?"

"He said, 'You don't want me to shoot you in the face, do you? You're cute, honey.' "

"What happened then?"

"I said thank you and then I gave him my money. He took it and left."

"Did you push the silent alarm?"

"No, I was, you know, shook up. I just said 'Have a nice day' to him."

"You just stood there?"

"Yeah, for a minute, and then I turned to Sheila and said, 'I've just been robbed.' "

"What happened then?"

"Nothing, not even after I told Cheri on my other side."

"Then what?"

"Well, I said it a little louder: 'Jeez, guys, like, I've just been robbed.' And the guard came over."

"Did you ever attend a police lineup and identify anyone as the robber?"

"Wow, I couldn't pick anyone out."

"Do you see the man who robbed you in court?"

"Hey no, it's just, like, I can't do that. I was, like, in shock, you know."

"Thank you."

The witness stepped down and walked slowly out of the courtroom, her presence breaking the heart of a twenty-something juror who fell in love with her on the witness stand. I recognized the look on his face. He knew her name. I wondered if he would try to call her after the trial.

This bank robber had some hopes because no teller could identify him, but he had made a problem for himself by wearing a shirt with sleeves short enough to cover only half of his tattoo, a wingspread falcon under which were the words "We always die in vain." The security videotape showed the robber's arm with those very words tattooed on his arm. I would have liked to know the story behind that tattoo, and so would the jury, but I doubted the defendant would remember—you have to be very drunk to get a tattoo as stupid as that one.

4.

THREE WEEKS AFTER the Plymouth incident in the hospital, Charity asked to meet Dave, and Dave agreed. He had the sense to pick the Underground Wonder Bar just off Rush Street at 2:30 in the morning. With the stairs leading down to the entrance, no one can see who is inside the place without going in, and even when you are inside, it is dark enough to pass unnoticed. It is usually the only place in the white people's part of the city that has live jazz after two in the morning. The late-shift piano job was popular among musicians because they could work another gig on the same night and show up afterward at the Wonder Bar. After one o'clock, the audience was tired and rarely sober, except for some people just off work from other clubs and restaurants who showed up to drink, flirt, or listen. Nobody paid attention to anyone else in the bar. The sight of a white man and a black woman sitting together wouldn't be a memorable event.

The late-shift pianist decided to do nothing but Disney tunes beginning with "Whistle While You Work" at a tempo so fast no one could have sung the words.

"I don't know what to do with Trimble anymore. His mood's worse all the time," Charity said.

"Is he getting better at all?"

"Real slowly. And he hurts. And he blames every one of us," Charity whispered.

"Hey, it wasn't anybody's fault, except maybe his own. He should have worn a shirt that didn't burn. You told him to roll over on his stomach when it started to burn?" Dave asked.

"I tried to roll him over myself, and I yelled at him, too."

"I said it to him ahead of time."

"You don't get Trimble," Charity snapped. "He's just very good at what he does and he never, never says he made a mistake. Anything goes wrong, it's got to be somebody else's fault. That's why he got in trouble at work."

"Pardon me, but he must be hell to be married to," Dave told her.

"No. No. He's fine. Marriage is a thing he's good at. All I had to do was take the blame for…whatever. I always said 'Sorry, baby,' whatever. You know, it's just words."

"Can we do something?"

"No. I just needed to say this to someone other than myself."

"You afraid of what he'll do?"

"No, I don't think so. Well, I don't know. He could say the wrong thing accidentally. There's that nurse Bonnie hanging around when he visits the hospital. He likes her."

The two of them sat morosely, in leaden counterpoint to the upbeat piano version of "You've Got a Friend in Me." Dave always remembers the tune that was playing whenever anything happens. "Let's get out of here," Dave said.

Outside Charity looked very down. Dave wanted to help. I would have wanted to help too, if I had been there.

"Want to ride around for a while, see some city lights?" Dave asked.

Charity shrugged. Dave took her arm and led her to his small white car.

Dave's Mustang drifted through the north side of Chicago. The late May day had been very hot and the night not much cooler. Along Michigan Avenue, the closed stores were mostly dark, except for the occasional punctuation of startling color like the windows of Escada. In Wicker Park to the west, every store light was out and the storefronts covered by grates, but on the side streets lights were on, and entire families sat out on stoops and porches and sidewalks, babies asleep in parents' arms, to escape the heat.

They stopped for a moment in front of the Bop Shop. He should not have stopped. He should have driven until exhaustion overtook him and then escorted her to her car.

"Remember this place?" he asked. "I want to tell you . . . that time we touched, I felt . . . I don't know . . . like never before . . . I wanted to say . . ."

Charity lightly put her hand on his shoulder. She shouldn't have done that either. I would miss a hundred such signals but not Dave.

Dave drove east to the lake.

Lake Shore Drive was nearly deserted. They cruised from the Gold Coast north to the Edgewater Beach Apartments. The lake would look like black glass, and there would be a freighter from Wisconsin easing south to Gary. The high-rises on the west are somber towers brightly lit only at their feet, with gardens inclining up to the marble-and-wood lobbies. The city's most romantic drive in the wee small hours. And things got worse.

After turning around at Wilson Avenue to drive south, Dave and Charity saw a skinny young boy, about seven, walking shoeless and shirtless on the Drive. Dave abruptly stopped and slid out of the car. He moved slowly to keep from frightening the child. He talked the child into his arms and carried him to the narrow back bench of the car.

"He won't say anything. I'm taking him to the fire station," he explained.

On the way, the little boy stared at Charity and took the hand she offered.

In the fire station, the boy tried on a helmet and played with a hose nozzle while Dave talked to the battalion commander who would call the child-welfare officers. The child waved at Charity, who had stayed in the car.

When Dave got back in the car and headed onto Lake Shore Drive, he told me he could not stop himself from saying, "I live near here, a couple of blocks."

I was livid. My throat was so constricted that I had the voice of a frog when I told Dave what he had done was immoral, stupid, dangerous, unworthy of a snake, and disgusting.

He knew it, too. I could tell from his voice and all when he told me. And from the fact that he had knocked on my front door at sunrise. "I'm not going to take advantage of Trimble. He's our partner, and he's hurt and helpless." He meant this. I noticed he did not say that Trimble was a good man, a worthy fellow, part of the team, or a friend. I wouldn't have said those things either, not now. Wc owed Trimble a debt for past services—that seemed to be it, all of it.

"Charity?"

"She thinks the same way. We're betraying Trimble unless we stop."

"Yes. You are," I said.

Dave found his own way out of my house. Charity would not keep at her adultery if she thought it was wrong. She was willing to rob a bank for the same reason I was willing to rob a bank—it wasn't wrong under the circumstances. You could criticize our moral baselines; a moron could do a good job of that. But at least we had moral baselines.

I stayed in place for a time, thinking nothing. I finally remembered I was uncomfortable in my wife's chair. I stood up and wandered through the room, watching my feet step across the parquet floor. I went to sit in my chair. There were fires inside me, which Dave had ignited.

Then it was cool and I saw Ellen sitting in her chair. She fixed her eyes on my face. She stayed this time, longer than she had ever stayed before. We started to talk—that is, I started to talk to her. I told her what I had done and what I was thinking. I left out most of the details. My wife knew them as well as I.

"Why are you angry at Dave, and only at Dave?" she asked. Before I could recite all my lawyer's arguments about Charity's ordeal and Dave's ability to seduce women, she left.

Charity was as wrong as Dave, but I could no more condemn Charity than I could condemn Ellen. I willed myself to stop thinking about the risk that Trimble would crack open, destroy himself, and take us with him. I willed myself to stop thinking about Charity.

5.

THE LONG WAIT after the big score is obviously something that has to be done right. The experienced professional criminal would know that it is a tough proposition.

The first weeks, my crime story was always on my mind, even when my work or my social obligations forced me to pay attention to something else.

A judge works closely with five people every day—two law clerks who each spend a two-year term; the secretary, the courtroom clerk, and the court reporter are permanent. They know your persona. They would notice a change. I labored to maintain the same voice, the same face, the same Paulie Devine in chambers right after the robbery. They deserved something better than a morose, distracted judge. And they might have to testify someday about what they had seen and heard in the times after the great theft.

The case of *United States v. Luytens* was a hit of crank. Ludwig Luytens was a wondrous man with a stratospheric IQ. He thought he could defeat any criminal charge. Small, twenty-eight, thin, even frail, with wispy hair, he smiled often and had the look of someone recently cured of a wasting disease. But you might fear him if he were holding a sawed-off shotgun and wearing a mask, which it appeared Ludwig Luytens often did.

With all his brains he chose the criminal career of carjacking—a low-return business that subjects you to the ridiculously high risk of being shot by an armed driver or having to take care of a baby you find strapped in the backseat of your newly stolen Mercedes.

An undercover officer/fence testified that he bought the

jacked cars from Ludwig, whose fingerprints were found all over the cars. Ludwig said he just delivered them to the fence for the real thief and was paid thirty dollars a car. No victim could identify Ludwig as the carjacker. He wore a handkerchief over the bottom half of his face.

Ludwig decided to represent himself. That way he could tell his story to the jury without having to worry about answering difficult questions from the prosecutors. His strategy was based on two principles: one, that whatever the prosecution wanted would not be good for him; and, two, what it did not want would always be good for him. The first principle is usually valid. The second one is not. The prosecutors did not want to call a carjacking victim to the stand. Acknowledging that the victims could not identify the carjacker, they just wanted Ludwig to concede that the victims would testify that they had been carjacked. Ludwig said no. He wanted them on the stand to admit that they could not identify him as the carjacker.

Ludwig was very gentle in court, showing the jury that he was not a fierce masked man with a gun. One victim was a woman with an earnest air about her. Her rounded face displayed her intense concentration and her determination to answer to the very best of her ability.

"You did not see the lower two-thirds of the carjacker's face?" asked Luytens. Mrs. Rosen said no.

"And you saw a police lineup," Luyten said, "and you could not identify anyone then."

"That's true."

He raised his voice a bit and asked, "So you do not know who stole your car?"

Mrs. Rosen did not pause. "I think you did," she said.

"Huh?"

"Well, I've been watching you move around the courtroom and I've been listening to you all this time and now I know it was you."

The verdict was inevitable at that point, and Ludwig may have known it. His tactical errors will certainly be clear to him one day in the prison yard.

I could be standing there with him.

Ludwig did have one fine moment in court. He was scribbling away on a legal pad while we waited for the verdict. Tearing the sheet from the pad, he taped it to a courtroom chair and pushed the chair up against the paneled wall. The marshal went over to look at Ludwig's note. He had written, "Don't use this chair, the bottom is broke." And it was broken. I remembered this act of decency when I passed sentence.

Tony Plymouth appeared in the back of my courtroom during a Tuesday-morning docket call. I nodded at him. Afterward my courtroom clerk told me that the detective from the Serena case wanted to know if I could see him in the near future. He left his phone number and said he just wanted some advice. He was in the federal building all day. I told my secretary to call the detective and tell him he could come up in the late afternoon when my hearings and sentencing were finished. At lunch with one of my favorite law clerks, I was unable to eat a crumb.

The Serena case had netted a ton of media, some of it on the front page below the fold. Some Sunday newspaper essayist had used the detective as a starting point to discuss the Gypsies of today, the Gypsies of America, and Gypsy culture. Tony Plymouth had a few seconds on *Nightline* and a few minutes on the local news. He said he didn't really know that much about Gypsies.

When he arrived, we sat in my small study. I was listening to a collection of Bill Evans piano pieces. Spread before me were the papers from a difficult case about a series of currency trades of the Swiss franc and the Japanese yen, the kind of case where the winning margin is measured in a tenth of a point. They were for show. I could not concentrate on them knowing I was soon to meet with the detective who worked so closely with Bonnie Owens, who nursed Trimble Young. "Ah, Detective. What's happened to you since Serena?" I asked him.

"I'm pushing to start a major fraud squad. An old idea, but after Serena they're asking me to write some proposals." He made several small circles in the air with his right index finger and looked at me with his blank eyes.

"So it might work out for you."

"Well, the thrill is fading, but I felt good enough to leave town on a furlough—first time ever."

"Where did you go?"

"Judge, I drove the California coast," he said, now smiling at me almost boyishly. "I just let it all go, except twice I was in the real world. I stopped up at Pelican Bay to see a prisoner; the guy ran an electronic funds transfer scam from inside. And later in Los Angeles I saw this producer who wanted to make a Gypsy film, like *King of the Gypsies* only better. I met a couple of distant cousins."

"There's going to be a movie?" It would upset Bill Serena to be outed to millions of people. Someone out there might know where Serena hid his dough.

"Maybe," the detective said, "but I hated *King of the Gypsies*."

"Let me know if you need an entertainment lawyer, Detective."

"Don't really care about the movies. I'm still working on my fraud squad idea. The command sees that they can take the cases to federal court and still get some credit, but they want evidence that Serena's case was not a fluke before they put up the money for the unit. So I need something else." He made a left handed circle in the air to finish his thought.

"I see."

"I found something. A suspicious fire at the Federal Reserve Bank. I'm thinking it's some kind of personal-injury scam— this bank employee gets himself burned a little and files a big lawsuit. I pick up lots of stuff that way. You know, that's how I first got on to Serena, a little scam with his son's broken leg. I do this tour of the emergency rooms every week, looking for funny stuff."

As he spoke, I was rigid as a board, trying to convey zero body language. He was calm and earnest, his eyes searching my face. Was he looking for signs of guilt or signs that I approved of his work?

"That's a new one. Is that a common police procedure?" My voice was as even as the horizon on the lake.

"Not common, but there's some of it in the big cities."

"And this turned out how?"

"Well, they were funny-looking wounds, which is what spurred me on, but my idea didn't pan out. It turns out that you can't really get a lot of money when you get hurt working for the federal government—just monthly payments from some compensation fund at the Department of Labor—and, if you sue the G you get a hearing in front of a judge without that jury around to give you a few million. You knew that, right?"

Tony Plymouth looked at me and raised his brows.

"Yes. I did." I did not raise my brows or blink. I moved only my lips.

"Then the guy doesn't file for anything. He's just getting disability pay, and they foot his medical bills. But those wounds still look phony, and a security guy at the Fed tells me that he thinks the fire was a little suspicious, since it started in the electrical system and the employee who got burned was their electrician. And then I thought of it." The detective leaned forward. "This fire, Judge, could serve as a cover for a robbery if the paramedics had to cart an injured person out of the bank in a hurry. Those gurneys and their pads could be used to conceal a lot of money. Thieves could stuff two or three million dollars into an empty pad cover and under the pad."

I got up from my chair because I had to move. Then I covered myself by asking if he wanted coffee or a Coke and did he mind if I had something. We split a diet something.

Jesus, Mary, and Joseph. He had guessed half of my plan. He was just thinking too small. When would he figure out the other half? My face betrayed me, I believe, but the detective took my reaction as one of surprise and interest. "It could be done, Judge. They could get a few million that way."

Yes, it could, Detective, I thought in response

"That much?" were my words. *This is good,* I was thinking. *If he made one error about the robbery, he could make other errors and, maybe, we were not playing suspect poker here.*

"Yes, sir. The paramedics had to be in on it. Ditto the employee's wife, a guard. The head of security there, Corman—I talked to him, and he sets up a meeting with the top man at the bank—Mr. Prindiville."

"How did the meeting go, Detective?" I was returning to my body. I was more like the boy fending off the faculty at Mater Dei. I was beginning to think tactically.

Some detectives take it as a sign of guilt if you sit and listen without speaking. You are silent, the detective believes, because you know everything the detective knows and more. This is trash thinking; people are sometimes silent because it is polite or because they are like animals frozen in headlights—they have fear without guilt. I had fear and guilt and I felt frozen in the headlights, but I'm Irish and I can always say something.

And then my secretary walked in. "Sorry to interrupt, Judge, but Don Leary and Mickey Gordon are both here to see you and they say it's an emergency."

My secretary, who is aptly named Mrs. Tiger, would not interrupt unless she thought she had to. " Hold that thought," I said to Plymouth, and I went into chambers.

Leary represented the plaintiff and Gordon the defendant. Leary wanted an injunction to stop Gordon's client from displaying something called BadAss 3.1 at the Speciality Products Show, a large industry exposition occupying acres and acres of indoor space at McCormick Place. The show would open in two hours, and I had to rule quickly; it was important. Only a bad judge would tell them that their issue might be important to them but it was not important to me. I went back and told Plymouth that I had to go to court. "I'm sorry to cut this short; if you want to finish it sometime, I'd like to hear the rest of it. Sounds interesting," I said, Irish Paulie Devine, through and through.

"Actually, I would," Plymouth said, his eyebrows in motion again. "I need some advice from you about what I should do."

"Just talk to Mrs.Tiger on the way out, and she'll give you a time to come back. I'd be happy to tell you what I think." With that true sentiment, I stuck out my palm; he stood up, we shook hands, and I walked him to the Tiger's desk and told her, "I want to see Detective Plymouth again. The two of you can pick the time." She would know that I meant "soon."

I would have enjoyed this case at any other time, but not right after an intrepid cop has just thrust half of your master criminal plan into the searchlight and left you trembling. Leary and Gordon were both former law clerks of mine. Here were my professional children who know better than anyone how I do my job, battling it out in my court—with me watching to see if they have learned my lessons and me wanting to be very sure to be the perfect judge. I suppressed my anxiety, tried to forget Plymouth, and spent an hour listening to each protégé of mine spend his or her intellectual power on the question of whether BadAss 3.1 would hurt the sales of Mr. Orange Head—a round plastic orange-colored ball with a cute face that, when touched, told short children's stories. BadAss 3.1 was the same orange color over a square shape with a cute face that, when touched, said things like "You smell like puke," "Your boobs droop," "Your dick is teeny." The question is whether someone would buy BadAss 3.1 thinking it was Mr. Orange Head, give it to a child, and then tell all their friends never to buy Mr. Orange Head. In the end, I told Mickey Gordon that her client had to change the color of BadAss 3.1 to avoid confusion. Of course she had known what I would do, and she came prepared with some handmade BadAss 3.1s. They were black with a green face, purple lips, and yellow eyes. I allowed her client to display them at the trade show if all the orange-colored product was destroyed. Leary smiled and said that was fine with Mr. Orange Head.

The case was closed, and I took Tony Plymouth home with me.

6.

I NEED TO know more about Plymouth, more than his smooth voice—he never seemed to breathe—and his clean, bland clothes could signify.

I reached out to someone I knew well from my time as a prosecutor: Lieutenant "Guadal" O'Hara, an excellent man. He was the son of a Mexican mother and an Irish father. Seriously ill during her pregnancy, his mother supposedly invoked the aid of Our Lady of Guadalupe—the apparition of the Virgin Mary who appeared in 1531. In gratitude, the boy was named Philip Guadalupe O'Hara. Of course, as he grew up, the name

Guadalupe disappeared from sight. It reappeared when O'Hara applied for the police department and thought he might derive an affirmative-action benefit from his middle name. He worked like a dog to relearn his high school Spanish and started filling out police board forms as P. Guadalupe O'Hara. One of the instructors shortened his new first name to Guadal. It stuck. O'Hara was smart and he knew that a memorable nickname gave him an edge in the police department, even if he didn't get a leg up from affirmative action in a direct way. I believe he told me that he has dozens of recordings of the song, spliced end to end on a single cassette which he plays at a loud volume in his office from time to time—"Guadalohara, Guadalohara."

"Hi, Paulie, how are they hanging? Your Honor."

"I am too dignified to notice, Guadal. I need to know about one of your brothers in blue."

"Ask."

"You know Tony Plymouth?"

"He worked for me a couple of years. You want to know what?"

"What kind of cop. He did a good job on a case I heard."

"Always does a good job, a little monomania there; he really cares about his stuff, really fucking cares." Guadal was very forthright, which right now I appreciated very much. "No limit on the hours he puts in; he couldn't give a rat's ass if he gets paid for the overtime. A zealot, not a crazy zealot; he's a Mountie, always gets his man."

"Why'd you say 'zealot'?"

"Well, he has got this fraud squad unit; he won't let go of it. They try to turn him off it but he won't budge and now, I hear, he might get it."

After the Guadalohara call ended, I thought I needed a drink. I needed Ellen more.

Ellen saw the beginning of me the way I am now. She was calm when I was angry. Later on she was able to detect, from my face, just when I had what she dubbed a "Prindiville Moment." By then she had put Redding Prindiville III in some wastebasket she kept for the bad things in her life. Of course, she did not know that Prindiville had lied to her when he told her that he was not the primary reason she had had to live through four years of accusation and trial. She did know that he could have stopped her ordeal and refused to do so, and she had enough reason to despise him for that alone.

The first time she heard his name, she laughed. Few people in the Midwest walk around with two last names and a roman numeral.

"He's from Vermont," I told her. She had just received the report blaming her for the the investment trust fiasco, and I had wanted to know just who this man was. "He is related to three or four governors, a nineteenth-century United States senator, a famous congressman of more recent vintage, and various local leading lights. His father was chief justice of Vermont and is supposed to have single-handedly created the rules that govern skiing accidents."

"Whom have you been talking to, Paulie?"

"Lois Carson, at Northwestern Law School. She had Prindiville as a guest speaker in her government regulation class."

"The law of skiing accidents?"

"Probably the most sizable legal task you could perform if you were on the supreme court of Vermont," I said. "Some of the story may not be true—it could be the usual Washington, D.C., newcomer's tale about how important his family was in Muskegon or Des Moines or whatever. A federal prosecutor in Vermont told me that the family had money but had sunk from prominence over the years. He also said that Redding wanted to restore their former glory but that his family isn't going to finance his political ambitions."

I speculated to Ellen that Redding Prindiville decided he had to leave Vermont, make a name for himself, and return to Burlington primed for politics. He must have had some clout, because the Comptroller of the Currency took him out of a law firm in Burlington to make him deputy general counsel. I heard he was trying to go to the Federal Reserve Bank, ambitious to become a governor of the Federal Reserve.

"So he'll go back to Vermont and run for governor on the claim that he had guided the nation to prosperity."

"Now you're kidding me."

"He could fool the voters into thinking he was responsible for good times. It could be a good bet. Presidents have been making that bet for years."

"Come on, Paulie. You think the Vermonters, whatever you call them, will be falling on their knees in gratitude to someone for his service to the American monetary system?"

"Stranger political careers have been made."

She shook her red hair. She often did that. She knew it made my heart speed up.

"You never told me what he looks like, Prindiville?" I asked her.

"Very distinguished, almost six and a half feet tall, a narrow well-shaped face with light brown hair and surprisingly kind eyes. Misleading eyes. So he might succeed in politics on his looks," Ellen said.

"I hope not in a place like Vermont, where you have to meet the voters face-to-face. Unless he could spend a fortune on first-rate handlers. Personally I'm praying, praying that his political ambitions will take him home away from you."

"When was the last time you prayed, Paulie?" Ellen asked.

I hit her with a pillow.

Prindiville did not go home, but he did make it to the Fed first as general counsel and then as president of the Federal Reserve Bank of Chicago, which made him a member of the board of governors, a plan well executed by him and for him.

7.

"THIS GUY, THIS Prindiville, the head of the Fed I told you about—a dickhead. He listened to me. Yeah, he gives me the serious face, the fortune-teller face. He waits until I finish and then he drops his mask. He looks at me like I was a bum wanting a handout. He starts in with his sarcasm. He thinks I'm nuts."

Plymouth had come to see me the very next day. He must have been anxious. He was wearing street clothes—running shoes, khaki pants, blue-checked shirt, and a worn blue sport coat—no wrinkles anywhere. We drank coffee and he had started right in, maybe because he was concerned about another interruption.

"What did he say, Detective? Why did he think you were nuts?" I was a portrait of an intellectually intrigued listener, exhibiting perfect calm.

"He runs it down like this, Judge. He says 'One, nobody robs the Fed. Two, I don't think anybody deliberately sets himself on fire unless he's a Buddhist monk circa nineteen sixty-five. Three, they can't get the money out. Four, we used to burn money here at the Fed—we know how much the ash is supposed to weigh. We weighed the ash; we found eight hundred ten million dollars' worth of ash, more or less.' Then he just sits there. It was a closed case to this guy. So I say, 'Could I ask you something?' 'If you must,' he says. I ask, 'Did you examine the scene for evidence of arson?' He answers yes. I'm pulling teeth here. I ask, 'And?'

"He says, 'The electrical switches and wires were melted. We don't know what went wrong. There were readings of surges, and the safety systems failed. This sort of event does happen. The equipment is dated. It was a small fire that damaged walls and burned money and, incidentally, saved us the trouble of destroying some of it. We did think there was more smoke than there should have been, but it doesn't matter.' I say, 'Why not?'"

I am listening, blinking my eyes normally, nodding at the right time. I am listening very closely. I am just listening.

"He tells me, 'Suppose someone made smoke to obscure our surveillance cameras—that's what you're thinking? I can see you were.' He's right about that. 'You recall what I said, I said that no one robs the Fed. I did not say no one ever attempts to rob the Fed. You think somebody made smoke to cover a robbery? Okay, they *didn't carry it off!!*'

"This guy is yelling at me. It rocks me back, and I see him give off a little smile when I move. He stops yelling and finishes off. 'They never got the money. We followed the ambulance to the hospital. We searched it and we searched the electrician's clothes . . . I see you are unconvinced . . . You want to talk to the security people on duty?' I nod. He says 'Go ahead. Spin your wheels. You can try all you want, mister, but you can't rob this place. When you think you have some evidence, not guesses, but evidence, you can come back to see me.'

"I got up and got out of there." Tony Plymouth peered at me. "You mind that I'm telling you all this?"

I shrugged. I didn't want to show my elation even though he has run up against the other half of my plan, that the Fed won't admit the theft, and he can't get around that.

Tony Plymouth cracked a small grin, a novelty on his face. I must have raised my eyebrows questioningly. "When I got outside his door, I whispered, *'Ac tu nashvalyi, tiro tcud ac yakha.'* "

"A Gypsy curse?"

"Yes, Judge." Now he was smiling. "But it's the wrong curse because it means 'Be thou ill; let thy milk be fire.' It is a curse for a woman. My grandmother taught me the little I know. She must be laughing at me in her heaven."

Too bad, I thought. Prindiville deserved a nice effective curse.

"What's next, Detective?"

"I have one shot left at the bank, the security director. Ernest Corman, an unhappy trooper. He doesn't like this worker or his wife, the guard. She was an affirmative-action baby. He said she got promoted because she filed a case in federal court. Plus there is a brick on Corman because of the way the evacuation was handled on the day of the fire. He's done rising through the ranks with that brick weighing on him."

Wheezer, clumsy, vindictive, now scared. He was always a danger to us. "Does this Corman think there was a robbery? Does he believe your theory?"

"Hell no, Judge! What's in it for him? But he asks who might be a suspect. So I tell him anybody who was there, even you, but just between us, I'm looking at the electrician. He volunteers to help."

"What can he do to help?"

"Not a lot. But I went to tech services and I got this."

Tony Plymouth then reached down into his square document case and pulled out an odd-looking device, all tubes and gauges. "It's a sniffer, like the thing to check for leaks in air-conditioning, but this one is calibrated for the smoke chemical that was found in the money rooms. I talked to the arson investigators. The smoke might have come from the paint and the ink, but I'm thinking somebody might have put a little extra chemical there. If they did, they would have had to store the chemical somewhere. Corman can take this sniffer anywhere in the bank. If he finds the hiding place, maybe we can track it back to the person. And I tell Corman to sniff around places where people can see him, and maybe he'll get some funny reactions."

"Is that where you are right now, Detective, using the sniffer?"

"No. And this is where I need a little advice about what I should do here. I don't know the federal stuff the way you do. If the Federal Reserve gets upset enough, can they stop me? Will it get the FBI and the others upset? The bad part is I could look like fool if I'm wrong. I could be right and not be able to prove it. Either way somebody could make a big thing about it, and it would guarantee that there would never be a major fraud unit in the police department. What are my risks here?" I saw him make a slow right-handed circle in the air, and he looked either ingenuous or disingenuous—I couldn't be sure.

A chance to tell him to drop it all. It would have been good advice, not the best advice, but good enough. Yet I did not do it. Plymouth might know more than he was telling me, and my advice to drop the case would be evidence against me. There was the little tantalizing reference to Charity's lawsuit. If he had looked at the file, he would know I had been the judge. And it would be no great trick for him to find out that I had known the paramedic on the scene, Dave Brody, since we had turned double plays at Mater Dei.

I tilted my head to one side as I do in court when I want the lawyers to know I'm thinking about what they've said. My arms spread like those of a law professor about to make a point, and I told him that he ought to try the sniffer. It would be Corman and not Plymouth who would be blamed. I told him that my impression of Tony Plymouth was of an officer who would not ignore a crime simply to advance his own career. If he let it go now, he might find it difficult to live with himself. "See what happens with the sniffer, and then come back and talk to me." I slowly sipped the dregs of my coffee. "No one in federal law enforcement cares much about any other part of federal government. If you get something good—really good—the Federal Reserve won't be able to stop the FBI. If Prindiville calls to complain, they'll listen and laugh after they hang up. Just as Prindiville is doing to you. This make sense to you, Detective?"

"Yes. I think it does."

"I don't mean to rush you," I said as I stood up. "If there is anything else..."

"No. It's been a big help, talking to someone like you." He laughed, cocked his head at me, got up, and left happy.

I finished my day and went home to go to bed, nauseated and hungry in the same moment, my eyes on the coffered ceiling in the bedroom, calculating and recalculating my position.

8.

Delphine: *Hello.*
Osoberto: *Hi.*
Delphine: *My love?*
Osoberto: *Yes, as you are my love.*
Delphine: *Have you heard from Paco?*
Osoberto: *No, I am fearful.*
Delphine: *It will be well.*
Osoberto: *Keep trying to reach his wife, so she can get the papers.*
Delphine: *All right. And... and I called my mom to ask her to light a little candle.*
Osoberto: *A good thought, and...*

Delphine: *All right.* Ciao, *my love.*
Osoberto: *I call again in an hour.*

Delphine: *Hello.*
Osoberto: *What's up?*
Delphine: *Dear one, nothing, I have been calling.*
Osoberto: *This is bad. I left the car abandoned. It's all going sour.... What was I going to tell you? Oh, I've been calling too and getting no one.*
Delphine: *Perhaps they are out together.*
Osoberto: *This is my hope. One calls and no one answers. We'll see what I will do.*
Delphine: *Then you might not come to me.*
Osoberto: *Yes.*
Delphine: *But you must call me.*
Osoberto: *Yes, my dear.*
Delphine: *Trejo did call.*
Osoberto: *What did you say?*
Delphine: *That you went out, an errand for our baby, some milk. It is true. The milk is gone.*
Osoberto: *I will bring some immediately.*
Delphine: *No. Don't you think it could be dangerous?*
Osoberto: *Our child.*
Delphine: *No. My love, I'll prepare and give him juice ... already I have prepared apple juice and everything.*
Osoberto: *All right.*
Delphine: *You sound sad.... Should I keep calling, what should I say?*
Osoberto: *Tell her that I urgently need her to come to me, a taxi, but now.*
Delphine: *Yes.*
Osoberto: *But today. It has to be today.*
Delphine: *I call now.*
Osoberto: Ciao.
Delphine: Ciao.
Osoberto: *Wait, you are the love of my life.*
Delphine: *Oh, Osoberto.*

Oddly poetic, isn't it, if you do not know it is a dialogue between two criminals. It took place before I had even conceived of my great robbery.

The clicks of the telephones disconnecting were the next and last sounds on this tape of Delphine and Osoberto. They were sharp sounds, much louder than in real life. Someone must have turned up the gain on the recording machine just before Delphine and Osoberto hung up. Everyone in the courtroom looked up when the two clicks snapped out of the speakers, as if in the primal response of our ancestors listening for the breaking of twigs by deer in the forest.

According to the prosecution, apple juice was a code for cocaine and milk for heroin, and Delphine and Osoberto were narcotics conspirators badly imitating an ordinary married couple. The assistant United States attorney and the FBI team, all hardened aging grown-ups, could not believe this sappy conversation was legitimate—that any married couple in their late thirties would utter "You are the love of my life" or "Oh, Osoberto." It's true that Ellen and I did not say such things, but we felt them, and I knew early on that the minions of law enforcement were wrong on this one small detail. Anyone with an open mind could see that Delphine and Osoberto were mad with love for each other. They had an infant girl for whom apple juice was nectar. They were also narcotic traffickers. Specialists in dodging the Internal Revenue Service, they were particularly desirable to Paco Marquez and his wife, who were not answering the phone because they were then in a lockup in the Metropolitan Correctional Center, our local federal jail, more than willing to testify against anyone, even each other. Paco and wife would do five years and the faithful pair before me would not get out of jail until their little girl was a high-school senior. This was depressing me so I switched gears and used the case to remind me of the necessity of not being overheard, and to be clever in the code words I use.

I picked up the phone after I adjourned court. "Dave, let's go hear some jazz."

We went to the Metropole in the Fairmont Hotel, a nice club that, like many clubs in big hotels, is often nearly empty even when it offers great music. We heard Jeremy Kahn's trio. The club has two corner tables far from the stage and not close to any other table. We broke a cardinal rule and talked while Jeremy played "The Jitterbug Waltz."

"What now?" Dave asked me when I explained Plymouth to him. Dave was keeping his hands quite still, folded in front of him.

"I don't think we have to do anything," I said. I had decided to believe this. "This whole deal depended on the Fed never admitting that anything had been taken. I don't think Prindiville could even admit it to himself."

"Sure, but..."

"Why tempt fate? But do tell Charity. See her in person," I told him.

Dave raised his face to me, a schoolboy braving the priest's gaze after having been caught with a girl in the library or, just as bad at Mater Dei, going down the up staircase.

"I'll meet her for breakfast, you know, to ask after her and her husband whom I so bravely rescued. I won't be the first firefighter to have a meeting with a grateful wife."

"Fine. I would keep to our original agenda. The issue here, Dave, is that Plymouth is not under the control of the Fed. I don't think he can knock down that wall, but..." I felt like making one of Plymouth's little circles in the air, but Dave would not have known what it meant.

9.

CHARITY WAS READY for Corman, who came the next day.

Money does not stand still. The Fed's money rooms had to be open for business a day after the fire. The Fed had done what it had to do to put itself back in business and left everything else for later. All the electrical cables and panels were on temporary shelves and, except for the floor, nothing was cleaned up. Corman came marching around with some *Star Trek* mechanism, sticking it into every corner of the damn place and taking notes. He wouldn't tell Charity what it was for when she asked him. "Something for the front office," he said, smirking. Corman went into the surveillance room and put the sniffer on the floor. Charity felt she might throw up.

She kept her face turned sideways to Corman but used the last bit of her peripheral vision to watch him. He kept his face flat except for a single moment at the end when he frowned, which to Charity meant that the plastic bag had kept the wafers safe and no residue was left at the hiding place.

Corman walked out and Charity felt the start of a sensational headache, caused, she thought, by keeping her eyes on Corman. She went out to spy on the locker rooms from the women's washroom. Corman was in for a surprise.

The chief of security must have seen the sniffer register wildly in the money rooms the way it was supposed to but not anywhere else. In the guards' locker room, he would run the sniffer all over Charity's locker and there find nothing. Then Corman opened his own locker to store the device—and the gauge shot to the top of its range. Now it was his turn to quaver and feel sick. Charity saw him rip everything out of his locker and run the sniffer over it all. Charity watched him look under the empty locker and find the wafers. She heard him say, "She must have planted them here. And fingerprints." He used his knife to scrape them off in one piece. He probably thought about sticking them under Charity's locker. Charity would have put them right back in his locker if he had tried to do it. He pried the blade under one wafer and scraped the knife under it. The wafer crumbled; each one in turn crumbled. Charity saw the crumbs fall to the floor and heard Corman say "Shit." He scooped the crumbs into an envelope.

Charity wondered if he would be stupid enough to tell Detective Plymouth that he had found them under Charity's locker. But he wouldn't be that dumb. Corman shuffled into the men's room, and Charity heard the toilet flush twice. Then Corman came out and left the locker room with a sick look on his face. After a minute of slow breathing, Charity went to discover if Corman had left anything she had not managed to see when she was in hiding. She got a pain pill and swallowed it dry and, dropping to her knees, looked underneath Corman's locker and then her own. Nothing. Her headache left her.

Corman would not forget that technically he was a suspect. If he reported finding the wafers under Charity's locker, he might get caught in the lie on a federal polygraph, his career would be in trouble, and Charity would become known as the intended victim of a supervisor's lie, which would make her bulletproof for several years. Even Wheezer Corman would know that.

Charity met Dave and me at the O'Hare Chapel. We sat in tranquil silence in comfort until an older man and a younger woman who looked like his daughter walked into the room, looking startled that they had entered a chapel, and sat down without seeming to notice the three of us. When we left, they did not look at us. We decided we would have our meeting on the Blue Line, riding the subway back to the city, which was sparsely used at that time of night. I learned about Corman as I looked out over the lower-rise, residential parts of Chicago, which seemed as endless as my conspiracy was turning out to be.

"This has to be much harder for you than any of us expected, and it's not over," I told her. Dave nodded and smiled at her. She smiled at him in return. I tried to find her eyes, and she found mine first. I had faith in her steadiness, and I was sure she had faith in my judgment.

The train descended into its tunnel, and we swayed along with it. "Maybe Tony Plymouth will come by your place for free sandwiches and advice," Dave suggested. "And if he doesn't, maybe that'll mean he's dropped the whole thing."

"Corman won't forget," Charity said over the din of the train.

"Tell me about Reverend James," I said to Charity.

"I tell you that, then you know why I am the way I am. How I learned not to look back."

"If you know that, Charity, then you know more than I do about myself."

Dave put his hand on Charity's hand. "I'd like to hear it, really, if you don't mind too much."

Charity looked briefly at both of us and shrugged. I wonder if she thought we needed to know what she was going to tell me. I doubt she was telling her story for her own comfort.

"I'm Mama's only girl, born after my two brothers. Daddy died. I'm just four, don't get it about Daddy. We live on the south side of Chicago on the edge of Chatham, not exactly black middle class but getting close. Daddy drove a large truck to and from Buffalo. Man worked as many hours as he could. He was a fool for insurance salesmen. When he died, the insurance policies kept us in the house and off welfare. The last year of his life, his heart got too weak, so he stayed up in our sun parlor. He rested on a daybed and when I come toddling in, his big old face give me this big smile.

"When Daddy's gone, Mama needs a man to help out. Either she turns to Uncle Edgar, the mechanic, Daddy's brother, or her brother, the Reverend James. I got Reverend James and all his rules for me. Whenever the Reverend James disapproved, Mama had to disapprove too. And no middle ground at all. I figured I do whatever they wanted and they'd leave me alone in my spare time."

"That sounds like me," I said, leaning against the plastic seat and rocking along with the train.

"What's that mean?" Charity asked as quietly as she could over the noise of the wheels. She looked directly at me.

"I never wanted to be told what to do, ever. Like high school—I didn't fight the school. I did whatever they told me and I did it so perfectly that they decided I could be left alone because I was so perfect. That was my strategy."

"It wouldn't work with Reverend James. Never got credit from that man. You in the choir, you go to Bible class, then you go to Bible camp. And that Bible camp, I'm reading what they tell me, so I ask why God put the tree of knowledge of good and evil in the garden if he didn't want Adam and Eve to eat the fruit, and why God let the serpent talk Eve into eating the forbidden fruit? Is God setting up Eve or setting up the serpent, and, by the way, how come the Bible says Cain is the firstborn and in another place says the first son was Seth? No one cares about the Bible; they just care what the deacons and such are saying." Charity's voice could cut diamonds.

"I sneak out to see Uncle Edgar about two hours a week. He

teaches me how to drive a truck in the auto graveyard next to his shop. Now Mama sometimes catches me with grease under my fingernails and finally Uncle Edgar told me to stay at home, the garage is no place for a girl. He had to because the Reverend would command his flock to boycott him. Reverend James and Mama can't be beat by me, and I couldn't fool them. Reverend James said I had insolent eyes."

I wonder if my Ellen had the same trait as a child, a precursor of the cast of eye that Ellen and Charity shared. I was captivated by it, but some men would be terrified by it in a woman, fearing whatever disarms them.

"What happened then, Charity?" Dave asked. I could hear the trace of scandalized desire in a voice I recognized from Mater Dei when he talked to girls more worldly than the lasses of Blessed Lady.

Charity looked at Dave as if she had known him at age sixteen.

"James was doing this to everybody. He wants people to follow his orders without ever admitting he was giving orders, as if the community is giving the orders. 'If you don't prepare yourself to be a good Christian wife, Charity, you'll be letting the community down.' If you didn't come along the Reverend James would preach against you, 'the demon trying to destroy the community.'"

She vocalized a sound like an angry nicker from a horse. "What community? If there was one, why wasn't it able to keep drunks off the streets three blocks away, or drug sellers or gang bangers? In the pulpit, the Reverend James was more concerned with telling the quarter of the congregation that was on welfare that they should skip a meal a week to support the church."

"Very Catholic," Dave murmured, "the mortification of the flesh, the path to sainthood. Was anybody trying to save you?"

"You couldn't save me, sweet boy." Charity laughed. "I even made trouble in Bible camp. The Lord God comes down to earth as two men to visit Lot in Sodom. The Sodomites come by and start yelling that the men be sent out so the Sodomites could know them, and God refused. I ask the deacons why God would refuse to let the Sodomites know them, because I figure that knowing means having sex. The deacons put me on the next train home. I just had to get a scholarship and get out."

"Who gave you the scholarship?" Dave asked her.

"The Urban League. I went to Howard University, so I could be a black female engineer."

"So you got out."

"Reverend James had done his damage. College was too free, too easy. I needed somebody to fight against, an enemy, you know. I drifted from great grades to good ones. I lost part of the scholarship. Mama refused to replace the missing money, but I wasn't going back. That's when I went to the Army."

"And the Reverend James, you see him?" Dave asked, studying her because of instincts I knew too well; she was beautiful as she spoke.

"I drove around the old neighborhood. The church looked better than ever. The streets around it looked worse. I live in a white neighborhood. And I don't like chapels." She grinned at that.

She left the train at Clark and Lake streets. Dave and I stayed on for three more stops, got off at Jackson Street, took the glass elevator up to Dearborn, and walked the twenty feet to the courthouse door. I thought if the detective was suspicious that Charity would have to prepare Trimble to deal with it. She could handle it.

"You see why I fell for her?" Dave asked quietly. The question disconcerted me, and I dropped the security keycard I needed to enter the courthouse. I stopped abruptly and said nothing while I picked up the card from the sidewalk.

"Yes, of course I do," I said, recovering my composure. "Who wouldn't fall for a woman with that soul and those looks? I trust her and I care for her and you deserve someone like her, but Dave..."

"I can't have her. I know," he said in his smallest voice. "I didn't get off the train with her, Paulie."

I was not worried about Charity, because I knew her. I worried about Dave because of the vacant, uninhabited places inside him. But he was above all a professional who knew how to set a fire without getting burned. Trimble, however, had been literally burned. He was in thrall to Charity, and Dave and I now understood why.

10.

I WENT TO lunch with former law clerks. Norbu is Tibetan; he looks every inch the monk and often wears saffron ties to cement the impression. He likes the air of mystery it gives him when he walks into a courtroom. Then he opens his mouth to talk in the flat midwestern speech of Iowa where he was raised. He said he had the three big *I*s in his favor: intelligence, inscrutability, and Iowan. Norbu was about to leave the United States attorney's office in Manhattan to join the New York office of my old law firm; he was following my career path. I hope he never robs the Federal Reserve Bank of New York.

I saw Charity once. Her skin seemed even blacker. There is an old story that coal-black women and men are not appreciated in America either by blacks or whites. I remembered that two black songwriters, Fats Waller and Andy Razaf, wrote "Black and Blue" with a bitter lyric: "Browns and yellows, lucky fellows, ladies seem to like them light." She gave me a report on Trimble, still difficult but not impossible. Afterward she said I had seemed to be on her side from the first moment she saw me. I told her a judge tries to appear sympathetic so that when I have to tell someone that his case is legally weak, the truth is easier to accept. When we parted company in front of the diner she said, "You were on my side, you were. I knew it then and I know it now." I confessed to this.

Another day I lunched with another former clerk who worked very hard as a lawyer despite an inheritance that could have financed the construction of an aircraft carrier. This clerk had an agenda. His sister, he said, was a neurosurgery resident at Northwestern, and he and his sister wanted to suggest, just suggest, that I meet the chief of neurosurgery, a sensational woman named Maeve Nolan—an unmarried woman, of course. It was a quiet time, I was no longer myself, and I said yes even though I might have to think of a cover story for the broad white scar on my hand—my daily physical reminder of my life of crime.

After a few days, I invited Plymouth to lunch.

There was a quiet table in a little dining room alcove at my club, which I needed because I intended illegally to record the conversation. The tape would let me dissect every word, every pause, every slip of the tongue. I wouldn't have the chance to talk to Plymouth a dozen times, and I could not ask him a hundred questions.

Secret tape recording is a class-four felony under Illinois law. Every time I played the tape might be another crime, but I would not be violating my judicial oath. I administer justice impartially, and the oath doesn't require me not to rob banks. After I listened to it a few times and took my notes, I burned the tape, and by destroying the tape I destroyed my crime.

Tony Plymouth came ten minutes early, a cop thing. He dressed in a much nicer suit than he usually wore, making himself look as if he belonged to the club. The detective seemed thinner than the last time I had seen him. The hair was still tightly curled and his brown eyes were as opaque as I remembered. He stood very erect. He was a little shorter than I, but we seemed to meet eye to eye at the same level.

I told him I wanted the lunch with him to learn the rest of the Bill Serena saga. I told him I assumed the other matter he and I had talked about hadn't gone anywhere. He shrugged at that. I didn't push it. We ordered iced tea, salad, and pasta as we talked.

The detective's voice had a nice range. He could probably growl at suspects and purr at witnesses, a lucky trait for him.

"After I made detective I did a year in general assignments, then on to fraud, partly to watch the Gypsies. Every big department has someone to watch the Gypsies. I catch up to Serena when he nearly kills his own kid. Did I tell you the whole story about that? No. Well, one day I'm doing the emergency room routine looking for insurance fraud—injured guy calls his lawyer before he calls his wife, you know. I like the nurses. They see how a cop can get all wrapped up in the job, just like they do. One day I meet this woman, Bonnie Owens. Easy on the eyes, short hair, never stops moving. She's got one of those raspy voices—ex-cheerleader voices, I call them." Plymouth smiled and, keeping my face amiable, I tried to decide if he was baiting me or not with the mention of Trimble's nurse.

"Bonnie gets a father into emergency with his son, fifteen—very serious injuries, two fractures, one in the hip, and internal bleeding. The boy is hurt and feeling sicker by the minute. He asks if he is going to live, and he's practically spitting with anger at his dad. The nurse thinks child abuse. They sedate the boy for surgery on the bleeding thing. When Bonnie cuts off his clothes, she finds a hospital wristband from Loyola, up in Maywood. The band's got the boy's name on it and that day's date." Plymouth draws a circle in the air with his finger. "She checks up at Loyola and finds out the kid was admitted there with the same injuries earlier that day. The father checked him out against medical advice. She decides to play detective herself and visits the boy after surgery. She makes the father leave the room and she gets the whole story from the boy."

"Wait a second," I said as our food arrived. "Is it a problem, a Gypsy going after Gypsies? Your parents think you are embarrassing your own people at all?"

Tony flashed a brief confessional smile. "My parents were striving young Americans working to make it into the non-Gypsy middle class. My grandparents no longer lived the Gypsy life, but they were sentimental about it—even went to visit the shrine of Saint Sarah, patron of the Gypsies, in the Camargue in France. At the City Colleges I read up on the Gypsies. The Nazis killed a lot. Then government regulation in Europe and assimilation put a big dent in their life. There are still Gypsies who never learn to read or write and keep their kids out of school and teach them to steal, or, in America, teach them to live off welfare, but that culture is slowly going away. They are good people—clean, smart, quick on their feet. I don't have to draw pictures for most Gypsies. They figure things out for themselves."

They figure it out for themselves, like Tony Plymouth drawing conclusions from what Bonnie Owens tells him. Yes, they do. What kind of luck is it that she winds up with Trimble?

"The boy skipped school with his buddy to go to Blessed Lady Girls School where, I remember from my high school days"—Plymouth grinned and ate—"there is a mythical place where you can peek into the girls' locker room. There is no peephole. The kid climbed up the outside wall and fell off the wall. The boy landed on concrete, and his buddy carried him to a park bench and called home. Serena took his son to Loyola and, after he hears the diagnosis, tells the boy that it could mean a lot of money if they have a better version of the accident. The father decides to start fresh at another hospital. The son hears the doctors say how dangerous this could be. The move hurt like hell, particularly when Serena has to put a fresh pair of pants on the boy so that the new hospital can cut them off just as the doctors did at Loyola. The boy was so angry that he told Bonnie Owens, 'I am going to fuck off the money.'" Plymouth's face hardened in anger. "Gypsies aren't perfect, but they don't risk their kids' lives—ever."

"So that's how Serena got into your books?" I asked.

"No. Bill Serena was in the files already with lots of clean cons reported by private security guys who had no way to prosecute."

"What happened to the boy?"

"He healed up. There was a lawsuit, but the lawyer dropped it before anyone had to answer it. The kid was as good as his word; he blew off the money."

"And so how did you finally assemble enough to pinch Serena?" I asked.

"I had a string of Gypsy acquaintances who had Serena's knife at their throats one too many times. Many Gypsies don't like to go to the police to complain. Lots of police won't arrest one Gypsy on the word of another. They have too much experience that the Gypsy accuser disappears before the court date, unless it's rape or murder. Serena's enemies told me where to find him and my partner and I ran surveillance, which is what really did the trick."

"You just watched him," I said. "How could you know it wasn't going to be a big waste of time?"

"Instinct is part of it. I trust mine." Plymouth gazed into my face, and my stomach clenched its fist. "Plus Serena doesn't want any other way to live but to con."

Plymouth's voice was clipped with contempt.

"I have to say, Detective, I will never forget those two trials," I said, leading him into my territory.

Plymouth broke into a wide smile, his first. "Judge, the federal investigation was the best thing I ever did. And that lawyer, the one Serena hired for the accident case, reminded me that it was a case of mail fraud, so I could go to the G with my case and get out-of-state court. The G cares about the fraud stuff I work on, and the things they were able to do were great—tax returns. The funny thing was, with all his false names, Serena filed just one return under his true name. And he reported all his income."

There was a pause while the detective seemed to think. "By the way, Judge, you have a reputation with everybody in the G. The federal prosecutors told me you were the most pro-prosecution judge in the building. If you had a different image I don't know if that prosecutor, Mason, would have listened so carefully to you."

"Every little bit helps. And don't hesitate, Detective, if you need anything from me. The department needs more officers like you."

Plymouth beamed, looking as innocent as a child, guileless as a monk. I believe him perfectly capable of concealing his thoughts and intentions. He might still be pursuing the bank investigation and I might have come on his radar screen by now, but I would not know unless he wanted me to know. On the other hand, he did not try to get any information from me, and that allowed me to digest my lunch. The bad news here was that he launched an investigation of Serena and pursued it for months on instinct. He could do the same with his suspicions about the Fed. He could be close on my trail. I admired him. I wished the police would transfer him to homicide or robbery or narcotics so I could admire him from afar.

I had Dave Brody take a photograph of the two of us as we left the club. I saw him standing across the street, looking like a tourist getting a picture of the famous building that housed the club. Now both he and Charity would know Tony Plymouth on sight.

11.

CHARITY WANTED TO meet me. I refrained from meeting her at the diner or the chapel because I knew now that Tony Plymouth had his Gypsy acquaintances and I saw them everywhere. Instead I spoke to her on the phone. "Write down a list of any difficulties you might be having with the consent decree, anything at all, even if Prindiville would have a good explanation. Can you do that?" I asked.

"Yes. I have to see you very soon."

"Write up the list, then file a motion yourself to enforce the decree. Then you'll see me."

Four days later Charity was in chambers along with the lawyer for the Federal Reserve. She told me in a rote voice about trying to be assigned to another shift than the one her husband was working part-time and about the persistent harassment by Corman. The Fed lawyer explained why none of that mattered because the Fed sincerely wanted to abide by their agreement.

"May I talk to each side separately?" I asked. Both of them nodded. No one has ever said no to this question when I have asked it. "Miss Scott, you may go into the study and close the door. Mr. Westridge, you can remain here."

Charity left. I raised my eyebrows at Westridge.

"Judge, honestly I can understand why she is nervous, but

she's crying before she is actually hurt. And I don't think she's going to be hurt."

I looked as if I cared about what he was saying. As soon as I could decently do it, I stopped his recitation of the herculean efforts of the Fed to accommodate Charity and Trimble. "I'll talk to her," I said and moved toward the door to the study.

Alone with Charity behind the closed door, the charade could stop. It was extreme, but I turned both television and sound system on. Eddie Palmieri's Latin jazz did not go well with *I Love Lucy,* but it would be hard for Tony Plymouth or any other curious party to overhear us. Then I realized that having two sound covers for our conversation was itself suspicious and I clicked off the tube.

Charity sat on the edge of a red leather chair behind my writing desk. I took the blue easy chair and looked out at the Palmer House. "It's Trimble," she said unhappily. "The burn healed, but there's damage to the nerves in his face. He has pain every day, not a lot, but every day. He has to take Vicodin. He's probably addicted. Except they try to switch around with Percodan and Contin. When he takes enough to kill the pain completely, he's too doped up to work, and he wants to work so he lives with the pain through his shifts. That scar on his face bothers him worse than the pain. He's still looking for a plastic surgeon. He and I, when we are in the bedroom—he turns out the lights." Charity faltered slightly. "He's never done that before. He uses a little green makeup on the red part of the scar."

"Exactly what has happened?"

"Last week, I came home and he was very quiet. I asked about the doctor, and he told me he got a new prescription. I asked if anything else happened and he yelled at me. 'Why do you want to know?' He just shouted. I stopped talking. I'm scared about where a long talk might lead us. But he pushed it when I told him I just wanted to drop it."

"And what?"

"He said, 'Yeah, drop it.' He has a little sarcastic whine now. I tried to calm him down. 'I know you're hurt, Trimble. I love you; I want you to get better,' I was saying. It made him worse. He reminded me that I got him into a 'deal where nothing can go wrong,' and he just went into a rage, his face turned red, and he shouted as loud as he could, almost in my ear, *'Something sure went wrong!'*" Charity stood up and turned her face to the wall. She might have been crying.

"What did you do then?" I asked after a minute.

She turned slowly. "Nothing, because he started shouting again, but it wasn't words. He was in pain. The stress set off his facial nerves. He sank to his knees and started squeezing his face. He let me hold him. I just sat and rocked back and forth with him, like he was a baby. You know he never shouts, Judge, never."

"What do you want me to do to help you, Charity?"

Charity was trying to keep her face strong. "I don't know. He blames Dave Brody and you, too, except he doesn't know who you are. He spends all his time at home except the three short days that he puts in at work. He may be blaming me, too. I just fret. He may be talking on the phone with that nurse from the hospital. I don't know what he tells her."

She was speaking so much faster than she usually did, but she did sit down again, and I froze a bit when she mentioned Bonnie Owens.

"He buys a lot of travel magazines, a six-inch stack each month. When he was little, he was supposed to go to Six Flags or Disneyland and he couldn't go, broke his leg. And his mama and papa never took him at all. He told me about that a few times. He's losing patience. Well, he never had any patience; he just abided along with me."

"And he doesn't want to wait five years?"

"Right." Was it possible that the five-year wait might also be too long for Charity? I didn't think so. I could not be sure. It didn't make a difference in what I would do.

"Have you some money put aside, some savings?"

"Sure."

"Spend some of it. You don't have to save for the future. Make your life better now. And consult some expensive pain doctor."

"I'll try that, Judge."

"I'll see to arranging another meeting like this. Stay here while I speak to the Fed lawyer."

"Yes." Her voice was still unhappy. It hurt to hear it.

"If the lawyer talks to you, tell him you hope it will work out. Be sure to say you have no personal grievance with him. There's no reason to multiply your host of enemies at the Fed."

As I walked out I touched her shoulder, chiseled ebony. I hoped I felt her tension abate.

Back at my desk I informed the lawyer, "I've spent some time with her. I think she's willing to give you the benefit of the doubt. Just play fairly with her, and this case will stop plaguing us all." I sounded grumpy, which wasn't hard. "The two of you return in nine weeks. Meanwhile, all is peaceful."

"We will try to back off a little."

"Sounds very good to me, Mr. Westridge."

12.

Two days later, Charity and Trimble were tromping around the swell woods surrounding the American Club near Kohler, Wisconsin, a resort well above their means. Neither of them had ever been in a steam bath or had a massage; now they had them every day. The resort crowd was so upper middle class that Charity was unable to catch anyone looking askance at their interracial presence; everyone was studiously sophisticated.

Charity reported to Dave that Trimble's pain lessened and he laughed once in a while. In one of her phone calls to me at my chambers, she told me, and not Dave, that her husband resumed touching her without first turning off every light in the room.

When I saw her face-to-face, I asked her if it was going better between them.

"I can't be sure. Trimble, bless him, always been beautiful—baby, boy, and man and he knows it. You should see the photos.

He loves being looked at, this perfect white man with his tool belt, running around fixing things. The way he walks now, tucking away one side of his face, he's thinking people are looking away from him."

I turned away to think of some wise thing I could say about this, and I could think of nothing. She broke the silence, and I looked at her. She spoke very softly, and her eyes were unfocused.

"A lot of women want to try him on for size, and I think a lot of them did before I came along. I don't know how they liked it, but I think I might be the first one who was good for him. After we got together, he was real happy gliding around in his own world with his audience and me. Now, he thinks, he's lost one of them and me, I'm what he's got left, baby."

She sat there unmoving, and I touched her shoulder. I would have done more to help her, but I had no idea what that might be.

The Wisconsin idyll must have disappointed Tony Plymouth, who spent a day, maybe more, watching through binoculars. Charity saw a man who looked like him parked in the farthest reaches of the hotel lot. She glimpsed his form when she walked out of the indoor sports center and started to jog back to the hotel. She turned a corner, then stopped to hide behind a pump shed. Shortly thereafter, she saw Tony Plymouth leave his vehicle and walk to the hotel. Charity jogged back to the hotel and found Plymouth's empty car with his binoculars resting on the front seat.

Tony Plymouth had clearly decided not to let his Fed investigation slide. If the detective trooped himself all the way into Wisconsin, he was beyond the stage of casual interest. Plymouth had clamped his teeth onto us and would not let go anytime soon.

Charity got Trimble and walked around the resort looking for Plymouth. They saw him sitting in a corner of the reception area. She told Trimble that he was the police officer who might be investigating the robbery of the Fed.

"Oh yeah," Trimble said. "I talked to him last week."

"Really, baby? What you say?" asked the ever cool Charity.

Trimble had left his house to walk to the drugstore and the grocery. When he turned onto the neighborhood's main commercial street, Tony Plymouth pulled his car up and barked out Trimble's name. Trimble stopped and looked.

"Hello, Trimble. I'm Detective Plymouth. I need to talk to you. We can do it in the car. I'll give you a ride to wherever you're going."

Charity had warned him about Plymouth. I had asked her to do so despite the risk in telling Trimble that Plymouth thought a robbery had occurred; if Trimble decided to talk, he would then know whom to contact. But if Trimble was so enraged that he wanted to confess, he could go up to any police officer in Chicago and have himself heard and understood.

"Look, Mr. Young, here are my star and my ID. It's better to do it out here than in the station. Honestly, you don't have a choice."

Trimble decided he would look guilty if he refused to get into the car. He was right.

Tony Plymouth put the car in motion after Trimble told him where he was going, but he pulled over a block away from the drugstore. To me the whole scene meant that the detective did not have much to go on, that he was trying a risky move, one that would let his targets know that he was on their case. Usually it is best to investigate crime the way the best criminals commit crime, with stealth and undercover. Interrogations in a car are not recommended. A car is too open; it is too easy to look out the window and to hear the sounds of the street. Trimble would not feel isolated from the rest of the world. The detective was stuck behind the wheel. There could be no dramatic gestures, no stomping around, no pounding a table.

The automobile interrogation also meant that the detective was still alone on the case. An interrogation in a car can sometimes work but there ought to be two officers, one to keep driving on a freeway while the other did the questioning. That way the suspect wasn't going to think he could simply leave by opening a car door and getting out. Plymouth could keep on driving, but then he couldn't see Trimble, and he needed to see how Trimble reacted.

"I've been wanting to talk with you for a while. You mind if I call you Trimble?"

"What about?"

"It's okay if I call you Trimble?"

"What do you want to talk about?"

"The fire, Trimble. What else?"

"What about the fire?" Trimble folded his arms across his chest, beating a rhythm with his fingers against his upper arms.

"I've done a thorough investigation. There are a lot of odd things about the fire," the detective observed.

"All I know is I got burned." Trimble told Charity he was very edgy despite the two pain pills he had consumed before breakfast.

"There was a lot of smoke, much more than there should have been."

"I wouldn't know," Trimble said.

Plymouth kept his eyes on the windshield, watching people cross in front of him. "And it was an electrical fire, the kind of fire you would know how to set. Why don't you admit you can understand why I would be a little suspicious? That's not much to admit, is it?"

"I didn't set the fire." Trimble unfolded his arms. He fiddled with the outside mirror control and peered into the mirror to see who was walking along the sidewalk.

"Let me tell you, Trimble, I think you did it and you planted a chemical that increased the amount of smoke . . ."

Now Tony Plymouth was staring directly at Trimble, who sat as still as he could.

"I think you planned to sneak out with a whole bunch of money. Your wife would help you. She knows how to get money out."

Trimble started to relax because he knew the detective was just guessing. I don't think that Tony Plymouth would have failed to notice that Trimble was easing up, and I would bet that the detective's heart fell a bit. If Trimble relaxed, then the detective would know he had gone wrong. But he would not know how and he would take another guess.

"The robbery just went wrong," Plymouth said, his voice almost lacerating. "The fire got out of hand, and you never stole anything."

Trimble felt safe. Instead of feeling safe, he should have gotten out of the car and left.

"The fact is, you set the fire, damaged property, and put lives in danger," Tony Plymouth told him. "It's still a serious crime, Trimble."

"Why would I set a fire to burn myself?" Trimble asked confidently.

There was an answer to that one. "Because you figured that nobody would search you if they took you out in an ambulance and your wife could take the money on the way to the hospital."

"That's crazy."

"You never figured you'd get burned so badly, did you?"

"No."

There was silence. Trimble saw a smile grow on the detective's face. Tony Plymouth said, "That's exactly what I thought happened."

"I mean I never set a fire, and I never figured to get burned at all. That's what I mean."

"Okay, you told me what I wanted to know."

As Trimble left the car, the detective got out as well. "Trimble, if you help me, I can help you." Trimble started to walk away. "You know, if you did get the money, it doesn't seem to be doing you a damn bit of good," the detective shouted after him. "All I see is a guy who's hurting. Don't be a sucker, Trimble."

Trimble told Charity that he never looked back. Charity, who has good sense, told Trimble that he did fine.

So Plymouth knew, and he watched them in Wisconsin.

Part Five

Retrial

1.

"I HAVE TO ask you something, Maeve. You never seem to eat anything that requires cutting with a knife. Is this a surgeon thing?"

"What do you mean, Paulie?"

"Suppose you do a bad job cutting a steak—suppose you even cut yourself with a knife—and soon it's all around the city that the neurosurgeon is klutzy with a knife, and that can't be good."

She laughed, a small tinkling laugh. "You have found me out. I only use a knife in the privacy of my own kitchen."

This was our third meeting. I didn't feel I could call any of our encounters a date. One late lunch for a first meeting, one early dinner for our second meeting, and tonight a long schedule, starting late: we saw *Sideman* at Steppenwolf, a play about a jazz musician, then a meal at Vinci, close to the theater, and then Pops for champagne, the most beautiful jazz club in the world, although the elegant blue arch that bisects the ceiling isn't that nice for sound. We would be very tired at the end of the long night; I hope I hadn't planned it this way to avoid sex. Maeve was barely over five feet tall but looked taller because she was very thin, from her fingers to her toes. What she looked like without her clothes was difficult to tell, because I always saw her in opaque, heavy fabrics. When it was cool, she wore gloves. She spoke very rapidly, expressing opinions on everything; she asked questions and listened to answers, but something about her made you think you should answer as quickly as you could. Her short black hair must have taken thirty seconds to fix in the morning, and she didn't waste much time with makeup. She didn't need to; with her very clear skin, hazel eyes like mine, and nice features, she would be good to look at the first thing in the morning, or so I guessed.

These meetings were hard to arrange. Her medical services were in demand. I ask to see her. She would call back. "Paulie, how about Wednesday at seven-thirty? It's my only free time for the week. You all right with that?"

Given the limited menu, I said yes.

"I've checked on you, Trimble." Tony Plymouth said to the electrician one day in the grocery store. "You got your same house, your same car, you don't seem to do much, you go nowhere. I think your partners must be holding all the money. A smart guy wouldn't let his partners hold all the loot. Why trust them if they don't trust you?"

Trimble walked away after Tony Plymouth finished talking.

At the Pancake Place, Plymouth appeared next to Trimble at the counter.

"A lousy cheap pancake for lunch, Trimble. You could afford better. Here's a thought, Trimble. The Fed would pay a reward for recovery of the money; I hear it's ten percent. I hear you can do it anonymously. You do it through me, I'll see you get the reward. Then the money is honestly yours. You can spend it in the light of day." Trimble paid his bill and left without finishing his meal. The detective had told a small lie. The thief cannot collect the reward.

Finally at the door to the drugstore: "If you are the first one to tell me what happened, you won't go to jail. If one of your partners tells me first, then you will go to jail." Trimble started to move away as he heard Plymouth add, "I know about the paramedic. Can you trust him?"

As long as Trimble was telling this to Charity, we were relatively safe. Maybe he was telling it to Charity because he wanted her to go with him to the police, but Charity didn't think so.

* * *

The day after he met Trimble at the drugstore, Plymouth walked up to Dave Brody at a firehouse.

"Look, Brody, I know you hit the Fed and you got millions. I also know you have a lot of partners, too many partners, and one of them is going to take my invitation to the dance and make a deal and the rest of you go to prison for years and years. Why don't you be the first guy? You have a hell of record, saving lives, doing good, and you might get probation. It's the smart thing." The detective said all this, Dave reported, very earnestly.

Dave said, "I don't have the faintest fucking idea what the fuck you are talking about and I have no fucking desire to dance with some fucking detective, so fucking arrest me or fucking go away."

Plymouth smiled and withdrew. Trimble was his shot.

At the second chambers conference on Charity's case I told the Fed lawyer that Charity was not going to pursue her latest petition. We might need a little goodwill at the Fed so Charity would have leeway.

As we pretended to confer on the case, Charity reported that Trimble was more pleasant but he was buying books on plastic surgery, reading them, and throwing them out. He rarely slept through the night, and he often rejected whatever Charity offered to do for him—get his pills, rub his back, bring him ice, or make love.

"If there is an emergency, phone here and leave a message that you are calling for the Celtic Lawyers' League. I'll call you at home that night," I said.

"You see, Judge, I don't know if I love Trimble anymore; maybe it's all used up."

"You still have some feelings for him?" I asked, while thinking how I'd like to ask the same question about her feelings toward Dave.

"I do. I do." She shook her head up and down, tight little nods.

"It could be what you're feeling is love under stress, still love, just changed a little. Love does that," I suggested.

"It's more like sympathy or guilt I feel."

"How can you tell?"

"It's never fun to be with him. I just know that I would feel worse if I left him. I got him into this."

Her night with Dave a while ago, which she did not mention to me but which Dave had come to my door to declare at dawn, had to be unforgivable to her: Trimble in the hospital for rehab and Charity tumbling in another man's bed. It would be better to forget that night. I wonder if the memory of it came back to her, as it did to Dave; always unbidden just as my sexual images of Ellen arrive uninvited. As vivid as the living moment, the relapse soothes me for a few moments until I suppress it before it slices me open. I would not ask Charity about any of this.

Dave had asked Charity to meet him late in the afternoon the previous week at the Moosehead just east and north of the Loop. She might have thought there was business to be done, but Dave simply needed to be with her.

They did not stay long at the Moosehead. The music can be good but the air was smoke filled, people were loud, and the interior lights had a reddish tinge. It looks too much like the hell that the two of them had heard about on a hundred Sundays in church.

They needed a quiet green forest glade on a sweet summer day—very hard to find in Chicago. They drove three and a half miles north to Belmont Harbor and walked among the trees and the big boats there in the cold water and the runners weaving through the paths. With the sun in an open pale blue sky, the light in Chicago is bright, not bleak. They did not make love, they talked, but Dave would tell me that they knew the boundary between them had disappeared. My insides churned like wet cement. That boundary was the key to our survival.

In my living room, we sat on metal and cane Mies chairs and talked it over.

"Dave, you going to cross the line where that boundary used to be?"

He said nothing.

I looked at Dave and I thought: There are always changing shifts and overtime and compensatory time in an organization as big as the Fed. It would be simple for Charity to sneak time from her job and from Trimble to give to Dave. They could be with each other often. They could make love and talk and spend the time holding each other in the quiet of the day. Dave could convince himself that this would help her endure Trimble.

Dave and Charity would be fearless in love. Dave reminded me that I picked them to help steal a hundred million dollars precisely because they were fearless.

My father warned me years earlier, "There are no unmixed blessings, boyo." I heard his voice now.

I could foresee it: a room in a downtown hotel, a nice room with bright chintz, pulling clothes off, touching, carrying, pushing, squeezing, then moving in nature's cadence and then stopping, resting, and warming each other.

This was very attractive idiocy. Dave was wrong about Charity. She would keep to her Baptist tenets of sin and faithfulness even when Dave buried his sense of culpa. The boundary between them was still intact for her even if it had dissolved for him. She might make love with him, because she was a woman who wanted to be with a man and Dave knew as well as any man how to invoke that desire, and Dave would be better for it and Charity would be worse. Each time would make her worse. The time she spent back with Trimble after her tryst with Dave—these hours would finish her off.

"You love her, Dave?"

"Yes, Paulie." He raised his gaze from his feet to my face, and I thought again of all our double plays.

"Yes," I said.

Dave, in love, believed that he would fulfill any woman he loved. It was his faith. He had no religion I knew about; he had only that blind faith, unshakeable by fact. He had loved the grand witch Bridget Ryan for a long time and he did not fulfill her anywhere but in the bedroom, but even as he gave her up he believed she could never surpass him. He could understand that Charity's spirit might quail at abandoning Trimble, but he would be certain that he would bring her peace.

We shared some wine. We talked a little baseball. We listened to Cyrus Chestnut play some piano. Dave was enjoying our friendship. I was buying time. I did not appeal to reason or to ethics. "Dave, you can't become Charity's lover. Trimble will know. He may not know it's you, but he'll know. He'll turn from an angry man into an insanely angry man, and his only way of destroying her will be to go to the police or worse. He won't care if he destroys himself as well. He won't care if he destroys you. If he does find out it is you with Charity, he will be delighted to do in the both of you. When you are in jail and Charity is in jail, you will not be together. You will not be able to love her or help her. Can you imagine a magnificent woman like Charity in prison?"

My voice was taut, frayed twine. Dave heard me, but he gave me nothing other than silence.

"You will be in prison. Charity will think it is her fault. It will torment her. I am your oldest friend. I will think it is my fault. It will torment me whether or not I, too, am in jail. You will be in prison. Prison is hell."

He shifted in his chair. I was watching him so intently that my temples began to ache.

"I am your oldest friend. I conceived this entire plan, and I saw to it that it was completed. I am responsible for what happens to you."

Not a sound from him or a move.

"I am your oldest friend."

Finally, a slight shake of the head, up and down, not side to side, a yes from Dave Brody, I was his oldest friend.

"Stay away from Charity. Stay away because I ask you to, because we owe each other too much for you to refuse. Do not tempt her. Just as you would not have tempted my wife, Ellen. Please, I ask, do not make love to her."

"All right, Paulie." He agreed so quietly that I could barely hear him. I did not want to make him repeat it.

I turned away for a minute, glanced at the mantel, examined my hands. Then I looked at Dave and felt my confidence waver a touch. I could make it easier. "Dave, this is not forever. It's just for a time, now, until it is safe."

We had another drink and listened to more music and let the tension dissipate.

2

I BEGAN THE day with a run along the lakefront. The water was high and I got tired of trying to keep my feet out of the waves spilling over the breakwater around Chicago Avenue, so I jogged over the footbridge at North Avenue and went into Lincoln Park. I was tired when I finished two miles at the Lincoln Park Tennis Club on Diversey. I slowed when I saw Prindiville playing tennis, as I had occasionally. He cheated on his line calls sometimes.

I hoped Dave had an exhausting day on his shift—many exhausting days—and a lot of mandatory overtime. It would be good to take up his nights with jazz—even a trip to New York, the Vanguard, the Standard, the Blue Note, Sweet Basil, Birdland, Smalls. I could kill a week in New York if I had to get him away from Charity.

When I got to the office I found a voice mail message from Tony Plymouth, who wanted some advice about "Fed Chief Prindiville and some other things, if it wasn't too much trouble." I retrieved my tape recorder from my wall safe. I picked the large office of my chambers. The tape recorder was in open view on my writing table, but the detective could not see that the spools were moving.

Plymouth had managed another meeting with Prindiville, who must have enjoyed putting the detective in his place. In Prindiville's utopia, he would be at the top and his occupation would be to see that other people became acutely conscious that they were in pigeonholes well below him—that would be his ideal labor of love.

Prindiville had another person sit in on the interview, a

prover, to back up whatever version of the meeting that Prindiville would recount. Of course he picked Corman.

"This Prindiville was a wiseass right from the start," Plymouth said, leaning forward, his eyes brighter, less blank. "He asks, 'Have you found all that missing money we allegedly lost? If you've found even a little bit of it, that would be good news. Who knows? We might be running short any day now.'

"I stay cool, I need something from this guy, so I sort of beg him to listen and just keep an open mind. He didn't let up much. 'I hear it all,' he says, 'aliens seizing control of the money supply. Negro clerks putting poison on cash we send to the white people in Minnesota. I don't need another story taken out of the thin air. You aren't a nut, but you are a detective with a gut instinct, and that's almost as bad. Tell me what you know, not what you guess. Try that for a change. I'm listening.'"

Plymouth was animated now, as if he were telling me about the Cubs in the World Series. I listened neutrally while I tented my fingers in front of my face. "I have nothing to lose and who knows, so I lay it out. I tell him the theft started when the thieves started an electrical fire, which Trimble Young could do in a lot of ways. They planted smoke-bomb material to get mucho smoke from that fire, and then Trimble set a small controlled fire on himself to create an emergency. He had to do this because he couldn't carry much money out. The emergency gave his wife a good excuse to run to his side. So right at the time he needs it, Trimble gets another pair of hands to grab cash while the smoke is screwing up the security cameras. And she gives an order to get the paramedics, and that is the final thing that they need. The paramedics brought down the gurney. They stuffed the money into the mattress pad—it was the only place they had to put it. They could have shoved five or six million into the stretcher. So the paramedics are in on it. I tried it myself, and that's how much bond paper I stuffed into a mattress cover—same volume as a gurney pad. Then they run out of the vault and into the ambulance with the security people holding the door open for them. I don't blame the guards; I would have done the same myself."

That made sense, I thought. What a good plan. "What was Prindiville doing when you said this—smiling, laughing, turning up his nose? And what did he say to you, Detective?"

"He kept a straight face, Judge, but his sidekick, this Corman, he looked interested. When I stop, Prindiville asked me, 'Are you deaf? Didn't you hear me ask you to tell us what you can prove? Where is the proof? . . . Am I going too fast for you?' He's an icy one, that Prindiville.

"I told him that, logically, it was the only way it could have been done. He says, yes, it is more logical than the maharishi yoga mystics who are teleporting currency from the San Francisco Fed to build luxury ashrams. But no proof.

"I'd be a big dumb ass if I didn't expect him to say that, and I did have a piece of evidence. What I had, Judge, is that I've been talking to Trimble, the electrician who got burned. It's pretty clear he was burned worse than he thought he would be, and I had reason to believe he was unhappy about what happened. And I don't think he was the leader, so there is a chance he is angry at whoever got him into it. When I said this, about Trimble not being a leader, this Corman popped out with 'That's true. He especially was not a leader around the bitch.' Corman shut up when he saw Prindiville glaring at him. I jumped right in with my only real piece of evidence.

"You see, this Trimble slipped up when he talked to me. I told him he never figured he'd get burned so bad. He didn't give me the blank look or ask what the hell I meant; he just said 'no' as in, 'No, I was surprised by how bad the burns were.' And he knew he had said the wrong thing; his face went red, and he told me that he didn't mean what it sounded like he meant." Plymouth paused and looked at me as if I could issue a warrant this minute. "It's not enough to take to court, but it tells us that this thing ought to be pushed hard."

Be calm. Press fingers into one another. Breathe slowly and don't be like Trimble.

"Prindiville didn't give a shit. He says, 'Pardon me for asking, Detective, but did you find any goddamned money?'

"No, I didn't, I said, and I wouldn't until he took this seriously and admitted there had been a robbery. It's the only way you can turn up the heat on Trimble or Charity, I told him. If they know you're after them then Trimble will crack or someone will, or they'll grab the money and head for the borders. I could see this jerk start to laugh.

" 'I don't want to ruin this for you,' he says, 'but I must remind you that we searched the ambulance and secured the gurney, and we searched it too and there was no money, not even spare change from someone's pocket.' He pulls out a thick report with a fancy computer graphic cover depicting a flame.

"The title was *Final Report, Storage Vault Fire Incident* in big letters. He dropped it on the table, telling me, 'I'd like to give you a copy of this to take with you, but you know federal regulations. We aren't fools; we looked in the pad. It was all foam rubber.'

"They switched pads in the emergency room, I told him. He said no one saw it, and a lot of people were watching. I said they could have made the switch outside. He says how is it no one saw some guy walking around with a big pad weighted down with five million bucks. Then Prindiville said something that made sense."

"He did?" I said. My voice sounded hollow.

"'Might I also point out, Detective, that we know Charity and Trimble did not have any stolen cash. We searched every paramedic around the emergency room. So now there is another mysterious person committing this noncrime.'

"I got up and got out of there."

I crossed my legs carefully. The detective still could not conceive of the size of the theft. But he might eventually think of a handmade gurney, a larger theft, a wider conspiracy. Plymouth was not surrendering.

"Judge, you remember the husband and wife at the Fed, the two who I made for a big robbery?" he asked.

"Yes."

"You remember the wife got promoted because of some lawsuit?"

"I think I do."

"You were the judge who had that case. I pulled the court file."

Going through the court file in *Scott v. Board of Governors of the Federal Reserve Bank* he would have found my opinion, when I refused to throw the case out. In those kinds of opinions you assume that the plaintiffs are truthful, so the opinion would present Charity's case in the best light possible.

He wondered whether I would have some insight into Charity and Trimble. So he came by to ask, he said.

This could be true, or he could be telling me that he knew I was involved. "What case?" I asked him.

"Two people sued the Federal Reserve for employment discrimination. You ruled in their favor some time ago. You remember the case?"

I fought off an unexpected tremor. It had never happened before, not even when I was in the Army and I slipped into the house of an East German secret police officer to retrieve a tape recorder. I counted on the fact that I have trained myself to look as if I am thinking about and genuinely interested in anything anyone brings to me, no matter how little thought or interest is required. Plymouth could buy that act. "I have had a lot of cases, Detective. But if you tell me something about the case, I might remember."

"The plaintiffs were Charity Scott and Trimble Young."

"Names are the first thing I forget."

"She was a black security guard; he was a white electrician. They said they were being harassed because of an interracial marriage."

"Yes. I do remember that case."

Tony Plymouth tilted his head.

"There was proof of discrimination," I said, "more of it against her than against him. The man never got along well with his bosses. Her career was fine until she started up with him. The matter should have been resolved before it ever arrived in court—the Fed had administrative hearings and they knew what the evidence was, but sometimes they need to have an outsider, like a judge, tell them what to do." When I stopped talking, I realized I had said too much. So why stop now? I added a small lie: "The Fed officials were willing to listen and to change their position."

"From my experience," Tony Plymouth added, "I don't think they're willing to listen."

Now I felt a slow roll of nausea. Perhaps I wasn't nervous. Chills, nausea, maybe it was the flu. Tony Plymouth was a true cop. I wanted him out of the room. "I wouldn't trust my memory of that case anymore," I said, a little too hurried, "except that I thought the plaintiff was right but the law was not much on her side. I have no idea whether she or her husband would be able to commit a robbery or even willing to do it. I'll reread the file if you want me to."

"I would appreciate that," the detective answered.

As we walked toward the door, Tony Plymouth said, "I wanted to ask—you think the Supreme Court leaned over too far for the suspect, too far against the police with suppressing evidence even when it is the truth?"

"Yes, they did, way too far, but I have to do as the Supreme Court says."

"Right, Judge," were his parting words. His eyes were back in their blank poker-player cast.

I had a patent case before me, a huge case and a plausible reason to cut off the meeting. There were large boxes labeled "Conway Packaging Patent Cases" sitting on my love seat. I was going to end the interview as soon as he asked a single question about me. I didn't bother listening to the tape. I knew whom I was dealing with now. Mrs. Tiger picked that moment to walk in and see me burning the tape in one of the few remaining ashtrays in the no-smoking federal courthouse.

"Gosh, Judge, are we burning incriminating tapes?"

"Yes, Mrs. Tiger, we are," I said, and she laughed. She did not ask another question; she left, as a good secretary would.

It is, as my mother would say, "ill fortune of Irish proportions" that it is Tony Plymouth who now investigates my crime. I wonder if the next time I see the detective, he will try to arrest me. I think I could outrun him. I see myself with my robes flying as I run out of the courthouse and the detective pants to follow. And I have no sense of humor.

"Judge, it's Senator Kray calling."

I pulled away from Conway Packaging patent papers and reached for the phone. "Hi, Dan, what's up?"

"You, Paulie. You're up," said our avuncular senior senator from Illinois. "I want to push your name for the vacancy on the court of appeals. I hear the White House doesn't have a candidate who can be confirmed. But I don't want to start this deal unless you want the job. And you have to tell me now. I see the President in two hours—I mean, that's all the goddamn notice they give me." The senator always acted as if he were under siege as he martyred himself to his constituents. "My agenda is one item, the Hillside Strangler intersection west of the city, but that's a highway money issue, which means I got room for one people issue, so how about it? You're a good judge—at least, that's your reputation, and I personally think you're okay and you know what I think of lawyers. Always need sensible people up there. What d'you think?"

In his rush of hail-fellow rhetoric I was thinking how I was trying to avoid a bank robbery rap and I couldn't believe the timing of this phone call.

"Well, Senator, it's an honor—" I began.

It was an accident, really, that I was sitting on the bench in the first place. I had always suspected that federal judges rarely came from the ranks of those who, like me, had only a vague idea about how to get the job. I wanted to be a judge for the power, responsibility, and interesting work, but I did not want it enough to learn more about obtaining it. If I had learned, I would have known you can't plan on being a federal judge any more than you can plan on funding your retirement from lottery winnings.

The managing partner of my law firm had a very clear grasp of the mechanics of judicial selection and no interest at all in having a judgeship for himself. A year came in which two candidates vied for the favor of a United States senator who would recommend one of them to the president of the United States, who would in turn nominate that candidate to be a United States district judge. The senator had decided the next judge should come from a large firm. It was the big-firm turn. He was not very picky about judges. The senator did not like deciding; it disappointed many worthy applicants and thrilled one winner who, as a judge, could never return any favor to him. His successor, Dan Kray, was, I believed, a little more choosy, but then again Kray was about to endorse a multiple felon for the court of appeals.

My senior partner despised both of the two likely nominees. Each of them had been his rival in lawsuits and deals over the years. To defeat them, he adopted the tricky strategy of trying to shore up the support of whichever one lagged in the senator's favor, while bringing up unkind rumors about the front-runner. When the two candidates slew one another, my senior partner proposed my name. He liked me, although that was the least of his reasons for putting me forward. My appointment would be seen as a sign of his power, and my visible career as a lawyer made my confirmation more likely than that of any of the others in the firm who would be willing to take the pay cut that went with the office. I became a federal judge with virtually no effort on my part. I was thirty-eight years old.

I was happy about winning the prize. Ellen was very proud of me.

The court of appeals was interesting work, and, if you are already a district judge, the judge makers will always give you a quick look as a possible appeals judge. A district judge might be facing odds of thirty to one against going to the court of appeals, compared to the odds of a thousand to one against his or her becoming a district judge in the first place. I would miss the action of the district court, and I would miss the sense of unshared responsibility that the trial judge has to accept. On a court of appeals, you can do very little by yourself; you always need at least one other judge to go along. I did not want the job, but I was obsessed, maybe for good reason, but still obsessed with the robbery and its consequences, and because I was looking for something to take my mind off that subject, I told Dan Kray to put my name into the hopper. If I were convicted as a bank robber, Dan would be embarrassed and so would the President if he nominated me, but that would be the least of my sins.

3.

TRIMBLE, AWAKENED AT four a.m. by a headache, turned on the light and took a pill. Charity reached her hand to his, to hold it. He tore his hand away.

"You all right, baby?" she asked.

"No," he replied, short and sharp.

"Aren't the pills working?"

"Not the pills. It's the money. You ever seen the money yourself—I mean, actually seen it?" His voice was trembling; she thought it was rage.

"No. Not actually," she admitted.

"How do you know there is going to be any money for us in four years?"

"We all agreed."

"I don't trust anybody."

"I do," Charity whispered.

"I want to see the money."

"That just increases the risk, baby."

"What happens if we wait all these years and then there's no money? What are we gonna do, go tell the cops?" Trimble's voice had an acrid tone now.

"I don't know if I can arrange it. Honestly I don't, Trimble."

"Tell them if I don't see the money, I'm going to the cops and cut a deal."

"Trimble, I love you, baby," Charity answered quickly. "This is wrong. You can't do a deal with the cops without getting us both thrown in jail."

"That's not what Detective Plymouth says."

"That man has been trying to lead you astray for months, baby. He doesn't care about you. Just looking for a promotion, that's all. How come you're believing him now?" Charity was caressing him now, her hand on his spine as if he were a spooked cat. She avoided the grayish, damaged skin of his arm and shoulder.

"Fuck believing him. I'm just wanting to see money. I'm calling him unless I see cash. Your friends, they'll listen to that. That I believe."

Trimble wanted what he wanted. "Why can't we use some of the goddamn money now, right now?" he went on. "Your friends downtown tell you eighteen million is too much. It's my share, right? Okay, I buy that, but why don't I get to hide my own share myself and spend a couple of hundred thousand a year? You could hide your share, too. You could quit your job and we could get out of here, go to fancy places."

"You don't think Detective Plymouth would notice that?"

"Not if it was just two hundred thousand."

"He wouldn't notice that I quit my job?"

Charity took one of Trimble's pain pills.

"I want to see the money. I mean it. Talk to those guys soon, will ya?"

Charity swallowed the pill. "Yes, I will."

She leaned over to kiss him. She did not like the phrases "my share" and "your share."

"I love you, baby," she lied then.

A switch had just been thrown, and she was dark inside.

I received a message from the Celtic Lawyers' League. When I returned Charity's call Trimble picked up the phone, and I used my gruffest voice to ask for Lieutenant Scott.

"This is Lieutenant Scott."

"Can we speak?"

"Not really."

"He is standing there?"

"Yes, he is." Charity turned from the mouthpiece of the phone, and I heard her say, "They're asking if you're okay." I heard Trimble mutter, "Yeah, yeah."

"We need to meet, I assume?" I asked.

"Yes, sir."

"Urgently?"

"Yes, I'd say so, definitely."

"Buckingham Fountain then, at three."

"I'll be there, sir."

Charity told Trimble that she had to go in for the evening shift. Trimble did not give a damn. In the afternoon he took a nap. Charity held his hand, hoping to calm him. When she got up from the bed, Trimble slept on. His bottle of pain pills was open; he breathed slowly and deeply. She moved quietly, trying not to wake him. In their living room, she passed a small writing desk with a blotter, a pen lying on it and, in the wastebasket, some paper torn into tiny pieces. She thought he was probably trying to write a letter to Tony Plymouth.

Sitting in the wind-driven spray of the fountain, she whispered her story to me. I told her to come out to meet me and Dave Brody at the cabin that evening.

The Taste of Chicago festival was long over, and the place was peaceful, the weather mild. "Come after dark; take special care you're not followed. If you are followed, turn your car around and lose yourself. Don't go home. He's expecting you to work the evening shift until eleven."

We three met in the darkened cabin. Charity looked worse than she had in the afternoon. Her ebony skin had a slight tinge of gray as she repeated her story for Dave. Her voice was completely flat.

Dave spoke first, in the soothing medical voice he used to keep accident victims calm. "I can see his point. The idea was we would do the job and then go back to our old lives for five years. He can't go back, and he's sick and bitter."

"And?" asked Charity.

"It happens to firemen who get hurt on the job and have to quit. They keep getting paid; it's not enough. They turn sour. It's common," Dave finished. "I've seen it before."

"Does it work itself out?" I hoped aloud.

"I never saw one that did. When they start to go, they drink, they whack their wives and kids, nobody wants to be with them, they drink more, smoke dope, they wind up alone, just them and their disability pay." Dave watched Charity while he gave his prognosis, and I wondered if on some level he wanted Trimble to fail so badly as a husband that Charity would have to leave him.

Dead silence. Dave broke it.

"I don't want to say this, Charity, but we have got to get away from this somehow. Otherwise, all of us, including him, are going to be ruined. . . . He isn't Trimble. He is a different person." Dave was speaking slowly. I could tell he was pained by what he was saying, but he was also cold in a way I had not seen before.

Then I realized Dave meant we had to kill Trimble.

Charity read him the same way, and she sat on the filthy floor.

There was no sound now other than crickets and our inhales and exhales. Charity's eyes reflected light. I could not see if the light arose from tears.

"I think Dave has a point, Charity."

"Yes," Charity said in a choked voice.

"How do we..." Dave wondered.

"Let me think..." I stalled for time. I would not say another word that night.

As we prepared to leave, emerging from the spring gloom of the musty cabin, Charity asked the open night air for its opinion. "So now we're murderers?"

The reply was silence; nothing was settled. We had traveled very far since last June.

I wanted to get angry again. At Ellen for leaving me, at every foolish hypocritical and grandiose Brother I knew from Mater Dei, at Prindiville, at Maeve Nolan whom I could see on Wednesday night if I wanted to, at foolish venal defendants or the careless, uncaring government. I needed the sort of case that comes up to you, shakes your shoulder, and yells in your ear.

United States v. Seth Aranow was prosecuted by Alfred Dodd Pullman, the assistant attorney general, Civil Division, an appointee of the President and not simply an aide to the attorney general. One does not often see such an officer appear personally in federal court. Pullman, the son of a congressman, had been a New York county prosecutor from Westchester with a national reputation for toughness. He was in the Civil Division because he wanted to broaden his experience. Apparently he was being groomed for something. He had been assigned some very public cases. Even I, in the far-off Midwest, had heard of him. His work in the courtroom, when he did some of it, was excellent.

In the middle of the first substantive hearing in the case about a Department of Agriculture whistle-blower, Trimble Young walked into the courtroom and I was shaken enough to call a quick recess. As I left the bench, I saw him sidle up to my minute clerk. He wanted to see me, I was told. I said yes, and he walked into my chambers.

"I have, Judge, I mean I need, well, a question—can I ask you, is it legal, you know, to ask. I don't know anyone else—it's important."

Of course, it isn't legal for a plaintiff in a lawsuit to ask advice, but who was I to tell that to Trimble? "Go right ahead, Mr. Young. I don't know if I can help you, but I'd be glad to try." I tried out a winning smile, and I spoke slowly as though he might have trouble understanding me. He pushed his hand through his silken hair and then just stood there.

"Let's sit down, Mr. Young. Why don't we, right over here?"

He lowered himself into the red leather chair from which he could see a very angry Lake Michigan. The water looked gray on the swells and chops.

"What is your question?" I asked very softly. I sat in the chair closest to him and canted in. We were almost shoulder to shoulder.

"What I mean, this is just an 'if' question," he said.

"Sure, I understand, an 'if' question."

"It's about the court case, over my job. You know it."

"Yes," I said, "I believe I remember it—your job, was it at the Federal Reserve?"

"Wow, you do remember. It's about that job." He was pleased.

"Is that why you came to me?" I held my breath to keep from showing my fear that Trimble thought I was the author of his troubles.

"I don't know who to go to—you're the only law person I know."

I waited for more and then, when it came, it came in an unexpected way, with quickly spoken words: "Suppose I knew about something real bad at the bank and maybe I know 'cause I did a little bit of the bad things, but it wasn't my idea and I wasn't in charge or anything and it wasn't my fault because I didn't understand what I was doing, and my question is, could I still keep my job over there?"

"The answer is probably no. I could not stop them from firing you," I said.

"Well, now, what if I came forward and told them about this bad stuff, about which they don't know. What if I, you know, revealed it to them, could I keep my job?"

All this time he was pushing his hair back and sideways. He started to tap his feet, alternating right and left; I could not hear the tap on the carpet, but I saw the little tremors and I looked down and then I peered at his face, all the while considering my answer. On his face were a few graceful, crescent-shaped scars along his jawline from chin to ear. They had not puckered; they were faintly red and looked to be fading. He was not going to be severely disfigured. What was setting him off?

"Mr. Young, I am afraid the answer is still no, but I have to tell you I am assuming you are talking about bad stuff, not something minor." I spoke the truth. "Is there anything else you want to discuss?" I asked.

His appearance changed; he compressed his lips, stopped fidgeting, and balled his hands into fists. "No, thanks for your . . . I mean, thanks, but I better go," he said rising and striding to the door. I walked with him out to the hall between my chambers and the judge's back door to the courtroom.

"You can talk to me again, if you think it is important," I said to his back as his stride became longer and faster; maybe he did not hear me. He turned left to the elevators. I pushed open the door to the courtroom and someone said, "All rise."

Seth Aranow was a whistle-blower, a small, roundish goofy-looking guy—a Disney cartoon of a man. Whistle-blowing is a noble act rarely undertaken by noble people. When somebody blows the whistle on his employers, you usually find he was on the verge of being fired or demoted or he is trying to make trouble for someone he doesn't like. The government said Aranow was trying to blame someone else for his own negligence.

Cases usually reveal themselves to me in one fell swoop—that is, if you consider a three-week trial or a four-hundred-page motion for summary judgment to be a fell swoop. In the opening statements at trial, each side sets forth its proposed final draft of the truth and then I see which one is backed up by the evidence. Often I think I know which one is the truth before I hear the evidence. One version makes sense and the other does not. I hear the evidence, which I am paid to do. I listen with the hope that I will be surprised.

Aranow was an export officer at Agriculture detailed to clear large-scale agri-product shipments to Third World countries who were paying with foreign-aid funds or loans. Impure soy-based baby formula went to Africa; a dozen babies died in West

African nations; many more became gravely ill. News stories moved to the front pages when Seth Aranow told *The Washington Post* that the government knew of the high risk of contamination when it approved the shipment. He told reporters that, as the father of two small children, he was having trouble sleeping. He said the shipment was related to an arms trade that the United States made with one of the African countries.

The government reacted to the story with a denial and then with a lawsuit. Pullman was demanding a prompt hearing, to which he was entitled. He asked for a short date. I gave him the following Monday, a very short time to wait.

4.

WHEN THE SUN cleared the watery horizon, I went marching through the woods by the cabin with my mattock, stopping here and there to swing the pick over my head into the earth. I stopped to check its diameter of every soft spot, looking now for places to bury things. I came out of the woods, dripping wet. I sat on the rear porch, closed my eyes, and tried to catnap as I waited for Dave.

When I opened my eyes, I saw Dave's unhappy face.

"I found some new spots in the woods, Dave."

Dave bowed his head slightly, looking as though he wanted to say something and, thinking better of it, moved to a seat next to me. He would sense my pangs, my distress radiating outward. Dave had seen my sadness before; a new element was my disquiet. I tried to find the right word to describe my state of mind; "perplexed" was what came to me. It had to be the first time I was perplexed in my life since I was little.

"You remember my Uncle Seamus?" Dave asked.

"No."

"The one who went to prison?"

"Oh, that one. I don't think I ever met him."

"When he was an old man, he told me he made three mistakes in his life."

"Those were?"

"He didn't wear a mask, he didn't wear gloves, and he didn't work alone. The last mistake, he said, was the biggest one."

I looked back into the woods, turning this over in my mind. Then I said, "He was quite right. It's first-rate advice, all one needs to know, both technically and morally." I was beginning to notice a certain pontifical quality in my speech—had it always been there?

"What's the moral part of it, Paulie?"

"If you never join with weak people, ones you do not know well, then you will never have to do this..."

"Do you think Charity will hold up?"

"I guess so. When Trimble lost faith in her, he lost her, finally."

Dave fell silent, thinking of Charity free, I suspect. "The money has lost a lot of its flavor for me, you know, Paulie."

"Yes, maybe give it to Catholic Charities or the Salvation Army. You might drop eighteen million in the deposit box along with a bunch of old clothes."

We barely made a faint smile out of it, two bemused Irish in search of the confidence they had weeks ago, when they were young.

"Let's start digging." I said.

"Let's start doing something."

The two of us stripped part of the earth from the hole. It was nothing as hard as the work of digging the hole. We went down through the two feet of dirt and uncovered a small portion of the cash packages. We rested in the cabin, with myself standing at the windows now and again scanning the surroundings with my binoculars. The day was growing bright.

A half-hour later, Charity arrived. Dave moved out of the cabin, and I stayed hidden. Trimble would surely recognize me after our meeting. I felt supremely dignified, a grown man crouching down to hide in an unused summer cabin, breathing stale, dusty air. I peeked out. Charity had arrived alone, and so I showed my face.

"Where's Trimble?" Dave asked.

"He wanted to drive by himself."

"Christ Jesus. You think he's bringing a posse?"

"He wants the money, so I guess no." Charity's voice was drab.

I retreated when Trimble arrived. He seemed to fly out of his nondescript sedan, looking like wrath incarnate. Get close to him and I bet you could have seen him shaking with the emotion of the encounter with Dave and the cash.

"Hey, I'm alone." Trimble's voice was loud and sharp. He took off his coat and his shirt and dropped his pants. The burn scars on his arm and shoulder clearly marked his flesh, reddish and gray, roughly textured, but not very large "See, no transmitters, no signals to the cops."

Dave and Charity stared.

"Get over here, Dave. Check for yourself." I had not expected this aggressiveness from the silent Trimble.

Dave did not hesitate. He searched Trimble very thoroughly, and then he searched Trimble's car. He found nothing.

"Now, can I see the money?" The whine that I had expected crept into his voice.

Dave pointed to the open hole in the ground and handed Trimble a trowel. Trimble worked rapidly until he saw some of the money become visible. It took no time at all. Reaching down he pulled out a plastic bag containing a million dollars. He grasped the bag and looked over his shoulder, a cagey sort of expression replacing his anger.

"I know you want to kill me," he told his wife and Dave. I noted how he was starting to glance at the cabin once every few seconds.

"No, we don't, Trimble," Dave answered. "We want to reason with you."

"I would never hurt you, baby," Charity added.

"Well, you did hurt me. And you want to stop me from hurting you."

Charity, using her sweetest voice, began "But Trimble . . ."

"Well, forget whatever fancy plans you got. I wrote a letter telling the whole story. I left it with a lawyer. If I die, it goes to the police."

Charity put her hands to her face. Her gesture emboldened Trimble. "Yes, yes, think about it, cunt bitch."

Dave's face bloomed with fury at the insult. He pulled out a gun and cocked it.

Charity seemed to skate across the ground between herself and Dave, and her contact with Dave sounded like a forecheck at a hockey game. Dave collapsed beneath her, and his gun flew to the cabin porch. I flinched. Holding Dave on the ground, Charity looked up at Trimble. "I won't let them hurt you, baby." Trimble appeared to believe her. At least he looked impressed.

"Get off me, Charity, for Christ's sake!" Dave shouted.

Charity stood and pulled Dave up with her.

"God damn you," Dave yelled, struggling to quench his anger at Trimble and shake his body loose after the tackle. "Your share is eighteen million. You can fucking have it."

Trimble's rage played out. His face slackened and he looked old and stupid. Rage builds on resistance, and Dave had stopped resisting.

"Not here," Charity told Trimble. "You should be out of the country. We'll give it to you in Canada. Then you go to Switzerland and you stay there. I can come after a while." We had agreed she would say this, but still it seemed wildly imperfect to me that she would utter these words.

Dave said, quietly and firmly, "If you come back, I will kill you."

"I'm supposed to go off to Canada and trust you?" The whine was back.

"No, no, don't you see? If we don't deliver the money, you can go to the cops."

"I'll need some money to go up to Canada. I want to start leading the good life now. I'll take this package here as a sign of good faith." The voice was clearer now, but the expression on his face had morphed into a slight smirk.

"You take the package, and I'll shoot you here and now." Dave moved to the gun, and Charity did not stop him. Trimble stayed unmoving.

Charity started to plead. "It'll work out, baby. Just empty all of our bank accounts, take the pension money, too. Take it all. Pay me back out of your share. That's a guarantee you'll get the money."

Trimble hesitated, his hand suspended above the package of hundred-dollar bills.

"Look," Dave said, his voice calmer, "you do want the money. What's three days more to wait? If you didn't want the money, you would have brought the cops today."

Trimble shrugged and walked off, looking at nothing and no one. He drove away. I rose painfully from my crouch. Even my eyes hurt from looking out with such intensity. Charity and Dave trudged toward the cabin.

Inside the cabin, Charity sat on the floor, her knees pulled to her chin, arms wrapped around her legs, rocking slightly, her eyes on a window. From her position she would see treetops and clouds. Dave walked slowly from one wall to the other, keeping away from Charity. I moved to the window, to bring myself into Charity's sight line. I looked out on the lake.

"The very thing," I said, "going to Canada. How much money can he pull together from your accounts?"

"Right away, about twelve thousand dollars. If we tap IRAs, that kind of stuff, he could take twenty-five or fifty, but he would need my signature."

"Charity, the more money he takes, the better."

"Yes, I can see why he would relax with the money in his hands." She sounded like a mother with a hyperactive child.

"Right, but I had another reason in my mind. If he crosses the border with more than ten thousand in cash and he fails to declare it, he commits a violation of federal law. If he ever gets to the police, I want him to have committed as many bad acts as possible. It will give the police a little pause before they believe him. And give us a little time."

Dave Brody gave me a wry smile. He loved these tricks with the law.

"There's more, Charity." I concentrated on the lake outside. "You have to see a lawyer and complain that Trimble has taken all the money without your permission, that he has stolen everything and you want a divorce. I'll get some cash to you. Pay the lawyer extra money to file the papers in court on the next day.

The divorce dispute is a reason why we can argue that Trimble would lie about you to the police."

"Damn, Judge."

It was a damned sort of thing to do, a final severance of Trimble and Charity, I thought to myself, as I gazed at the lake through my binoculars and I saw Tony Plymouth on the opposite shore watching the cabin through his own binoculars.

I felt almost nothing when I saw him except a frisson of fear I swallowed. It seemed somehow appropriate that he should be here, so close to the cash and the criminals—the next step in the game. I had no notion how long he had been there. I doubted that he could have found out about the cabin except by following someone up here. He might have tapped a telephone illegally. I thought he was not that sort.

He could have followed anyone up except for myself. It was so early when I drove up that there were no other cars in sight for the last few miles up to the cabin.

I told Charity and Dave to stay away from the window, and then told them why. They reacted as I had, it seemed, with tense weariness and not surprise. Neither of them had noticed a car following them. I hoped it was Trimble he followed. If it were Trimble, then Plymouth had not seen me.

If Tony Plymouth had randomly picked today to follow Trimble around, his best possible hope should have been that the two of them would wind up in a bar where Trimble might drink himself into indiscretion. Plymouth would be thrilled beyond belief to see Trimble's route to a place far out in the country, a hiding place. He must have found the dirt road to the cabin and followed it until he saw the sign warning POSTED, NO TRESPASSING and the large metal plaque saying THE MULLIGANS' WEEKEND SHOWPLACE.

He would have had to back up. It is not against the law to trespass in open fields without a warrant, but the Mulligan sign meant that these were not open fields but a home, and even if he made no search, he would be unable to testify about the things he saw if he was a trespasser when he saw them. He had obviously found the public boat ramp on the opposite side of the small lake, where he was standing when I saw him.

The confrontation would have been nearly over by the time he arrived at the ramp, I calculated. The cabin would block his view. But he should have been able to see Charity and Dave, and he knew Trimble was there. The detective would know, absolutely know, that there had been a crime. There was no other reason for these three people to meet in this out-of-the-way place, a two-hour drive from the Chicago city limits. He might have seen my shadow in the cabin, the fourth thief. If the robbery plan had failed, the thieves would not be meeting. They had to have made it out with some money. He could guess where the money must be. It was still not enough for a warrant. But still.

In the decrepit two-room cabin, I stood unmoving with my binoculars on Tony Plymouth as we worried and talked softly as I told them what I was seeing and thinking. The window was too dirty to be seen through from where he stood, but he might detect movement. My arms were starting to ache.

"I ought to follow Trimble," Dave said.

"Why?" I asked

"We need to know where he is going to be and when."

"We do know already. He's going to be in a hotel, a very nice hotel, in Canada in three days. He'll tell us where he is because he has to—otherwise we can't deliver the money to him. We're going to defeat him when he goes to Canada."

"I damn well hope so, Paulie."

Charity was wordless.

Charity left.

We wondered if Plymouth would leave with her, which he did. That would mean he had followed Trimble. He would track Charity if he wanted to find Trimble again. I did not want to think about what it would mean if he'd waited around after Charity had left or what we would have had to do about it.

Dave was calm now. I asked him how he would do what he was going to do to Trimble. Trimble surely expected an attempt on his life. I did not want to know, really, but I didn't want Dave to think I was putting all the moral burden on him.

"I'll rent a room in the same hotel. Then I'll leave a package for him at the front desk and wait until he picks it up or a bellman takes it to him. That way I'll find his room. I'll take my gear with me, the firefighter coat and helmet and a respirator. I can slide something under his door to smell of smoke and then call him on the house phone and tell him an alarm is triggering on his floor. I go to his door. He looks out, sees the firefighter, and opens the door. I hit him with the butt of the fire ax. Then I drown him in his tub. Maybe they'll think he died by accident. I'll be gone."

It sounded terrible to me. It sounded good to me. "Okay," I said.

We left separately. I was the last to leave and drive home. At three in the morning, I finished the last of my paperwork. I would be ready for the motions and the lawyers on Monday. I had been awake for twenty-two hours.

There was a time when I had talked myself into believing that it was boredom that led me to start down the path of crime. I would trade what I was feeling that Monday morning for a decade of boredom.

5.

DODD PULLMAN WAS redfaced and a little over-weight. He handled only the important moments. Arnold Lawton, the gremlin from Justice who handled the routine parts, was patently odd. He spoke very softly. He showed signs of agitation, even dismay, if it looked as though the sessions in court would extend past his regular five P.M. quitting time. He had some power over the minds of men that made it difficult for them to remember his name. I called him Lawson, Lawler, Larson, Lubin, and Lowman. Unless he stood in front of me, I found it difficult to locate him in the courtroom though I knew he was there. Pullman could be sure that this man would not steal his glory.

Pullman first asked for the return of the papers Aranow had taken to prove his case to the press. A security surveillance tape showed Aranow using a screwdriver to break a lock on an office door and then enter the office. Inside the office, he forced open file cabinets and pulled out papers, then he went to a computer, turned it on, sat there for quite a while, punching the keys; then he took some papers from a printer and left. Aranow had also accidentally erased another export officer's file so a shipment of medical supplies to West Africa was delayed.

Aranow was staring at the floor. Silent and limp, as if his spine had melted, he looked less heroic than before.

When I wafted off the bench for the lunch break, the first slip of paper I saw on my desk was a note that Detective Plymouth had called to see if I could spare a few minutes before noon. Weariness suffocated anxiety. I slipped a new tape into the recorder and asked my secretary to call Plymouth. He was in my study in less than ten minutes.

"There was a robbery. No ifs, ands, or buts. I followed the electrician, and I got lucky. He met up with his wife and the paramedic, someplace in the sticks. They looked like they were arguing. I saw shovels. They could've buried the money out there." His voice was as sharp as a lancet.

"You have enough for a warrant, you think?"

"Your opinion is better than mine."

This seemed merely to be a detached, purely legal discussion, like those about Bill Serena.

"Well, let's see, there's a small chance the warrant might be good, but I'd get some advice from a prosecutor, someone you know and trust. You are, in fact, going to have to say something about the fact that the Fed doesn't think it's been robbed. If you conceal that fact from the judge who issues the warrant, then that's bad."

"Yeah, I don't think I've got enough," Plymouth said. "It's one thing if I find the money. I don't see them coming into court and telling a judge they want it back. They can say it's their dough, but they know the judge is going to ask how they came by a few million dollars and why, if it is honest money, they buried it in the woods next to some old wood cabin."

"The very thing, but if the money is illegally seized, the investigation is over, and you won't get a federal task force. There won't be any legal way to prosecute the thieves. No publicity, no credit to pass around, no good reason to start up a major fraud squad in your department. And, you must know, you will not be getting a thank-you note from the Federal Reserve Bank of Chicago. It won't be like the Serena case, not in any way." I delivered all this strongly to convince him not to go digging at the cabin.

"I know that."

If the stakes were not so high, I would have felt as if I were Plymouth's buddy, the two of us mulling career prospects at the coffee bar in the detective squad room. "Let me ask you—most police like the work a lot, but they look to get assigned to the stuff they like best, and to get promoted. Are you like this, a little bit at least?"

"Yeah, sure. I'd like to be the sergeant or the lieutenant in charge of a fraud unit."

"So you want to be careful not to let the department think you went on a wild-goose chase?"

"Yeah."

"So be careful."

"Yeah."

"You're not happy right now. You do good work, but no one can win every time."

"I'm just not sure what to do. It's a big thing to me."

"Can you tell me why?"

"Well..."

He was off the track for a moment, and he seemed like my other best friend.

"You don't have to. I'm not your priest. But it helps to know why you take one road rather than another, and talking about it helps you to know. I'll keep my mouth shut."

So he told me about a day he worked for Guadalohara, who could not give him any help pursuing some pigeon drop artists preying on the elderly with a forged winning lottery ticket. Guadalohara needed his twenty detectives for a showy house-by-house canvass to find the killers of three white college students; they couldn't safely tell their influential parents that their nice kids were dealing cocaine, shorted the Royals on the pay-off, and got themselves killed. Tony stood alone in a drugstore watching a little park where the con artists work.

"I spot the con artists, two overweight, freckled redheads, one male, one female, with an elderly woman who was leaning forward straining to hear. I knew the pitch: she and her brother had a winning ticket, you can see the number in the *Sun-Times,* and we need money to get me and my baby back to my family, who have never seen the grandchild because my husband is so mean and violent. Problem is that hubby works in yonder Jewel. Please cash it for us. By the way, could you let us hold your watch or ring so we can be sure you will bring the money back? They wait until she enters the store before they run away. The average take was less than four hundred dollars. The victims feel old and foolish. Some go into their shell and never come out. I saw the old woman hand over her watch. I called for two uniformed officers. Just before the uniforms came up behind the couple, I yelled out, 'The cops are here!' The two mopes bolt, but they didn't get very far. As I come up they say, 'We're clean.' The girl told me to fuck myself. 'So, why did you run?' I asked. 'Fuck you,' she says. The old woman asks if she has to go to court. Could not be happier when I tell her yes. Something to do for an old lady. It could have been a tragedy, and now it's an adventure."

"Very neat work." I told him.

"That wasn't the end of it. To top the day off, I go back to the drugstore to pinch the cashier there for theft from her employer. While I was watching the park I saw her running a routine scam with the register tapes whenever the customers pay with a check.

"'One hell of a day,' Guadalohara said, but he didn't care much. It got to me. For years, I got very drunk every night; it took me from midnight to three to get that way. I'd wake up at six and take six aspirin with a half glass of red wine which I laid out when I went to sleep. If I got out of bed without taking my aspirin and wine, I'd get a headache like a spike entering my goddamn head at the chin and going up. I was getting sick from doing the same thing over and over again and for my supervisors who didn't give a rat's ass for the work I did. The Serena case took me right out of that. I want that Fed case; you can see why. Besides, I like to prove I am right." He traced several circles in the air with his left index finger and shrugged.

"Anyone who is any good feels that way," was all I said when he finished. He thanked me after our talk was over. I don't think he would have shared that story with me if I was now a suspect.

6

AT ELEVEN THE next day, Tuesday, after I had managed four hours of something like sleep and had been awakened by Dave Brody telling me that Plymouth had spent his evening sitting in his car across the street from Dave's house, a group of very well dressed lawyers greeted my secretary and said they had an emergency.

Roan Corporation had been buying up many shares of Mercer Protection Systems. In response, Mercer had a plan to use the corporate treasury to buy its own shares back from the public and keep them out of Roan's hands. Roan said this was an illegal self-tender offer designed to keep the Mercer executives ensconced in their plush suites, all to the detriment of the suffering shareholders of Mercer, who deserved the value and dividends that an effective management could provide. Mercer said that Roan was looking to get greenmail. Mercer was unwilling to yield to extortion and buy Roan's shares at a huge profit to the sharklike Roan. Roan said I should order Mercer to stop buying their own shares. Mercer said I should let them go ahead and, while I was at it, order Roan to stop buying.

Whenever many expensive lawyers come to chambers at eleven with a new case, it is an urgent matter. The lawsuit was filed the first thing that morning, but the case would not be docketed and assigned to a judge until a little before eleven. Such cases almost always involve trading on the public markets—shares, bonds, pork bellies, soybeans. The judge has to decide what to do, if anything, before the market opens the next day—he gets the case at eleven, to decide it by the end of the day.

This pressure is exciting, and it occupied my mind until seven when I decided that Mercer was not violating any laws and they could keep buying shares. The Mercer executives had experienced death and resurrection. They floated out of the courtroom. I could go back to spending the waking hours brooding over the rightness of killing Trimble Young.

I managed three hours of sleep that night before my fear forced me awake at one in the morning. From one until dawn, I rethought my way through every method I knew to investigate my crime.

In his property crimes office, just south of the Loop, Tony Plymouth knew that Trimble was no mastermind. He had to wonder whether Dave or Charity was up to planning the theft. He knew there had been another paramedic in the vault. The other paramedic would be a fourth thief, maybe a professional, the planner. His name might be in a police intelligence file.

Trimble, Charity, and Dave were not in any intelligence files as thieves. He would get Charity's military record and her Fed file and find nothing. Plymouth would go to the computers and start searching databases for the very short list of thieves who lead groups to steal from heavily guarded sites and have the ability to broker hot currency for cold currency. He would check this list to eliminate the names of those who are dead or in jail. My name would not be on his list.

The detective would look for something or some person he could focus on. He would call New York, Los Angeles, Washington, and the few other places where detectives like him work in the vineyard of thieves. These calls will knock some more names off the list—people who would not hit anything federal, people working only on the coasts. In the end he would have some names, and he would pull whatever information he could find on each of them. This would lead nowhere. I could hope that he would find one or two names that would be worth a look and divert him, but then he would be unable to link any of them to the three thieves who were in his sights.

If I was lucky, he would stop there. But I had been lucky with Tony Plymouth just once—when he did not see me at the cabin.

He would, eventually, remember he had one other place to look. There was an electrical fire and smoke, and Plymouth believed it was deliberately set. Plymouth would ask an arson investigator to help him.

I fear this most: the arson specialist would know Dave Brody's name. There would be not a scrap of hard evidence, but one of Dave's intermediaries, one of those problem solvers for troubled businesses, might trade Dave's name for a favor from a cop. The police always want to know who is doing what, even if they can't do a blessed thing about it. If Dave's name came up, it would be inspiration for the detective to go on climbing the mountain.

If Plymouth knew about Brody, he would realize that there was nothing he could prove. As good a bet as Brody is for the crime, he would have no leverage on Brody. Plymouth was so careful and so committed here that he would then reread his files and come upon some words I wish I had never written.

In my opinion deciding that Charity had enough evidence to take her case to trial, I said:

> *Taking plaintiff's evidence at face value, I would say this case would not be here in court if the management of the Federal Reserve Bank of Chicago had not been so consistently blind to what was happening on their very premises. The administrators were never engaged in willful discrimination or willful harassment; they were engaged in willful disregard of what was in front of their noses, of what could be seen with only a modest effort to look, an effort that was not undertaken even when it was urged on them by plaintiff Scott and her witnesses. It was and is Federal Reserve policy that neither discrimination nor harassment occur, and since this was a clear policy, the managers therefore believed there could be no problem. Federal Reserve officers were trained not to harass or discriminate. The Federal Reserve had done everything it thought it had to do to prevent these things from happening, and so it believed they did not happen.*

Tony Plymouth, fully steeped in his case, would read this and know something very important. He too had talked with

Redding Prindiville, taken his measure, and seen what I had seen. The Fed chief would not admit that the crime had occurred, even to himself. The detective had probably realized some time ago that the success of this bank robbery did not depend so much on knowing how to steal the money. It relied on knowing how the victim would react. No one would anticipate that reaction better than Judge Devine.

This fact itself would mean nothing until the detective saw some tie between Dave Brody and me. That would not be hard if he dug a bit into the life Dave had lived before he was twenty-one, and there was an easy place to do that.

He would want the fire department files. If he asked for them he would get them, but someone would inform Dave that the cops had pulled all his files, personnel, fitness reports, run reports, and his partner's files too. The detective would not care about that. When he saw Trimble, Charity, and Dave together, the detective knew that he had lost the element of surprise against Dave.

The detective would read the fire department files as they are compiled, in reverse chronological order. He would decide that Brody's partner was the kind of kid who could win forty million in the lottery and not want to quit the fire department. From Brody's stellar record as a firefighter and then as a paramedic, the detective would see why no one wanted to push the torch charge against Dave.

The final papers were the background investigations when Dave and his partner each applied to join the fire department. When the background investigators went around the neighborhood to find out what people had to say about firefighter candidate David Brody, they talked to his closest friend, one Paul Devine. I remember giving that interview, and I remember signing the handwritten version of it that the investigator presented to me. Tony Plymouth would realize I was a common factor in the lives of all three of his suspects, and I would become a candidate for the fourth thief, the leader of the gang—an unlikely candidate, yes, but still a candidate.

Apparently, Tony Plymouth was well into this process. This morning, the day Trimble left for Canada and his suite at the Four Seasons hotel in Montreal, Dave Brody called to tell me that the police had just taken his files.

When I began my time with the Serena case, I was upset with the government people I was beginning to see too often. At the time of the trial, I was very pleased to see an officer like Tony Plymouth. In those days I thought there were not enough Tony Plymouths in the world. Now I think there is one too many.

7.

ANOTHER SHORT HEARING for Aranow. Pullman wanted to break down media support for Aranow. You do better with the media if you feed them in small bites, if for no other reason than that each small bite is a separate story on a separate day and the news hole that media must fill is enormous. A little piece at a time lets the story build nicely for the reporters; with each new tidbit they reprise the older bits. The reporter gets longer stories and you get public repetition of your case. Today Pullman called the assistant secretary of state for African Affairs, who told the truth.

"The President for Life," began the witness, "is our ally. He told us that he wanted news reports about a large arms deal on favorable terms. Our policy precluded such sales on bargain terms. He told us that he did not want the arms; he wanted the news reports about an arms deal to help his negotiations with his unfriendly neighbors. He said that I was a poor listener. He intended to announce the arms purchase and merely wanted us to confirm or at least refuse to deny the truth of the reports. I asked him if he did want any weapons, and he said that he did not trust his own army with the artillery or the planes or the small missiles we had come to talk to him about."

"So no arms deal was made?" Pullman asked him.

"Neither made nor intended."

"Would it have been possible for Mr. Aranow to have confirmed the existence of the arms deal?"

"No." The assistant secretary looked as though he was thinking. Then he said, "He would not know. He could only guess, and he accused his own government on the basis of a wrong guess."

The tone of the media coverage changed. It went from "Aranow, man of courage and conscience" to "Whistle-blower story springs leaks."

Plymouth walked into my courtroom in the middle of an afternoon and sat through two hours of a trial over whether the unusual shape of a noodle could be legally protected as trade dress. There were many boxes of dried pasta lined up on my bench. I raised my hand to him in what I wanted to look like a friendly greeting. If the detective was waiting this long, then I must be a suspect. I suppose it was a point of distinction for me, the first federal judge to be suspected of bank robbery.

When court recessed, Plymouth walked smartly toward the bench. I decided it was better to stay and wait in the courtroom for him. If I left, he might think I was running away. We stood at the clerk's side desk looking at each other across a table holding every possible shape of noodle. Tony Plymouth took a breath and opened his mouth. He was not going to let me speak first, a way for him to exercise some control on the judge's turf. Many lawyers try the same tactic.

"The robbery of the Federal Reserve. I want to talk to you about it."

I hoped that the tired but untroubled expression I always wore at the end of the day was still in place. I raised my eyebrows in inquiry. Let the detective go first. It was my courtroom, and we would operate under my rules.

"You know the robbery I mean?" Plymouth asked.

"The one you told me about. Does the Fed admit it now?"

The detective must have regretted that he already told me his whole theory. If he had not, he could confront me with the story and look for some flicker in the eye, some fear, some pride, something that told him that I already knew the story. He did try to get some reaction by surprising me with a name.

"I wanted to ask you, Judge—do you know a paramedic named Dave Brody?"

Following my rule about speaking only the truth, if not all the truth, I said, "Detective, Dave Brody is one of my oldest, closest friends, ever since childhood. Was he one of the paramedics at the Fed the day of the robbery?"

Tony Plymouth reacted as I had wanted him to. The disappointment was written in his eyes. He needed a lie from me so that he could brace me with the truth—as in "Funny you denying knowing him, you vouched for him at the fire department." Instead he said, "Yes, he was, and one of the robbers has agreed to talk to us. I wondered what your opinion is of your friend Dave Brody." He was trying another tack with me: tell a lie and hope I believe it and say something stupid.

"Honestly, I don't think he's the type to think of robbing a place like the Fed," I said.

I hoped, perversely, that the detective would admire the hurdle I cleared in making another true statement. But he would not know that I was always truthful. He would not infer that I might only be saying that I thought of the robbery and Dave went along for the ride.

"Well, thanks for your help, Judge. I may have to talk to you again."

"Detective, how much did they get away with? What did you say last time?"

To my relief, he still gave me his very low six-million-dollar figure. I feared that Trimble might have told the story to the detective, but I realized that he would not do so as long as he had a hope of getting his money.

"That's quite a haul," I said.

"Yes, sir. It is. Get you a lot of time in federal prison."

"It would in this courtroom. Good afternoon, Detective."

8.

AS THE CASE resumed I was still surrounded by noodles, half listening to the arguments until the end of the day when Charity and I met at the Palmer House, a massive brick hotel, close to the dead center of the Loop. It is well run, brushed up, and updated, a maze created by many renovations over nearly a century.

On the sixth floor there were pay telephones in a cul-de-sac corridor. The surrounding meeting rooms were not being used, and the corridor was deserted. We met to hear from Dave in Canada. Had he killed Trimble by now? If he hadn't done it, then what? Hadn't we already decided? Charity glided into the empty corridor. Her smooth gait was unchanged, but her skin was not so deep a black, her facial bones not so sharp, and her presence not so strong. Dave had driven twelve hours to Montreal. This day we were to murder her husband.

Charity waited. I waited. I could sometimes see myself reflected indistinctly in her eyes.

When I reached for the phone, I said the first thing that came into my head: "If I call this off, we'll still have some time before the worst happens, but Trimble is a fool and will be caught and will tell."

Charity said nothing. The decision was left to me. I had never loved Trimble. I would not be losing him as she had lost him. She had chosen Trimble and trusted him, and she might have believed that Dave and I should not pay the price of that mistake. She would accept blame she did not deserve, a noble trait. She seemed the only one of us with any nobility left; this was my thought.

I called the Four Seasons in Montreal and asked for Carl Crosson, Dave's alias. The phone rang, and then I was transferred to voice mail. I tried every five minutes for half an hour. Charity spoke once. "Doesn't he have a cell phone?" Must be Trimble was already dead and Dave was on his way back. I ignored my nausea and dialed the cell phone number even as I decided that doing it was idiotic. Trimble is dead, someone may find out he was murdered, and Tony Plymouth will get a cell phone record showing that Dave got a call in Canada about the time of the murder. Dave answered before I could hang up.

"Where are you?"

"Outside Montreal."

"I thought you were already there. You are checked in."

"I was. Now I'm coming back."

"Is it done?"

"No."

"Did you say no?"

"I said no." I nodded and Charity said, "Praise God." I saw relief in her eyes.

"What happened? Is he there?"

"Yes, I found him. I couldn't do it."

"Neither could we," I said, sure that it was true of Charity and believing it was true of me. "Thank the Lord, Dave."

"Yes, whatever, but I couldn't."

I put my hand on Charity's shoulder and brought her closer. I put my hand on her face, brought her ear to my lips and whispered, "Trimble is alive. Dave couldn't do it. Dave is coming home." Charity turned into me and embraced me. We stood entwined. It was almost a lover's embrace, and I became embarrassed and pulled away.

"We've got to call Trimble," she said, coming out of her cloud.

He picked up on the first ring. She told him that she and Dave had work emergencies and could not bring him what we had promised. We would deliver it in Chicago and trust him to leave the country on his own. He said he would be back when he felt like it, after he had his car and driver show him around the town. He said he enjoyed living on $1,500 a day.

* * *

I was late for my date with Maeve and rushed into the lobby of the Drake Hotel to meet her. "There was something I just had to do," I told her. "I'm terribly sorry, and I really am happy you waited."

"Look, Paulie, I don't need an excuse," Maeve said, looking up from a medical journal she had spread on the cocktail table. "I waited because I allocated this time to be with you. I would have waited, reading my journals, for a long time. And if this happens one more time, I'll wait then too. But I'm never going to allocate any more time for you after that." She smiled sweetly. "I'm a doctor, I'm scheduled, and that's that. The only way I can do it."

"What would you like for dinner, Maeve? I know the owner of Tru. We can eat in the kitchen."

She whipped her journal shut and stood. "No, the time for dinner is used up. Let's go straight back to my place."

We had sex in her bedroom, its huge windows overlooking the Lincoln Park Zoo. When the clock hit midnight, she said, "I'm on call now. I'm going to try to get as much sleep as I can." Within ninety seconds she was sleeping so quietly that I wondered if she was breathing. When the phone jarred us awake at four A.M., she was dressed and out the door in less than five minutes. I left with her, disheveled. She reminded me that on Friday, I was to be her escort at the black-tie fund-raiser for the hospital and I was to meet her there at nine on the dot. "I want to show you off, Judge," she said, and kissed me, her lips firm.

I thought I wouldn't sleep, so I drove to my chambers.

9.

PULLMAN CALLED ARANOW to the stand. He went straight to the point.

"Do you still contend there was an arms deal?"

"I guess not."

"These shipping licenses, for the baby formula—who signed them?"

"I did."

"Did anyone else sign anything, a memo or an order?"

"No, but my superiors told me orally to sign it."

"Orally, not in writing?"

Aranow said yes in a quiet voice. Pullman commented, "How convenient." Aranow's lawyer objected, and I sustained the objection. Pullman apologized for commenting rather than asking a question.

"Why would they tell you to sign, if there were no secret arms deal?"

"Don't know, but they did."

"This shipment of formula had caused death and sickness among helpless infants about which you feel awful?"

"Oh yes," Aranow answered.

Pullman turned to me. "Your Honor, Mr. Aranow could not endure his own responsibility, and he looked for someone else to blame. A very human thing to do, Your Honor, and if he convinced himself of this and found some solace in it, we would not be here. His sin is that he publicly passed his own blame onto others and damaged the reputation of two other Agriculture employees, and he also created a diplomatic nightmare."

Pullman's conclusion sounded right to me. Aranow's lawyer

had only the word of Aranow who, by now, seemed a dumb cartoon character with an anvil hanging by a thread almost visible above his head. His lawyer's last-ditch effort was to subpoena government files for me to look at and search for some other reason to ship the baby formula.

Pullman professed reluctance to give me the files because he needed to discuss the diplomatic ramifications with his superiors. He asked for time to consult with the deputy attorney general. I said yes. Many lawyers with weak cases like Aranow's will go on a fishing expedition with no good reason to think they might find something that will help their case.

That evening I drove south to visit an old friend recovering from surgery at the University of Chicago Hospital. As I was leaving, I saw Aranow's wife and children in the waiting area next to the emergency room. In court she was bitter faced; I could not tell whether she was upset with me or the government or her husband.

Now she rose from her chair and came toward me, rage in her eyes, her face turning furiously red. When I got to the reception desk where a security guard stood, I stopped walking and turned to her.

Her voice was very hoarse. "You...you...you...you... bastards...bastards...bastards..." Then it fell away and her eyes emptied, her cheeks paled. I walked away. I felt sick and trembled.

Aranow had tried to commit suicide. He left a note about his insurance policies. He was in a coma from which he might or might not awaken.

10.

IN THE EARLY hours of that Friday morning, just before the dawn, after a little side trip to the airport, I drove up and down Lawrence Avenue and then on Addison Street, far west of Wrigley Field—commercial streets full of small establishments with cheap rent and no walk-in trade. These are supply houses; you phone in the order, and they deliver. At night, the street is lined with delivery vans, small trucks, pickups, and station wagons, each one with lettering on doors and side panels. No one thinks they will be stolen, with all those painted signs on their sides.

I looked for a Jeep, a white Jeep, like the one that I was driving. I knew no one would use a Grand Cherokee Limited like mine as the company vehicle, but all I needed was a white Jeep. It took nearly an hour to find one, parked in front of Toomin's Slicers, a storefront displaying two old-fashioned meat-slicing machines—Hobarts, they were. The faded paint on the door promised "slicing machine parts, repairs, all makes and models, all work guaranteed. Thomas and Michael Toomin."

I pulled my Jeep to the rear of the Toomins' old Cherokee. Then I jumped out into the chill of an early-fall day and quickly unscrewed both license plates from the Toomin Jeep and replaced them with two plates I had taken from another car in airport long-term parking less than an hour before. It took less than ninety seconds. I brought the Toomin plates with me. At home, using Ellen's graphics printer, I made a sign for each of the car's front doors. They said TOOMIN'S SLICERS. They looked exactly like the VAN SCOYK SANITATION signs I'd made for our earlier raid on the garbage dump.

I phoned Dave to tell him I was coming, and I met him at Printer's Row, half a mile from the courthouse. The old buildings used to house big printing companies; now they housed people in condominiums. Dave had bought three lofts for investment; he was always doing some improvement project for a tenant. We drove a hundred yards to the railroad bridge, rolled onto the frontage road, and stopped to put the Toomin plates and the Toomin signs on my Jeep.

"Paulie, you think these are the Toomins we know, the ones in our old parish?"

"I don't think so. They were plumbing contractors."

"Idiots too, I seem to remember," Dave remarked.

"That's what they'll say about us, Dave, if we get caught."

We needed to retrieve the money to get Trimble's share and to move the rest of it to a place unknown to Trimble. I reset all my Friday cases.

Charity had taken the train into Union Station. We met there. She climbed in the backseat and fell into a deep sleep. The trick of the veteran soldier—sleep when you can. Dave and I went over my plan.

Traffic was light in the later morning, an easy trip. Dave asked me if I thought that Trimble would try to dig up the money himself. I told him I thought no. After we showed him the money Charity had stayed with him, more or less constantly, until she saw him board the plane for Montreal, and even then she didn't leave the airport until she saw the aircraft push away from the gate. Anyway, that kind of action was too daring a move for a man like Trimble. Trimble would make a deal with Tony Plymouth rather than take the money. He would look to Plymouth to lead him, the way Charity had.

Did I think he would have already talked to Plymouth? No. He would wait until he was sure we would not give him the money.

Why did we have to move the money now? Dave knew Plymouth could not get a warrant. He had no evidence. We knew he had discovered the truth, but his instinct, intelligence, and judgment would not help him get a search warrant. A police officer needs hard evidence or else the word of a reliable and usually disreputable informant. But clever as he is, Plymouth would manage to search the place without a warrant. He would find out whose cabin it was, then charm the old woman who owned it, who would be delighted to cooperate with the police. If, in her great age, she somehow remembered me, her husband's lawyer friend, she might call me to ask for advice about what to do. But I could not count on that.

After the conversation we rode in silence. For all the desperation of the moment, we were pleased with ourselves. It is something worthy, to put ourselves at risk because we could not take another man's life. We were thieves but not murderers. But it was not suitable for a boast, and neither Dave nor I could call his father to report, "Hey, Da, I'm so proud that I'm a thief and not a killer." Hence our silence.

We dropped Charity off at the town diner.

The cabin and the land were undisturbed when we arrived a little before noon. The day was cloudy but bright, and the air had grown warmer. We exchanged pager beeps with Charity to make sure she was in place where we had left her. We picked up our spades and began. The earth was not compacted, so we could work quickly. My Grand Cherokee was pulled up to the lip of the hole. By the time the money packs were visible, both of us were beginning to breathe harder, and I was sopping wet. Charity should be ordering coffee in the little shop and staring out the window while we dug.

In less than an hour we had packed the money into boxes and put the boxes in the Jeep. It was a tight fit.

"Start closing the hole. Let me check the house," I said. Dave picked up his shovel as I walked into the cabin. On the floor I saw footprints and swept them away, then wiped every surface. At the last moment I looked to see if anything had dropped and rolled under the worn-out furniture, and I found two pieces of paper slipped down behind a three-drawer dresser: the computer graphic for the construction of the money trays and the diagram of the gurney. I had brought them here when we first hid the money. I forgot them, but there was nothing to identify their source; I had used a standard drawing program. I put them in my coat pocket as I went out to help Dave;

I started to gasp. I had not taken a breath since I'd found the papers.

All the piled earth was back in the hole, but it was barely half filled. Even after we carried shovelfuls of loose dirt over to the hole and threw it in, the job looked done but it wasn't. "Anybody steps on this, they're gonna know there was a hole here, Paulie," Dave said, sweating, nearly breathless. True, but I shrugged and went to get more dirt. What else was I going to do?

At Carson's Pantry, Charity looked up from communing with her coffee to see what were clearly two unmarked squad cars, with Tony Plymouth in another car following them slowly down the tight S turn of the Interstate exit. She went to the pay phone, dialed, listened, punched in, and hung up. She wandered out, moving slowly until she was out of sight. Then she started to run. She would have to do the mile to the cabin in five minutes.

Dave's pager beeped and showed the number "1." He yelled, "Paulie!" and held up the pager for me to see. We stopped spreading leaves and twigs over the ground, ran to the Jeep, and threw the shovels in the backseat. I got behind the wheel with Dave beside me.

I could not find the keys to the car. Knocking on my door were nausea and panic, the thrilling highs of the criminal's life.

I tore at my clothes and myself. Rather than slide out of the car, I plunged out, landed on all fours, and skittered to the ground over the money pit. While I scrabbled in the dirt, Tony Plymouth must have been near the turnoff to the cabin. I calculate he was turning in when I found the keys in the dirt. Slipping and straining, I got to the Jeep, started it, and pulled slowly into the woods. I pulled behind a high mound in the pine woods. Dave and I left the Jeep with its doors open and its motor off. We were afraid the cops would hear us driving away. We crawled up the mound until we could peek over the top of it.

When Tony Plymouth and his friends arrived at the cabin, the only trace of the Jeep would be some leaves in the woods, kicked up by the wheels and floating to the ground.

If the cops saw the leaves, they paid no attention. Cops

swarmed all over the cabin. Plymouth had finally gotten some help to work his case. They searched every inch of the cabin and the grounds. One of them signaled to Plymouth. He pointed to the hole. "I bet something was buried here," I heard him say. "All the earth is real soft."

"Dig it up and sift through it," Plymouth commanded.

Dave and I watched as the cops, like prospectors for gold, shoveled up the sandy earth and put it through a screen. They found stones, pebbles, and little scraps of plastic. We heard a crackle in the underbrush and started—it was Charity, who crept in beside us to watch the search. We were all sweating from exertion and anxiety. The ground was cold enough to make me shiver. The day was clouding over.

After ninety minutes, every police officer except Plymouth packed up and left. The detective wandered around, looking disconsolate even from a distance, when he spied two scraps of paper on the ground. I saw him abruptly kneel down and examine them. As far away as I was, I could discern the detective's smile. I felt my pockets; the computer drawings were missing from my coat. They must have fallen out when I was bent over trying to find my keys. Out of good police habits, Plymouth searched about and saw two depressions on the sandy leaf-strewn ground. His eyes followed what he might think were faint marks made by a car. Plymouth started to follow the trail. Moving slowly and erratically, the wide grooves in the leaf beds were probably difficult to stay with. But they were the tracks of the Jeep.

On the low hillock, I whispered, "Let's get to the car."

"He'll hear us," Charity hissed.

"If we don't go now, he'll see us; that's worse—he'll be a witness."

All three of us slid down the mound to the Jeep. The storage space behind the backseat was packed with money. As I made sure the roller cover hid the money from view, Dave smeared some mud over the back plate. Our panic had subsided and we got in noiselessly. Then I started the engine. I let the car drift forward and took off slowly over the rough ground.

Tony Plymouth would react to the engine sound by running to it, but the Jeep would already be out of sight. He would have to run back to his car to give chase along the Jeep's tracks, but his squad car would not do well on this very rough ground. Soon we heard his undercarriage scraping the earth and a cracking of a small tree.

The Jeep careened down a small rocky slope.

"Where's the road?" Dave asked, bouncing like a ball in the front seat he shared with Charity. His voice rumbled with the bumps on the rough ground.

"I don't want to get on the road," I said wrestling with the wheel. The Jeep nearly tipped as it moved over a large stone that marked the corner of a peach orchard. "If we get on the road, the cop will get on the road, follow us, and set up a roadblock."

The Jeep bumped hard over tree roots. A peach fell into Dave's lap, through the open window. Charity wrestled with a seat belt, trying to fasten it. Dave leaned to look over my shoulder. "We are going five or six miles an hour. This guy can catch us on foot."

"He can't run fast—this is all orchard here and grapes," I said, my voice breaking with each rut and furrow. "The ground is covered with roots and vines. It's rough as hell, you may have noticed."

"Right, Paulie." Dave's head thudded against the dashboard.

Charity's head banged against the roof of the Jeep as it jumped over an irrigation pipe. She turned to look out the rear window. "His car just passed by the entrance back there."

Dave turned around to look. "He's backing up, I think he must have seen us."

I wrenched the Jeep through a gap in the trees. We slid down a wet and muddy slope. The Jeep started to tip again. "Lean right," I shouted.

The Jeep stayed upright and started up the opposing slope, which I knew led to a vineyard. We were trespassing, another crime. At the top of the slope, I backed up to the head of the vine rows and turned into the field of grapes. There were fifty wooden posts in a row, deeply planted in the earth six feet apart; each served as anchor to a row of grapevines which wound over metal wires stringing from the posts. Each vine row had several posts, and the space between each row was just big enough for the Jeep. When I pulled into one of the middle rows, the heavy growth hid the Jeep from view. It also slowed us down to the speed of a child walking home with a very bad report card.

Now we were fleeing the law at a speed of two miles per hour.

The Jeep rocked down the lane. Bunches of grapes smashed against the sides and the windows. The windshield was awash in grape juice. The only clear line of sight was out the rear window, and that was where Charity spotted Tony Plymouth and his police sedan coming down the row behind us. "He's there, and he's going faster than we are," she said.

I looked in the rearview mirror to see Tony Plymouth jounce through the row, looking like an insurance salesman riding rodeo. "Not for long, I hope. Tell me when you can read the numbers on his license plate. That's when he may be able to read ours."

"Not now, not in—whoops!" Charity cried.

The squad car bucked up nearly a foot in the air. Plymouth instinctively turned the steering wheel. This had no effect because his front wheels were in the air. When they hit the ground, the car veered off into a heavy vine and crunched to a stop. We heard the engine race as the detective pushed on the gas. The squad car started forward again, but he went too fast and the enormous gnarled vines bumped his tires off their tracks into a wooden post and another dead stop. Tony Plymouth reversed and, lucky this time, moved cleanly out of the row.

I stopped. "Dave, get out of the car. Go to the outside edge of the rows and tell me what he's doing."

Dave tried the door. It wouldn't open, caught against a vine. Dave slid out the window and stumbled his way to the outside row. I resumed my slow creep down the row.

Dave gestured as he spotted Plymouth, now tooling along the flat ground between the orchard slope on his right and the vineyard slope on his left. The ground was flatter and wet, and I knew Plymouth would be able to drive faster. Then the front of the squad car dipped suddenly. The rear of the car came up; I heard a loud splat as it came down.

Plymouth's car made a popping sound as it pulled free of the mud. Then I heard a metallic splash and a splutter as Plymouth's engine stopped, thanks to what I thought it had to be: backwash ponds from leaky irrigation pipes. The water flooded and stopped the engine, and we heard water gurgles and Plymouth's loud curses. From the echoes I heard, it sounded Hungarian.

Dave caught up to the Jeep, panting, smeared with grape pulp, and I stopped.

"Dave, wait to see what he does. If he uses his radio or a phone, give Charity's pager a beep—use number one." I tossed Dave my cell phone.

Dave seemed confused.

"Stay out of his sight, see if you can break his police radio. Get yourself home."

"How am I going to do that?"

"Go find a farmer's daughter," I said.

Dave shook his head in mock disgust and jogged back to his lookout. I throttled the Jeep into motion in its lowest gear.

I suspected Tony Plymouth wouldn't radio in for help. Most cops who put a squad car in a pond would rather pay for a tow out of their own pockets and avoid the embarrassment.

Charity caught sight of him, running hard, his clothes catching on the vines and drenched with grape juice, but he did catch sight of the Jeep and he saw Charity.

Interesting news, but I was already going as fast as I could. "Is he talking into his radio?" I asked her.

"No, sir, not that I can see."

I came at last to the end of the row, and with a bone-jarring bounce, the Jeep landed on a dry tractor path. To the right and ahead was open field, to the left a patch of tall grass. I went left, at fifteen miles per hour. The ride was so rough that Charity's head was bloodied when it hit the window post. Charity saw Plymouth run out into the tractor path. He was very far back, but now the tractor path was abruptly ending. I had to turn either back into another vineyard row or into the field of grass. Charity watched Plymouth. "Lord, this guy is like a terminator."

"A what?"

"You don't go to the movies."

"Not much."

"He's gonna catch us."

"Oh." I chose the grass field.

The grass came nearly to the roof of the Jeep and we slowed agonizingly, knocking down the grass as we went. After some seconds, out of the corner of her eye, Charity saw the shadow of Plymouth, moving in the tall grass off to the side of the Jeep, still behind but getting closer.

"He's running faster than you're driving."

I pounded the steering wheel, hunched down, and slewed off to the left, but I could only go a few feet before the woods stopped our progress. Then I reversed to my original direction. Plymouth moved out into the path made by the Jeep. I realized that the flattened grass actually slowed him down; it was like running on pillows. He started to talk into the radio.

"He's calling in. Must be trying to get help."

"This is a good time to pray, Charity," I muttered.

Plymouth pushed the transmit button on his radio. He hit the radio and tried again and hit it again. He probably got static but no squelch sound.

Dave had killed the radio. He had jimmied open the trunk of the squad car and poured water all over the police radio, and he used the tire jack to smash parts and tear wiring. Plymouth's handheld radio is like the one Dave had for years; it transmitted to the main radio in the car, which used its power to broadcast the message over a long distance. No radio in the trunk, then Plymouth can't transmit to any police headquarters.

"He stopped."

The detective knew his radio didn't work. This, I think, stopped him. He would get no help. He would be spent. He knew Trimble was not going to be in the Jeep. There were three people in the Jeep, which meant the fourth thief was here, one whom Plymouth had to get sight of right now, if he could, to confirm what he already knew, to give the detective something to say, under oath, on the witness stand.

I kept on a steady course. Tony Plymouth started moving again, a slow lope this time, following us, not closing on us. We cruised out of the grass field onto another tractor path, and I went left toward another very large grove of trees, an apple orchard. The trees were widely spaced; the ground was smoother. The Jeep was well down the road when Plymouth emerged from the tall grass. Dave came around the edge of the grass field. The Jeep, its pursuer, and the man assigned to watch the pursuer all occupied a separate point on a single straight line. I saw it all in the mirror.

This was not good.

I rolled us into the orchard and lost sight of Plymouth.

I drove through the orchard, past the U-Pick farm office, and onto the road.

It took four minutes to drive two and a half miles into Apple Creek Village. The parking lot for the Orchard Bowlium was empty. A sign said BOWLING LEAGUES BEGIN NEXT MONTH. I coasted behind the building. Charity and I changed the license plates and tore off the Toomin signs. Plymouth would call for a roadblock. He would never get it with what he had, but he might get a radio broadcast order to stop a Toomin Jeep, if he saw the license plate and the Toomin signs. Trying to clean off the car with two towels was beyond us. We drove off.

"We'll take the back roads," I said, easing back out on the roadway. We drove for a short way and I saw a self–car wash with all the bays empty and I drove into a bay. We washed the car. That at least was easy. A few seconds later, Charity's pager showed the number "1."

"It's the number one. The cop got to a phone or a radio, I guess," she said.

I just kept driving. In seconds I saw what I needed. On the right was a sign heralding JOHNNY LADD'S USED CAR CONNECTION. I drove past and parked out of sight of the lot. Crawling into the backseat, I jammed my hand into the storage bay and pulled out a ten-pack of hundred-dollar bills from the robbery. "Charity, either I'll be back in five minutes or I won't be. If I'm not back in five minutes, take the Jeep, drive on, and meet me at the underground entrance to the Fairmont Hotel." I took the Toomin plates with me.

I rushed to the car lot. It was stupid to do this; the adrenaline was the culprit. In front of me was a 1985 Olds 98 with 110,000 miles on it and a price tag of $850. I took a step toward it and was quickly met by the very vigilant and smiling Johnny Ladd.

"A real find there," he remarked, aggressively conversational. "I won't lie to you, lots of miles, yes. But you get basic transportation plus a lot of extras."

"Yeah," I growled, trying to disguise my voice a little. "How about seven hundred?"

"No can do, friend. I'd lose money. But for you, I can go for eight."

"Maybe, but can I take it now and do the paperwork later?"

"You ain't gonna try to give me a check, are you?" Johnny Ladd grinned suspiciously. " 'Cause it's gotta be certified."

"I'm starting a new job. My wheels broke down. I sort of need it now." I said, trying to sound like a fortyish loser, hardened yet needy.

"Friend, if I'd known that, I woulda stuck with eight-fifty."

"Can I have it now? Clear the title later?"

"You got cash?"

"Yeah."

Ladd looked askance at me.

"I knew I needed the car today," I said. "I went to the bank." I twisted away for a moment and then turned back holding $800 in fifties.

Johnny Ladd counted it all out. "Friend, you had more to spend, didn't you?"

I nodded.

"Wish I'd guessed that . . . But you go tell people that Johnny Ladd treated you right. I'll get you the keys and a receipt."

The time crept until Ladd came out. "Be sure to come back so we can title this."

While Toomin's Jeep and its plate number started coming up on squad car computers and on police radios all over the area, Charity drove to Chicago along rural roads. In my frayed Olds I ran the Interstate at a safe five miles per hour above the speed limit.

I went directly to Toomin's Slicers, driving my newly acquired basic transportation. After what Plymouth had seen, I didn't want to be spotted driving a Jeep anywhere near Toomin's. By now it was late in the day, and I hoped to find the Toomin Jeep near where it had been that morning. And I did, quickly reattaching the correct plates to it. There were stains on the front plate. I touched them with wet fingers and tasted the stain. "Grape juice," I thought; good corroboration that it had been the Toomin Jeep that Plymouth had chased around the orchard. I barely got back to the Olds parked on a side street when I saw a half dozen police officers converge on Toomin's Jeep. Another half dozen knocked on the door of Toomin's Slicers. One of them held the long piece of paper on which state courts issue search warrants. I took the Olds back down the side street and headed off to meet Charity.

We connected on the same underground streets where I had first proposed the theft to Dave. I gestured for Charity to follow me to a salvage yard. It was nearly deserted, but open. Its owner was always in trouble over receiving stolen cars, and he wouldn't be too picky if he found an old used car on his lot without plates, so I parked it, wiped off the steering wheel, door handles, and gear shift, took the dealer plates off, and left.

On the way back east to the Loop, I spun the dealer plates into the river.

The adrenaline supply was running low, and I was feeling my exhaustion. I drove the Jeep on the west side of Union Station where a large Loop FedEx office stays open late on Friday. I parked close to the office entrance but out of the sight of anyone inside.

"We really going to ship the money?" Charity asked.

"We can't keep carrying it around ourselves," I said.

Charity got a cart from the FedEx office and came back. "You know, FedEx has the right to open the packages. They do sometimes," Charity warned.

"It's a chance we have to take. And the U.S. marshal is going to X-ray for bombs, too. Another chance to take. We have no choice."

Some of the money was ready to go in some FedEx boxes we had packed with the cash. We filled out the shipping slips. The addressee was the Honorable Paul E. Devine. I gave her the rest of my bills.

"Pay cash. Tell them you have run out of account slips."

We made four separate stops at Mail Boxes stores, splitting up the shipments to make them a little less memorable.

Charity brought the boxes in at the last place on North Avenue. Closing my eyes, I managed to doze until she got into the car and woke me by asking, "Are you sleeping?"

"Yes . . ."

"How come you had so much cash?"

"I started collecting cash in case we had to give Trimble something more. And emergencies and such. This shipment has my name on it; I couldn't use the Fed's cash."

"Got any leftover?"

"No."

"Then we have a little emergency. We don't have enough money to send them all. We have one small box left over. It's in the back."

I did not know what to do other than shrug and drive Charity to the east side of the station, so she could catch her train home.

I patted her arm before she exited. "Dave will get in touch. I'll worry about the box in back. It's just the last four million dollars."

Charity laughed as she said good-bye.

I guess Dave waited for the Greyhound bus in Apple Creek Village.

On my way back to chambers, I stopped at a Walgreens to buy a box of plastic garbage bags. In the underground lot of the courthouse, I ripped the shipping label off the FedEx box and used all the garbage bags to envelop the box. Then I went upstairs, showered quickly, dressed in my dinner jacket, double-breasted, without a cummerbund, then back down to the lobby and I took a cab to the Fairmont where the benefit was being held. I arrived at eight fifty-eight. Two minutes later Maeve appeared in a silken thing that displayed her graceful body, very thin and nothing too large. She introduced me to a few doctors and I introduced her to a larger number of rich people, lawyers, and businessmen. We were very handsome together that night. Maeve was methodically networking, a skill optional for federal judges, but I did my part. We danced and left near the very end of the ball and went to her home and took off our clothes and finished quickly. She was tired, I was running on empty. I was glad to be with her. When I was with her, Ellen stayed away, and having spent myself in a full day of criminal misconduct, I was not ready to commune with my beloved. The phone rang for Maeve sometime after four, and I left with her. It was not as bad as it sounds; I was so exhausted, I could not sleep for the hour and a half that it was dark and quiet in her apartment.

I cabbed it back to the courthouse, recovered my Jeep, and went north to Uptown where Broadway is less crowded and stopped in a little strip mall, where I added the four million dollars to the garbage in the large Dumpster. The bags overlapped head to toe, so that nothing could fall out. When the loot rested on top of the pile inside the dumpster, I stood on the bag and forced it down to the middle of the pile.

Not so easy come.

The two weekend days were very hot for fall; the thermometer touched eighty-five. I hibernated in my house with the thermostat set at sixty degrees. The sky was incandescent. I did not feel the heat, but I resented the intrusion of the light on my seclusion. No police knocked on the door. Tony Plymouth did not call. Maeve did not call. By Sunday night, I could not sleep anymore. The heat had broken. I then realized how scatterbrained I had been on Friday; dumping four million dollars in a dumpster because I was too fatigued to see that I could have carried it up and left it in my chambers.

Where was Trimble, and why was there no word about him?

There was some work to do on a case I was supposed to begin tomorrow. The file was thick and I looked carefully at every document in it, even the unimportant ones. In time I forced the case into my mind.

On the way to work this morning, I stopped to call Charity. Trimble was still in Canada. He would be touring Toronto. Some Canadians he had met told him that Montreal went dead when they started speaking French and the English speakers moved away. There was more to do in Toronto, and he had engaged another suite in a Four Seasons hotel to do it. Trimble would wait until he was ready.

Charity said he did not trust us but he was no longer so angry. He was buying clothes, being chauffeured about, using a trainer and a masseur at the health club. Charity thought she heard a woman's voice in the background. In her way of telling me this, I discerned some pleasure in her at the fact that he was doing better. It had to end fairly soon. He'd carried $28,000 with him into Canada. The money would not last more than ten days at the pace he was spending it.

In my chambers there was a double pile of mail, Friday's and today's, and a few phone messages. Each of my clerks had a draft opinion on one of my cases. I read them carefully and approved them. Ordinarily, I would make marginal notes and add a sentence to the opinion or a comment to the clerk about the opinion. The opinions were fine, but I was too distracted to do more than change a single phrase in each one, to let them know I had actually read it. Some judges joke about signing the clerk's draft opinions without reading them, and all clerks wonder now and then if we actually do so.

For many years, we had a judge here, an amiable, deranged fool. Then he became better. The lawyers thought doctors had stabilized his medication. Actually he stopped composing his rulings and issued draft opinions without reading them. His reputation began to improve.

Just before trial began, the FedEx boxes arrived. I announced that they were family papers that my parents wanted me to keep. I let Mrs. Tiger put the boxes away in my storeroom. My secretary liked to pump iron in the federal building gym, and she seemed to relish hefting paper that was heavier than she could have imagined.

11.

HOWARD BRACE AND his family-owned corporation designed, produced, and sold a billion dollars a year worth of small, patented components for a variety of products. Now what they produced was a messy case to distract me, a family fighting over control of a business. For decades, the Brace men had invented things. The Brace wives had run the company. At issue was a new computer hardware connector designed to replace the metal pins that get inserted into metal rings. The new connector looked like a tuning fork, and the plug looked like a slightly twisted ribbon. The ribbon did not touch either tine of the fork when it was inserted. The twists in it slowly pushed against the tines to make contact. The lawyers gave me a large-size model of the plug and the receptacle, which I often pushed together and pulled apart during trial.

Howard Brace, older engineering whiz, was the big man at Brace. His wife, Karen Hamilton Brace, was chairman. Their son, Wallace, invented the new connector. He showed it to father who simply said, "It won't work." He never gave his son a reason, so Wallace told the family that he would go out on his own and make the product. The other dozen or so Braces intervened because they thought the invention might work. The family forced Karen Brace to hire lawyers to sue her own son to stop him from competing with Brace Corporation. Wallace, like all the Braces, had signed a contract saying he would not go into competition against the company for two years after he left the company.

Everybody who mattered was in court. Howard, a rotund grandfather type, had a pleasant, uninterested look on his face. Wallace had the beginnings of his father's face. He watched the entire case as sharply as a border collie watches sheep. Karen Hamilton Brace sat at the Brace company table, but she had selected a seat as close as possible to her son, almost in the dead center of the courtroom. She alone would look at me. She must have hoped that I could somehow save her from this family nightmare. Maybe Charity once had the same hope of me.

It was a case in which large interests of both commerce and the human soul were at stake. The day was a gift to me. I was not interrogated or arrested. I was a true judge in an important case. Why wasn't this enough for me?

There had been no lunch break before the trial recessed, and I went for Thai food at the little place in the DePaul University downtown center. The music school is in that building and groups play at the lunch hour. I bought a newspaper to read

while I ate. In a gossip column was an item saying: "We hear
that a Chicago detective who made a name for himself last year
has got another hot fraud case, and this time the target is a hero
firefighter. Fire department brass are preparing for damage control, burned because it is a case of fire insurance fraud. Got it,
folks? THE FIREFIGHTER IS SETTING FIRES."

I paid quickly and left my lunch uneaten.

Dave Brody was working that day, so I could not call him. If
he was not working, then it would be too late to call him. He
might be in custody. He had to make the call to me. The rest of
the afternoon I diligently cleared every piece of paper from my
desk, did a half hour on a rowing machine, and carefully re-
arranged the mess of papers in my armoire. I did no work on the
trial case; it deserved the efforts of a judge whose mind was not
in turmoil.

In the early evening, Dave Brody arrived at my house. Neither he nor I much cared if someone saw him come to see me in
his time of trouble. Usually we go down to the office in the
basement. But Dave started in as soon as I opened the back
door, and we never made it downstairs. "You see the article,
Paulie?"

"Yes. Can there be any doubt it's you?"

"My battalion commander called his brother in the cops to
find out what's what."

"Did Tony Plymouth give anything up?" I put my hand on
Dave's shoulder for a moment, and he paused to take a breath.

"My commander's brother is very straight. He went up to
Plymouth and tells him why he was asking. Plymouth tells him
they have one of the insurance consultants who fingered me
along with all of his clients." Dave's voice sounded the same,
but his words were short, blurted sounds. "The department is
taking it to the federal government—mail fraud, he said. You
know, the insurance claims and the checks to pay them were all
sent by mail. Plymouth said he had a message for me, that it
was not too late to make a deal for myself. Who he's got, I don't
know. Any one of these guys could be wearing a tape recorder.
I'm afraid to call." He sounded as stolid as a soldier reporting
on a battlefield maneuver gone awry.

"I have to ask you. Did you stop, you know, doing them
when I asked you?" I spoke as slowly and calmly as I could.

"Right."

"When was the last one you did before that?"

"Almost a year."

"So it's at least two years from today, the last one?"

"Yeah."

"In the last six years, how many?"

"Four. I did about one a year, all over the Midwest."

"All for the same insurance consultant?"

"No, two of them."

"If Plymouth has his hooks into a consultant, it's one of those two. There's a five-year statute of limitations on these crimes. Even if you allow for the time it takes to pay the claim, it won't go back more than six years."

"Can I find out which one?" Dave asked.

"Not without sinking yourself," I replied.

"Jesus, Mary, and Joseph, what a mess." Dave, who had stood very still, meandered around the room. Now he looked more crestfallen than panicked.

"He doesn't have you yet. There's time—they have to have a grand jury and subpoena witnesses and records. You'll get to know who their witness is because it will become known on the street which company is involved. When you know the company, you'll know which fire it is, and if you know which fire it is, you'll know which consultant used you. We could beat this thing on the square in court."

"I'm a fireman who sets fires. I'm a firefighting fucking arsonist. You think about it. That's what I chose to be, a firefighting fucking arsonist. I've got me to blame—no one else."

"You were careful. No one was ever hurt."

Dave shrugged and sat down on one of the chairs. I gave him coffee.

I told him what I guessed.

Tony Plymouth had this consultant in his pocket for quite a while. That was why he felt he could move on the cabin by the lake. I was wrong when I thought he had done it out of desperation. He wanted to frighten us and then hit us with his leverage on Dave. It meant he could try to start a race between Dave and Trimble. The first man through the door offering testimony would have a deal. The second man through the door would wind up with large legal bills and a long prison term. It was the best he could do with what he had. The prosecutors liked his track record, which gave him greater leverage. The Gypsy detective story gave him access to the media, which allowed him to plant that story in the paper.

But he could tell no one his real purpose—to pin the Federal Reserve robbery on us. If he says anything to the prosecutors or the press, the Fed will deny the whole theory and his persona switches from solid police officer to wild-eyed eccentric. He wouldn't be able to get subpoenas issued against me or Charity or Trimble. Therefore, we had time.

It was a long speech, and it sounded so great that I convinced him and myself.

12.

I WAS IN chambers before the sun was up. I checked the money boxes—intact, unopened, and stacked in the back of the room.

I was ready for the Braces.

The character of Howard Brace lay at the center of the case. His son was a reasonable fellow who was not trying to make anyone's life miserable, including his father's, and certainly not his mother's. He was a Brace, genetically programmed to invent things that were tiny and useful, to see those things made and sold, and then to be praised and rewarded for his work. He could not understand why his father was standing in his way.

Howard Brace paused for long periods before answering questions. Regarding Wallace's invention, he just said, over and over, "In my engineering judgment it won't work." Other members of the Brace family attributed the dispute to the bitterness of old age, Howard's resentment toward his son's brilliance. Howard Brace heard this evidence with an untroubled face. I thought something was wrong with him. He was a Trimble who would never listen to reason.

Karen Hamilton Brace was not called as a witness. She must have been sitting in court ready to murder her husband and son for the pain they were inflicting on her.

The evidence and arguments finished at three in the afternoon. Now I was to decide who was right and who was wrong. I would spend most of Thursday thinking about the decision unless I had to think about Tony Plymouth. I would announce my decision on Thursday afternoon if neither I nor Dave was under arrest.

Maeve called. "I know this is short notice, but I'm suddenly free for dinner, just dinner. I have to be back in the hospital at ten. Meet me at Spago."

"Do you mind if I bring my oldest friend?" I asked. "You'll like him, and I'm supposed to have dinner with him."

"Why not? I can be flexible, despite what everyone says."

I hurried to call Dave, who would be in need of cheer. If the two of us were alone, then we couldn't escape, but in the company of Maeve we could try to be normal for a while.

13.

DAVE WALKED IN wearing his best suit, blue with a touch of gray thread, an off-price Brioni. He looked like a bar mitzvah boy except he was way beyond thirteen and, at least once in his life, he had accepted Jesus as his savior. He lit up the lights in Maeve's eyes, I thought, but she might have been staring at his tie, an expensive silk, in a diamond pattern of eight colors. The shirt was good, too, not the usual Dave package deal—he looked invulnerable tonight.

I felt fine; my troubles were disappearing in a red wine called Pahlmeyer, which Maeve had ordered. "Maeve, you take my breath from me. And Paulie, how are you tonight?"

Dave looked as he had at Mater Dei–Sacred Heart mixers. "Maeve, I have known Paulie since school days, and I have just one thing to say to you: You ought to leave this stiff right now and come away with me. Let's give it a try." Dave spoke with utter seriousness. He did this once when I was dating Ellen.

"What would you do," I asked him then, "if she said yes?" He answered that he would get up and leave with her. "If she said yes to me, you would not be wanting her, now would you?" Dave smiled. Maeve took a second or two to reach over and squeeze my hand as Dave sat down.

Through the rest of the evening Dave and Maeve discussed what they did and then proceeded down the list of appropriate general subjects, which did not include investigations of free-lance arson among Chicago firefighters. I said little because I saw Dave's mood lifting and I needed to rest. It was going well. Maeve called the hospital and excused herself somehow from being there at ten. I was hungry too, and while the two of them were talking I ate most of the bread on the table and wondered why, even now, neither Dave nor I had a gray hair on our heads.

"You ever been married, Dave?" Maeve asked, sounding both flirtatious and professional.

"No, Maeve. How about you?"

"Someday maybe. You have a particular girl?"

"No. You have some suggestions?"

"Oh, I have somebody for you. I'll give Paulie her name," she said.

"You know," I said, "Dave has plans to marry. He is going to Europe to find a noblewoman to propose to. He wants somebody named Hohenzollern. He wants to have a title—a good plan I think."

Maeve looked at me, head cocked to one side, as if to ascertain in what way I was serious.

"Really, Dave, tell me more. I have always wanted to be Contessa Dottore Nolan, Maeve of Rome."

"My current plans, Doctor, are to become a *Grossherzog*," Dave said.

"Meaning?"

"Grand duke, my friend Paulie tells me. I just like the name."

"*Grossherzog* Brody. You will be one of a kind."

"That's why I ordered the Wiener schnitzel, a *Grossherzog*-type dish."

I interrupted to point out that he had ordered the Wiener schnitzel because it is the largest amount of food you can get on a plate at Spago.

We had a good time. The three of us walked down to the Jazz Showcase to hear Russell Malone, a great guitarist who might have noticed three half-smashed adults occasionally stifling a laugh.

14.

ON THURSDAY I considered my decision in Brace.

I reread nothing, no transcripts or expert reports, no lawyers' briefs. Instead, I re-created from memory the big moments of the trial. I made a mental first cut of a movie of the important things that were said and how the witness looked and spoke. I watched the movie, reediting, cutting some lines, putting others back. The mind is much faster than the eye and the ear. I could replay two days in court in a few minutes.

If you keep rerunning, keep editing, then the right point of view sooner or later emerges. The fair judge starts cutting the movie without being committed to a particular point of view. I forced myself to do this. And I could never agree with myself about how it should end.

Then I recalled that Wallace's lawyer had tried to move Howard out of the case because the lawyer thought that without Howard, the case would be settled quickly. The corporate by-laws permitted the board of directors to insist on a medical examination of any corporate officer. The bylaw existed so that the corporate officers could go to someplace like the Mayo Clinic for a few days, get a complete checkup, and have the corporation pay for it. It had never been used to force an examination but it could be, I thought. If Howard Brace was out of action for a few days, then a deal could be made. During the trial, Wallace's lawyer stood up in court to say that the directors had breached their duties by failing to insist upon a medical determination of Howard's fitness to serve as CEO. That lawyer never expected me to do anything about this claim of breach of duty. He was just trying to drive a wedge between Howard and the rest of the Braces. Now, for me, it was an opportunity to make peace.

If Howard could be taken out of the decision, then an amicable settlement could be reached. And Howard might be able to accept that what is done is done. More to the point, the Howard Brace I saw on the witness stand could not have been the man who brought success to the Brace Corporation for twenty years. The doctors might be able to find a problem and either fix it or force him to retire.

I would tell them that I would have a further hearing on Tuesday to decide the case. Then I would suggest that the directors consider the question of a medical examination of Howard. Of course, they did not have to agree, but such a suggestion is never ignored when the federal judge is going to decide what a trade secret is worth.

The lawyers heard my ruling at the end of the day. Lawyers are not paid to agree or disagree with decisions. They want to know who wins and if the judge has said something they can use for their client in the future. They suspected that by delaying the ruling I meant to say that either side could still win and a settlement might be best. All the Braces looked puzzled except Howard, who was toying with his own model of the connector, and his wife, Karen, who smiled at me and then quickly covered her mouth with her hand.

I had to keep busy until Monday. That meant I had to take

work away from my clerks and do more of the first drafts of opinions myself. I walked into the law clerks' office.

They pile the work on their bookshelves. They live in a forest of paper. I used a tape measure to select the tallest stacks of paper. Those were the cases I took back to my office. The clerks were taken aback and pleased. Given that the anniversary of Ellen's death was coming soon, they probably whispered among themselves that Judge Devine wanted to smother memories of his dead wife in reams of paper.

On the way home, I made my call to Charity, this time from a phone in front of Fitzsimmons Surgical Supply near my house. She answered promptly in her soft telephone voice, so at odds with the rest of her firm kind of beauty. "Trimble is coming back to Chicago next Tuesday. He doesn't want to stay with me. He'll call from his hotel."

On Saturday night Dave Brody and I went to the Green Mill to listen to loud music until four in the morning. We talked over the politics of the city, the game of baseball, and the state of the world, never mentioning Tony Plymouth. Since the conception of my crime, I had parted company with human commerce, save for the tiny part of it that was assigned to my courtroom. Germany could redivide and turn Berlin into Sarajevo, Milan could secede from Italy, and Barcelona could secede from Spain—I would have barely noticed and not cared at all.

I had reached a saturation point, like very old people, well into their nineties, who stop thinking much about death. You see them in court. For years the law presumed any gift made within three years before death was a gift made in contemplation of death and thus the estate paid more tax. A lawyer could try to disprove the presumption. I saw it happen. A man of ninety-seven years gave a huge sum of money to his family members. He wrote in his journal about funding his grandchildren's business and his expectations for its five-year growth—how he was going to be darned upset if in five years they hadn't done right by his investment. His death occurred a few weeks later when he had a first and fatal heart attack.

He was a first-rate businessman with not a trace of senility. How could he have not contemplated death? The psychiatrists all testified that the greatly aged are different. For adults the drumbeat of impending death grows louder every year and we worry, until the nineties, when the drumbeat stops. The enormous human capacity to worry is not inexhaustible. You just finish worrying about death. On that subject you have run out of fuel, as I had about Tony Plymouth.

Dave Brody made the newspaper again on Sunday, in exquisite, if unsourced, detail. The story identified the firefighter suspected of arson as a paramedic with a string of awards for extraordinary service. This distinguishing characteristic would leave the cognoscenti with about two possible choices for the target of the investigation. The fire commissioner would already have been told who it was, Dave said to me when he called to tell me to turn to page three of the Metro section, but he had not been told he was relieved of duty. I suppose they felt he was not a threat to set fires now, and his work was saving lives; there would not be any criticism for letting him continue to save lives until they put him on trial for arson.

Dave had not yet received a subpoena himself, but he had checked with friends and found out that the federal grand jury had subpoenaed two arson investigators from the fire department. One of them had worked the Bridgeport Brewery fire. The incident had been less a fire than an explosion that Dave had created by damaging a pressure release valve in a brewing vat, which in turn tore open a gas line, the contents of which ignited from sparks created by flying pieces of metal. The insurance consultant was a man named Lester Trippi; the insurance payoff was in the multimillions. The owners took the cash and never rebuilt the brewery.

Lester could put Dave in prison, but that was no sure thing; it was not bankable. It would be the fraud broker Lester's word against that of Dave the hero. That might be enough, but the prosecutors would look for more, ruling out any alibis for Dave, which would be easy: Dave had no good alibi since he was the one who set the fires. They would also interview all of Dave's acquaintances to see if he told them any of his secrets. Perhaps most damaging, they would go over his finances very carefully, where they would find money Dave could not account for, the seed of his dowry for Princess Hohenzollern.

This could all take a few months. Dave could then run to

Brazil or some other place with no extradition to America. In a few years he could use the millions that were his to spend. This was not what he had in mind, marrying the impoverished but noble Princess Whatever in Switzerland. There would not be any pictures of Dave and the royal bride for Bridget Ryan and her father to see. It was still better than prison.

Dave listened to my analysis of his options. He did not seem relieved. He did not seem that worried either. "I did not turn out to be much" was a phrase he used. I agreed that he had done wrong but he had never killed nor injured a single soul. This, I said, was redeeming. He did trust me to tell him when it was time to get the hell away. "Do you think I would see much of you in Brazil, Paulie?" he asked.

"I'd like to go quite often." I smiled at him.

"Do you think I would see much of Charity in Brazil?"

I had no answer. We ended the evening when we stopped down at my chambers. We went into the storeroom. We repacked all the money and made a special package of eighteen million for Trimble. I gave Dave a box with eighteen million dollars to deliver to our erratic partner in crime.

15.

I LEFT WORK at noon on Tuesday for the rest of the day. The Braces wanted more time to continue with their case.

There was no reason not to meet Dave openly, so we had lunch. People would agree it was natural that he would come to me, his longtime friend, the federal judge, for help. I could not preside in any case where he was on trial. As long as I did not represent him, I could offer him advice and friendship.

Nor would our relationship raise any red flags with the federal prosecutors. If Tony Plymouth had mentioned his suspicions of me, he would not have gotten as far as he had with the government lawyers in suits. The head prosecutor would think Tony Plymouth was crazy, but being the kind of man he was, he would have asked if the detective actually had photographs of me caught in the act of robbing the Fed. Trimble was a menace, but not on arson charges against Dave. The detective had tried and failed with Trimble and now he was using the old arsons to lean on Dave because he didn't know how close he had come, and might yet come, to roping in an angry Trimble. Dave said, "Christ, if Trimble goes, that's the end of Charity. He can take her out."

At lunch I told Dave we had to scour out my basement. If the place was searched, the police would use vacuum cleaners to find any shred of metal or glass from the gurney or the trays to use as evidence. We would have to destroy the hard drive on my computer.

"I made a mistake," I told Dave, who was trying unsuccessfully to finish his lunch. "The detective laid his hands on my drawings, you remember, the trays and the gurney. If they get a warrant, they may be able to find the originals on the drive."

"Didn't you delete it?"

"They have people who can undelete it, sometimes."

Finally, and worst, I absolutely had to destroy my wife's modeling kit. I had already taken apart the model of the vault, but someone who had all the pieces might be able to figure out what it was.

Cleaning the basement was tedious and noisy. I was grateful that I had no furniture with fabric to vacuum. It was all wood except for bright orange hopsack pads that Ellen had put on the seats of six chairs and two benches. I regretted having smashed the glass trays. Little flecks of glass could stick anywhere. We ran the cleaner over the walls. Ellen's cushions had to be thrown away. I could never ensure that the cushions were completely clean.

While I practiced my criminal handicrafts before the robbery, I had covered the partner's desk with a plastic drop cloth. I hadn't been worried about trace evidence; I wanted to keep Ellen's desk untouched. It is my shrine for my wife. It is irrational to create a shrine out of the petty physical remnants of a life, scraps really, but all shrines to the dead are irrational, even the Taj Mahal. It is the source of their power, the irrationality of it. I packed up the drop cloth with the orange cushions in a large rubber storage tub.

We ran damp cloths over every inch of the room and threw the cloths into another tub. The mop heads we used on the floor went into a tub. After a final vacuuming, the cleaner itself went into a tub. At the end, I would drive through alleys all over the city and dispose of the contents of the tubs by depositing them, bit by bit, in other people's trash containers. There were two areas where the garbage was collected on Wednesday, and there I would leave the gleanings from the basement.

Then I turned to my computer and unscrewed the top, exposing the inner array, and removed my hard disk drive. I would shatter this thing and drop the pieces where they couldn't be recovered.

"Now, are we done?" Dave asked.

"Close." I looked at my watch. Three hours of cleaning. "She's going to get you on the cell phone?"

"She has caller ID. When he calls, she'll know where he is. She'll ring the cellular, and I'll go to him."

"We don't want him to pick the meeting place if we can help it."

Dave was neatly scraping the dirt from under his nails. "Did you think, Paulie, when we started . . . ?"

"No, I thought, if anything went wrong, it would be something in the bank so we would be caught then and there. We'd wait five years, and the statute of limitations would expire. At most we would have a tax problem we could avoid by going overseas."

There was a rueful look on Dave's face, and I wondered if there was such a look on mine.

My last task was the modeling kit. I knelt at Ellen's side of the desk. The right side of the desk had three drawers, and on the left side was the typewriter well, where I opened the door to remove the modeling kit. It was missing.

I started to look for it, not telling Dave about the vacant space where the kit belonged. I scanned the typewriter well on my side of the desk, then each drawer of the desk and all the cabinets in the basement. Dave went upstairs to get a Pepsi.

Could we get money from Coca-Cola by blaming our criminal-ity on Pepsi or money from Pepsi for keeping quiet?

The modeling kit was still missing when Dave returned to the basement.

"Tony Plymouth is in his car, sitting there across the street."

"Nice to know that." I spoke in my calmest voice.

The modeling kit had never been out of the basement, and tonight it was not in the basement. I glanced at Ellen's desk and then stared. The desktop looked a little different, but not in any way I could identify. The desk set items might have been a half-inch out of place. It was inconceivable to me that Ellen's desk had been searched. The desktop did not look that different. It might have been disordered when I used the drop cloth. I opened the drawers.

They were not as I remembered them. In the center drawer I found the line drawing of myself, the piece Ellen had been fin-ishing that last night of her life. One corner of the drawing was crumpled and slightly torn. It had not been damaged today. It did not catch on the drawer when I opened it.

I went on with my examination of the desk. The whole elab-orate piece of furniture sat on five-inch legs. Lying on the floor, I took a small flashlight to examine the underside of the pedestals. There I found a small microphone and a transmitter. It did not appear to be very sophisticated. Not state-of-the-art law-enforcement equipment, rather something commercially available. It might work well enough. I had no idea how long it had been there.

I beckoned to Dave, put my finger to my lip to signal silence. I pointed to the underside of the desk. Flattening himself on the floor, he looked where I showed him to look. He got up and shrugged.

I had overrated the character of Tony Plymouth. He did not have enough to get a warrant for my house, either to search it or to bug it. I thought he was a man who worked entirely within the rules. Now I knew he was another sort of man, a cop with-out integrity.

My fury rose, rose hard, and I wanted to obliterate the man, split him open and rip him like a lion ambushing an antelope. I felt the fury through my backbone, in my skull, my fists. This was not the anger I felt toward Prindiville; it was rage over the desecration of Ellen's drawing of me, her loving act that I could still touch even when its creator was in the grave. The invasion of my sacred place, the profaning of my shrine. Plymouth would die, and I would kill him. I saw myself killing Plymouth, and it was sweet. I was on fire with rage. I was paralyzed with rage. My sight was clouding over. I was not talking, I could not form words. Dave Brody wrapped his arms around me and dragged me up out of the basement before I started shouting threats into the microphone. I could have killed Trimble myself then and had a good lunch at my club right after I did it.

My heat was so intense it could not endure. When it plunged to cold, I was exhausted. I threw up in the kitchen sink and lay down on the tiled floor.

The cellular phone rang. Charity told Dave that Trimble was at the Downtowner Inn of Diversey, the mid-north side. Good. I had something less than lethal that I had to do.

"I wonder who the cop will follow from here." Dave mused. I walked down to the basement to get a document case. In it, I put the disk drive and a ball-peen hammer. There was a tremor in my legs.

Before we walked out, Dave looked through the window to see Plymouth sitting in his car.

We instinctively stopped to shake hands, a formal act we had last performed on the day I was sworn in as a judge. Dave left first. He was in his car by the time I opened my garage door and drove out in my second car, a judge's car, a dated Olds '98.

Dave drove east through tree-lined streets and past the expensive brick city homes between the DePaul neighborhood and the lake. He flew along and, at this speed, it all looked like a wall of green and dark red with an occasional flash of sunlight off the brass fittings that everyone in this neighborhood used for architectural accents. Tony Plymouth never followed him. Alone, Dave could go to the Downtowner about a mile away and watch for Trimble.

16

I DROVE SLOWLY and in the opposite direction from the one that Dave took. Tony Plymouth followed. As long as he followed me, he couldn't be following Dave, which consoled me. I sped on to test the detective. The detective kept up. Turning west on North Avenue, I headed for Clybourn, one of the few diagonal streets in the city. It was once an entirely industrial area; now it was mostly stylish residential, a swirling neighborhood with new buildings, new stores, new mall—a good place to lose the detective.

The Downtowner Inn sits on Diversey; like Clybourn, it is a hip street. The neighborhood was closer to the lake and Lincoln Park than was the Clybourn corridor, but with older, more expensive buildings. There were young people here, but only because of the nearby high-rise rentals. The Downtowner was a survivor of the time when the neighborhood was less cool and the stores had names like Polski Travel, not Centre Court Racquets. The Downtowner had cleaned itself up and catered to out-of-town parents visiting their kids in the city.

If Trimble hadn't called Charity at home, we would not know where he was staying. He probably asked a cab driver to recommend a hotel on the north side. Dave intended to deliver the money to Trimble at the hotel; since Trimble was not expecting this, we did not think Dave would encounter a police trap.

Trimble pulled out of the parking lot the instant Dave parked on the opposite side of the street. Trimble headed west on Diversey and roared past Dave. Dave shifted and started after him. Trimble was too fast, and Dave lost sight of him until he came to Halsted and Diversey, where Trimble, in a Camaro, was caught by a red light.

At the same time, more or less, my Olds moved at forty-five miles an hour; the speed limit was thirty. Tony Plymouth didn't pull me over. He wanted to know where I was going. He would stop only if this little chase got reckless.

I turned into a shopping center with a huge grocery store and a dozen small shops. The area was apparently all new to Plymouth, and he didn't know that the place was built over an old railroad siding. The developer left the tracks intact in the parking lot; the exterior of the stores were designed to look like antique railroad station buildings.

Plymouth could not see my brake lights go on, the parked cars blocked his view. When he whizzed into the lot, he hit the tracks at twenty miles an hour. The elevated rail bounced his car in the air, and he bottomed out on the second set of rails. The sound was awful, and I had to grin.

As I came down the opposite direction in the adjoining lane, Tony Plymouth reversed, cracked the rails again, and fishtailed around to return to Clybourn, farther behind me but still there. I had a wild hope that his car would explode, maybe a cracked gas tank and a spark from the rails.

As buildings became more and more industrial, I angled very sharply into a machine-tool company's empty lot at nearly fifty miles an hour, and the Olds slid halfway across the lot. Tony Plymouth followed. I reversed direction north on Clybourn.

There was no traffic in that direction, and I pushed it up to seventy.

I made a soft right at Racine and then a hard right down Armitage. To the left was the expensive DePaul area, to the right mixed housing on its way to becoming unaffordable to the people who lived there. Another sharp right, and a little faster while Tony Plymouth chased my Olds until we reached Maud Street. As the detective entered the street, he couldn't see the Olds; instead he'd be distracted into believing he'd gone to rural Mis-

sissippi, because the houses were shacks, lots vacant and overgrown, a few with cars up on blocks and people, unemployed
people, standing amid stray dogs nosing for something.

The people stared at him and his squad car. He would know
he wouldn't get far asking these people whether they saw where
the Olds had gone.

Trimble looked back at Dave, who was stuck three cars behind.
Their eyes met, and Dave saw fear. The light showed green. Trimble was first in line, and he was fast on the pedal. Trimble was not
trying to meet Dave; he was trying to lose Dave. Trimble saw
Dave's murderous urge and not his moral inability to carry it out.

Trimble was running from death, and Dave was chasing him
just to hand over eighteen million dollars.

Trimble had to stay away from Lake Shore Drive and the expressway; it was too easy for Dave to follow on those roads. He
had to lose Dave in the neighborhoods. He needed luck to do it.
Trimble was not a north sider; he didn't know these streets.
What he did know was that the only dead ends around here
were the streets that come up against the north branch of the
Chicago River. He had to keep his eye out for bridges, and he
didn't care if a cop stopped him. Both vehicles raced along Diversey, weaving around slower traffic.

Trimble drove onto a less crowded street. The two cars sped
like Formula One cars on a tight grand-prix track, weaving
through neighborhoods, past industrial zones. On Elston, a
wide diagonal street, the cars reached ninety miles an hour and
Trimble must have wondered, "Where the hell are the cops?"
But Dave was lucky, or maybe the luck was Trimble's.

Trimble turned on North and went over the bridge, then
went left into a riverside factory district. It was a mistake—the
area was utterly deserted, rough pavement and open ground.
The cars bounced over steel tracks and every turnoff dead-
ended at the river or at a rail crossing. The area itself seemed to
come to an abrupt stop at a bridge embankment.

Trimble thought he was driving down a funnel with a
blocked drain. He tried to slew around and reverse direction,
but Dave blocked every move, a ballet of cars ending up each

time with Dave's car interposed between Trimble and his freedom. Finally Trimble just accelerated toward the embankment; he would rather die in a crash. Dave followed him until he realized what Trimble was trying, and Dave slowed.

At the embankment, Trimble saw only the pylons of the bridge set far too closely together to drive through. He aimed the nose of the Camaro squarely at the cement base of the pylon closest to the river.

He hit a large mound of earth ten feet from the pylon.

The Camaro climbed the mound, but the earth was soft enough to slow the car and catch a tire, throwing it sideways and bringing it to a bone-breaking stop.

Trimble then saw that behind the mound was an equipment track, narrow but flat, running between the pylon and the river bank. He took the car through the open track. On the other side was a street that would take him onto the bridge, where he could cross to the west side of the river and turn north.

Dave could not see the track from the place where he stopped. He thought Trimble had driven into the river. Dave finally saw the track and drove along it carefully. He looked for Trimble and saw his car stopped on pavement. Dave's tires were on soft earth. Trimble knew he could not be caught now.

Dave decided that he would wait. Trimble put his head out of the window. "I know you're trying to kill me! It ain't so easy, asshole. Is it, asshole? You want to fuck my wife! That's why you want to kill me!"

Trimble was shouting, and Dave was afraid someone would hear. He put his hand out the driver's side window and levered himself out of the car, keeping his hands above his head. "No, man, I want to give you what you asked for."

"Bullshit."

"No. Let me show you. I can show you from here. I won't move any closer." As he spoke, Dave took the money box out of his trunk and held it in his arms.

Trimble peered at the box. Dave watched him think.

"Open it up!" Trimble shouted.

Dave lifted the top Trimble could see the cash.

"Let me give it to you now, Trimble, and we never have to see each other again."

"You think I'm stupid. I put my hands on that box, and you bang me over the head. There's nobody around here to see us."

"Trimble, I'll deliver it anywhere you want."

Trimble said nothing for so long that Dave thought the cause was lost.

"You bring it to my house," he yelled at last. "You come in wearing tight clothes so I can see if you got a gun! You can be sure *I'll* have a gun. Just bring that box."

"Fine, I'll do that. Trimble. Can I call you to set a time?"

"Yeah! Do that. Soon."

Trimble drove away.

I was hidden in an alley of overgrown weeds that looked like they came from alien spores, a half-block away from Maud Street. I watched Tony Plymouth go by. I stopped myself from driving head-on into the driver's side of the squad car. I could probably crush him. I would be arrested for murder. It was hard as hell to keep from doing it anyway. After a while I nosed out and twisted down a series of alleys until I reached Sheffield and went north. There was the patient detective waiting at the corner of Armitage and Sheffield. He must have deduced that the only way out was Sheffield and had taken a chance that I wanted to go north. It was a fifty-fifty shot, and it paid off for him.

This time I rolled slowly back up to Clybourn, turning onto Cortland, gliding past the plant of an old client of mine at the law firm, a large manufacturer, incongruous in the middle of a new condominium kingdom. It had its own rail siding where locomotives came to do business and a blast furnace that could be seen twenty-four hours a day through the open doors of the plant. Tourists drove by the place to see the real Chicago. Its owner had retained me a dozen times when I was in practice. I drove to the office around the corner on Southport. Plymouth followed.

I waited until I saw a yellow light start flashing on the plant storage building across Cortland. It was a signal given every half hour, when a small trailer on rails carried inventory between the buildings. There was no driver; it was automated. It blocked traffic for half a minute. If I moved in front of it, missing it by inches, the detective could not follow.

I took a harsh fast breath and I executed the move, then I drove into the open plant to the spots where the management parked their cars. Leaving the car, I carried the hard disk drive to the door of the blast furnace and tossed it in. I did not need to break it up with the hammer. Then I stopped off to visit my old client.

Tony Plymouth must have braked his car and run out past the rear end of the trailer. He jogged down to the open plant door, where we caught sight of each other as I mounted the steps to the plant offices. He pivoted on his heel to return to his car.

He would have to wait for a while to use it. The automated trailer would still be stuck in front of it. The automatic safety system halts the trailer when a car gets too close, as my car did. He would have to wait for someone to come from the plant to move the trailer.

If Dave was right about the time of day, the detective would have been standing by his car when Trimble drove his Camaro over the Cortland Street Bridge. It would have been a bitter moment for him if he had seen the car and Trimble inside it. The detective was gone when I left.

17.

AFTER ALL THE excitement, I looked at my mobile phone and saw I had two unanswered calls.

The first was from Maeve, and I called her back. "I need you Thursday night," she said immediately. "The medical faculty foundation directors' dinner. It is important to me."

"If it's important to you, Maeve, it's important to me," said Judge Devine, the reliable escort.

Mrs. Tiger had called to say the senator was in town and, by chance, he was having dinner with the White House counsel and a judicial nominations staffer from the Department of Justice. I should come to dinner. Kray had picked a good restaurant and a time that allowed me forty-five minutes to clean up and get to the dinner. Kray's assistant answered his phone and expressed great delight that I would be able to join the senator. To me, it was a distraction I had to endure to present my ordinary public face to the world.

Back home, I dressed the way laymen like to see judges dress: lace-up shoes, dark suit, white shirt, and modest tie, the way a smart police officer dresses when going to court. Ambria is one of Chicago's best dining places and is sited in a fine old apartment hotel, not in the restaurant colonies scattered on the north side, opposite the Shakespeare Garden, grown up around a statue of the bard, and near Maeve's apartment.

"How would you define the qualities of a good appellate judge?" asked the DOJ staffer. What kind of nitwit would ask a question like that at dinner, or anywhere? The kind of nitwit who is not far removed from his high-school days, and this kid might have been twenty-five.

"Patience, open-mindedness, good legal skill, clear writing style, and the ability both to disagree without being disagreeable and to change your mind when you think the other judge is right," I said without having to summon up more than two brain cells. "That about wraps it up."

"Yes it does," Tom Kray said.

The White House counsel rolled his eyes at the kid. This was not a job interview in the classic sense. They could read my opinions and find out the way I think. The point of dinner was to see if I had two heads, and if I was the kind of person who could sell himself, if need be, to the Senate. They would try to figure out who might object to me—labor or management, plaintiffs or defendants, environmentalists, conservationists, and so on. If I wanted the job, I had to sound as if I was firmly in the middle and that any side has a fighting chance to win my vote—except the criminal defense bar, whose opposition is sometimes a benefit to a candidate. It is not politically wise these days to pay attention to what criminal defense lawyers think about judicial candidates, which is too bad because they often have good insight into the character of a judge.

So I told light and fast war stories of cases past and present, selecting each one to advance the point about how fair-minded I was. The White House counsel paid attention as I interspersed my tales among their endless poring over what was happening in Washington, which fascinated my three dinner companions and, if I worked at the seat of government, would have fascinated me too. Tonight it was just making it harder for me to fight sleep. It was two semipleasant hours and when we left, Tom Kray grasped my elbow and whispered, "We have a fighting chance here, Paulie. You did good today."

I spent three hours looking for and not finding another microphone in the kitchen or bedroom. It was enough. Two safe rooms.

Dave came by at eleven in a bleak mood. This time it was the accusation by Trimble—*You want to kill me to take my wife.* This had echoed in his mind; he could not let it loose, and he had decided that it was true. "The best measure of your guilt, Dave, is not what you wanted but what you did," I said, but he wasn't listening very well and my power to persuade him was fraying.

I kept Trimble's money with me. Tony Plymouth was closer to being able legally to search Dave's house than to search mine. Obviously he would not stop at an illegal search to learn the truth, but the money would be unusable evidence if it were illegally seized.

My best hope was that if the detective found the money he would keep it. He would be a thief, too, and could not continue to pursue us. I wanted to believe that Tony Plymouth would not steal, that he would break the law only to punish those who broke the law first, but I once thought he would never break the law for any reason and I was wrong; he had violated my Ellen sanctum.

I tried and failed to work after Dave left. Around one I started to use the rowing machine. After forty minutes my heart hammered, and I was light-headed and nauseated again. My fury at Plymouth was as strong as ever, but I could think again. I could calculate his ruin and destroy him without destroying myself. I took a very hot shower. I didn't want to sleep too long, so I wrapped myself in a gigantic terry-cloth robe and dozed on the bedroom floor.

The sun woke me Wednesday morning. My body was unhappy with the hard floor and to appease it I spent another fifteen minutes in a hot shower, thinking of the microphone in the basement. It would remain untouched. It was best if Plymouth did not know that I knew of it. He could not have heard anything too damaging. But he had heard enough to corroborate Trimble's confession if the belligerent electrician decided to talk to the police. Yet there was no reason to believe that Trimble would talk. The way he spent money in Canada was reassuring to me. He would want to live high on his eighteen million dollars. Charity had said that he had discussed investing the money in some Swiss-based mutual fund. He had sent away for booklets on how to hide money from the government. Trimble had ordered the materials in his own name, a bad way to start and another piece of corroborating evidence. But he had probably spent $2,000 a day in Canada. If he doubled that outlay (and he could), he would exceed his income. He could fall in love very often and give extravagant gifts to deplete his treasury. Worse, he could fall in love very deeply and share his secret with a lover who did not quite cherish him and who might see a reward in her future.

Trimble's departure from the country would be dangerous in another way. Where evidence of a federal crime is located outside the United States, the law sometimes suspends the operation of the statute of limitations; if Trimble took his money overseas, the five-year clock might stop and the government might have forever to prosecute us. If Trimble stayed in this country, a detective like Tony Plymouth could find out how much the electrician was spending and then run to the Internal Revenue Service. Ever since the Serena case, Plymouth had contacts at the IRS.

So I thought, sitting in my ornate and uncomfortable chair in my large main chamber, aggravating the discomfort that came from having slept on the bedroom floor. I rose and walked into my study. I have no notion why it was so, but I was able to work on a huge paper pile of a case I had taken from my clerks.

In the afternoon, I learned that when Howard Brace had gone to the hospital, his only complaint was a lot of pain in his joints. He was getting cortisone to reduce the swelling. While he was being treated, the Brace Corporation directors and Wallace Brace made a deal, and then Wallace went to the hospital for a face-to-face reconciliation. Howard still insisted that Wallace's device would not work for long, but he gave reasons, something having to do with the curve of the strip and the alloy of the tines of the receptacle. He drew diagrams and identified moments in the structure, times and places of force and resistance. Wallace patiently tried to show Howard that he was wrong. He failed. Instead, Howard convinced him. When Wallace asked his father why he hadn't said these things early on, Howard could not say why. Wallace showed Howard a copy of the father's trial transcript. Howard read it and said, "Well, Wally, I don't blame you for not paying attention; I sound like an idiot in this transcript."

On my way home I phoned Charity, who had moved into a Holiday Inn just west of the Loop. Trimble had curtly asked her to leave their home. Still, he had called her four times since she had left, once last night and this morning, then at noon and after work today. The noon call was made to her office at the Fed. He was friendly, asking after her, promising to pay back the money he had taken to Canada, and suggesting that she ought to replace the furnace after he left the house for good.

On Thursday, Dave Brody called Trimble, who told Dave to meet him at Trimble's house at six-thirty that evening, wearing tight clothing so that Trimble could see Dave was unarmed. Before entering the house Dave was to turn around slowly so that Trimble could examine his back as well as his front. Trimble would have a pistol. Dave called me from home. "Can we meet at your house after my shift?" he asked. "I need some advice about these newspaper articles." The prosecutor could play a tape of that conversation until the tape machine broke and it would not incriminate anyone. I didn't think that Plymouth would tap a phone; he would know that Dave and I would be circumspect.

At eight A.M., I read another morning-newspaper article about Dave's case and, much worse, an editorial demanding prompt action from the police and prosecutor. The tone was exceptionally strong. If the firefighter was innocent, the writer declared, the public should know soon. The speculative stories were ruining the image of the fire department. If the firefighter was guilty, then he should pay. The editorial writer used a biblical style. I was surprised that he did not open with the line that a firefighter who was an arsonist was an abomination unto the Lord.

At four o'clock, Dave arrived. He had a copy of the morning paper but never mentioned the editorial. We talked in my bedroom. Dave recounted the conversation with Trimble. "Will we be safe if I complete delivery and Trimble leaves the country? Even if Trimble spills all his secrets to someone, the Fed is still going to deny that there was a robbery. They're gonna say Trimble was crazy."

"Yes, they will—if Prindiville is still in charge," I said, but Prindiville, an ambitious man, would want to move on to something bigger and better. "The next man won't be so committed to the proposition that the robbery never occurred. If it happened on Prindiville's watch, it does not harm the new man to expose it. You get credit for finding the errors of your predecessors and correcting them yourself. The end of it is that Trimble could find someone to listen to him and try to make something of his confession. We have to hope he'll never confess."

The box of Trimble's cash was on the bed, lying there between us. Dave had a small athletic bag with him. "I've got a gun in the bag. I'll repack it under a layer of hundreds. He could be mad enough to take the money and kill me." Dave looked at me. "Don't worry—I absolutely won't shoot first."

He asked me if I had some duct tape. I went downstairs and when I came back with the tape, the box was ready. Dave took the tape and sealed Trimble's box with a single strip across the top.

It was too soon to leave. Dave should not be early. If Trimble saw Dave arrive much before six-thirty, he would think it was part of some plan to do away with Trimble Young. So we sat there.

The money sat on the bed like an unwelcome houseguest. I did not want to look at it. The two of us went to the kitchen, where each of us drank a beer. We passed a couple of hours in the recitation of our earliest years together. The pain of adolescence had transformed itself into a residue of funny stories. It was the best mood Dave had been in since Trimble had departed from my game plan.

When the time came, we carried the money to Dave's car in my closed garage. Dave turned to me and grinned. "Look, Paulie, this will come off fine. It'll be good work."

He was amazingly calm for a man with a gun and eighteen million dollars in his possession.

"Be careful that you're not followed," I told him

He gave me a forgiving look. "My friend," he said, and got into the car.

Dave started the engine. I opened the garage door, and he glided out into the street and turned right.

I went upstairs. Anxiety and the lingering anger at Plymouth were wearing me down; I thought I would take a shower and wait for news from Dave.

I pulled back the shower curtain and found a mound of cash in the tub. It appeared to be about two-thirds of what had been in Trimble's box.

I suddenly knew what Dave's good work entailed.

I ran halfway down the stairs and vaulted over the handrail. I banged through the garage door, dove into my Olds, and started the engine with my right hand while punching the garage-door opener with my left. I drove out into the street. I didn't bother to use the remote control to close the door.

I raced to Charity and Trimble's house through semibad traffic; it never jammed to a full stop but it crawled at random, inexplicable intervals. I was cool; pounding the steering wheel does not help. It took me twenty minutes to get there.

Plymouth was already in place, sitting in the driver's seat of his squad car. He trained a small set of binoculars on Trimble's building, the drapes undrawn in a large picture window. Trimble and Dave stood with the box between them, characters in a tableau. They were moving their hands with their heads cocked a little to one side as men do when they speak. I thought I could see Trimble holding a gun against the back of his leg, ready to use it if he had too.

By this time I was out of the car, my eyes fixed to the window, praying that Dave would open the box, just show Trimble what was in it, and get out of there. I readied myself to distract Plymouth while Dave escaped. But I knew my prayer would be unanswered.

Dave did open the box. He reached in, and I saw packets of money scatter. Very bad; Plymouth could see it. Then he held up a small, square package and showed it to Trimble.

He dropped the package back into the box. In the same instant he grabbed Trimble's gun arm, and wrapped his other arm around Trimble, embracing the electrician, who tried to wrench away. Trimble failed. Trimble pulled the trigger on his pistol, six times, as quickly as he could. Dave held the gun arm tightly against Trimble's side, and the shots had no effect. Trimble jerked himself toward his front door; he dragged Dave with him for a few feet. I ran toward them; I stopped. I knew.

Trimble's living room exploded. Orange flame filled the room in a nanosecond. The roof rose from the house, rose six feet before it collapsed back into the flames. The walls didn't move, the window shattered but the glass flew only to the edge of the front lawn.

Dave must have used a shaped charge.

Tony Plymouth and I thought the same thing. A murder-suicide destroying the only promising witnesses the detective had found to prove his case. He would believe that. I would bear a truer knowledge.

Standing there on the curb, the flames warmed my face but consumed themselves so fast that I soon felt coolness and tasted ash. I calculated that Dave took six million to blow up. If the money, or its ashes survived, Tony Plymouth would think that was all the loot, the six million we had stolen. He would have two dead thieves with all the money. What would he have left against Charity and me? Dave must have thought of this horrifying gambit for a couple of days. I could not see that he had found his life worthless because I valued his life as highly as I valued my own.

Tony Plymouth called in a fire alarm. I stood in the street unmoving and grim as night.

The detective finally turned, saw me, strode toward me. He stopped less than a foot away. He stared at my face. I was unable to return his stare.

"You had no idea, did you?"

I stood still, glancing at the dying inferno Dave had wrought.

He yelled, "You didn't know he was going to do this, you didn't!"

I saw his outrage, his fierce narrowed eyes. He looked like he was struggling to keep from attacking me. The band of flesh between his hair and his eyebrows was scarlet. His ferocity disarmed my own anger at him.

The insight had been instantaneous and terrible when I saw the millions that had been left in the shower. Dave had not taken enough money to pay off Trimble; Dave had condemned himself. Dave was going to kill Trimble and then kill himself. It was the only way he could kill anyone; he had to punish himself for the murder. I had been certain he would shoot Trimble and then himself. In the mad ride out here to stop him I figured out why he had taken a third of the money. He left himself and Trimble as a sacrifice to Tony Plymouth. When I got there I thought I had time, because there had been no shooting yet. The explosion was the deepest shock of my life.

This was nothing to tell Plymouth. Tears were coming to my eyes. I ignored them and walked away. Plymouth followed, shouting after me like a street preacher in the Loop. "He was your friend! You got him into this! You made him dead!"

I walked past my car. My vision was going. I heard the fire sirens coming.

"This character, Trimble—you think he would have been blown up if you had left him alone?"

I walked on.

"What are you going to tell Charity, Judge? Chalk it up to experience, lose a husband, lose a house, live a life on the run, all courtesy of the leadership of the great Judge Devine?"

The sirens were very close. I kept walking. Plymouth was getting close.

"You fucked up people's lives—you ain't just a thief, Paulie Devine. You ashamed at all, buddy, or is it just a little mistake in the plans? Too bad about Dave, but life goes on. Not for *him*, for *you*, Judge—life goes on."

I stopped.

"This doubles your take, doesn't it? That's a good side. I didn't think of that; it's a good day for you."

I turned and circled back around him to my car. He circled with me. The fire engines turned the corner and stopped in front of Trimble's house.

"A piece of work you are, the great judge. You make a fortune, your friends make the grave."

I walked on, almost to the car.

"I ought to look at the way your wife died. Awfully sudden, wasn't it? And she had a lot of insurance, I hear."

I pivoted on one foot and swung my fist at Tony Plymouth's jaw. He tumbled to the ground. He was still.

I didn't care if he was dead. People were around, but they all were looking at the dying fire now being drowned by the fire department. I moved to my car.

When I opened the car door, I looked at Plymouth. He had risen, holding his jaw, looking at me with his blank eyes. Maybe because of that illegal microphone in my basement, he let me drive on. In my rearview mirror I saw him walking toward the demolished house, unhurt.

Maybe Charity would think that Dave did what he did for her as well as for me. I resolved then, in the car, never to tell her that I was at the house and saw Dave blow himself and Trimble into bits.

As I drove back into the city while the night came, I called her at the Holiday Inn and told her that Trimble and Dave were dead. Because no one knew where Charity was staying now, if I hadn't called, she would have seen it first on television or been told by someone like Corman when she reported for work. She gave me her room number.

In a half hour I knocked on her door. She sat down without my speaking a word. "Trimble and Dave died in an explosion at your house. The house is destroyed." Her head dropped. I couldn't see her eyes. She held her face in her hands and slowly compressed her torso onto her thighs. She slowly tipped over on her left side and ended up in a ball on the cheesy hotel room sofa. The air contained only some rough sounds of her breathing. I sat down on the bed.

She stayed there so long that I thought she might have known what Dave had planned to do. But Dave would not have told her, he didn't tell me, and she would not have abided his plan for a moment. "Do you know what happened?" she asked.

"Yes." I gave it up. "I was there." I told her everything.

"I should go home. There'll be things to arrange. I want to see, you know."

It pained me that I could not drive her home. We walked together to the Fed for her night shift. By now people would know, and they would take care of her. I thought to hold her, but that seemed forward and she was stone. "Stay here. Don't go home Charity," I said. "I am so very sorry, Charity. They are in God's hands." We were standing on Jackson Street, fifteen feet from a front entrance to the Federal Reserve.

As I walked back to the Holiday Inn to get my car, the mobile phone vibrated in my pocket. I answered.

"Hi, Paulie. This is Maeve. . . . You're not here. Good night."

Her tone was steely and her pause was designed to let me speak, just a pause before the shot was fired.

Part Six

Postjudgment Motions

1

WHEN I DREAMED, I stopped Dave Brody on his way to Trimble's house, curbed his car on Damen, pulled in front of him on Fullerton, yelled at him through my car window when we raced down Elston, and I always got him; and then I always woke up. Once I delivered money to Trimble in Montreal and saw him off on a plane to Geneva. He was telling me how happy he was to let me invest his money for him, just before my alarm clock went off on Friday morning.

The weekend was for funerals. Trimble's funeral would be reasonably well attended. Die in your thirties, and you usually draw a couple of hundred people.

Dave Brody, hero firefighter and paramedic, drew a crowd of thousands, many in fire department dress uniforms memorializing a fallen public servant. All were convinced that the bad rumors about Dave were untrue, public suspicions never supported by public evidence washed away by the special presumption of innocence accorded to the dead. His mother was no longer alive, but his father flew up from Sea Island, Georgia, or some such place and was one of hundreds of faces familiar to me as were so many alumni and faculty from Mater Dei to whom Dave had been a hero since he was fourteen. I was still trying to let it all blur together, so I cannot be sure if I saw Bridget Ryan. Maeve came for Dave, not me.

I spent my waking hours in my chambers. The cases were a good distraction. I did not think at all about how Dave Brody's act would play out in Plymouth's crusade.

Trimble had probably not written a letter about the Fed to a lawyer. If he had written it, it would have not been admissible evidence and the lawyer would not have given the letter to any-one else for fear of being sued by Charity for publishing a libel against her.

The Brace litigation ended. I had been wise. The doctors had ordered an MRI for Howard Brace. In time, they found a benign tumor in Howard's brain that had caused a swelling in the brain. Some traces remained. There was talk about the areas of the brain named after Broca and Wernicke and a hypothesis that the swelling might have impaired the ability to articulate certain thoughts. They would never know, because they did not test for this when he entered the hospital. The cortisone reduced swelling in the brain as well as in the joints. Howard was able to tell Wallace that the device would wear out quickly and how it might be fixed. His son listened and agreed.

When I left my chambers, I thought I saw a small sign of metal fatigue on the pieces of the large-scale model of the device that I kept putting together and pulling apart.

More of these days in my court and I would not have robbed the Fed, a fine thought to have and believe that day.

All was quiet in the outside world.

2.

SHORTLY AFTER I first met Ellen, when I was try-ing so hard to get her to warm to me, I contrived a trumped-up wrangle between our two prosecutors' offices and had Dave Brody also show up just when the meeting was ending. Then I arranged to have myself called out of the meeting, leaving the two of them together. I was a fully grown man doing all this set-ting up just so I could hear Dave Brody tell me whether or not she was as wonderful as I thought. I also privately hoped that

Dave would tell her things that would make her think I was worthy of her.

The office where I left them was the smallest one in a long row in the criminal division. I walked into a larger conference room next door and sat quietly with my forehead pressed against the outer window. You can sometimes hear what is happening in the next office if you do this because there is one continuous piece of glass sealed to the common wall. I did hear the sound of talk, and I did make out a few words. Dave must have been closest to the window because it was his words I heard.

"My best friend ... A good friend ... Smartest guy I know ... Maybe ... thinks he knows everything ... Full of himself. Well, I would say ..." I was beginning to get a headache. The two of them were starting to laugh. Who was charming whom and was it at my expense? "He does have a sense of humor ... Women in his life, you're kidding ..." More laughter.

My head was throbbing, and I recognized the pain: an ice-cream headache. The window against which I had flattened my forehead was freezing cold. As I left the conference room I bumped into a paralegal who said, "What's wrong with your head, Mr. Devine?" I turned to a secretary, borrowed her mirror, and saw a huge white mark on my forehead. I edged back into the conference room to slap myself on the forehead to restore my skin color, my cosmetic repair work impeded by the ice-cream pain in my head. I didn't want Ellen to see me looking less than my best. I had forgotten to close the door and a newly hired assistant United States attorney, a young man whom I was supposed to mentor, caught me slapping myself. He was intelligent enough to look away. Did he still think he had chosen the right career?

When my forehead appeared normal, I walked back into my office. I told Ellen that my boss had agreed to all her suggestions to resolve our profoundly important conflict. Then I walked her to the door and asked her if we could progress from lunch dates to dinner and a movie. She paused and said she would think about it, but for now we could stick with more frequent lunches. As she stood in front of me, my eyes followed her perfectly straight nose down to the slight off-kilter smile that whispered across her lips for an instant.

After she left, Dave Brody put his feet up on my desk and

told me that she was fine, far too good for someone like me. My duty, he told me, was to give her phone number to him. He had felt honor bound to tell her what a worthless package I was, he said. Even after Ellen agreed to accept a dinner date, I never felt that I was the only one in her life. I could never assume that she would be available. I could not possess her. I was surprised to be content with the fact that she possessed me. I was Paulie, the paragon of Irish independence, under the thumb of no man and only one woman. By the time we slept together, I was madly in love. I think she thought she was doing a favor for a decent guy. We were fine lovers and, in time, she saw something in me, and her soul opened to me, as had her body, tinged with thousands of tiny freckles and silken from head to foot. I was very happy about that, I was.

When we had grown so close and so loving that I knew I could tell her anything, I chose, with my usual artful grace, to tell her that she was the hot Catholic girl of my high-school dreams and, so that she would understand the context, I told her how I had figured out who would be hot with whom. Dave Brody gave it a label, the theory of interfaith lust, that teenaged girls had sex in those days only with those boys they will not marry, boys of a different religion.

I intended to ask her to marry me that night, but first I was trying to make her laugh. I often tried and failed to convince her that I had a great sense of humor. That's why I told her about the hot girls, and she did laugh hard. She stroked my cheek and said, "My family are Orangemen, Protestants every one of them." I sat quietly, not wanting to make myself even more of an embarrassment to all men. "So about your theory. I'm sure you are right, Paulie, dear."

I should have known she was not Catholic, but neither of us cared to talk about religion and people in Chicago whose names are Doherty rarely go out of their way to say they are Orangemen.

I used to say that I was permanently relieved from my Catholic guilt when Ellen refused a Catholic wedding; I could blame it on her. Ellen said, "Honestly, I have never seen in you the slightest trace of Catholic guilt nor any guilt at all, but I am sure you are right, Paulie dear."

3.

JUDGES WILL TELL you that being a judge is a
lonely place in life, that you lose all your old friends because
you are afraid of influence on your decisions. This is false; you
don't lose many friends except in the normal way, as they die or
retire and move away. The truth is that you can't make any new
friends because the people you meet now are usually people
who might want something from a person who wears a black
dress every day at work and you never know why they want to
be your friend. You have no way to replace the friends you lose.
I went on the bench with just two close friends, Ellen and Dave.

On a mild winter morning Charity called. We had met now and
then to go over the legal things that come with the death of a
husband. We went to the Midland Hotel, a nice place in the
Loop where it was simple to walk in and rent a room without
being noticed. Her legal troubles at the Fed were fading; she
scarcely saw Corman, but the atmosphere there was still unset-
tled and the death benefit for Trimble had not yet been paid.
The only reason her case was still pending before me was to de-
ter anyone, meaning Wheezer, from retaliating against her. It
was good to talk about the common weight we carried, two
dead men on our shoulders.

We would meet Sunday at the Midland when the Loop
would be empty. She now lived in a small rental apartment just
west of the Loop, but the building had a doorman; I could not
go there.

"That cop, Plymouth, he was around the Fed on Friday," she

told me as she perched on one arm of the overstuffed chair in the junior suite. "I saw him walking out with Corman. He was saying something and the Wheezer was shaking his head, like 'no no no.' The Wheezer was looking like it was plenty of trouble." Charity shrugged as if to indicate: Your turn to say something.

I leaned my elbows against the small desk where I sat. "Did you check the visitor logs?" I asked.

"Indeed I did, and Plymouth had checked in a half-hour before. And I saw another visit listed about a month ago. He was there to visit the Wheezer. Now what?"

"I don't know what," I said as evenly as I could. "This detective could do anything; the rules don't matter to him." Look what he had done to Ellen's desk.

"Judge, the rules don't matter to anybody excepting somebody like you and even then, you know..."

"Yes, I know," I admitted. "I'm glad I have the money at the courthouse, because nobody is going to let him search my place without a warrant and it would be hell to get a warrant for somebody like me."

"So we do nothing and wait?" she asked as she slid down to the blue-checked seat pillow of the chair.

"That was always the plan."

What I feared most as I left that Sunday was something I kept from Charity: whatever that microphone had picked up in my home. Was anything incriminating on it? If Plymouth dared to play it for Wheezer, what would the Wheezer do?

On the elevator ride back up to my chambers, I heard Dave's voice come unbidden into my head. Crazy, but I was prepared for crazy conversation now.

Was that the beginning of the end, Paulie, when I bonked Charity?

Damn that's crude, Dave.

It could be then I began to feel terrible about myself... But it might have been worth it.

What's the point here?

I'm dead, I'm trying to look at the bright side, the good things. So did I screw it all up that night?

It was Plymouth who screwed us up, Dave, no one else.

I enjoyed the trick of my mind that let me talk to Dave. It went by too quickly. I waited for more and when I felt my unconscious was not going to revive him anymore, I turned to my Monday cases.

Can the government prohibit people standing outside the courthouse from smoking cigarettes? A reformed smoker became head of the General Services Administration in Chicago. On his way to his office in our courthouse and federal building, he was "overwhelmed," he said, by the haze of smoke lingering outside the doors to the courthouse. So the GSA chief barred smoking anywhere within fifteen feet of the building. Federal control of federal land, he said. Television declared it to be the first outdoor-smoking ban in the nation's history. I doubted that, but historic first steps make better stories.

After three months of a grace period and another three months of issuing warnings, the police of the Federal Protective Service started issuing tickets. If someone refused to put out a cigarette, the FPS would move in for an arrest.

The media loved the idea of smoke-free outdoor air. But they would not be cheering when the police arrested some nice old geezer for smoking outside our front door. They would ridicule the building police. Many laws draw applause when they get passed and jeers when they are enforced, unless, of course it's a lawyer who gets nailed. Inside the court family, we feared the arrestee would be Judge Uhler, a fine, ninety-ish semi-retired judge who stood outside the courthouse door three times each day and smoked his cigarettes. Someday a new fellow from the police might ticket Uhler; the new fellow would not know he was a judge. A lawyer's suit to invalidate the regulation ended up, gloriously hyperbolic, in my courtroom.

In the lawsuit, the GSA administrator pulled out every stop—Clean Air Act, the Pure Food and Drug Act, and the common law of nuisance abatement. It was all drivel, and the government lawyer knew it. No federal law prohibited smoking out-of-doors. The GSA did not have the power to stop anybody from smoking outside the building except to prevent fire or explosion. The whole purpose of the hearing, which wasted a week, was an opportunity for the GSA director to show how much good faith he had had when he'd promulgated the no-smoking regulation. I could then write, as we judges do, "While his purpose was laudable, the law simply does not allow him to ban smoking outside the building."

Legally it was one of those cases that did not have two sides. I spent the hearing remembering things. On Friday morning, when the lawyers told me they were finished with their arguments about smoking and the rights of man, I announced my inevitable ruling and went into my study to look at my perfect photograph of Ellen.

When one of Ellen's biggest deals in Asia was ready to close, we went to the K-Club in the Caribbean, where the water poured over one end of the pool and seemed to flow into the sea. Ellen rose from the water one day. In the dazzling heat, I saw her as a fabulous mirage and I felt light-headed, my wife of fifteen years, floating in glory, and I photographed her.

Those nights were a series of dares, reversions to adolescence. The first evening we walked into the forest—the jungle, I suppose. I thought it was just a walk, but Ellen pulled a blanket out of her backpack and threw it down on a small patch of yellow tallgrass. She walked on the blanket and turned to look at me. I stood there like a fool. She cocked her head. When I went to touch her, she stopped me and started taking off my clothes. We started with me on the bottom and switched positions several times. The blanket and the ground made a slippery surface. In the moonlight, she had no color, and she was beautiful in black and white.

On the last night, the moon was gone, and she led us down to the beach. She walked naked from the cabin. Anyone could have seen us. We heard voices within feet of where we lay. We took very little time, and then we plunged into the Caribbean. On the walk back, she remarked, "I wonder if anyone is watching us. They could see our silhouettes." She pulled me down onto the sand and we started again. This time it was slow and this time I lost none of my senses, as I usually do. I heard her and watched her and felt her and inhaled her and tasted her even as we finished. We half crawled back to our cabin and fell into a deep sleep on top of the bed. In the small hours of the morning, we awoke, chilled by the night air and chafed by the sand that covered our bodies. We stood in a warm shower and half dozed leaning against each other, holding each other. That memory is as alive for me as the memory of the robbery.

We went home from the Caribbean, happy with each other. The day after we landed in Chicago, the Asian deal fell apart.

Three days later she pulled it back together, making it bigger and better. Choctaw Chip would dominate the Asian market, and she bought up an overlooked and valuable bandwidth technology as part of the deal. The Secretary of the Treasury said the deal was rich enough to reverse some negative trade balances and he wanted the deal announced in Washington. *BusinessWeek* took photos of her for a cover story. She had moved from lawyer to industrialist, and the kids who ran her company gave her all the credit. It was fine for her. A little time in the sun, outside the shadow of Judge Devine. She would have gotten there a lot sooner if it hadn't been for the lost four years that Prindiville's action cost her. I would have been the big deal-maker's spouse. Ellen was sheepish when she admitted she might enjoy that for a while, and I was happy as a clam.

On the morning that the *BusinessWeek* story ran, Ellen had mumbled "good-bye" when I left at six A.M. to run at the gym and then go to my chambers. She was sleeping in and taking a later flight to Washington for the press briefing scheduled for the half-hour after the stock markets closed. I had rehearsed her until two in the morning and she was very ready to shine. But she missed the big day. When her secretary called at eleven, I rushed home to find her completely cold. I agreed to an autopsy. I wanted to know. The burst aneurysm was in her ascending aorta. She just missed her moment in the limelight.

Jesus knows I can't put anything out of my mind. I think there must be something rational or, at least, coherent about my recent life. I tell myself I am a smart guy, which everyone thinks is true, and I ought to be able to figure it out, something buried in me for a while. Maybe a really smart guy wouldn't try.

From the beginning, I grew up in comfort. Paulie Devine, the only child of a construction contractor and a freelance writer for women's magazines. You can probably guess which was my father and which was my mother. Kate Devine read Irish works to me; these were my bedtime stories. Thomas Devine often came into the room to listen to the rhythm of my mother's speech. What I remember from my earliest days is the lilt of her voice and the faint smile on his face.

In my boyhood house was a basement storeroom, where at

age twelve I discovered a depiction of Saint Ignatius of Antioch. It was very badly painted, a bloody red mess showing Ignatius being torn apart and eaten by wild beasts. Ignatius seemed to be smiling during it all, which made the sight of the thing even more gruesome. No wonder it was hidden in the basement, stored behind two sets of golf clubs dating from the 1930s. I showed it to my mother, who turned quickly to my father.

"Tom," she said. He looked at her. She pointed to the painting and raised her eyebrows and went back to her writing.

"Ah, Paulie," my father said. "That is Saint Ignatius of Antioch. This painting was sent to us by my father. It belonged to his mother, my grandmother. She was very religious, and this painting hung in her parlor in her home in Ireland. He sent it to me to remember her by, but I remember her quite clearly without this painting which, you may have noticed, is very poorly made. Your mother thinks it is depressing and ugly, and I agree. I just can't bring myself to throw it out, because it's a family heirloom. So I hid it in the basement and I want you to put it back where you found it. Of course, you may look at it yourself anytime you wish as long as it stays in the basement. Is there anything else you want to know?"

"Who is Ignatius of Antioch?"

"Ask the brothers at school."

I was a fairly obedient child, and I returned the painting to its place of obscurity in our house. The last time I saw it was the day my father asked me if he might put it in my storeroom when they moved to California. I am sure it is still there in whatever hiding place he could find.

Anything so gruesome that it had to be hidden would attract the curiosity of any twelve-year-old boy, especially when his father discouraged discussion and his mother shuddered when the object was brought to light. Brother Connelly, on the other hand, was eager to help me find out anything I wanted to know. He knew nothing himself because Ignatius of Antioch was not familiar within his order. Yet I was one of the bright boys in school and I think he must have believed my interest in an obscure saint, martyred in the second century, might be a very good sign that the young Paulie Devine had potential for the priesthood.

Brother Connelly and I went down to the small library on the second floor of the school. Amid the dark wood shelves and worn tables, we consulted books on martyrs of all stripes and found Ignatius, Bishop of Antioch, whose death in the 107th year of Our Lord provided circus for the Romans who watched him being eaten by leopards. He is known to history for a letter he wrote to the Christians in Rome. He was in chains when he composed it, while being transported to Rome in the company of the leopards who were to kill him. Christians should not interfere with the Roman plan to put him to death in the Coliseum, he wrote. "Please let me be thrown to the wild beasts. I am God's wheat. I am ground by the teeth of the wild beasts that I may end as the pure bread of Christ."

Brother Connelly must have been alarmed by my reading of this letter, worried that it might thwart my priestly calling. None of his students would ever believe they could do what the holy Ignatius had done. I think the Church has always lost a few of us every year because the young do not understand that you can be a good Catholic without being a saint, without being anywhere near to sainthood. Most of my classmates would think poor Ignatius was just crazy. The young were to be taught of the mortification of the flesh, but the lesson had to be taught lightly. But Brother Connelly could not read my reaction to Ignatius's letter.

I admired Ignatius, though not precisely for his faith. He was a man who was willing to do whatever he had to do to get what he wanted. I thought this must be bravery, and manhood. It was not exactly what my parents meant to teach me, but it was what I heard and learned.

4.

HI, PAULIE...
How is it, being dead?
I miss Lysette. Do you see her?
No. She is in New York, I heard, singing.
Did you see her after I died?
Actually, I did. I remember now she was at the funeral.
Was she sad?
I thought so.
The first time I met her, at the Gold Star Sardine Bar, that bright green dress, that straight pitch-black hair, those eyes, those lips, I could hear the goddamn song in my head. She liked cold air on her skin, she said it made her tight. I'd have to push myself into her. She'd keep her eyes open. I want her now, shaking a little until I touch her...
Christ almighty, Dave.
Damn it, Paulie, you don't have to look so sad. I'm dead, it happens...and the robbery, that was a ride, the noise and money boxes starting to crack open. A hell of a way to end a career, and no innocent victims.

Now, at least, I was sure it was not Dave. He would never have talked about Lysette so explicitly. The real Dave's ghost would have stayed longer to keep me company.

By late Sunday morning I ran out of paperwork at the office, not the best time for this to happen. I was learning, to my dismay, that being alone was too hard for me. I had understood loneliness the way a physicist understands the inferno at the center of the sun. I knew I could be alone one day when I was old and filled with fine memories. But I was still young. My new friends, the files, had deserted me. I stewed at the office. I played computer games, and I stared at photos. I was anguished, "vexed," my mother would say.

I walked the short distance from the courthouse to the Midland Hotel when it was time for me to meet with Charity.

A bright cool January Sunday, downtown Chicago nearly deserted of pedestrians. I slowed my own walk and felt the sun. I looked for Tony Plymouth as I circled the block in which the Midland sits. I saw no one watching me, and I went into the hotel.

The lobby is small, built with an older style of elegance. Both elevator doors were open. I went to the fifth floor and knocked on Charity's door.

She wore very pale denim, more white than blue, a long-sleeve shirt buttoned to the neck, and loose jeans. Holding a heavy, hardcover book, she stepped back and pulled the door open. The drapes were closed, and only the floor lamp was on, creating a small circle of light over a large easy chair covered in chintz. Even in good light Charity's face was hard to read, but before she shut the door, I saw there the calm acceptance I did not have.

The door latch slid into its seat with a snap. Charity waited, looking at me. I stood immobile. She sensed something; her lips parted a little, a look of surprise. A panic filled me and I grabbed her, jamming her against me. She put her hands on my back and pressed in. Moments passed.

I had no idea of what to do next.

"Do you want..." I said, hoarse. I had not spoken a word to anyone since Saturday afternoon.

" 'Want' is a very funny word."

Somehow we moved a foot or two toward the wall and bumped against something.

We broke a lamp. And we parted. Good luck, I think; it had felt fine to hold each other, but it would not have been fine if we had done more. Charity smiled and patted my shoulder.

"I think I'd like to sit down."

"You take the chair, Judge."

She sat cross-legged on the bed.

"You still love your wife?" she asked.

"Yes. I will until I forget her, and I can't see how I would do that."

"Lucky. I don't love Trimble. I forgot why I did love him. I must have, because I wouldn't have married him otherwise. You know I slept with Dave?"

"He felt very guilty."

"You think he loved me?" Her voice was faint, not quite girlish.

"He was beginning to love you. He might not have permitted himself to love you completely because he could not have you completely. It was the way he thought."

"How'd you deal with it, when she died?" she asked the ceiling.

"I didn't deal with it."

"Were you with anyone after?"

"No one special. We have to talk about Tony Plymouth," I said.

"Where do we stand?"

I told her at last about the microphone and the missing modeling kit. She deserved to know everything.

None of what Plymouth had was enough to justify charging us with a crime. We had less than four years to go before we were safe. Charity still had her job, some insurance payouts, and, after the death of Trimble, she could stand the lingering Fed unfriendliness.

"Is there anything he can do to hurt us?"

"Dave made one mistake. I think his idea was that he would destroy Trimble and himself and with them he would destroy about the same amount of money that Tony Plymouth believed was stolen from the Fed. Not all the money would be vaporized. There would be scraps and a lot of ashes. The amount of money might be estimated. The detective would discover the destroyed money, and he would believe that Dave and Trimble did the robbery and no one else was involved. That would explain why the two of them had all the money."

"So?" Charity asked.

"Dave was not thinking clearly. The traces of money just prove to Plymouth that there was a robbery, and it gives him something to take to Prindiville. They might finally open an investigation."

"But you said there's no evidence against us."

"If Detective Plymouth is willing to burglarize my house and plant an illegal bug, both of which are felonies, he will not hesitate to commit perjury to get us into trouble. Do not speak to him under any circumstances. If you do, you are likely to be arrested, and then you will read in a police report that you had an attack of conscience and confessed the crime to the reporting officer who will be Tony Plymouth.

"We can't be seen together. Tony Plymouth will be able to prove that the explosion was calculated with great care, designed to limit destruction to one very small area but also to be completely destructive within that area. He will be able to prove that this was part of Dave Brody's stock in trade. He has a witness who can testify to Dave's skill as an arsonist for hire."

Charity listened, even though I was sure she knew where this would end.

"The detective will argue that we conspired to get rid of Trimble. And we fiddled with Dave's bomb so that both men would die. Trimble is out of our way, and we get to split Dave's share of the loot. He will try to leverage another investigation out of this, anything to get the Fed to listen to him. He can stir up the insurance companies, the ones that covered your house and Trimble's life. Even if the criminal investigation goes nowhere, he can ruin our lives."

"Yes, we're in a terrible place," Charity said flatly. "I want to go somewhere else."

"In time, in time." My last words as I walked from the room.

5.

I DECIDED A dispute over a claim of faulty design of a racing sailboat that foundered and sank when it was leading the annual Mackinac race up the length of Lake Michigan.

I presided over a criminal case involving a man who, using inside sources to get two account numbers, was able to wire-transfer several million dollars from one of our leading banks to his own account in Vienna. Why he thought he could succeed was beyond my ability to conceive. It was the bank's own money that he stole. Did he think they wouldn't notice it? Or that they wouldn't notice that it went to someone who was not entitled to it? If you are going to do what he did, you have to delude the bank into thinking that the money they are holding for Joe Smith was transferred to Joe Smith, and then you have to delude Joe Smith into thinking he is not yet supposed to receive the money. Then you might have a few days to get the money into your pocket before anyone notices the accounts are out of whack. But that it is very hard to do.

Abdullah Fergerson would have some stature during his fifteen years in prison. He did sort of have his hands on $12,988,500 for a few hours.

I did not stop thinking about Charity. It would not be possible to be together without shame.

I was in my study when Charity called. She had to see me now.

The cafeteria in the Board of Trade building was the closest good place to meet. We might be seen together, but no one could say we were trying to hide in that crowded place. There were open booths for us, and Charity started to speak before we sat down.

"The detective was waiting outside when my shift ended at three," she said in her tight military voice. "I walked away from him. He walked beside me. I couldn't think of how to avoid him."

"What did he say? Did you speak to him?"

"I didn't say anything. He had his sermonette." He told her she had lost a husband, a home, a career, and a sense of security.

"He said I would never know whether one of my partners would turn me in. If I had the money, I couldn't spend it here. The tax man would come after me. I would have to leave the country. 'You have lost your place here; you will have no home.'"

That was indeed the kind of point an American Gypsy would make to an African-American, both feeling this might be "their" only country.

"Did he ask you a question?"

"Not really, other than saying, 'You know this, don't you?' I didn't answer."

"You remember anything else?"

"The most important thing, at the end. He put his hand out to stop me and he whispered so low I could hardly hear him, 'Listen, I'm giving up on you for now. But I'll be back to watch you, and you won't know when. Don't spend it all in one place.'"

"That's it. 'Don't spend it all in one place'?"

"That's it. What do I do?"

"Follow his advice," I said.

Tony Plymouth could not use the tape recording; an ambitious, unscrupulous detective would not want to push an investigation that would not result in a conviction. The death of Trimble and Dave made the case an unacceptable risk. Thank you, Dave.

6

I FOUND OUT from Lieutenant Guadal O'Hara that Plymouth had gone on furlough. He and another Gypsy police officer were in eastern Europe discovering their roots.

But soon, as the acting chief judge, I granted immunity to Lester Trippi, the witness that Tony Plymouth had discovered he could use against Dave Brody. Trippi's cooperation was the reason that Plymouth could plant those newspaper stories about Dave. I authorized the government to install pen registers on four telephone numbers. The pen registers would record the phone numbers of all persons who called those four telephones. The papers told me that Tony Plymouth was still working on his federal cases. The prosecutor's goal was to roll up every consultant who solved business problems by hiring arsonists and rooking insurance companies. I could not tell the assistant United States attorney that he had put the case in the hands of a rogue cop.

I signed the papers and asked for Lester Trippi to be brought into my chambers. He appeared to be the kind of man Dave Brody would deal with—trim, clean, and clear-eyed with an open, honest face that was a real asset to a criminal. "Do you understand, Mr. Trippi, that you no longer have the right to refuse to answer questions put to you in the grand jury? I have granted you immunity so that you cannot use the Fifth Amendment."

"I understand, Judge."

Did he know that I was Dave Brody's friend?

As Trippi walked out with his lawyer, Dave's voice arrived in my head.

Hi, Paulie.

I was thinking about you, Dave.

Don't get maudlin, now. It's very insulting to the dead to see living people cry.

I still see the bomb going off.

Hell of a piece of work, nothing but me and Trimble and the one house. My final piece of work and one of my best.

I thought you did it because you were disgusted with yourself and you figured you'd save me and Charity.

Yeah, yeah, that was part of it. Now that I'm dead, that arson stuff's not so big with me. I must have been a little out of my mind.

But you went along with the robbery because you wanted to get out of setting fires.

Not entirely, Paulie. I made good money with the fires. I liked the robbery. It was a giant payday and the rush the day we did the bank, that was like the combined rush from setting a million fires. I knew it would be great.

You liked setting fires?

Anyone who does it likes it. What I figured out after I died is that I like crime. Might have done more.

You're just trying to make me feel better about your being dead.

No. You're just trying to make yourself feel better about my being dead.

7.

CHARITY FILED ANOTHER motion against the Fed. The lawyer for the Fed asked for a conference where Mr. Prindiville himself would appear. Charity swore that Ernest Corman told her not to bother taking a promotional examination because she would never be promoted as long as Corman was there, and Corman had twelve years before he would retire.

The following Monday at four, Redding Prindiville and Charity Scott presented themselves. After my customary request to meet separately with them, they agreed, and Charity went into my study; I followed her in, shut the door, and asked what the hell had happened.

"One day, right straight out, Corman comes up and says that to me, no promotion. He smiles. I wonder if they got something on me and I start to check. In the records room, they tell me that every one of my time sheets, my shift reports, and my incident reports is pulled routinely and sent to Corman. I thought you should know."

"Yes. I should."

I sat on the sofa. Charity sat next to me. She took enough space to permit her to turn and look at me as she did when I spoke to her. It was still too close for me, and I got up. Then I felt like a fool, so I offered my hand to help her up. It was an offer to touch her. She knew. She ignored the hand and rose up into what became a crushing embrace. I had never felt such strength in a woman's arms. We parted only because it was hard to breathe.

Standing close, touching face-to-face, time passed. It was unbearably sad.

I left to talk to Prindiville. He was examining the large vase of silk flowers I kept on a side table. They were perfect copies of living flowers, the illusion aided by artificial water in the bottom of the vase; the artisan had darkened some clear plastic. The texture of the acrylic shimmered a little in the light, giving it a watery look.

"This fooled me."

"It fools everyone at first glance."

"You have to get very close to it."

"That's true, Mr. Prindiville."

He came back to his chair, and I asked him if he had read Charity Scott's petition.

"Yes, Judge, I've read it. None of that matters."

"Are you telling me that this was just one of those unauthorized remarks, the threat that Corman made?"

"No, sir. He was authorized to make it. In fact, I ordered him to make it. It is a false statement. Corman is going to Washington to work there. It's a real step up, and I got it for him."

I was sorting papers on my desk. When I finally looked up, I saw that smug grin on his face: the same one he used on the old lady who was late cashing in her Treasury bills.

"Corman said that because I wanted to see you. I knew it would precipitate one of your settlement conferences."

Prindiville opened a small document case. He pulled out the pieces of Ellen's modeling kit. You could see some of the pieces still had the shape of the money carts, and one of them looked like the gurney. The base plate had two of the markings I used to show where the vault walls were located. He pulled out a cassette tape and a small tape player.

I said nothing. I fought my emotions. Who the hell was I to be enraged? This jerk Prindiville hadn't robbed banks, hadn't gotten anybody killed.

"You know what this is, of course." He pointed to the modeling kit. "You have never heard the tape. Let me play it for you." He inserted the tape, pushed the rewind button. In seconds, the machine stopped.

"Voice activated. No dead spots on the tape." He hit the play button.

Now, are we done?

Close. She's going to get you on the cell phone?

She has caller ID. When he calls, she'll know where he is. She'll ring the cellular, and I'll go to him.

We don't want him to pick the meeting place if we can help it.

Did you think, Paulie, when we started . . .

No, I thought, if anything went wrong, it would be something in the bank so we would be caught then and there.

We'd wait five years, and the statute of limitations would expire. At most we would have a tax problem we could avoid by going overseas.

Tony Plymouth is in his car, sitting there across the street.

Nice to know that.

The tape hissed on for a moment, and then the machine stopped.

I was partly relieved that this was all he had. It might not be enough to convict. It was enough to make trouble.

If there was no robbery of the Fed, there is no case no matter what he has. If Prindiville declares that a robbery occurred, the whole world changes. The burned money in Trimble's house corroborates the fact of the robbery. The tape corroborates the involvement of Dave and myself in some serious crime. Dave was in the Fed vault on the day of the crime. The modeling kit establishes which crime it was that Dave and I had been talking about on the tape.

The case might never come to court because the modeling kit and the tape were illegally obtained, but I would face the prospect of having law enforcement go over my life and affairs for as long as I lived. They would do everything they could to see that I did not get away. They would do the same with Charity. They would be right to do so. The money was forever lost to Charity and to me and so was whatever chance I had for peace in my life.

He could make it worse; Prindiville could claim that the tape and the modeling kit were not obtained by the government. He could say they were anonymously mailed to him, and it must have been the work of some private citizen, maybe even Dave Brody, who was so consumed by remorse over the robbery that he committed suicide. Tony Plymouth might back up Prindiville. It was not a bad story, and some idiot judge might believe it and let the evidence go to a jury. If a private citizen like Dave

Brody made the tape and stole the kit, the evidence would be admissible.

Was Prindiville here to gloat over my downfall? Were there agents waiting to come in and arrest me in the presence of Charity, a dramatic gesture to frighten her and get her to testify? Was Prindiville wearing a recording device?

I said nothing.

Prindiville grinned once more and began to pack up his exhibits. He stood up and walked to the door. "Why don't you enter an order dismissing this case? Trimble is dead. We agree not to discriminate against her."

When he was gone, I escorted Charity into my bathroom, turned on the shower, and told her what happened. I did not ask her to take her clothes off to see if she was wearing a wire.

8.

I LEFT THE city to visit my parents in the semiwarm desert outside of San Diego. They were pleased with their lives and still mildly proud of what I had made of myself.

Back in Chicago, I kept looking for signs I was being watched. If they had subpoenaed my bank records or tapped my phone, I would not know. If they had a search warrant, I would know about it but not until they executed it. The only location where a search warrant would have done them any good was my chambers. I was counting on that being the very last place they would try.

I spoke to Charity from pay phones. She had seen nothing. Wheezer Corman had left Chicago.

I heard several IRS cases in a row. The first three all concerned the ways in which drug dealers could appear legally to enter or leave the United States with large sums of cash. One witness, an IRS expert, testified in each trial.

"Agent Bradford, are there any general investigative principles used by the IRS?"

"We always look at money that goes to a taxpayer and money that comes from a taxpayer and goes to another taxpayer and, of course, we look at money that comes from the government and goes to taxpayers in the form of tax refunds. There is an old rule in investigations. It is 'follow the money.' The IRS is concerned with crimes that are committed for financial reasons, so our basic principle is to look at money that is in the hands of individuals or corporations and then to see what happens to it. We stop looking when the money gets into our hands at the IRS."

"In this case, what did the IRS do?"

"The law requires that anyone who crosses into or out of the United States with ten thousand dollars in cash has to declare it. If you declare it, you can't be stopped. Eventually, of course, the IRS gets reports of these entries and we investigate. Here someone created a dozen fictitious taxpayer files using social security numbers legitimately assigned to persons who were deceased. Then false identification documents were prepared and then imposters would enter the United States and declare that they had large sums of cash. These phony taxpayer files could be used for nearly twenty months before the alarms would go off. Eventually we installed a computer program to check for the suspicious creation of taxpayer files. I would prefer not to give the details."

I liked this testimony, including the nice touch at the end about not giving details. No one had asked the witness to give details. His comment was his way of telling the jury that this was important government work, a military secret in the war on drugs. A good way to make the point.

All three prosecutions led to convictions by jury. The trials together took just eight court days. I had time left over to wait and worry and grieve.

9.

In mid-March, Prindiville called me in chambers. "Judge, since we no longer have a case pending before you, I was hoping we could have lunch," he declared.

I was not going to say no. We agreed on the University Club. Prindiville occupied me with colorful stories of Vermont history. The only words I uttered during lunch were "iced tea" and "the chopped salad." Prindiville closed lunch with a suggestion that we walk down to the Bath Department and use the steam bath. I agreed. He was going to show me that he was not wearing any sort of microphone. Perhaps he noticed the absence of conversation at lunch.

In the steam bath, we were alone, wearing the club's bathing suits.

"You know I don't want the robbery of my bank to become public knowledge," Prindiville remarked. "We are on the same side."

"Mr. Prindiville, what do you want?"

"Money. The money would make me very happy."

I said nothing.

"You took more than five or six million dollars. You burned hundreds of millions in the vault. Why would you burn so much just to cover a relatively small theft? And why would a man like you take the risk for six million dollars? You're probably worth nearly that amount anyway, or you could be if you went back to practicing law. I think you made a special pad for the gurney. Looking at the model you made, I think you fabricated a special gurney. Then I figured in the space you had in the air tanks attached to the respirators. I reckon one hundred million dollars."

He had thought of the air tanks and I hadn't.

"I would not want you to do anything desperate. I am reasonable, Judge. I want fifty million. Say yes or say no. Decide now."

I nodded yes.

"We will discuss the method of delivery day after tomorrow. Let's have a swim that morning at the Union League Club."

I nodded again. He left and I stayed until I could not bear the heat.

There were sixty-three million dollars left in my storeroom. I had thrown four million in the garbage, and Dave destroyed another six million. Prindiville wanted fifty million. There would be thirteen million left for Charity and me.

Let him have the money. He would give up the modeling kit and the tape. If he wanted to keep a copy of the tape, he could but it was not much use without the modeling kit. It was no use at all to him if he took the money. He would not be talking to anybody; he would be too busy spending money and not wanting to explain how he had acquired it. That was a good way to think about it, and that was what I told Charity.

I was betting, too, that he would have to divide it with Plymouth, who also knew of the robbery and from whom he got the tape and the modeling kit. I would like to have known if he told Plymouth how much money he thought I took and how I did it. If he hadn't, he could give Plymouth three million and claim it was an even split.

10.

THE POOL AT the Union League Club is kept cool because the real swimmers doing their quarter miles and more do not want to have their strength sapped by heated, comfortable water. When I arrived wearing my bathing suit, Prindiville was swimming strong strokes. His lap counter showed him at three hundred yards plus. I would not join him. The few times I had been forced into that pool, I would have to stand under a hot shower for two minutes before I dove in.

When he was finished with his 440, we talked at one of the sitting areas near the pool. Prindiville was on a high—pink, shiny, breathless, almost boyish. His time for the swim, he said, was very fast for him. He knew he was getting his fortune. He was a winner. He would restore the Prindiville fortune, and he would buy himself a governorship or some such thing. I even sensed a sort of lukewarm New England sentiment toward me. He was victor, I was vanquished. Of all people, I would appreciate the genius of his move. He spoke in a low, calm voice.

"The idea that someone could steal millions from the Fed was unthinkable to people in the building. A lot of people might daydream about doing it. I was prepared to accept that someone might think of a good plan, a plan that security did not anticipate. The Gypsy was very convincing, and I liked his idea." Prindiville threw his towels on the floor and stood up to slip into a dry robe. He grinned at me. "What he wanted me to do would have been an embarrassment to my administration. You'd think a Gypsy could have figured that one out." Prindiville lowered himself into his chair. "When I saw he was very hard to discourage, I half hoped he would bring forth a solution to the crime. He would have been easy to co-opt. In the end he brought me burned money, enough ashes to satisfy me that there had been a robbery. He had no proof against anybody but Brody. And that was not until after Brody was dead."

You're leaving something out, I thought.

"The detective always thought it was Brody and Scott and Young, and he thought there was a fourth man, a mastermind. He was putting pressure on Young and then on Brody. I thought Brody would go back to the mastermind. I told Corman to put a tail on Brody. Corman told me about you."

"And?"

Prindiville sighed. "I'm afraid Ernest Corman was not very aggressive. But he did want to go to Washington, and he was not going to go until I had my answers. You should have seen how desperate he was, the elaborate ideas he had, but all those ideas took men and money to nail my criminals. I wanted it to be my little secret. Old man Corman—his men call him Wheezer—had to take care of it himself. You know what he did, of course. You must have found the microphone by now."

"I am sorry," I said.

Prindiville thought I did not understand what he said and he started to repeat it. I waved him silent. I was apologizing to Tony Plymouth that I had thought he would trespass on the law.

"It was a riot when he brought me the tape and the modeling kit. He was as pale as he could be and his hands were trembling. You know, you could really hear him wheezing. He didn't listen to the tape. He was finished, and he begged me to send him to Washington. The man was no good to me anymore, and I sent him on his way. It was all too much for him, breaking into your house. When Plymouth later told me about the burned money and Brody, I knew what to do."

"What now?" I asked. I felt simple. There was something purifying about having my plan seen so fully; maybe it was just the effect of chlorine air wafting off the pool.

"The exchange must be worked out carefully. Perhaps at the airport. There are always reams of suitcases and boxes. You could bring them, I could take them away and I would, of course, give you my briefcase with the tape and the modeling kit. Keep the case with my compliments. I like the airport because it's safe, and it will be difficult to bring a weapon past security."

"Mr. Prindiville, what you want is heavy and voluminous. It will be conspicuous at the airport."

"You have an idea?" His voice was so polite.

"We will store the goods in a public warehouse, one of your choosing. You can inspect the goods, and then the container will be locked in our presence. I will get a warehouseman's receipt for the goods. You will receive the receipt when I receive your materials. I like your idea of the airport. We can make the exchange of receipt and your briefcase on the far side of the security checkpoint."

He agreed. He would call me within a week with instructions.

If I had still then believed I was entitled to be angry with Prindiville, to judge him, I would not have been so calculating. I could not have controlled myself.

11.

THE NEXT WEEK, I had a jury back to hear the case of a tax protestor accused of criminal tax evasion—a small blessing, this jury trial, because I do not have to pay such close attention. The case did have a moment worth remembering.

The prosecutor said, "I have heard your lengthy explanation of your defense. Could you restate the gist of it, Mr. Norman?"

"I guess I can try," the defendant said. "It starts with the Sixteenth Amendment, the one that legalized the income tax. It never was properly ratified. You research the history, right, it was fraudulently certified by the Secretary of State. You look back more at the founding of this country and what do you find? It is pretty clear that white, Christian men were not to pay any tax but property tax. I know this sounds racist and anti-women, but it is the historical record, what the Founding Fathers intended. I have nothing against black people. I don't even think it's fair, but I do know it is the law."

"You argue that white Christian men do not have to pay income tax," I said. "But women, black men, and all Jews and Muslims do have to pay?"

"Yes, Judge, because that is my natural law right. And you know, those others do not have to pay because the Sixteenth Amendment is a fraud. You know, Judge Devine, you are a white Christian man yourself. You should not be filing tax returns either."

"Thank you for that hint," I told him.

The jury later told me they had poured coffee that had been delivered to the jury room and discussed why the federal government did not provide more low-fat snacks along with the coffee.

The jury unanimously voted guilty in less than a minute after the coffee had been poured, and signed the verdict. Some jurors exchanged telephone numbers, promising to get together. At last, one juror remembered that they had to knock on the door in order to tell the marshal that they were done so that they could get out of the jury room.

12.

I LOADED THE money into my Jeep. I used a rolling cart from the clerk's office. When I passed in front of the security monitors that surveilled the judges' private elevator, it would look like case files. Two nights passed fretfully with fifty-four million dollars stored in my easily entered garage at home.

On Friday I had arranged a settlement conference for which two men and one woman had traveled a combined thirty thousand miles to attend. An internationally known executive was hired from Chicago to save a British company and, on the verge of saving it, her employers sold the company to Australians, who did not like her compensation package and fired her. They said unkind things about her competence. She said even unkinder things about the Australians. All these unkind things were said in the papers filed in the case, which were under seal. Before the seal was lifted and reputations were put into play, the lawyers wanted to try settlement. The woman from Chicago and the Australians despised each other, speaking of each other as if they were like the characters in Euripides' Iphigenia plays, the ones who spit on the stage every time they mentioned the name of Helen of Troy.

In the midst of my shuttling between the parties, Prindiville rang my private office line and told me to meet him at Cheops on Halsted Street in an hour. I had expected that he would arrange to surprise me, to do it on short notice, to prevent me from scheming.

I had no time to spend on the settlement conference. I did what bad judges do; I abandoned reason and went to fiat. To the Australians I said, "Pay her the two years' salary left on her contract, but not the bonus. Buy her a flat in London for her asking price. Agree never to speak of her to anyone. She will agree not to work for a direct competitor for three years. Including the flat in London, this deal is worth two-point-one million dollars. She will give up a claim for a profit-sharing bonus, which might be worth nothing, or worth four million." To the Chicago woman I said, "Take the money now and keep quiet about them." These were not suggestions; they were orders, and all three parties were too frightened to say no. There must have been some visible ferocity shining from my eyes. Each side said yes, and it was over in less than five minutes. Mea culpa.

I made my arrangements and left the chambers while the lawyers were still shaking their heads at the sudden end of the case.

* * *

Cheops was a good choice, on the north side, west of the lake, near the expressway to O'Hare Airport, an old warehouse with a mock-Egyptian façade, pillars in the shape of a pharaoh, and a pyramid motif stamped on the tiles. Part of the warehouse had been rebuilt into rows of storage rooms for the needs of high-income people in small urban homes who needed a ready access storage space with real security, more than a chain-link fence and a Master lock on a metal door.

Prindiville was waiting. He had reserved a room to be rented in my name. The contents would be listed on the warehouseman's receipt. The possessor of that receipt would be entitled to remove those contents. There was a modern refinement, a customized bar code pasted on the receipt.

Prindiville and I and the Cheops customer-service man unloaded the boxes from my Jeep and loaded them into a storage room. I placed the boxes in the room and numbered them but refused to let Cheops examine the contents. He explained to us that if we did not allow him to itemize the contents, then they were effectively uninsured. Prindiville told him they were sensitive and confidential family records that had no monetary value, and the Cheops man walked off. Prindiville opened each of the boxes, which were not all of the same size. The largest held six million, and the smallest held four. Prindiville was pleased; he wore his smugness clearly on his face. "I don't even care if you undercounted," he said. He finished and we called the Cheops man who delivered the receipt to me.

On the loading dock, we stopped at my Jeep. I showed him my briefcase, a small plastic square with a combination lock.

"We will trade briefcases at Gate B 30 at O'Hare, the United Terminal," I said.

"Yes, if we do it now," Prindiville said promptly. "I'll follow you. I hope I do not see you using a phone."

The trip was slow. I did not use a phone.

We both parked in the Airport Hilton driveway, half a minute from car to terminal. If you give the doorman twenty dollars, he'll let you leave your car there for half an hour.

We stayed a few feet apart walking through the center terminal and then into the United Terminal, arriving together at security screening. I stood in front of Prindiville. As our turn came, a spectacular woman dressed entirely in gold lamé crashed the line in front of me. Her hair was done in long braids decorated in beads. I looked back. Prindiville was amused.

She put her canvas bag on the X-ray conveyer belt. I put my case on the belt, and I saw Prindiville drop his just when the buzzers started going off. It was the lady in gold.

She spoke in a loud voice, not angry, laughing and challenging. "What you want me to do? Take it off, honey? You want to see what I got?"

She was drawing a crowd.

"You got your wish, baby." Judging from the gasp of the crowd, she had started to take off her clothes. I wasn't watching. I was opening her canvas bag and removing a plastic case that was the twin of my own. I stuffed my case into her bag. I grabbed Prindiville's case and started toward Gate B 1 in a half run carrying Prindiville's case and the twin of my case. Prindiville must have been watching her, because he just stood there. He was supposed to be watching her.

I hoped he would not see it was Charity. Her jacket was off, displaying a sequined black halter. Her pants were far enough down to show the top of a sequined bikini bottom before the guard told her she could go to her gate.

Prindiville realized I had his case and he gave chase. He did not catch me until I had stopped to open his case in the empty B 30 gate area and seen that he had brought the modeling kit and the same tape he had showed me in my chambers. He was very angry.

"You tried to cheat me."

"I plead guilty, Mr. Prindiville. I saw a chance."

"I ought to make you give it all to me." He had the rare ability to be sniveling and overbearing at the same moment. His anger was gone in an instant. He realized he had a chance to play with me and he did. "Tell me why I shouldn't. You know, I wouldn't even take the cash from you. I'd just make you burn it in my presence. You're good at burning money."

"Please, someone will hear us. You have what you want." I was pleading. I handed him the twin case I had taken from Charity's bag.

He liked pleading, and he opened my case and removed the

warehouse receipt and saw it was one with the eight numbered boxes.

Prindiville waved his arm, dismissing me. He went ahead and I followed, but not closely.

He drove back to Cheops. I wondered how he thought he would manage to put all the boxes into his sedan. I was tired of thinking about him. I drove down to my chambers. I know Prindiville went to Cheops and surrendered his receipt. He went to the storage room and found the boxes exactly as we had left them. The closest box was a small one with four million. He opened and caressed the money. He relaxed. He opened the other boxes and found a single brick in each one. His expression grew progressively more downcast. I would have thought he was clinically depressed by the time he had finished. Yet he did not forget to take his four million dollars with him.

Just before Cheops closed that night, I went there and reclaimed the fifty million Prindiville and I had placed in the adjacent storage room. I suppose I could have left it there, but Prindiville might be annoyed enough to phone in an anonymous tip to Tony Plymouth after he spent a day nursing his injured ego. I picked the lock to the other storage room with the fake money boxes, and I recovered the video camera that Charity had planted in the room when she had rented that room before Prindiville and I had arrived at Cheops. She'd arranged and numbered the boxes according to the way we had planned.

Charity had used taxicabs throughout the day. She wore a plain brown pants suit to fit over her gold lamé outfit. She changed in washrooms. No matter how close you park your car at O'Hare, you get away fastest in a taxi. I gave her more time by making Prindiville follow me all the way to B 30. By not giving up too easily, I tried to make Prindiville believe he had gotten the real goods from me.

I knew he believed he had triumphed because I saw the expression on his face each time I played the videotape of Prindiville with his millions and with his seven disappointments. He came to my office to see the videotape on Monday morning after my secretary called him to tell him the final dismissal order in Charity's lawsuit was available for pickup, as indeed it was.

The only flaw in the plan was the man at Cheops. He would remember the box people and their multiple visits in and out. He would remember the seven empty boxes with bricks when the thirty-day rental ran out. But no one would ever ask him.

Charity asked why I did not let Prindiville have the whole fifty. We would still be rich.

He was an arrogant man, I answered, a man who would not think he could be caught at anything and a vain man and a hateful man. He'd be careless because he would figure he could talk his way out of anything. Someone would find out about his money. And he would have plenty of enemies who would try to exploit any possible negative in his life. He was vulnerable as Trimble was vulnerable; they would both give someone a good reason to ask a question for which they had no good answer. Four million dollars would not attract that kind of attention. These were good reasons. They were not the only ones. I robbed a bank to spite men like Prindiville. I would risk a great deal to keep him from a full victory over us.

I repacked the money in the case files in my storeroom.

Three and a half years to wait.

13.

ONE DAY THE whistle-blower Seth Aranow awoke from his coma and his case revived along with him. Pullman still needed time to confer with the attorney general about the files I had asked to see. He apologized for not doing so after all this time had passed but everything, he said, had "gone in the deep freeze after Mr. Aranow went into a coma." Come back then in four weeks, I replied, and tell me what Washington wants to do.

A short time later, Ben Golden asked me to have lunch with him upstairs in his chambers at the court of appeals. He had a funny story to tell me. He finished his lunch in short order. He had the same lunch every day that I knew him, a small bowl of dry Wheaties and a glass of iced tea with lemon. He is thin and strong. At sixty-eight he looks fifty. I wish I had his self-discipline. I wish I could do what he did when his wife died. He goes out with many fabulous women. I wish I had his legal mind.

Ben had gotten a call from his friend former Senator Clayton. The Senator heard from Congressman Pullman; the congressman told the senator that his son needed advice from Judge Golden. The senator wanted to help Pullman, who was supporting the senator's efforts to ban tobacco subsidies.

Ben met Dodd, who told Ben about the Aranow case and then asked about how to handle the files issue. There were diplomatic secrets, and he feared I would release them and ruin our relationships in Africa. He asked how he could persuade me to get this done.

Before talking about Aranow, Pullman broke the conversational ice by dropping the name of the attorney general, speaking of a new policy of appointing only those who were already judges. Pullman said that they would broaden the field by considering senior judges to fill vacancies. Then they talked about Aranow. As Pullman was leaving, he turned to tell Ben they expected the retirement of the Chief Justice of the United States by the end of the year and that one other justice would leave with him. This, he said, was going to present a difficult choice for the President.

Ben dissolved in laughter the moment the door closed behind Pullman. "This idiot Pullman, where do they find them?" Ben asked me. "He was offering me a shot at the Supreme Court of the United States. Does he think that I would ever buy the idea that someone of his rank could play in that league? Does he think I would ever buy the idea that the President would put a third Jew on the Supreme Court? Does he think a sixty-eight-year-old wants to start a new career in a job where it takes you seven years to have an impact? He thinks we are all fools." That was clearly true.

"He was offering a seat to you too, Paulie."

I nodded, but Ben and I both knew that a district judge like me had not been appointed to the Supreme Court in the last hundred years or more. I could not bring myself to laugh because I was furious at Pullman.

"I called Clayton, who was shocked, but he admitted he had heard that Pullman was a really fine lawyer who believed that the only way a lawyer could commit malpractice was to have leverage and fail to use it."

"The very word." I used my mother's phrase for "that's right."

This Pullman was not just another political jerk promising what he could not deliver; he was corrupt, and he was trying to corrupt me. Well, I was already corrupt, in a sense, but he was trying to corrupt me as a judge.

Ben and I had a way to deal with this. One of Ben's former clerks was now a senior lawyer at the Department of Justice. I asked for a favor, a favor to advance the cause of justice. After some weeks, I received some documents, a file from the Department of Justice addressed to Dodd Pullman but "mistakenly" delivered to me. I "mistakenly" failed to read the name on the envelope and read the file.

The infant formula was shipped overseas because no one in Agriculture wanted to stop it. The Bowdan Company needed those shipments to be made. The price of shares was down. If the formula went out, there would be one uptick in the quarterly report; units shipped would skyrocket. Of course, no one thought the formula would really be very harmful. It would be just a little substandard, and Bowdan was a large contributor of soft money to the President's party.

In court, I told Pullman I had received this file meant for him and inadvertently read it. I recited the gist of it for him, but I sanitized it. Putting all the details on the record might bring all the President's power to bear upon Seth Aranow to sustain this case. The Justice Department file would be disavowed, and Ben Golden's former clerk might be found out. In the end, the truth would probably prevail, but some of the wrong lives would be ruined.

It was enough that Pullman knew I had the file. He would drop Aranow. I would not put the file in the record. Only Pullman would take some heat. He would take more if the file became public. He was the only sure loser now. He knew it. He was walking in Aranow's shoes.

"I'm sure you will agree, Mr. Pullman, this case is over."

"Yes, Your Honor," he replied in his bilious voice.

I called him to the sidebar and signaled to the court reporter that this was off the record.

"Mr. Pullman, you have destroyed a man's reputation. He is dead broke, without a career. He was a fall guy you needed for political purposes. Now when you go back to Washington you are going to be the fall guy. Find another line of work, Mr. Pullman."

Find another line of work: that is the worst thing a judge can say to a lawyer, worse than finding a lawyer in contempt.

A couple of months later, I dropped an envelope with $100,000 in Aranow's mail slot. I put a note with it that read "from a friend," and then another note, a lawyer's afterthought: "Be sure to file a gift-tax return." I do this sort of thing once or twice a year now. It helps a little, giving money to people, but I am still alone.

Except for things like this, the money was untouched.

Dan Kray called to tell me that the vacancy on the court of appeals would not be filled until next year. He would call to see if I was still interested. I would not be.

In the next two years I heard an exceptionally large number of IRS cases. Sometimes I have pondered a bit about the IRS—the pressures on it, and its response. The IRS, confronting drug dealers, protestors, and refund scams, has devised a useful operating principle. As many IRS witnesses testified in my court, they work hard to control the money that passes between the IRS and the taxpayer; money is easily accepted by the IRS but paid out only with difficulty. Many people have to approve any significant payment. Yet there was one glitch in the system. There was just one last gatekeeper with his list of code numbers for cutting checks and transferring money by wire; he was supposed to decide only when money would be paid. He was not to decide whether it was to be paid to a taxpayer. But he had the numbers and if he fed them into the computer, the checks would be issued, no matter what.

I wondered if someone could take the IRS by diverting large refunds that would not be expected and thus not missed for a few weeks. I wondered if someone could clip a few million out of the presidential campaign funding checkoff fund, money that is not coming from or going to taxpayers and, for that reason, not so tightly controlled. I wondered if an unhappy IRS gate-keeper would help me do it.

Epilogue

Orders Terminating Case

I STILL HAVEN'T hit the IRS, and I try to stick to the law in my work. I usually do what the judge is expected to do. But I do go where I should not.

The correct and proper judge in me is broken beyond repair. Mitchell Lang saw this.

Lang had been Serena's lawyer. He used the law sadistically. Any lawyer will invoke, has to invoke, the law to the pain and detriment of others. But Lang took joy in it. He would engage in a brutal cross-examination of a rape victim even if a gentle one would have been better for his client.

In my court he represented Reza Chalani, a man accused of advance-fee loan fraud. Chalani would set up an office in some city and advertise that he could secure loans for start-ups and troubled companies. He represented to his clients that he would use his access to Middle Eastern oil money to finance those whom all banks had refused for loans. He would guarantee that the loan would be made, but insisted that one or two points had to be paid in advance to Chalani. The fee had to accompany the loan application. He made as many deals as he could and as quickly as he could and then he skipped town with the money. Chalani knew no Arabs; he was Persian, but his Iranian contacts were penniless. He just moved on and repeated the fraud in another town. He was prosecuted on multiple counts of mail and wire fraud.

During his trial the federal agents uncovered the location of a small cottage Chalani kept north of Waukegan in Lake County. I gave them a search warrant, which they served on Chalani in the courtroom about a minute before the search was to begin. When I recessed the trial, Chalani went to lunch and never returned. It was an intelligent choice for him to make. He knew the agents would not discover any evidence of his frauds; he knew that, instead, they would find a number of photographs of unclothed women. Posed photographs of terrified women. In some of the photos, the bruises were apparent. You could see tears in their eyes. The backgrounds suggested that some of them had been taken in the cabin. In a day or two, the police knew he was a multiple murderer and wanted him in custody now.

We went ahead and finished the trial of Chalani. A defendant cannot stop his trial simply by walking away. The rule is that the court waits for a day or two and then resumes the case. Mitchell Lang slyly taunted the agents and the prosecutors who were certain he knew where to find Chalani. He had taken control of all of Chalani's assets when he undertook the defense, and Chalani needed to have contact with Lang for money to live on. Lang never answered the question of whether he knew where Chalani was hiding. He could have simply said, either truthfully or not, that he had no idea where Chalani might be. Instead he hinted that he might know something; or, on other days, that he did know very much but that he was worried about the legality of revealing what he knew.

When a week had passed in the trial, I asked to see the prosecutor and Lang in my chambers for a conference where I would meet alone with each side.

Mitchell Lang sat in a large padded chair in my study, the small room in back of my chambers. His suit was made of a slightly iridescent fabric that clashed with the worn blue fabric of the chair and, it so happened, with the $5,000 cowboy boots he wore. In fact, Lang's whole persona clashed with the accepted model of humanity. His demeanor showed that he expected some fun out of driving me to distraction with the problem of Chalani's whereabouts.

Our conversation began with Lang telling me that he expected me to lean on him about Chalani and threaten him with the loss of every case he ever tried in my courtroom and I would probably bad-mouth him with all the other judges. This would not work, he told me.

"I thought about that," I replied, "but some of your clients ought to win their cases, and I wouldn't punish them because they were foolish enough to hire you. A lot of your clients deserve better than you, Mr. Lang."

Lang was silent. I told Lang that I was going to do two things. First I was going to order him to reveal the whereabouts of Chalani and, when he refused, I was going to find him in contempt and lock him up on the spot. It would take him a few hours to get the appeals court to release him on bond. It would not matter whether he was given a bond or not, because a few hours was all the agents would need to search his office. I told him about the search warrant that the government had asked to issue and to look for clues to Chalani's whereabouts, that I had refused to sign it because it was legally insufficient. Then I told him I would sign it, and I said I would keep him locked up in the little holding cell hidden behind the panels of my courtroom, and I reminded him that there was no telephone in that cell so that he could not call anyone else to have them clean out his office. I honestly doubted Lang would have a record of funds he provided to Chalani, but I was certain he would have several things that he wanted to hide.

Lang knew that searches of lawyers' offices are not easily approved by the courts and even if the agents found incriminating evidence, it might never be legally used against him. Nevertheless a man like Lang would have papers and objects that he and some of his unforgiving criminal clients would never want law enforcement to see, even if they could not be used in court. "The Royalton Hotel, Fourty-fourth Street in Manhattan," Lang said.

I asked Lang for his cell phone and told him to call in an anonymous tip to the FBI. He did, and the two of us waited silently for a long time.

The hour we spent in each other's company was grotesque. I pointed to my bookshelves. He ignored the offer at first. Then he rose to retrieve some hardback reprints of the Prince Valiant comics. He seemed absorbed in the books, reading steadily.

My intercom rang and my secretary put through the special agent in charge of the Chicago FBI, who told me that Chalani had been shot to death while resisting arrest in the Royalton Hotel. I repeated this to Lang, who kept on reading until he completed the volume he held in his hands. An act of silent insolence to which I thought he was entitled.

Obviously I never told anyone how it came to pass that Chalani, the serial killer, met his end. Lang never told anyone either. Whether he violated a legitimate confidence of his client is
debatable, but he did not want anyone to know how afraid he
was of what someone might find in his office.

Every week or so I walk into my storeroom. I look at the boxes.
All of them are labeled CONWAY PACKAGING, a case that finally
closed last year. When I open a box, I can see all my millions
bearing the face of Ben Franklin looking up at me. I have no idea
what to do with my share of the money. Once in a while I se-
cretly donate a little to the undeserving losers in my courtroom.

For a long time after Prindiville walked off with his consolation
prize, I neither saw nor spoke to Charity except for brief telephone check-ins.

Charity left the country with a year and a half left to go on
the statute of limitations. She went to Trinidad and Tobago. Her
mother had died. She had no reason to stay. Death and disaster
had left her with $350,000. It would bridge the gap until she
had millions.

I drove her to the airport. We held hands in the international
terminal. "This is very hard," I said before we said good-bye
and kissed lightly. It was no lie.

When the statute of limitations passed, Charity flew back to
Chicago and bought a large boat and hired a captain. On a
cloudy night she and I loaded twenty-nine and a half million
dollars onto the boat. The next day she started the complex
journey to the Mississippi River, then down the river to the Gulf
of Mexico and finally to the Caribbean Sea. She made several
stops in the Caribbean to make deposits in countries with strict
bank secrecy laws. She bought some land in Belize. She packed
a case with a million dollars that she had kept as a reserve and
neither invested nor deposited. She docked at St. Martin. There
she dismissed the captain and gave him a plane ticket back to
Chicago. She stayed at a very nice place called La Semana
while a broker sold the boat for her. Then she flew back to
Trinidad.

I have heard that she lives with the Minister of the Interior and serves as a consultant to the local police. She is building a very large home.

Redding Prindiville bought himself the nomination for governor of Vermont. His advertising was good, but first-rate political consultants told him that Vermont was a state where a candidate had to meet the voters one by one and shake their hands. He paid good money for this advice, and he followed it down to defeat as I had hoped he would. The voters met him, they knew him, and they walked away from him. He practices law in Burlington. I have heard he is campaigning for the next federal judgeship that opens up in Vermont.

Did I have vengeance on Prindiville? Was he even chagrined by my robbing him or sorry about what he did to my wife? In the end, I gave him a chance to grab the gold ring for himself. Prindiville would never be sorry and neither is the system in which he first thrived. All I had was that I was able to sit face-to-face with him, both of us knowing that I had beaten him out of tens and tens of millions of dollars.

I feel a little less guilt about Dave Brody. Worse things could have happened to him, including prison and public disgrace. He could have died committing arson for hire. The fact that I knew he had become a criminal and had enjoyed it might have been one reason I decided to rob the Fed—to be like him as I had wanted to be on the baseball field and with women and men. Yet I am still responsible for his death. While worse things could have happened to him, they might never have occurred.

I remember most the words at the end. "Look, Paulie, this will come off fine. It'll be good work." And his last words: "My friend."

Detective Tony Plymouth is now Sergeant Plymouth. He has a good chance, I am told, to become Lieutenant Plymouth. I give high praise to Plymouth whenever I speak to my friends in the police. There is a major-fraud squad, and he is second in command. He does testify in federal court. He could wind up in my court. I wonder what each of us would think would happen when he was on the witness stand. I would like to talk to him, but I am sure that it would not go well.

I saw Tony Plymouth last night at Pettiford's, a new jazz club in which I had invested. When Stefon Harris finished the first set with a fast blues, the detective rose to leave. On his way to the reception desk, he saw me. Without a pause, he walked over and bent to speak in my ear.

"I know it had to be your deal," he whispered, "all along, your deal, I know."

He moved around to face me. I think he'd had a couple of drinks.

I was beyond prosecution—the statute of limitations had run. But still I held back. I said, "Maybe, you know. Maybe you just guess."

"The next time, Judge, you won't have a buddy who'll blow himself up to save you."

"What next time?"

"Something will set you off." His voice was louder now. "I know your ways. I won't be fooled by the robes."

"You are a little drunk, Detective."

"But you are sober as a judge, and I know you understand me. You could find a reason to do something bad, a good reason, good enough so that you won't care if somebody gets killed."

He was wrong. I have never gotten over that caring. Enough of this. I stood to escape his contempt and walked out past him.

At the door, I saw Johnnie, the club manager, who smiled.

"Jazz always takes away your troubles, don't it, Judge?"

Not anymore.

Afterword

I HAVE TAKEN some liberties with the current geography of Chicago. Some of the unused and underused land, particularly near and along the North Branch of the Chicago River, has been gentrified or developed in other ways. In this book I have demolished a bit of the building that has taken place and restored some of the grit and a few of the open spaces suitable for car chases. I have also deliberately misdescribed some of the aspects of the Federal Reserve Bank of Chicago because I did not want to write a complete and accurate description of how one could rob the Fed if one were willing to do so.

Michael H. King, a truly gifted lawyer in Chicago, told me that he had a good idea for a movie involving a federal judge robbing the Fed of millions of dollars. The judge, he said, would take, under cover of fire and rescue, a lot of money that was destined to be destroyed and, so, would not be missed. The judge, he said, would be tripped up by a cop who had the habit of checking emergency rooms. I thought he was right, and he is still diligently working to make the movie. It occurred to neither of us, then, that his idea would give rise to a novel. When Neil Russell, a fine writer himself, said that I ought to make a novel out of it, I thought it was a swell idea, mainly because Neil Russell did not bother to tell me how much thought and effort it would take to do this. When I realized the truth, I had become too close to Paulie, Tony, Dave, Charity, and everyone else to abandon them.